SALT ON THE
MIDNIGHT FIRE

Salt on the Midnight Fire

Liz Williams

NewCon Press
England

First published in June 2023 by NewCon Press,
41 Wheatsheaf Road, Alconbury Weston, Cambs, PE28 4LF

NCP305 (limited edition hardback)
NCP306 (softback)

10 9 8 7 6 5 4 3 2 1

ISBN:

978-1-914953-50-7 (hardback)
978-1-914953-51-4 (softback)

Cover by Ian Whates

Editing and typesetting by Ian Whates

For Veronica and Trevor

PROLOGUE

Out on the island, the wind roared down the chimney and the fire leaped up. Elowen went unsteadily to the window and pushed the heavy cow hide to one side. The bay was black under a sickle moon, too thin and frail to cast any radiance over the water, and the clouds were racing. A light flickered out across the bay: once, twice, three times. She knew the signal and caught her breath, but her gasp was snatched by the wind. Elowen let the hide fall back and sought what warmth the guttering fire provided. The old woman had told her that she ought to be grateful, that she and her child had shelter here in this great gale, that she had come to the attention of those in high places, but Elowen was not grateful at all.

She knew she did not have a choice. Now that the Morlader had returned with his ships to harrow the coast, events had started to move again after this brief lull, carrying Elowen and her child with them as swiftly as a winter tide. There never had been any chance of turning back. The high sea thundered at the base of the rock and Elowen's thoughts, too, began to thunder in her head. Her vision went red, then dark. When it cleared, she found that she was sitting down, rocking the cradle to and fro, to and fro, but with too much force, so that the baby gave a small uncertain cry, more like a gull than a human child. The creak of the door drowned the little sound out.

"It will be midnight soon," the old woman said. "The Morlader will be here."

Elowen gave a mute nod. The old woman did not ask if she was ready; that did not matter. She grinned at Elowen.

"Won't that be nice?"

Elowen felt the signal flash again, sharp like a needle's prick in the centre of her mind. She bowed her head, to where the child lay, staring into the dark. Again, that seagull cry. And then, high above her in the church that crowned the island, the midnight bell began to toll.

BEE

I have broken my promise.

Every so often, throughout that spring, this uneasy thought had returned again and again to Bee Fallow. Hoovering the dining room, chopping vegetables, walking the dogs in the orchard, overseeing the building work on the barn conversion – whatever she had been doing, at some point the thought intruded.

I have broken my promise. I didn't mean to break it, but that's what I've done.

It was not as though it was a secret, either. She had discussed the subject at length, with her lover Ned Dark, with her sisters and their partners, and with her friend Vervain March. She had talked it through with the local Master of Fox Hounds and *de facto* lord of the manor Nick Wratchall-Haynes, and with her neighbour, Laura Amberley, who had secrets of her own to keep.

It sometimes seemed to Bee that she had discussed her broken promise with the entire population of the south of England: several people in London had also been made privy to her problem. Not all of those people were entirely human and at least a couple of them were no longer alive.

The one person whom she really needed to tell was her mother, Alys, but Alys was, once more, off a-roving, in pastures and forests unknown.

How frustrating.

The general consensus, whenever Bee did discuss it, was always the same: *we'll just have to wait and see. And hope.*

So on the evening of May Eve, old Walpurgis night, that was exactly what Bee was doing.

Luna's partner Sam had taken the placid piebald horses over to Amberley as a precaution. When he and Luna were on the road the horses pulled their van, and the pair usually resided in the field adjacent to Mooncote, but Laura Amberley would be looking after the piebalds that night. Sam had offered the excuse of refencing the back field. Bee had made sure that all the dogs were safely in the house, along with the cats, although these, unusually for their species, were rarely any trouble when it came to such occasions. They seemed to know that something was on the wind, secreting themselves in the nooks and crannies of the old house, lying low.

Bee could do nothing about the many birds, the rooks and starlings, bluetits and woodpeckers, the jackdaws which chacked and squabbled about Mooncote's chimneys, but she had to trust that they were sensible enough to keep themselves out of sight. Their numbers never seemed to be depleted in the morning, at least as far as she could tell.

She waited with Dark by her side, looking out over the back field. It was late in the evening now, the sun sinking into a rosy western light over the hills. At the top of the field stood Sam and Luna's van, now parked up with Sam's grandmother, Ver March, in residence. Most nights, Bee found it comforting to look out of the window and see the little light in the window of the van that was a candle, lit by Ver, but tonight the van was dark. She knew that Ver would be watching from somewhere safely out of sight; keeping the vigil with them.

The van was not the only structure in the paddock. A field shelter formed a small humpy shadow on a slope of tussocky grass and reed down by the stream. An absolutely ordinary English pastoral view. Except that it was not ordinary at all: for this was part of Bee's not-a-secret, that earlier in the spring she had bargained with the inhuman leader of the Wild Hunt, granting him access over this land in exchange for her life and those of others. A throughway, a corridor, a smeuse; linking the Hunt's patchwork territories together.

She had granted this access to Aiken Drum, goat-eyed, ram-horned Helwyr of the Hunt, because it was the least of the things that he wanted. There were other, bigger things which he had tried to take, and one which he had tried to stop: her sister Stella's quest in London. He had let Bee go free, on the condition that Stella would cease her search, and this Bee had promised him. But it had been too late: by the time Bee came home again, from up hill and down dale, Stella had found what and who she was looking for, and so Bee's promise had been broken before it had begun.

She did not know what this breach of trust would bring: perhaps nothing, but perhaps much.

*

"This is the third time the Hunt has ridden over Mooncote land," Ned Dark said and Bee knew that he was echoing her own thoughts. She reached out and took his hand, a strong sailor's hand, not like the hand of a ghost, which Ned was.

"Yes. Good Friday and then St Mark's Eve, and now."

"May Eve always was a chancy, unruly time. In my day as well as yours."

"Yes. It's changed its pattern." Up the road, in nearby Glastonbury, they would be celebrating Beltane tomorrow, with a May Pole carried ceremoniously up the High Street and no doubt a fearsome amount of cider and mead consumed while bonfires were ignited. Other towns nearby would be holding their own celebrations; Merriton, with its Oss, and Hornlake with a flower festival. These days, among modern pagans, it was a celebration of fertility and sex, but in older times, so Dark had told her, May Eve was a time when the fairies came to the world of men, with no good intent.

"They lit the balefires when I was a boy," Dark said. The pearl which hung from his earlobe, just above his ruff, stirred in a draught which Bee could not feel. "To drive the herds and the flocks between, to bless them as they went to pasture."

Bee smiled. "And what did the church have to say about that?"

"Why, the church said nothing at all, if it was wise. And old Father Merriam, who was priest at Hornmoon in my childhood days, was a very wise man."

"I heard the bells earlier," Bee said. "I think they're just practicing, though."

"The Hunt won't ride while the church bells ring."

"It's not quite dark, anyway." She watched as a flock of white egrets, which had been picking about in the field, whirled up and over the hedge, heading towards the water meadows beyond the church. "Oh, I'm glad they've made a move, at last."

"The evening star's out," Dark said. His face was in shadow. Bee felt a tingle of anticipation in the air, a sudden electric current. She sat up a little straighter. A hush fell over the sky, the last glow fading into the west. The evening star was bright and sparkling. Somewhere, an owl cried out: a tawny's fox-like scream.

Bee waited, remembering the other times they had sat here to watch the Hunt ride: the stream of grey horses with their horned and antlered riders, a great bull-headed man, the Hounds who were both man and mastiff, among them the Lilywhite Boys, the Helwyr's muscle: barely human and, as far as Bee could see, utterly malign. And sometimes, among them, riding pillion on Aiken Drum's great chestnut stallion, Bee's own mother, Alys Fallow. A stream of mounts and hounds and riders and beasts, heading over the land and up to the starways. A stirring sight, even if it chilled the blood: a transgression, a thing that humans should not rightly see.

And which, now, they did not. Bee and Dark waited, until Venus began to sink and the gibbous moon marched out, in company with the red and baleful eye of Mars and the spring constellations, but the Hunt did not come. They sat, silent and dismayed, until the church bells rang out the midnight hour over Somerset and the night fully claimed the land.

SIELLA

In Stella's thoughts these days was the Knowledge: that invisible map of London, its secret highways and passages and timeways and nexus points, which Stella's new friend Davy Dearly had received earlier in the spring, a long-overdue download from the mind of a ghost. After much deliberation and debate, Stella and Davy had put this knowledge of the secret ways of the city down on paper. They had both been wary of doing so, for various reasons.

"The thing is, I don't want to keep it to myself. I think it's selfish and you know my views on sharing information," Davy said. They had been sitting in the Southwark Tavern at the time, along with Stella's friend Ace. "Like, I am the one with ultimate power and only I shall be the bearer of the secret – fuck that. But, and it's a big but, there are plenty of people out there, and we've met several of them, who do think like that."

"Yes, and what happens if they get hold of you, Davy?" Ace said. "Some people wouldn't stop at torturing it out of you."

"Whereas if it's not exclusive to you…" Stella said. "Well, they could still do that, I suppose."

"They could *try*." Davy rolled her mismatched eyes, one grey and one blue. "But rats are sneaky. Seriously, there's a part of me which would like to put the cat among the pigeons and open source the whole thing. If everyone knows then no one's got the advantage – except there's a power imbalance in some quarters, know what I mean? Some people could do more with the info than others."

"Those people we met along the Thames back in the spring – the refugees from another time. They were pretty vulnerable. If someone knew, they could go after them…"

"And we don't know what they went back to. They were refugees for a reason in the first place. The Hunt drove them from their village."

"So what do you think, Davy?" Ace asked. "The knowledge was given to you. It's up to you, really, what you want to do with it."

"I've given it a lot of thought," Davy said. "And I do know what I want to do with it. I want to get a big map of the city, and make a note of everything I know, on little sticky labels, and put it on the map, and take it to Hercules Road. Because if it's safe anywhere, it's safe with William Blake."

"What about young Hob? He's still living at Blake's, isn't he?" Stella did not dislike Hob, whom they had met earlier in the spring, but for various reasons she did not entirely trust him: he had proved somewhat shifty. But now Blake seemed to have semi-adopted the young man.

"Yes, but he kind of hero worships old Bill Blake these days. Bill seems to have replaced Miranda in his affections. I was surprised he went back to Bill's, after she died."

Stella thought of Miranda with a shudder. She had been the ex of actor Ward Garner, had hated Stella's sister Serena, who was now going out with Ward. Even though Miranda had been the one to dump him. How unreasonable was that? But 'reasonable' and 'Miranda' had never really gone together. Stella could not find it in herself to be anything other than glad that Miranda was dead.

She said now, "I suppose Hob had nowhere else to go. And I should think Bill has all kinds of secrets he can keep from his house guests."

So this is what they had done. A carefully annotated map of London, with its secret entrances and exits, its passages and corridors and boltholes through time and space, was now lodged with William Blake, mystic and engraver and artist, in Lambeth, way back when and, with the exception of Stella and Davy, firmly out of the reach of the twenty first century.

"I don't know if you want to put it in a special box or a drawer or something, or under the floorboards or what?" Davy had said to Blake, handing over the scroll that they had rolled the map into. Stella had been relieved that Hob was nowhere to be seen that day ("Out on an errand," Blake had said).

But Blake told them, "Come with me."

Usually, Blake held court in his garden, which today seemed to be keeping pace with Stella's day and age: it was filled with white lilacs and through the open kitchen door the scent was overpowering. But now he ushered them into the house itself. Stella had previously glimpsed some of the rooms on the ground floor, filled with frames and engraving equipment, and the old fashioned kitchen alongside which Catherine Blake and her maid laboured over the laundry in the scullery. Did they ever long for a washing machine? Stella wondered. But she did not like to ask. She had never been further into the house, but now Blake led them into the hall. The house had a curious smell, beyond the odours of boiled beef and soap and the flowery scents drifting in from the garden: on a previous occasion, Stella had asked and Blake told her it was the wooden engraving blocks themselves, in conjunction with the ink. It was not unpleasant.

Now, Blake led them up the stairs, which had a small landing partway up, on the bend.

"Now you will know one of *my* secrets," he said, smiling. "Should I wish to keep a thing safe, I place it in here." There was a very small hole in the skirting board, a mouse's front door.

"Will it fit?" Davy asked anxiously. Even when rolled up, the map was quite large.

"Oh, it will fit."

Blake bent down and tapped the scroll of the map against the skirting board, three sharp raps. Inside the hole, Stella suddenly saw an eye, with a lizard's slit pupil, scarlet as a hot coal. She jumped back.

"Jesus!"

The mouse's front door expanded, swirling up in a funnel of black light. Stella gasped and stumbled, nearly missing her footing on the stairs and clutching Davy's arm, but the funnel engulfed them both. They stood on nothing. Stella saw galaxies swirling by, nebulas towered above her head, suns winked into existence and blinked out. Something was standing before her, its great mailed head bent down. She saw the muscles of its scaly shoulders twitch and flex, saw its beaked mouth open and the hard pointed tongue within. Paralysed, she felt Davy's hand close over hers and grasp it hard. Blake stepped past them, unruffled, and handed the creature the map.

"If you could look after it for us… really would be most grateful… your help always much appreciated…"

An urbane, English murmur: he might have been talking to his bank manager.

A great sun span, the dark was gone. Stella, hand in hand with an ashen faced Davy, was alone with Blake on the stairs in the old house in Lambeth.

"What –?" It was a squeak. *Do better, Stella.*

"What in the name of fuck was that?" Davy whispered, then added, "Sorry about my language."

14

"Quite understandable. Oh, my apologies, I suppose he really is rather alarming in appearance. But a gentle soul, despite his fearsome mien. Allowed me to do a little drawing of him once. I called it *The Ghost of a Flea.*"

"That's a sodding big flea!" Stella said. "He must have been at least eight feet high."

"Obviously, he's not a real flea. I don't know *what* he is, to be quite honest. Some kind of spirit – I do not care for the term 'demon', you see. So pejorative and are we not all brethren beneath the kind light of the sun?" Blake smiled at them. "Would you care for some tea?"

A whopping big brandy might be more in order, Stella thought, but she accepted the tea, which was hot and somewhat calming. Then they left.

"However," Davy said to Stella, on the way back from Hercules Road. "At least, one would think, the map would be safe with that thing. Can't see many beings wanting to ruck it up with *him.*"

"Was that an actual alien, do you think?"

"I have no idea. Maybe that's what these old timey spirits really are."

"I think you're right, though. I think the map will be safe."

"Also, it's not like I've downloaded it and erased my own copy. That's still in here." Davy tapped the side of her head. "So we don't have to have the map for reference, which is just as well, as I can't see me popping by to borrow it every five minutes after *that.*"

"I memorised as much as I could," Stella said. "I don't think I could do the full course of study you need to be a black cab driver, that kind of Knowledge, let alone the secret ways as well."

"Fortunately you won't have to. It's not every street that has some kind of portal to the otherworld or the past. It just *feels* like every street."

Blake had told Stella and Davy sternly that just because they now possessed a route to other times, this did not mean that they could gad about all over the timescape like Dr Who (Stella's thought, not Blake's instruction. She did not think Hercules Road possessed a television set).

"Absolutely not," said Davy.

"Absolutely. No. None of that. Too risky."

They did not mention this conversation for some time after leaving Hercules Road. But as they reached the end of the street and the twenty first century loomed into view, in the form of the pub called the Pineapple, Stella said to Davy, "So where d'you want to go first?"

LUNA

Luna stood at the sink in the kitchen of Mooncote, patiently washing the glasses from the night before and listening to the radio. Bee had left it tuned to Radio 4 and Luna could not be bothered to try and find some music. She listened to the news, which was as usual depressing, and then the shipping forecast came on. She smiled, hearing the familiar litany of names.

"Viking, North Utsire, South Utsire, Forties... Sea state, moderate... Winds, westerly to north westerly, three to four..."

Luna carefully rinsed out the wineglasses and placed them on the draining board as the rosary was ticked off. The Shipping Forecast was one of those things that made her feel all was well with the world.

"Visibility, good, sea state, moderate to fair..." One by one the names were recited, like a spell. *"Cromarty, Forth, Tyne, Dogger, Fisher, German Bight..."*

There would be storms, the Shipping Forecast told her, but not here, only in these distant coastal places. Then, in the middle of the forecast, came a sudden sharp cry. Luna jumped and nearly dropped a wineglass; she retrieved it just in time.

"...Rockall, Malin, Hebrides... Visibility, good..."

That had sounded like a seagull, Luna thought. In the middle of the Shipping Forecast? But *nothing* interrupted that. And it was read out from a BBC studio, not by some windswept gentleman in a sou-wester standing on a cliff top.

"...Fair Isle, winds northeasterly, Faeroes, Southeast Iceland..."

Luna listened but the sound did not re-occur. Perhaps it had come from outside the house. Seagulls did visit the fields around Mooncote, after all, seeking shelter from the gales in the Severn Estuary, which was not far away.

As the Forecast wound down, Bee bustled in.

"Thanks for cleaning all those glasses, Luna. You didn't have to do that!"

"You did everything else," Luna said, forgetting about her unease. "And also I feel that if I sit down I might never get up again." Pregnancy in the last few weeks was turning out to be an ordeal: Luna felt enormous and whenever she caught sight of herself in the mirror, she realised that she looked enormous too. Neither she nor Sam, the baby's father, were exactly sylph-like as it was and the baby promised to come out in the same sturdy mould. Scans had suggested that it was healthy, but neither Sam nor Luna had chosen to be told the baby's sex: as long as it was okay, that really didn't matter. She mentioned this again now. "Whatever it turns out to be."

"I think it's nice to be surprised," Vervain March, Sam's grandmother, said, coming in from the van for a cup of coffee. They'd had a long holiday, Luna thought, since she and Sam had arrived in the autumn and it was now May Day: the van would be taking root soon. "Better that way. More natural."

"Ha! Yeah, that doesn't really apply to me, does it? As long as it's not a bird," Luna said.

"More likely to be a human baby, one would think, whatever you might be able to turn yourself into. I never had any problems."

"Serena spoke to Ace's girlfriend in London, who knows about these things – she's sort of a goddess, after all – and she said it used to be much more common for people to give birth to animals. So I'm just hoping I don't lay a great big egg."

"The scans showed a baby, though?"

"Yes. But if you take a photo of me, you see a human woman, not a wren."

"Very true. Well, we'll just have to wait and see. Have faith. Though in what, I don't know."

"We do know several goddesses," said Luna. "As mentioned."

"I'm sure Lady Noualen would look out for you if you asked her to, and Mr Spare's Anione – what a nice woman she is, I thought – and those star spirits of yours, they'll be around as well, I expect. They've helped you before."

"That's true," Luna said, comforted. The prospect of labour, only a few weeks away, was daunting but she was a strong person: she hoped she could handle it. Her own mother, Alys, had given her advice and so had her sister Serena, who, after all, always looked a lot more fragile than Luna herself. Serena had said it was awful but only intermittently: "it just took rather a long time and I swore a lot, but darling Bella was worth it."

"Anyway," Ver said now, alluding to the reason for her visit, "Bee asked me earlier this morning and I shall be delighted to accompany you into Merriton today and see the old Oss. It's always a good idea to mark May Day."

"It's a lot of fun," Luna said. "When we were little, we used to alternate the Oss at Merriton with the King and Queen of the May at Glastonbury, but Bee says this year, it's the Oss' turn."

"I like a good Oss," said Ver. "But I hope, that should there be Morris Dancing, we avoid the unpleasantness of last time."

"So do I!"

Luna liked Morris dancers, but not when they turned out to be eldritch dog spirits who tried to kidnap you. "I hope they're normal, ordinary Morris Dancers," she added.

"What time would Bee like me to be ready?"

"It's nearly ten now. About eleven? They have food stalls so we can pick up a pasty or something when we're there."

"Splendid."

Sam was driving them to Merriton. Ver sat in the front with him, while Bee and Luna took the back seat. Moth the dog had been left behind, resulting in reproachful looks of woe. They headed west across the Levels, along lanes fringed with cow parsley and overhung with the vivid chartreuse of new oak. It was a high, bright day, slanting sunlight and high fluffs of cloud towards the coast. Merriton had been an old fishing port on the Severn Sea, but although a handful of boats remained, the little town was now home to a coffee roastery, two delis and a restaurant which featured regularly in the *Guardian* and whose prices always made Bee tut. As they neared the coast, the light grew: that chalky radiance which betrays the presence of the sea. Over a last hill and the sea itself was in view, the dull grey-brown water of the estuary sparking steel from the sun, with the dim Welsh shore beyond.

"There's always the issue of somewhere to park," Bee said. "Try round the back of Nat West, Sam."

"I'll drop you off," he said. "Then find a space."

"All right. Thanks!"

Sam dropped them outside the Crown Inn, facing the harbour, and Luna found herself in a throng of people. They retreated into a snicket running between the pub and the Post Office, but were obliged to vacate it almost at once: a green man, twelve feet high and operated by a number of nimble puppeteers, was coming down the snicket.

18

"Cheers, sorry, thanks," shouted a man. An older woman sitting at a table outside the pub said to Luna, "Do you want to sit down, love? There's plenty of room."

"I'm all right, thank you."

"*He's* very impressive," said Ver. "You didn't tell me they were going to have one of them."

"I didn't know. I've never seen a green man here before. He must be new."

He was, very obviously, a large puppet, otherwise Luna might have thought they were borrowing trouble. You never knew what might turn up at these events.

"Oh, hello, Luna," said a voice at her shoulder. She turned to see their friend, Nick Wratchall-Haynes, as usual tweed-clad and shiny of shoe, looking very much the respectable local squire.

"Hi! We got your text."

"Yes, I thought I'd pop over. See what was going on."

"The more the merrier," Bee said, but Luna knew that what she actually meant was, *the more the safer*. She drew Nick and Luna aside, away from the crowd and earshot and added, under her breath, "No show last night, by the way."

The hunt master's sandy eyebrows rose. "Really?"

"Neither hide nor hair."

"That's a bit disconcerting."

"I thought it was bloody typical," Bee said. "You're freaked out when they show up and then freaked out when they don't."

Nick gave a grim nod. "Yes, because you can't help wondering why."

"If it was such a big deal for them to have access to our land, why aren't they using it?"

"Agreed." Nick sighed. "It's always a delicate balance. I find that with the foxhounds. You're never quite sure how farmers are going to react – I do a lot of networking. But it's not the same thing."

"No, quite."

"I will say it's been very quiet since earlier in the spring," Ver said. "As though everything shot its bolt and is in recovery."

"It was the same after Twelfth Night. And then look what happened."

"You're not going to go looking for trouble, though," said Nick.

"Damn right I'm not. Oh, there's Laura!"

19

Bee waved vigorously. Laura Amberley's face lit up when she caught sight of them. She crossed the road. As usual, in jodhpurs and riding boots, she looked as though she had just got off a horse.

"Hi! Mum said you were coming. I hoped I'd run into you. I should have sent a text but it was all a bit of a rush getting out of the house..."

"Is your mum here?"

"Somewhere. And dad. But not Ben – my brother's burrowed into a recording studio like a Hobbit in its nest. Or hole. Whatever. Creating. Can't be disturbed."

"Well, that's a good thing!"

"Look, there's the Oss!" Luna said to Ver. It was progressing down the street: an enormous wheel covered in rags and tatters and leaves. Ribbons fluttered from it in the colours of May Day: green, scarlet and white. It had no head, just a pyramidal point covered in foliage. Under there, somewhere in the centre of the wheel and beneath the leaves, was a person. Luna could see his feet, clad in sturdy DMs.

"I've never known why they call it an Oss," Ver said, reflectively.

"No, it's nothing like a horse," Laura said, as they watched the swaying, whirling figure dancing along the street. "I don't know what it *is* like."

"Itself, perhaps."

Luna thought that the Oss was like the Mari Lwyds that they had met back in the winter, at Chepstow. She expected the tossing skirt to wheel up, revealing stars, another world. But the Oss passed by, playfully striking at spectators with a coloured stick, carefully avoiding the visibly-pregnant Luna. Accompanied by a Morris side, the swaying green man and a host of tourists taking selfies, it had soon gone down the street and out of sight.

Luna felt almost disappointed. The otherworld, with all its portents and signs, tended to make its presence felt on occasions like this. But the Oss was, thus far, all it seemed: a revived piece of local folklore, mainly for the benefit of outsiders. Nick Wratchall-Haynes was apparently thinking the same. Looking in the wake of the Oss, he said,

"I wonder how old that really is."

Bee said, "The actual Oss itself dates from the nineteen twenties. Grandfather told me that – the previous one got too old and fragile so the local cooper remade it out of a table top. Before that, I don't know – eighteenth century, maybe? A lot of these things aren't in an unbroken line: they come and go. When mother was a little girl, she said all the schools had a maypole, then it stopped for a bit, then it started again."

"I expect it just needs someone enthusiastic to take an interest," Ver said. "Like most community projects."

"A bit of old England," Nick said. "An anachronism. Makes us all feel timeless and nostalgic."

"You're right." Ver gave him an approving look. "But old England changes all the time."

"So I see." He was looking in the wake of the Oss.

"If you want to follow it, I can wait here for Sam," Luna said. There was a bench facing the harbour; she could look at the boats. Sam was, presumably, having problems finding a parking space.

"Are you sure?"

"Yes, go on. Have fun!"

Left on her own, Luna settled onto the bench. The harbour made a pretty scene, with the little blue, white and red boats stranded on the mud, waiting for the tide to come in again. A big herring gull perched on the harbour wall. It regarded Luna from one cold yellow eye and gave a harsh cluck. Looking at it, Luna found she had no trouble in believing that birds had evolved from dinosaurs. A couple walked past with a little dog, the terrier barked and the gull soared up with an affronted shriek. Luna watched it sail out across the harbour. She blinked. The sunlight was strong, but a shadow had fallen over her. Luna looked up and saw a man, dressed all in black with a broad brimmed black hat. She could see the harbour wall through his body. His eyes were empty sockets. He grinned at Luna and said,

"Stay away, girl. Or the gulls will be crying for your baby, too."

Luna gasped. A drum beat, and shouts. The Oss was coming back along the harbour; she felt the thud of the drum beat the shade away. The man was gone, whisked away in a handful of dust. Luna sat numbly on the bench, shocked. The encounter had happened so quickly that she'd had no time to protest. The Oss whirled and stamped, keeping trouble at bay, and then Sam was there. Luna stood up and buried her face in his shirt.

"How unusual," Bee said, when they got back home, "to have something that was supposed to be a nice uneventful day out turn into a horror story. Yes, I'm being sarcastic. Luna, are you sure you're all right?"

"I'm fine," Luna told her. "Bit scared, very cross."

"Cross is good! Nick, would you like some tea or do you have to dash?"

"Tea would be great. Thank you. And thanks for the fruit, too." The hunt master had been persuaded to come back to Mooncote with them and a bag of frozen gooseberries and one of blackcurrants now reposed on the kitchen table in front of him, in a chiller bag.

Bee gave him a look. "Well done. *That* didn't sound remotely sarcastic. You know as well as I do that this is self-defence rather than kindness. If I don't take last year's out of the freezer there won't be any room for this year's. We made wine, we made jam…"

"Incoming soft fruit! I wasn't here much last summer so Harris took a lot of ours and distributed it around the village. Until he realised that everyone else had far too much as well but was too polite to refuse."

"Stealthy gifts of gooseberries left on doorsteps in the middle of the night. I could just leave it for the birds but the Victorian housewife in me feels too guilty. Sam took a load into the Glastonbury community fridge but there's still a lot left. So I'm glad you're taking some of last year's excess. I'm sure Rachel will extend her housekeeping duties to turn it into jelly, if necessary."

The hunt master rubbed his hands through his hair, making it stand up.

"This is too normal," he said. "Especially after this morning."

"The calm before the storm?"

"I'd make the most of it, dear," Ver told him. "It won't last."

That night, Luna could not sleep. The final stages of pregnancy seemed to bring insomnia in their wake, just when she needed sleep most, and she kept remembering the shade and his awful words. Sam was out for the count and the lurcher, Moth, who had somehow snuck onto the bed, raised his long enquiring head when Luna got up and went as quietly as she could to the door. She went downstairs, made a cup of mint tea, and took it into her grandfather's study rather than into the sitting room. She felt like being enclosed. Being safe.

After his death, Abraham's study had not been kept entirely as he had left it. Under Bee's sterner reign, it was a great deal tidier. The piles of paper that had stood on the desk had now been filed or shredded: probably filed, Luna thought, knowing Bee. She smiled, remembering her grandfather talking about a fellow academic in his days as a university lecturer; how the old gentleman had kept a truly enormous pile of paper in the corner of his office. When he had died, or retired, Luna could not remember which, the staff cleared his office out and had discovered a desk beneath it. Abraham had not been quite that bad, but not far off.

She sat down in the captain's chair and found a coaster for her cup, then looked around her at the familiar bookshelves, at the old astrolabe that had been her grandfather's pride and joy: said to be Arabic, and acquired from a specialist dealer in Wells. Movement caught her eye and Luna stiffened, then realised that the movement was a tail: a long black tail like a bellrope, protruding from the bottom of the study curtains.

"Tut, you are not allowed in here!" Luna said. The tail gave an irritated twitch. Luna went over to the window and pulled the curtain aside: the black cat Tut sat upon the sill, lamp-eyed. He did not look at Luna. All his attention was focused on the orchard, which lay in the moonlight below. Luna could see someone walking there – a star? The woman wore a crown of roses and behind her, a few feet away, another woman was following, no more than a girl. Her face was white and quiet, and where she trod, small white flowers blossomed for a moment and then faded. Luna caught her breath, recognising the spirit that had grown from a huntsman's tooth earlier in the spring, who had trapped Luna and Laura and Ned inside the house while she sought to draw lightning and storm down upon it, for what purpose Luna still did not really understand. Simple malignity, perhaps. Nick had countered her magic and the Behenian stars of the Spring Triangle had taken her, made her a child again, but Luna had not seen her since. Now she walked in the wake of the woman with the crown of roses, as meek as a maidservant in the steps of a queen. Luna had to admit that she preferred her that way.

Tut's tail gave another twitch. The astrolabe creaked, making Luna jump. She turned to see it slowly turning, then settle into stillness. Luna watched, with the cat by her side, as the rose-crowned woman and her echo passed down the orchard and out of sight. They would, Luna suddenly felt sure, keep anything nasty at bay.

SERENA

"It's so cold!" Stella took a sip of her coffee, warming hands clad in fingerless gloves. "It's supposed to be *May*. April was warmer than this!"

"I spoke to Bee last night," Serena said. Wearing a parka, she was warm enough but she knew what her sister meant. "She says it's the Ice Saints."

"The who?"

"Ice Saints. St. Mamertus, St. Pancras, and St. Servatius. I think. It's their saints' days about now and ye olde folklore says it coincides with a cold snap."

"St Pancras, eh?" Stella said uneasily, huddling in her fleece. "I thought we'd seen the last of *that* part of town. Except for trains. And how is Bee? I facetimed her last week."

"She's fine. Except she's worried."

"The Hunt still hasn't shown up?"

"Things have come to a pretty pass, as Ver would say, when we're all twitchy because they *haven't* appeared."

"She asked Laura, but Laura didn't know."

"Laura is – still working with Noualen?"

"Yes, but she says it's like dreaming. Sometimes she's not even sure she's left her bed, let alone turned into a horse to carry an ancient goddess all over the English countryside."

"Must be funny, being someone's horse. In a non-dodgy, non-sexual sense, I mean," Serena added, somewhat flustered.

"Shades of the pony club. And not the one for kiddies. Mind you, it's not exactly normal to suddenly turn into hares or otters, either."

"No."

"No. Or rats." Stella waved in the direction of the wharf. "Talking of whom…"

"Evening," Davy Dearly said, stepping on board. "I got your text. Hello, Serena – nice to see you again." Today, she was smart in black linen and she carried an Apple laptop case. Her asymmetric gaze was amused.

"Take a seat. You want a beer?"

"I bloody need a beer, love. Marketing meeting. All day. In Shoreditch. Team building. Blue sky thinking. Mainly from men making the same point I'd made ten minutes previously."

"Oh, how annoying," Stella said. "I'm so glad I work for myself."

"Words were had. Young Mr Topham won't be doing *that* again, at least not with me." Davy accepted a beer. "Cheers. Anyway, enough of my tedious day at work."

Stella said, "It's Saturday tomorrow, and I wanted to ask you if you were up for a jaunt into town, Davy?"

"With a purpose in mind?"

"With a purpose in mind, yes. And Serena, if you want to come along, you're welcome, too."

"I'll have to pass," Serena said, a little reluctantly. "I said I'd go and watch Ward's rehearsal. Now that the theatre's been renovated after the fire, they're really cracking on with *A Midsummer Night's Dream*."

"No worries. Next time, maybe."

"Absolutely." Serena knew that Stella and Davy were hoping to explore: travelling through the palimpsest of time that had accrued upon London, those places where the city had worn thin. So far, they had been cautious ("don't want to rattle too many cages," said Davy) but now summer was coming and the city had been quiet, lapsing back into somnolence after the events of the spring, just as it had done after Twelfth Night.

"If everyone's ready to eat," Stella's landlady Evie said, emerging in a pinny from the depths of the *Nitrogen*, "I'll serve up."

STELLA

On the following morning, as agreed, Stella and Davy were again heading south of the river. They had been very good, Stella thought, and obeyed Blake's instructions until now, but honesty compelled her to admit that this might have been more because neither she nor Davy could decide when in London to go first.

Elizabethan? Been there and it stank.

Medieval? Been there, too. Dangerous. Also plague.

Dark Ages? Davy fancied pastures new but not, as she put it, pastures that were covered with shit and dead bodies. Even rats had standards, especially ones with human sensibilities.

Civil War? No, thanks, the whole Puritan witch-burning thing was offputting.

"Although," Davy said, "People accused of witchcraft were usually hanged."

"Oh, that's *so* much better. How about the Regency? Bit of costume drama? We might meet Jane Austen. Might encounter a dashing viscount or two."

"In parts of London during the Georgian period," Davy informed her, "there was one privy for two hundred people and many folk lived in cellars surrounded by their own filth. Also there was acid rain. From the copper works."

"There go my duke and bonnet fantasies, then."

Finally, however, the decision had been made for them. Stella had been to Brixton a few days before the dinner on the barge, to meet her agent and a client in a café about a gig. This had all gone smoothly and on the way home Stella, on a whim, had decided to stop off at St Paul's Cathedral and see what there was to be seen. She admitted to herself that this was skirting around the limits of Blake's instructions, for on a previous occasion the cathedral itself had taken matters under control and whisked Stella back in time. She was also obliged to admit that, in spite of previously expressed reservations, she was secretly hoping the same thing might happen again. Alarming though it was to have these temporal adventures, it was also intriguing and a bit addictive, if she was honest. All the same, Stella felt mildly guilty about her visit: it was breaking the spirit if not the letter of their promise to Blake.

However, the cathedral remained static in time and space, its grounds filled with tour groups and a small coterie of clerics, all of whom stayed resolutely modern. Stella did not go inside, but wandered about the grounds, eventually finding herself in Postman's Park, according to a nearby sign. Why a park, for postmen? Stella wondered. Perhaps this was a place for them to sit and rest their weary feet as they made their rounds. There were benches, and some formal planting, and a wall on which there were a number of tiled plaques. Stella went over to have a look.

The wall was Victorian, the tiles decorated with scrollwork and floral motifs. Each tile bore a story. A woman who had died in 1863, trying to put out 'flames on a friend'. A man who had died leaping from a steamboat to rescue a drowning child. Boiler explosions. Crashing locomotives. Stella read on, mesmerised with horror.

"I remember when they put this up," said a voice.

Stella turned to find her friend Mags, clad in hoodie and ripped jeans, and chewing bubblegum.

"Hello!"

"Yeah, it was some Victorian bloke. Wanted to commemorate all the people who lost their lives trying to save others."

"That's pretty noble. If depressing."

"Don't worry, they're in a better place," Mags said, absently. As an angel, she should know, Stella thought. "I dunno what it's got to do with postmen. Anyway, I've been looking for you. Bill would like a word. Don't worry," she added, seeing the expression on Stella's face. "You haven't done anything wrong! You're not in trouble."

"Legacy of school," said Stella. "Headmistress' office, Miss Fallow, now."

"You're like me – I always think someone's going to haul me over the coals."

"But you're an angel!" Literally.

"Even so. But no, he's not cross or anything. I think it's about Hob."

"Oh, right." Stella had not seen Hob for a while. The young man – if man he was, and not something supernatural – had been lying low since the events of the spring. Stella said as much. "And we didn't see him when we were last over there. Bill said he was out."

"He's been keeping his nose clean. I think he's got a lot of respect for Bill; he's not just putting it on. But Blake's been trying to find out who he is. Or what."

"He told us his mum was a model," Stella said. "And he grew up in Clapham."

"Yes, he said that to me, too. He also said he doesn't know who his dad was, which is fair enough. If this makes any sense, I think he thinks he's telling the truth, but Blake doesn't believe him."

"Why not?"

"Not sure, but he'll have his reasons. Anyway, he wanted you to do something for him."

"What's that then, Mags?"

"Trip to Clapham."

"Clapham? Not very exciting."

Mags grinned. "You might be surprised."

So that was where Stella and Davy were now heading.

"Blake's instructions were to get off the bus at the common and start walking north. It's a house, but I don't know which one. A big place with a turret. We'll know it when we see it, Mags said. But I can't think of anywhere round Clapham Common with a turret."

"Perhaps not now," Davy said.

"Ah. Is there an entry near here, then?"

Davy nodded. "Yes. End of the road. It's not like a sacred spot or anything. I looked it up on Google Earth once I realised it was there. I think it's in someone's flat."

"That could be embarrassing."

"Yeah. 'Hi, you don't know us, but we want to use your lounge as a portal to another time. Is that cool with you?'" She paused by a block of modern flats. "No, wait. It's not a flat – it's down there."

Cautiously, Stella and Davy made their way down into the underground parking area beneath the block. BMWs and Porsches were much in evidence.

"It's round here somewhere," said Davy. "I hope we're not on CCTV. I don't want to get arrested for snooping about someone's posh motor."

But suddenly, in the blink of an eye, the cars were gone. Davy and Stella stood by a brook, overhung by hawthorn. They were knee deep in cow parsley and buttercups. It was quite dark.

"Nice one, Davy!"

"So that would be your mansion," Davy said, straining to see. Then the moon came out from behind a cloud and things became a little clearer.

The block of flats had been replaced by a manor house, built of brick and dominated, indeed, by a turret. A long wall ran along a formal garden and beyond the house Stella could see the dim silhouettes of springtime oaks. Then she heard the clop of a horse's hooves and shortly a middle aged man riding a stout cob came into view.

"Elizabethan, yeah?" Davy murmured, looking at the ruff around his throat.

"Goes with the house. Hope he hasn't spotted us. Good thing it's dark."

But the man showed no sign of having seen them. He dismounted, and a young groom ran out and tethered the horse to a hitching post. They spoke, but Stella and Davy were too far away to hear the words. The man headed briskly to the house and was shown inside, but the door was left open. Davy and Stella looked at one another.

"Want to risk it?"

"We could have a little look."

As they approached the house, however, they saw that a gateway in the long garden wall was also ajar. A fragrant basket of rosemary and lavender sat forgotten on a bench.

"We could take that into the house. Pretend to be maids."

"It's the middle of the night. Also, we don't look like maids."

"You never know. Appearance changes when time changes."

Stella admitted that this was true.

"The thing is, though, they must know who the staff are."

"You'd be surprised. If he's a visitor, he probably doesn't even notice the maids. Not as people, anyway. Probably as the hands that bring him his beer at best and a pair of knockers at worst."

"I've never actually been groped by someone in the past," Stella said.

"There's always a first time, trust me. I have. Anyone even vaguely female's a target for a depressingly large number of the male population in most of history, as far as I can judge. I'd do the rat thing but that can be fraught with hazard, too – the number of boots I've had to dodge…"

"And I don't think I can change at will like you can," said Stella. "I've tried. Also they'd freak out if they found an otter on the landing."

"Yes, you'd be someone's coat trimming in no time."

Davy picked up the basket and they made their way into the house, meeting no one. The hallway was panelled and flagged, smelling of beeswax and old fires, lit by candles flickering in sconces along the wall. An oak staircase led upwards. Stella and Davy crept up it, trying to be quiet. They could hear voices coming from a room off the landing and avoided it, taking the staircase further.

"We're on the northern side of the building," Davy whispered. "I think this must lead to the turret."

"Do you know what Bill actually wants us to *do* here?"

"I think just have a poke about, perhaps. See what's to be seen. Mags said his instructions weren't specific."

Halfway up, they paused to look out of a small leaded window. The Thames was visible in the light of the moon, a broad grey ribbon threading through a maze of steep roofs. The spire of St Paul's could be seen to the northwest, ruling the skyline.

"This is before the spire got struck by lightning, then," said Davy.

"So this is about the same time that we visited before. Fifteen sixties?"

"Something like that. I think the spire collapsed in 1561, if I remember rightly. There's a lot of noise outside," Davy added.

Stella listened. The quiet of the house was broken by sudden hoofbeats, shouts and cries. They heard running feet down below.

"Up," Davy snapped. They proceeded swiftly into the tower. The stairs led into a large, square room, also panelled with oak but hung with tapestries. It contained a chest and a table, and two candlesticks. Both candles were lit. A portrait hung upon the wall, instantly familiar. Stella had last seen that chilly white face and flaming hair looking over the side of a barge on the Thames, but she had seen plenty of similar representations many times before: in school, in the National Portrait Gallery, on history programmes. And when they looked out of the turret window, they saw the original in the garden below.

"Oh shit," said Davy.

Elizabeth the Queen rode a white palfrey. She wore a green gown, embroidered with gold that sparked in the lamps held by the servants, and the light flashed, too, from a great stone on her hand, an emerald gleam. She was surrounded by men whom Stella assumed to be courtiers, young gallants and an older man with a forked grey beard, riding a horse as black as his clothes. Two women rode alongside the Queen and the palfrey was now guided to a mounting block. Elizabeth got down, not without difficulty.

"Christ, imagine riding a horse in all those skirts," said Davy.

"Whoever pioneered trousers for women was a saint."

"She's coming into the house. Perhaps we should try and sneak out while we can."

"She's not likely to be coming all the way up here, though," Stella said.

But Stella was wrong.

Stella and Davy went back to the door. Footsteps were coming up the stairs. Remembering their Hamlet, they dodged behind one of the tapestries: it was hung upon a rail, leaving just enough room for someone to hide. The footsteps, and the voices, grew louder.

"They're coming in here!" Davy hissed. Stella kept very still. There was a brief silence, then a voice said,

"Light the fire."

That was Elizabeth, Stella thought. She had heard the Queen's cold tones once before. She wished she could see, but a hole in the thickly woven tapestry was too much to hope for. There was the rattle of sticks and then, after a few minutes, the crackle of flames. Stella could hear people moving about, the rustle of Elizabeth's skirts.

"And you are certain this will work?" said the Queen.

A man gave a short laugh. "Nothing in magic is ever a certain thing, Majesty. But the signs are right: the moon is full, the tide of summer is on the turn, Mars lies in Aries and the vessel is prepared." Stella could not see him, but she was prepared to bet that this was the man in black with the forked beard. "I have had word from the Morlader; he has carried out his task."

"And do you trust this man, this 'Morlader'? Sir Francis has told me that it is the word for pirate, in the Cornish tongue?"

"He is a rogue and a scoundrel, like all his kind, but he has much to gain." A chilly little laugh. "After all, your coffers are deep and your ships are faster than his own."

"Very well. I know you have done your best."

Stella thought that there might be a faint threat beneath that statement.

"If you could move that table back a little, Sir Geoffrey, I would be most obliged."

Sounds of furniture being shifted and then a curiously precise scraping noise.

"This, as you will know, is our conjuration triangle."

Stella was now beginning to wish that they had brought Ace along. She had to remember everything that was said, to tell him later. Hopefully, there would *be* a later.

"Stand there," the man said. A childish voice replied.

"Here, master?"

Christ, there was a little boy with them. Why? The next moment, Stella's question was answered.

"Give me your hand." A pause. "The finger nail of this child is anointed with olive oil, your Majesty – see how I do it? The demon will be brought through this portal thus, via the hand of an innocent."

"And I must do the casting itself?"

"Your Majesty, yes, since it is you who desire the result. But we must wait till the clock strikes."

Stella held her breath. It was difficult to stand motionless; she was developing a new respect for life models. And they had only been there for a few minutes. To her relief, however, a clock did begin to chime, deep within the house. At the sixth stroke the man said, "Now, Majesty! Cast the salt."

A whisper of skirts, a hiss of fire. A thick smoke crept behind the tapestry, making it difficult to breathe. *Please don't let me sneeze,* prayed Stella. A slight movement beside her suggested that Davy was praying the same. The man began to call a sequence of names: "Paimon, Beleth, Vinea, Balan! O you kings and dukes of Hell! Agares, Amdusias, Malaphar! Open the way, I beseech you!"

Stella felt Davy give a sudden twitch. She reached out for her friend's hand and squeezed it. Davy squeezed back. The child gave a single sharp cry, as if hurt.

"Open the way!"

A great wind began to blow through the chamber, dispelling the smoke with the salt scent of the sea. There was rain on the wind, the smell of the great westerlies that blew up from Cornwall across Somerset, a scouring wind lashing the oaks and bending the knees of the reedbeds. The tapestry, however, did not move. The clock struck twelve.

As it did so, Stella felt the whole house shudder. The thick material which hid the room from her sight evaporated. She looked out onto a cold stretch of coast, a night sky racing with cloud, through which the moon dipped and the stars span. On the horizon, she saw an island, buildings perched on its summit, with the black run of a causeway linking it to the shore. Then, fast as a swooping gull, they were inside the building, which echoed with the sound of the sea.

Stella could see the room below: a circular space, illuminated by a fire in a great open hearth. A woman crouched beside it holding a poker. She gave the fire a stab and the wood flared up, sea blue and green. Driftwood, Stella thought; she had seen similar effects at beachside picnics. A second woman was sitting in a chair, her head bowed over a bundle in her lap. The woman with the poker stood. She was in her fifties and Stella thought that she had never seen a harder face: the woman's features might as well have been carved from stone. Behind them, in the corner, stood the tall figure of a man, dressed in black like a column of shadow. Sparks flared briefly around his face: Stella saw a haggard white countenance above a dark beard, but his eyes were empty sightless sockets. She swallowed a sudden lump in her throat. Bee had told her about Luna's encounter in Merriton.

"Elowen!" the hard faced woman said. It sounded like a command. A name? The seated woman did not move. The man raised a hand; there was a spark of marshfire green. In the seated woman's lap, the bundle stirred.

"*Elowen.*" She leaned forward and shook the seated woman by the shoulder. At last the woman looked up. Stella took a breath. It was Hob's face, pale and pinched, more androgynous in this female version, for there was little femininity in Hob's features. But the grey eyes and the curl of red hair beneath the woman's headscarf were the same, too – or was that a wimple, Stella wondered? She wore a rough brown dress.

33

"You know what you have to do." The woman's voice was implacable.

"No," Elowen whispered.

"A child of the Devil and you his consort? You know what you must do. Do it, now."

Elowen made a small, mute sound of protest. The man in black strode forward. Despite his blindness, he moved without hesitation or fumbling. He snatched up the bundle which, to Stella's horror, was a baby – she could see its face now – and thrust it into the fire. There was another shower of sparks, a handful of emeralds, thrown. Elowen gave a great wailing cry but the child made no sound at all. The tapestry came down, hiding the scene from Stella's sight.

"Now!" the man in the manor house cried, and Stella heard the Queen cry out: a shout of triumph.

"Seize him from the fire!" A new voice, bell-clear, not human. Stella was reminded of Blake's minion, the little demon whom the old man had once sent to aid them. Its sweetness sent shivers down her spine. "Now! Snatch him up!"

Sudden, rapid movement from the chamber and the strong smell of blazing wood. The wind abruptly died. Through the tapestry Stella saw an afterimage of a burning copper triangle, bright as fire and imprinted on her retina.

Silence. Then a wail split the air, a baby's seagull cry.

"Majesty!" said the man, in tones of deep respect.

"So!" hissed Elizabeth. "So, it is done! You did not lie to me, Doctor."

"I would not dare. Although I had need of caution."

"Understood. You are forgiven. And will be rewarded."

"Thank you, my Queen."

"As will you, Sir Geoffrey."

"I – thank you, Majesty." Sir Geoffrey sounded most unsure, Stella thought.

"You will, of course, forget what you have just seen. Sir Francis has explained this, I think."

"Yes. He has made it most clear."

Elizabeth gave a soft, nasty laugh.

"He would, my faithful Francis. Very well. The salt is cast, the child is mine. Let us take our leave so that you may rest."

Footsteps, mercifully going away, faded down the stairs. Davy nudged Stella and released her hand. Very cautiously, Stella peeped around the edge of the tapestry. The room was empty. She stepped out, followed by Davy. The grate was filled with old, dead ash. On the boards of the floor was the faint impression of a triangle, no more than a shadow, and as they watched, it disappeared completely. The room smelled of smoke and blood: the tang of copper. Down below, there was the resounding boom of the front door closing.

Stella ran back to the window, to watch the scene in reverse. Elizabeth was being helped back onto her horse, but this time she was holding something, a little bundle. As she turned, a small white face was visible, screwed up in preparation for an understandable bout of howling, Stella assumed. The cloth in which it was wrapped fell back, revealing in the lamplight a lick of bright hair.

"Right," Davy said briskly. "I think that's enough of this, don't you?"

"Totally. They're pulling out." The Queen and her retinue were trotting rapidly down the drive.

"And so should we."

They waited until the party had disappeared from view, then ran back down the stairs. Stella was on tenterhooks in case Sir Geoffrey, presumably the owner of the house, suddenly emerged from one of the rooms, but the hall proved empty. The front door was now shut but they located the kitchen, which was not empty: a woman lay sleeping on a pallet of straw. Stella and Davy tiptoed past her and out into the night.

SERENA

"Four nights will quickly dream away the time; And then the moon, like to a silver bow. New-bent in heaven, shall behold the night. Of our solemnities."

Serena sat spellbound in the stalls, watching as Ward and his colleagues brought Shakespeare to life. In this production, the dialogue of Titania and Oberon had been swapped, so now it was Ward who fell in love with Bottom, and Titania who strode about, manipulating events. 'Strode' was the word, thought Serena, for the actress who played the fairy queen, Maud Sonenclair, had recently come from the set of a blockbusting fantasy TV series in which she played a warrior general. Without heels, she could look Ward straight in the eyes and Ward was not short. She also possessed very long legs, substantial hips and a large bust: there was little that was fairy-like about her if one considered the fae to be tiny winged delicates. Serena thought she was amazing and sighed over her hair, which was waist length and pre-Raphaelite in both colour and style. She was also hilarious: Ward and Serena had spent several memorable evenings in the pub with Maud and her current girlfriend, a post-punk Geordie who was playing Puck. All in all, the production had a congenial, family atmosphere which was, Ward said, his favourite kind.

"I don't think the theatre partly burning down has hurt that. Kind of a 'we're-all-in-the-wars-together' Blitz Spirit kind of thing." He and the other cast members had participated in a fund-raiser in April, which had largely paid for the fire-damaged roof, as well as the aid provided by the Arts Council. Serena, who loved the old Pelican Theatre, had donated her dressmaking skills to some of the costumes for that. It made a worthwhile change from supernatural endeavours. And although Ward was frequently in despair over the success of rehearsals, Serena knew not to take this too seriously. A poor dress rehearsal made a good first night, she had heard, although they were nowhere near that stage yet. There was a wail from the wings.

"No, no, no, no, no, my GOD, Paolo, you're supposed to be a fairy named Peaseblossom, not some great clodhopping oaf…"

"Thank Christ for *Dragonholt*," Maud said into Serena's ear. She was sitting next to her, feet up on the seat in front, wearing ripped jeans and eating crisps. "Got me going on the old trapeze."

"They're called aerialists, is that right?" Serena said.

Maud nodded. "Want one of these?" She proffered the packet. "I'm not nearly as good as they are, mind you, but playing Valeria did give me some new skills. They sent me to circus school for a month. If the old thespian career fails I can always run off with the big top. Ooh, Paolo's giving as good as he's getting. Listen to that."

"Oh dear," said Serena, as the sound of raised voices escalated.

"It's only because Jonathan's decided to be a dick this afternoon." Maud said. "He's actually a very good director but occasionally he feels he needs to play one on TV, if you know what I mean."

Serena nodded. "Studied theatricality."

"Quite."

"Maud? Maud, where are you?" The first voice had now become querulous. "Darling, I need you here to talk some sense to this imbecile!"

"The great man summons," said Maud. "You can have the rest of my crisps if you want."

As the argument raged on, Serena wandered outside for a breath of fresh air. The Pelican was not far from the river, and she could smell the weedy odour of the Thames. It was a shame to spend the whole afternoon inside, although Ward had booked a riverside restaurant with a terrace for that evening and Serena was aware of the pleasurable anticipation of a night out. She wandered down to the river and looked over the water, leaning on the railings and wondering how Stella was getting on. She had turned her mobile on to silent for the rehearsal, but now checked it. There was a message from Bee. *Can u call me not urgent.*

Serena did not, these days, wholly trust 'not urgent'. She called.

"Oh, Serena, hi. Thanks for getting back to me. How are you?"

"Fine," Serena said. She gave Bee a brief rundown of the afternoon.

"Oh God, we binge watched all of *Dragonholt.* Tell Maud I am her total fangirl."

"I will!"

"Why I was calling, was just to say that I have had a text from the AirBnB woman in Cornwall and she's having to move us, for the two weeks in the summer, but it's only a bit further down the coast and it's on the beach. Or on the cliff, anyway, but definitely overlooking the sea. It's owned by some friend of hers who doesn't normally do B and B but she's going to be away. I don't know why she had to change the booking – something about American friends who always have that house and they decided not to and then they did. She asked me if we'd mind and I said no. Is that all right with you?"

"Yes, whatever. It's all Cornwall. As long as this other house is big enough."

"Bigger, apparently."

"And on the beach sounds amazing."

"I didn't think you'd mind that bit. So am I right in that Ward's not coming with us for the first week but he is for the second? What's actually happening with the play?"

"So. Second week, yes, and the play has seen yet another change of plan – I was going to call you about this. They're doing a night which is a one-off as part of the Glastonbury Festival fringe, at Pilton, on Midsummer Night's Eve itself. June 24th. So Ward says you can either come up to London to see it, or you can come and see it locally instead."

"That might not be a bad idea. I've been a bit worried about leaving Luna and going up to London, to be honest. She's due on the 21st – on the solstice."

"Well, if she hits her due date, she can either rest up at home while you pop out to the play, or come with you if she's up to it. Bring the baby in a basket."

"We might be hearing from Ward if it howls," said Bee.

"He once told me they're used to it with outside performances. I bet it will rain, too. How is Luna?" Serena asked.

"She's fine, the midwife says – all on track."

"And Mum? Any news?"

"Oh, you know Mum," Bee said. "Always away with the fairies."

When the call was over, Serena walked slowly back to the theatre. What an odd life, she thought. She remembered her childhood: Alys drifting in and out, but always somehow keeping her family together; Abraham the grandfatherly rock behind it all. Then Abraham had died, yet was still not gone, and Alys had disappeared on her own adventures, but Serena still felt that the family was a unit, even if one in different places. And occasionally in different times.

Ward had asked her, years ago now, if she had ever wondered who her father had been. None of the sisters knew, although Alys had said that they were the children of different men. Growing up, it had seemed normal, but recently, Ward had asked her again. They had been sitting in the Lion and Unicorn at the time, later one evening after rehearsal.

"I don't really think about it," Serena had admitted. "I did when I split up with Ben. I wondered if I was sort of heading in the same direction as Alys."

Ward smiled. "Nancy Mitford's Bolter."

"Oh God, don't say that! I can just see myself with a wig and a cigarette holder, picking up Spanish revolutionaries."

"I don't think you're the type," Ward said. "Cigarette holder, maybe, if you smoked. And anyway, can women really be bolters these days? Now she'd just be called serially monogamous."

"I don't see Mum as a bolter either. Or rather, she's stayed put and the men have bolted. Until now. She seems to be doing quite a bit of bolting these days."

"But she keeps coming back."

"Yes. Bee thinks she'll put in an appearance when Luna's baby is due. I think she will, too. Unless she's prevented."

"This – person. Aiken Drum. I don't like the sound of him."

"No, neither do I. Luna and Bee met him, you know that, and so did Ver and Sam. They weren't whelmed, to put it mildly. And Mum herself expressed some serious reservations."

"When she came back after vanishing the first time, you said to me that Luna told a friend that she'd been in a battered women's shelter – it's a thing people don't like to ask too many questions about, and they won't expect you to say where it is. Stroke of genius on Luna's part. Now I wonder what would happen if we actually *did* have to get her into a shelter. And are there such things, for women who fall foul of supernatural men?"

"That's an alarming thought. Ward, why did you ask about my dad?"

"Well, it's none of my business. Caro's mentioned it once or twice, but only in a sort of jocular oh-isn't-darling-Alys-so-*unconventional* way. I don't know what other people think – like the village post mistress, or the vicar – because I'm not in Somerset that much and, anyway, it's none of *their* business either. But there are some big questions, Serena. How did all this start? How did Alys suddenly stop being a wafty upper middle class single parent and turn into Feldfar, scourge of the eldritch hedgerows? And more importantly, to my mind, *when* did she start doing this? Given you all have, let's say, other natures, and your dads have never as far as I know shown up, one has to start wondering."

Serena nodded. "I know. You're quite right. And I have wondered. I hope I'm not Aiken Drum's daughter, for instance. Or that my sisters aren't. It crossed my mind that it might have been why he let Bee go, back in the spring. I didn't get the impression that Mum had known him for that long but I might be way off base. But you know what, Ward? I did discuss this with Stella recently and we think we'd rather let sleeping fathers lie. Stella said, you know, what are we going to do – launch some massive quest to find out who our True Parentage TM is, when we kind of didn't care before and now we'd rather not know? I haven't dared have one of those DNA ancestry tests in case a bunch of government goons in white hazmat suits swoop on the studio and bundle me into a van for experimentation. And the same goes for you, Ward. Your cousin's a horse."

"Jesus, tell me about it."

"When we were kids, I know this for a fact, we all had this thing at various times that our dads were going to turn out to be princes or film stars or rock musicians and they'd be ultra-glamorous and treat us like the royalty we hoped we might be. Until Stella said it's probably some local dodgepot fuelled by too much cider who's now a fat old farmer, and did we really want the disillusionment? Or some skanky hippy who plays the didgeridoo. No one's ever come looking for his daughters. Anyway, we had a father figure and it was Granddad."

"Stella had a point. I still haven't got over Laura and the whole horse thing. I don't know how I'm going to look her in the eye without making some stupid pun, for a start. 'Oh, hi, Laura – it's your round at the bar, care to pony up?'"

"Straight from the horse's mouth, if you ask me. I think you'd better rein it in, Ward."

"Serena!"

"On the other hand, it might be nice to have a stable relationship with your cousin."

"*Serena!*"

"And that was so unfair given that you've never said to me, 'oh stop haring around all over the place'. Or told Stella she's otterly lovely."

"I didn't realise you had such a thing for puns. Lowest form of wit!"

"I think that's sarcasm."

"I hope to Christ I'm not going to change into something, as well."

"I hope not, either. Surely you'd have done it before now? But it's all a little different with each of us. Laura started at puberty, mine was caused by fright, as far as I can tell, Luna's was triggered by the Hound, Bee's was kicked off by defending other people and Stella needed an actual artefact in order to change. With Stella's friend Davy it's hereditary and generational. And with my cousin Nan it seems to have been some sort of mating urge. It seems more common in women than in men," Serena said.

"But then there's the Hounds."

"Yes, true."

"What odd conversations we have," Serena said. "And what an odd family we are. A cross between a soap opera and a zoo."

Now, walking back to the Pelican, she remembered this conversation and smiled. Odd, but no one could say it was boring. And she had forgotten to ask Bee if she'd reserved a room for Alys when they went on holiday in Cornwall.

STELLA

Having witnessed Elizabeth taking custody of the baby, Stella and Davy were of one mind: Bill Blake needed to be informed, as soon as possible. On their return to modern London, therefore, they wasted no time. They swung by the Southwark Tavern, which was not too far distant, collected Ace, brought him up to speed and headed for Hercules Road.

"So how sure are you that this child actually was Hob?" Ace said, perched on the front seat of the upper deck of the bus.

"Well, hard to say, since it was just a kiddie. I don't know how you even tell which sex they are, if they're all bundled up. But the mum looked like Hob, and the baby had red hair and you know, Ace – process of elimination, Occam's Razor and all that. Who else do we know who has red hair and mysterious origins?"

"Also," Stella said, "Blake did presumably send us down to Clapham for a reason, and not just for the hell of it."

"I wonder what he'd got wind of," Ace said. "Right, this is our stop."

Stella supposed that it might be a false sense of security, but in spite of some of the more alarming aspects of the house, she was always conscious of a weight lifting from her shoulders when they went to see Blake. This must have shown in her face, because Davy said,

"Bit of a relief to hand things over to the old pitch and toss, eh?"

"Frankly, yes. You know I said I liked working for myself? But only when it comes to musical gigs and that. I don't really want the responsibility of magical London."

"Same here."

"This is the trouble with being Bohemians." Ace said.

"Well, you know what I mean. Anyway, I'm not a Bohemian – I'm a corporate gal, me. You and Stella might be artistes and all that."

"Mind you," Ace said as they knocked on Blake's door, "Bill was a bit of a rebel in his day. I think he finds his task somewhat onerous at times."

Stella worked up the nerve to ask, once they were in Blake's garden, still lilac-scented and drifting with apple blossom. Blake took a moment to reply, gazing ruminatively up into the trees.

"I took my task upon me gladly enough, but Ace is right. In my day I was quite the revolutionary. Perhaps I still am."

"Good for you," Stella, fellow iconoclast, told him.

"And yet the responsibility for others is never far from my mind. Yourselves, for instance. I am tethered rather than trapped, but I cannot travel far, and that is a burden, I admit."

"Why *are* you confined to this part of the city?"

"It was part of a bargain. I suppose the higher authorities did not want me running all over the country willy nilly. So now you and others, like Mags, must be my eyes and ears. It suits me well enough. I dream of Felpham, where I used to dwell. The Arun and the wide Downs, so open to the sky. The sea... I do miss the sea. But this city has always had my heart. Now, tell me what you have come to tell me."

Davy, with an admirable conciseness presumably borne of having to deliver corporate reports, explained what had happened in Clapham. Once she had finished, there was a short silence. Somewhere not far away, Stella heard the plaintive notes of a cuckoo. Blake smiled.

"Do you hear that? It is telling us something, perhaps."

"A cuckoo in the nest?" Ace said. "But whose nest?"

"Hob's never mentioned being, like, secretly brought up by Queen Elizabeth," Stella said. "He told us his mum was a model, died when he was little. And that he was brought up by his gran."

"Maybe someone else stole him from the Queen," Davy said.

"Either that or he was just lying. Which wouldn't exactly astonish me."

"We ought to talk to him," Ace said.

"Are you going to tell him what we saw?"

"No, I shall subtly probe."

But this would, as it turned out, need to be at a later date. Hob was not in, and Catherine Blake did not know when he was intending to return.

"Never mind," Blake said. "I shall speak to him, when he comes back. In the meantime, I have been thinking. You have done a good job, Stella, Davy. It seems you have been both brave and sensible."

"Mr Blake," Stella said, doing her best to look appealing, "I know you told us not to explore this – this network. And we haven't. A lot of history is scary, to be honest. But we would like to have the opportunity, without thinking we might be doing the wrong thing."

"We don't want to piss you off, basically," Davy added.

Blake was silent for a minute or so, apparently lost once more in contemplation of the lilac. Then he said, "I wonder now if I have been right to clip your wings."

"Oh! Does that mean we can go exploring?"

"Within reason!" Blake said, very stern. "Take Ace with you, should he agree."

"Yeah, I'm up for a spot of investigation. Where would you like us to go?"

"You said that the child came from a room in a castle, or fortress?"

"Yes. I only caught a glimpse of it, but I'll tell you where I think it was because we got this glimpse of it from the air – St Michael's Mount, in Cornwall. We're actually going to Cornwall, my family, on holiday a bit later in the summer. I thought I might check it out."

"Or we could check it out via other means," Davy said. "The only problem is, I've only got the Knowledge of London, not of the whole country. Do you know any other places on the network, Mr Blake?"

"I do not have personal experience. Follies and grottos, I believe, are often part of the ley ways, the coldharbour sanctuaries. And, I believe, some Martello towers."

"Chapels, too," Stella said. "And some old houses."

"And holy wells," Blake added.

"Still plenty of those around," Ace said.

"What, in London? Really?"

"Loads," said Davy. "I know them all."

"There's one in Mary Overie," Ace said, then added, in response to Stella's blank look, "Southwark Cathedral."

A holy well sounded nice and safe, it was within the bounds of a major church ("not that it means a lot," noted Stella, thinking of St Paul's) and it was in a part of the city known well to at least one of the team. Also, as Ace remarked, it had the great advantage of being in walking distance of the pub.

On the following Saturday, therefore, Stella and Davy took the clipper down to Southwark pier and walked along the bank to the cathedral. You tended to take it for granted, Stella thought, with all the tourist trade attention focused on St Paul's and Westminster Abbey, but Southwark was a perfectly decent cathedral in its own right: Norman, perpendicular (Stella and Davy had looked this up) and built of an appealing golden stone. They had seen it in a time when the huge buildings of modern London – the Heron Tower, the Gherkin, the Cheesegrater – had not even been conceived and when the cathedral, St Saviour and Mary Overie, had occupied pride of place on the south bank of the Thames. Now, for such a large building, it was strangely hidden, dominated by the towering glass immensity of the Shard.

They were perched on the wall which ran around the cathedral, eating wraps from Borough market prior to going inside the church precincts ('No Food and Drink Allowed'), admiring the hanging baskets, and waiting for Ace. After several days of showers, the clouds had rolled back and the cathedral gleamed in the sunlight. As usual on Saturdays, the market was crowded: people were having to shuffle in between the stalls and Stella was not surprised to see Ace approaching from a different direction.

"Afternoon. Sorry if I'm a bit late. Young Hob dropped by."

"Oh, he's finally shown up, has he? And how is he getting on? Did Blake ask him about the baby episode?"

"He's all right. I didn't ask him about the baby thing because I haven't had time to speak to Bill about it yet. I didn't want to step on Blake's toes by saying the wrong thing. Anyway, the lad seems happy enough at the Blake's place. He's a lot better off there than he'd have been with her late Ladyship. He's been starting to open up about stuff."

"Yeah? Like what?"

"He finally told me what Miranda stole that pissed off the Searchers so much. She wasn't able to tell anyone – Serena said there was some kind of spell on her tongue – but Hob has been doing some digging."

"What did she steal?"

"Her shape."

"Her *shape?*"

"Yes. Seagull. She wasn't a natural shapechanger, like Davy here or your sisters, or one who needed an item in order to trigger it, like you, Stella. She nicked the ability to change form from someone else and they weren't very happy about it, to put it mildly, and since they were apparently 'connected', as criminals put it, they called the Searchers in to do something about it."

"Do you know who this person is?"

45

"No. Hob doesn't, either. Or says he doesn't, but on this occasion I think he's actually telling the truth. He likes to think he and Miranda were thick as thieves and she told him everything, he was the trusted confidant, but I don't think she actually confided all that much. She was away a lot and not just on film sets."

"So when she died," Davy said, "do you think that ability went back to the original owner, then?"

"I've no idea." Ace looked up at the tower of the cathedral and added, "Shall we see what we can see?"

"Let's go for it."

Once inside the cathedral gates, the noise from the market was abruptly hushed, as though Stella, Ace and Davy had stepped into a soundproofed room. Above them, the cathedral bells tolled the hour: one o'clock. The air was filled with a strong, spicy scent.

"They have a herb garden," said Ace, unnecessarily.

"It's very quiet. Everyone seems to be ignoring the grounds – oh, no, there's a man, sitting over there."

Davy laughed. "Yeah, go and chat him up, Stella."

The sun had been in Stella's eyes. When she shaded them, she could see that the man was in fact a beaming William Shakespeare. In bronze, seated on a bench. As Stella watched, the statue was joined by a handsome black and white cat.

"Hodge," Ace remarked. "Replacing Doorkins Magnificat, the prior incumbent."

"You're well informed!"

"I like cats. As you know."

They walked around the northern wall of the cathedral, passing through the herb garden, fragrant with hyssop and rosemary and bay, to the shady coolness beneath the trees. Stella could now hear no sound from beyond the cathedral precincts, only the sparrows hopping around the branches. Traffic, voices and the distant roar of planes coming into Heathrow were all absent now. She wondered if the clock had already turned back, or if it was merely some acoustic effect produced by the trees.

"There's the well," Davy said.

It was contained within a low stone wall. Stella peered down it and saw her own reflection quavering in the dark water below. They waited. Davy's inner map, Stella knew, did not necessarily mean that she could open the doors and gateways between times and places, but the Knowledge gave her more of a chance to do so than was possessed by either Stella or Ace. They had gone into this in some detail, after the events of the spring.

"Anything?" Ace asked.

Stella saw Davy open her mouth to reply, saw a sudden shaft of light fall upon the well as the breeze stirred the trees, saw the water flash and shatter and then she was standing with her nose pressed to a clammy wall.

Stella stepped back. It was dim and there was a faint fish-like smell. The air was cool. It took her a moment for her eyes to adjust and when they did so she found that she was standing in a narrow passage, stone floored, its walls lined with shells arranged in swirling, lovely patterns.

"Davy? Ace?"

No reply.

"Shit," Stella breathed. Should she wait here, or try and find them? The passage was chilly. She didn't want to risk missing them, everyone running about after one another in what Ace was wont to describe as an Aldwych farce, but she could go a little way... Stella followed the curve of the passage around and found herself in a room, a dead end. The room had a high, arched stone ceiling and on the opposite wall a leaded window looked out over the sea. Stella went over to the window and craned her neck to see out. Open sea, then low, crumbly red cliffs, lined with trees. It looked a lot like Devon. Stella eased the window open, leaned out and squinted upwards to see battlements. She couldn't remember if there were any castles on the Devon coast... Below, the waves churned at the base of the cliff; she could hear the slap and smack of water against stone. A cold salt breeze drifted in. Stella withdrew.

The room was empty, with not even a stool or a table. She went to the door, intending to head back down the passage, but heard voices.

"...did not bring it, the Morlader will be angry..."

Stella knew that word. The Queen had helpfully, if unwittingly, supplied its meaning. A pirate. And probably the one who had menaced her sister Luna. Great.

"I should care, should I?" a second voice said.

"You would be wise to care. You don't know what he can do. If we..."

The voices faded a little. Stella held her breath. Both voices had been adult, and male. There was a scraping noise.

"Bring the rest in here, put it in the room at the end."

Shit, again. Stella peered around the edge of the door, to see two men with their backs to her, standing by a wooden chest. Both wore knee britches, loose shirts, headscarves, large curved knives at their belts. Black, greasy ringlets spilled onto the shoulders of one man; the other had a thick gold hoop in one ear. All they needed to proclaim their status was a peg leg and a parrot on one shoulder. Stella ran back to the window and shoved it open again. There was absolutely no chance of getting out that way without dying.

"He is angry enough as it is, I tell you." The voice was much closer now.

"This strife is none of my concern." The second voice was sulky, resentful. "What do I care of what happens ashore? I know nothing of the high moors and care less."

"Well, that matters little! We are all caught up in this now. Land and sea, a challenge between, and we must take the latter part, or risk a voyage down to hell. Is that what you signed up for?"

"You know as well as I that I did not. Should I be here now before you, otherwise?"

"Then swallow your medicine, bitter pill though it may be, and stand with the Morlader's crew, my good lad." There was the slap of a hand, as though the other man had clapped Mr Sulky on the shoulder. "Let's get on with it."

None of this made any sense to Stella. She looked frantically around the little room as the scraping sound intensified. Something, probably the chest, was being dragged along the floor.

"Stella!" She whipped round. A little door had appeared in one wall; Davy was beckoning. Stella threw herself through.

"Thank God for that. That door wasn't there before."

"No, I know. This place is like a bloody colander."

"There's another room beyond," said Ace. "Also lined with shells. It's one of those grottoes. Come and have a look." Stella was only too glad to do so. This was a much larger chamber, entirely decorated with shells above a cobbled floor. At the apex of the ceiling was a sun, picked out in yellow mosaic.

"I've been in a grotto before. But it was a chapel, not in our world, really." On that occasion she had found a captive star, Nephele, held in stone, and freed her to join her sisters.

"Serena went into one in Windsor Great Park," said Ace. "But she didn't go all the way in, if you remember – she thought it might be a trap."

"They're all connected," Davy said. "I know that now. But I don't have a map of the whole country, as you know. There aren't many grottoes in London."

"Are there any?" Ace asked, then answered his own question. "Oh, yeah – that one that Pope put in."

"Twickenham. But it's not a shell one – Pope liked mosaics. I think the nearest shell grotto is down the coast in Margate. That's quite famous. We went in it when I was a kid. But that's underground, no windows. There used to be one underneath Whitehall – I know this because I read up on them – but Cromwell abolished a lot of them. Too frivolous, probably."

"I can see why he got rid of them. There were these men – they looked like pirates. I thought they were going to trap me in there. Or chuck me out of the window. Or worse." Stella studied the wall, the patterned fan of shells. "This could almost be a map." She traced the maze of shells with a finger. There was a click in the air. Seagreen light flooded in.

Stella and her friends were somewhere else. Shell patterned wallpaper lay behind a small, ornamental cabinet.

"I was about to tell you not to do that," Ace said.

"Sorry!"

"If Davy's right and they're all connected, we could end up doing a grand tour of grottoes and end up having to take the train home from Yorkshire or somewhere."

"So where are we now? This looks like someone's house."

"It *is* someone's house," said a voice. "It's mine."

LUNA

It wasn't just the Hunt who hadn't come back, Luna thought, as she took the dogs down to the end of the field. The swifts and swallows weren't here yet, either. For Luna, they were summer's heralds; she missed that shrieking whisper in the skies and every day she had looked out for the first signs that they might be returning, to nest again in the barns and outhouses as they had done every year, ever since Luna could remember. The conversion of old barn to cider press was now nearly complete, but Bee and Luna had agreed to leave the half door in place, so that the swallows could zoom back in to their nests under the eaves.

But there had been no sign of them. Luna hated to think of their long journey ending in a volley of gunfire over the Mediterranean, or simple exhaustion. They were such brave little birds. She found that she kept looking up... Still, Luna told herself, there were plenty of other things to look at: the washes of pink and white hawthorn blossom across the countryside, in hedges and orchards; the buttercups springing from the scrubby winterised grass; the days drawing out into calmer, pastel sunsets. The candles of the chestnut trees along the drive were out now, flaring pale in the twilight and catching the evening sun to turn to gold, as if lit from within. Bee had picked handfuls of purple and white lilac to go in bowls around the house; its sweet, faint scent perfumed the air. And a couple of weeks ago, Luna had heard the first cuckoo calling, sweet and distant in a stand of oaks. She could hear one now, the faint, clockwork cry ticking the minutes away.

Now, it was evening. The days were too drawn out for Luna to see the first stars when she went down to settle the piebalds for the night, but the sky was cloudless, deepening to bronze in the west above the Severn estuary. As Luna made her way down the field she was hailed by Ver, who walked towards her over the rough grass, holding up her crimson skirts and clutching a bulging Tesco's carrier bag.

"Hello," Luna called. "How are you?"

"I'm all right, cheers, love. Look!" the old woman said proudly. She opened the bag to reveal the glossy spears and delicate flowers of wild garlic, along with nettles and cleavers.

"Pesto, nettle chips and tonic," Ver said.

"You didn't get that in Tesco!"

"I certainly didn't. Been out for a forage down by the church – there's all sorts along that lane. Luna, I wanted to ask you about something."

"Of course."

As they walked along the hawthorn hedge, the curds of the may blossom scenting the air, Ver said, "Luna – no one else uses that shelter at the bottom of the field, do they?"

"No, only me and Sam – we store the hay in it, as you know. Why?" She was conscious of a sinking dismay.

"It's just that I was down there yesterday evening, picking some cleavers, actually for a cup of tea, and I heard something moving about in it. Not like a rat or anything. Something big. I called out but no one answered. I wondered whether a sheep might have found shelter there. I had a quick look round the door but couldn't see anyone. I didn't want to go poking about, just in case. There are some funny people about."

"Very sensible," Luna said.

"Anyway, I went back to the van but just before the light died I thought I saw smoke coming out of the roof of the shelter."

"Smoke?" Luna said in dismay. "I hope not – all the hay's in there. There's no chimney or anything."

"Yes, that's what I thought. I went up to the house but I couldn't find anyone there either. You'd all gone out."

"Oh, sorry, Ver. Sam was working late last night and Bee and I had to go to Taunton to pick something up – the traffic was awful. We didn't get back until after ten."

"Not to worry. Anyway, I thought, be a bit brave, Ver. I came down here myself, but the smoke had gone and there wasn't anyone in the field shelter. I thought I must have imagined it. I thought I'd better tell you even if you do think I'm a crazy old woman. Well, I am, but you know what I mean."

"I don't think you're crazy," said Luna. "I think we should have a look, though. And not on our own."

Sam was working, and Bee had gone over to Amberley to see Caro. It crossed Luna's mind that her mother might have returned, but what would she be doing hanging out in the field shelter and not coming to the house? Dark might be around, but Luna wasn't sure how to find him; ghost-like, he came and went as he pleased. She spoke his name all the same, into the empty air.

Ver deposited the results of her foraging into the van and accompanied Luna down the field. Suddenly, she said,

"Ah, young man!"

For Dark now walked at Luna's shoulder.

"Ned! Great. Did you hear me? We think there's someone in the field shelter," Luna told him.

"There was marshfire down there last night. A blue flame, wandering."

"Marshfire or a soul?" asked Luna, thinking of the spark of her grandfather's spirit in the churchyard in Hornmoon.

"Marshfire. A hazy mazy ball of it."

"Hmmm," Ver said. "Did you investigate?"

"I went down the field but it had gone. The shelter was empty but something had spooked the horses: they were all at the far end of the field and they would not come closer. See, where they are now?"

He was right, Luna noticed. The horses were indeed in the corner of the field, as far as they could get from the shelter itself. Her skin prickled.

"Luna," Ver said, very low, "Do you want to go back to the house?"

Luna hesitated. Perhaps it would be best… but curiosity won. It was broad daylight and there were three of them. Not that this had stopped things from happening before.

"No," she said. "We'll take a quick look."

There was no sound from within the shelter. Ver took hold of the door and pulled it swiftly open. It was sure to be empty, Luna told herself.

But it was not.

STELLA

"This is one of the most civilised trips back in time I've ever taken," Davy Dearly said. "Unless you count the pub."

"I wouldn't mention that when Miss Parminter comes back," Ace said. "Given that she said they were teetotallers."

"Yes, no chance of sloping off for a pint here, Ace," said Stella. "And you didn't see those men earlier on. They didn't look very civilised to me."

"I'm sure there are plenty of local hostelries down on the waterfront. Probably pirate-tastic, as well."

They now knew where they were, and when: a considerable relief to Stella. Nor would they be obliged to travel the circuit of shell grottoes and other places that girdled the country, for Miss Parminter, after tea, would be sending them directly home.

"It might be a bit of an anticlimax, I suppose, but it's so nice to meet someone who actually knows what they're doing," Davy said.

"Thank you, dear." Jane Parminter came back into the room with a tray of biscuits. "Mary and I do try to treat our guardianship as responsibly as we may."

Stella, with the fire and baby episode in mind, had asked if they could be directed to St Michael's Mount, but here, Miss Parminter had perforce been less helpful.

"No one has been able to travel there for years. Why, by boat, yes – although all you will see is the old island itself. But through the shellways and the coldharbours, no."

"Do you know why?"

"No one knows."

So they had, for the time being, abandoned this plan. Stella thought that they could go to the Mount once they were down in Cornwall itself, on the ground. As if they were ordinary tourists.

Visiting this little building was like visiting one of your great aunts, if your great aunt lived in a magical octagonal house in the early eighteen hundreds. Miss Parminter had shown them around, very graciously for an elderly lady who had just discovered three outlandishly dressed temporal travellers in her drawing room ("Well, dear, it's not as though it was the first time"). The rooms of the little octagon were arranged around a shell encrusted gallery that occupied the second storey. Boxes and cabinets of shells, of moths, of feathers and pressed flowers took up most of the rooms and the eau de nil wallpaper, faintly striped or shell patterned, gave the house an underwater feeling.

They were also taken outside, into a sunlit spring day. Daffodils, shaken by the wind, ran along the garden wall and the long arm of the Exe estuary glinted in the light, but far out to sea Stella could see a squall of rainfall. From this perspective, the house was short and squat, its many sides making it resemble a truncated windmill, minus the sails.

"It's called A La Ronde," Jane Parminter said. "Because it is. Octagonal, anyway."

"It's actually octagonal, is it?" Ace asked.

"In truth it is neither octagonal nor round. Sixteen sides, in fact. The inner part is called the Octagon. We follow the day around; we rise at dawn in the east and pursue the sun until it sets over the estuary. Sometimes I feel as though we are winding a gigantic clock. Perhaps we are."

The name of the place rang a bell and Stella thought that the house might be still in existence in her own day – a National Trust property, perhaps? Back inside, through its many windows, she could see masted ships making their way up and down the river, white sails out against the sea wind as they ran towards the rain.

"You see, dear," Miss Parminter explained. "My cousin Mary and I have been most fortunate. We have a little money. We have travelled. We have done the Grand Tour, and visited such places as the Basilica of San Vitale, in Ravenna, which made a great impression upon us. On the ship coming home, as we crossed the Channel that you see in the distance, Mary and I agreed how wonderful it would be if we could set up house together, a house modelled on that marvellous church. We bought the land, had the house constructed – it was completed at the end of the last century, for we now find ourselves in 1810 – and she and I have lived here ever since. We have set up a chapel of our own and a row of cottages for distressed gentlewomen to live in – you could see those from the garden. We seek to allow others to benefit from our own good fortune."

Stella thought privately, and with annoyance, that there must be an awful lot of distressed gentlewomen in this day and age: not much else for them to do, except be dependent on some man. Good for the Miss Parminters.

"Our near relations think that we have gone quite mad and tell everyone that we are living in a hermit-like seclusion. It is true that we do not get out and about as much as we used to – we do not need to. All manner of folk make their way to us, along the shell-paths."

"Did you know, when you had this place built, that this was going to happen?" Ace asked. "That it was linked to the coldharbours?"

"Why no, although there were some legends about this district: we are not so far from Dartmoor as the crow flies, you know, and the Wild Hunt is said to ride upon the moor, among other stories."

Stella was careful to avoid Davy's eye at this point; she did not want to alarm Miss Parminter with reminiscences of the Hunt. Although perhaps 'alarm' would be the wrong word.

"Miss Parminter," she said, "Have you ever heard talk about someone called the Morlader?"

Miss Parminter said, "Why, yes, I have. It is the nickname of a notorious wrecker down Cornwall way, a pirate, too."

"Does he live in this day and age?"

"No, he has been gone two hundred years or more, but that means little – though he has died, yet he is still there." Miss Parminter gave a disapproving sniff. "Blasphemous, I call it. He dates from Elizabeth's day. I do not know him personally," Miss Parminter added, slightly reprovingly as though Stella might suspect her of hanging out with pirates, "but there has been talk. Perhaps you stumbled upon a lair of his, just as you stumbled upon A La Ronde."

"Yes, sorry again about that."

"As I say, we are used to it. When our first guest arrived, we were naturally most perturbed. Mary and I had gone to bed and to encounter a strange man in the house, when we were wearing nothing but our nightgowns, was quite alarming. I nearly hit him with the poker but luckily Mary held me back and we got talking. He was most apologetic, charmingly so."

"Who was he?"

"A magician, from earlier in your century. An Indian gentleman, though born in Bristol, he told us. A Mr Gambhir. Do you know him?"

No one did. Stella filed the name away for future enquiry.

"But there have been several travellers upon the ways, with various aims in mind. Only one or two have proved troublesome and we have had to learn some methods of dealing with them."

"I noticed," Ace said, smiling. Stella resolved to ask him about this later: the 'methods' were not apparent to herself.

"One young lady was really quite vexing. Have you come across her? A woman named Miranda Dean."

Stella sat up straight at this. "Yes. Big time." Then she thought that this phrase might not mean a lot to Miss Parminter. "I mean, yes, we do know her, or did. She's dead, though."

"Dead?"

"She fell foul of the Searchers," Davy explained. "I don't know if you know who they are."

"Why, yes, I do. How foolish of her."

"What did she want here?" Stella asked.

"Information. Although we are not ourselves magical people, by which I mean we have no special abilities and little specialised knowledge, although we have perforce had to pick up some tricks and fancies along the way purely for self-protection, we have cousins on the South Coast who have made something of a study of the Arts. Named Fane."

"I don't know them," Stella said, "But I think my sister might have met one of them once. In Brighton. Edith, I think. She probably isn't born yet. Although one never knows."

"Miss Dean was keen to force an introduction. To the Fanes in Sussex. She claimed kinship with a family known to me, as if presenting her credentials, down near Penzance. Name of Thorn. But that would be in your day and age and when I spoke to them in mine, they had indeed heard of her, but did not care to press the acquaintance."

This made Stella sit up a little straighter. "I'm going on holiday near Penzance later this summer," she said. "With my sisters."

"Then do take this. From me." Jane Parminter scribbled a note on a piece of paper, rolled it up and slotted it into a little shell that she took from a case: a creamy curl, spotted with chestnut like the markings of a spaniel. "If you should meet one of the Thorns, in your day or another, give them my note of introduction."

"Thank you!" Stella said, accepting her third token of the year. A coin, a prong of antler, and now a message in a shell.

At this point, there was movement in the hall, the sound of a door opening and the flurried noise of someone shaking out an umbrella before closing the door once more.

"Jane? Where are you? It has started to rain and we must bring the washing in."

"We have visitors, Mary!"

A second elderly woman appeared in the sitting room.

"Good day to you. That is as maybe, Jane, and I do not wish to seem discourteous, but the washing must still be saved."

"She's quite right," Ace said. "We ought to be going."

"Do feel free to come again, now that you know we are here. I shall open the path for you." Jane Parminter led them back out into the hallway, pulling on a wrap. But at that point there came a furious knocking at the door.

LUNA

The field shelter was dim and it took Luna a second for her eyes to adjust, after the sunlight. When she saw what was crouching amid the bales of hay, she gasped.

"What is it, dear?" Ver asked, close behind her. Then she said, "Oh my God."

Their visitor made an odd, whimpering sound.

"He's hurt," said Luna. "Oh, Ver. Whatever are we going to do?"

The dog was enormous. His side, grey-dappled like a horse's hide, heaved in and out like a bellows. He did not look up. His silver eyes were fixed on a point in the hay and his red-veined ears were flattened. One hindleg was covered in blood, both old and fresh. The stink of it filled the field shelter. Around his neck was an iron-spiked collar. Some of the spikes pointed inwards.

"Luna," Dark said. She felt his hand on her arm. "Be careful."

Luna nodded. She let Dark draw her back. There was a flash, a flicker and the Hound lay in human form, wrapped in a black leather cloak. He gave a yawning groan, like a bored dog; odd and unsettling in a man's face. But then, Luna thought, he did not really look all that human once you had time to study him closely. The long jaw, aquiline nose, and slitted eyes were more like a mask. His ears were set too far back, partly concealed by hair that had once been flame but was now the colour of dirty smoke.

"He's a Hound! A Lily White Boy!" Ver said.

"I will not hurt you," the Hound said, scornfully. He turned to look at Luna and she saw a semi-circular scar across his brow. This, then, was the Hound that Laura had, earlier in the spring, attacked in her equine form, bringing a hoof down on his head like a Medieval destrier, a war mare. The Hounds were so similar that Luna could not be sure if this was the same one who had tried to snatch her in Chepstow back in the winter.

"I can't trust you," she said.

The Hound grinned. "Wise. All the same, I shall not hurt you."

"What is your name?" asked Dark.

"I do not have one, ghost. I gave up my name when I became what I am."

"Were you not born a Hound, then?" Ver asked, with a slight pause. Luna was fairly sure that she had nearly added the word 'dear' to that sentence, but had bitten it back.

"No. I gave up all, to run with my master. That or go to Hell."

Despite her caution and fear, Luna was now becoming intrigued. "Do you know how old you are?" she said.

"When I was born, there was a rush light burning. My father was a slave to a man who ruled in the north. His sword was bronze. Much more was forest then. We lived in a round house."

Medieval, perhaps? Or earlier? Maybe even Bronze Age, given the sword. The Hound gasped and Luna saw a fresh seep of blood into the straw.

"And what injured you?" asked Dark.

"My master cast me out. I have displeased him." There was a dog's abnegation in his voice, a cringing note. "He tried to make me do what even I would not."

"I should think, frankly, that there's quite a lot of mileage there," Ver said.

"Let me stay here. I have nowhere to go. I will mend, given time."

"Don't let him," Dark said.

"The thing is," Luna said, "we have other people on this property— visitors, the postman, workmen. What if they see you?"

"I shall keep hidden from the sight of man. I promise."

"It's not just men," said Luna. "There are others. Spirits. I don't know how they'll react if they find you here."

"I shall take my chances."

"Your master – is he the one they call Aiken Drum?" Dark said.

"Yes. He leads the Hunt. For the moment. There are several challengers."

"The woman with the deer's antlers? Noualen?"

"She, and another. When I am whole I plan to seek the other out. I must be bound."

Luna was struggling not to feel sorry for him. It didn't sound much of a life but, from the sound of things, it might be better than the alternative.

Dark was evidently thinking ahead. He said, "You said your master cast you out. Will you be hunted down?"

"I do not know," the rasping voice said.

"Because obviously that is a worry if you are to remain here."

"It should not be for long."

"But if they do come, what then?"

"Then I am doomed," said the Hound.

Bee greeted the news that Mooncote had a new tenant with dismay.

"Oh God! That's just what we need! Sam's grandma I can obviously cope with. Dangerous fey huntsmen, not so much. And is he the one who grabbed me in the yard back in the spring that time, do you think?"

"I'm not sure," said Luna. "To be honest, they look very similar to me."

"I wonder if we can enlist the stars' help," mused Bee. "After all, they did come to your aid when you had the problem with that shoot thing. And this is their territory."

"Have you ever tried to summon the stars?" Luna asked.

"No. It has occurred to me, actually, but it seems a bit rude. And also I'm wary of pissing them off."

"I know what you mean. I didn't really summon them even then. I prayed to Arcturus, though, and she did come and help me."

"Hopefully he won't be here for long," Bee said.

"Hopefully no one will come after him, either."

STELLA

The knocking stopped. Miss Parminter frowned. Stella held her breath. Davy dropped to the floor, ran as rat up the curtains. Miss Parminter's eyes widened fractionally at this, Stella noticed, but she said nothing. Davy balanced on the curtain rail, clung, hung, and then ran back down. Human again, she whispered,

"There's a bloke at your front door and I wouldn't open it if I were you. He's got lit matches in his hat and a pair of flintlock pistols. Oh, and no eyeballs."

"Not the kind of blackguard I care to have in my house!" her cousin Mary exclaimed.

"What are we going to do?"

"That is the Morlader himself, Miss Fallow. Perhaps he has followed your trail? We cannot fight him, for he is known for his ferocity and we are not. But do not fear. We shall bamboozle him."

"How, Miss Parminter?"

"It will take a year and a day," Miss Parminter said. The knocking had started up again, a hammering on the door rather than any polite request for entry. Stella was about to ask what she meant, when Miss Parminter rose and, without any attempt at concealment, firmly closed the curtains. Then she opened them again and to Stella's surprise, it was now dark outside. The knocking abruptly ceased.

"What did you do?" Ace asked.

"I know," Davy said. She looked pleased with herself for a moment: star pupil. "The house actually is a clock. Miss P's rewound it."

"That is correct," Miss Parminter said, smiling. "And now we shall go into the next room."

The chambers of A La Ronde were small and filled with objects. This one held many feathers, neatly mounted on card and placed in cabinets. Stella saw the speckled plumage of an owl and the pale, delicate pink of flamingo. She wanted to stay and look at the feathers but this was not the time. Miss Parminter had produced a large pocket watch and was studying it. Outside, the sun was coming up. They went quickly on to the next room: painted blue, with the midmorning light streaming in. Watercolours lined the walls, many of the Exe Estuary, which Stella could see through the window. Roses bloomed in the garden and there was the distant clink of teacups. In the third room, more of the estuary was visible and white sails flew upon it.

By the time they had reached the twelfth room, the sunset light illuminated the opposite wall and highlighted the cabinets of shells. Stella wondered what she might hear if she picked up the big rosy conch and held it to her ear. The sea, or the sound of time turning? In an undertone, Ace said to her, "This house isn't big enough for twenty four rooms."

"I know. It's a TARDIS house, maybe."

"Can you feel it, turning?"

Stella thought she could, a kind of gentle inner wrench every now and then.

"As though we're being artificially cranked," she murmured.

"Presumably we are. Have you noticed that tree out there?"

Stella had. Down on the lawn, caught in the fiery sunset light, a copper beech blazed with autumn colour and the rosehips just outside the window were ripely scarlet.

"She's turning the year, as well."

"Yeah, but how many? I don't want to end up like that Irish fella – Oisín? – who crumples into dust when he gets off his horse. I remember Willie Yeats telling me about that one."

Stella was about to say, "What, the poet?" but it was once more time to move on. Not so much musical chairs, as musical houses. In her mind's eye, as if seen from above, A La Ronde was spinning like a top, whipped around by magic.

"Midnight!" Miss Parminter remarked, triumphantly. This room was painted dove grey and filled with samples of lace, which gave it a cobwebby, Havisham-like atmosphere. Outside, it was dark: only a dim lamp on the other side of the estuary betrayed, perhaps, the presence of a boat. They passed through the still, frosty hours of the morning. At three, Stella looked out to see the garden white with snow under the light of the moon. But as they came round to six again, the sky was growing light and in the garden the roses were in full and frothy bloom once more. There was an audible snap as Miss Parminter closed her watch. Then, with her guests behind, she marched to the front door and flung it open, but no one was standing on the step. Stella felt that they had been running from room to room for no more than an hour.

"Have we finished, Miss Parminter?" Davy Dearly asked.

"Yes. I have bought you time in this place. A year and a day, before the Morlader can find you."

"Thank you!"

"What did you mean, Davy, when you said he had lit matches in his hat?"

"I'm assuming they were matches. Blackbeard the pirate did it – I know that because of a documentary on the Beeb. Like little sparks of light. I should think it was a bit risky. Chances of setting your beard alight would be high."

"Before we were so rudely interrupted," Miss Parminter said, "I was in the process of sending you home."

"I should think you'd be glad to get rid of us," said Ace.

"Not at all, dear."

She traced a quick spiral in the air. "Should you become stuck in the grotto near Start Point, which is where you were earlier, a left-leading labyrinth should do it. Trace it with your finger upon the shells."

She had no sooner spoken than Stella felt herself in motion: a blur of watergreen, a fan of shells, the sea glimpsed through an open window – and they were standing by the well in Southwark again, with the cathedral bells chiming three o'clock and the noise of the market beyond.

BEE

Bee had considered trying to contact the Behenian stars before, had even tried a few small rituals. Lighting a candle, with a signature gem and a herb placed before it, rudimentary witchcraft. But the candles had flickered down and the herbs had wilted, without any sign of a wandering star. She had spoken to Dark about it, and to Nick Wratchall-Haynes.

Dark had told her, long ago, that he saw the star spirits occasionally, usually at night. They smiled at him but rarely spoke, and he did not see many other ghosts about the property, either. The girl in the rose coloured dress had not been seen since the autumn, when she had been instrumental in defeating a foe. Others – the woman in the garland of flowers, who carried apples in her lap – were even less frequent than the star spirits.

Nick said that he wasn't particularly psychic, that he sometimes saw ghosts around his own property but couldn't communicate with them, and that he had a basic working knowledge of conjuration.

"I'd like to have a chat with your sister's friend, Ace, though."

"He doesn't get out of town much."

"But he can do so, yes? He's not confined to the capital."

"No, he says it's mainly inertia, though. He and Stella went to Windsor a while ago so it's not like he can't go outside London. However, Stella's hoping to lure him to Somerset in a bit – to see Ward's play. Which I'm hoping you can attend as well, although at this rate Ward's entire audience will be composed of freebies to his friends and relations."

They were sitting in the drawing room of Wycholt, where Bee had come visiting to inform its master of recent events. The long windows were open to the sunlight and a huge bowl of pink roses, picked by Harris the gardener, decorated the table. Their scent was overpowering, welcome to Bee who found that so many modern roses looked lovely but had little fragrance. Occasionally, there was a distant crash, making the master of the house wince: Nick was having the floor of the library taken up and relaid.

"What are they *doing* in there? Hurling vases to the floor? Thank you very much for the offer of a freebie for the play, Bee, but I stumped up the £25 for a ticket."

"You didn't have to do that! Especially if you have to replace a few vases."

"No, but I believe in supporting the arts. And I don't think it's extortionate compared to London theatre prices."

Bee admitted that this was true.

"When is Stella coming down? On the day?"

"No, a day or so before with Serena and Bella and, as I say, probably Ace. Ward's rehearsing but he'll pitch up later with the rest of the cast and crew."

"A house party, then."

"We're having a family dinner on the evening they get here, to which you are invited. It'll be nice," Bee said, adding "As long as nothing goes wrong."

This time, Nick's laugh was rather hollow. "What could *possibly* go wrong? With an eldritch dog spirit holed up in your back field?"

"Luna is behaving *exactly* as she did when she was a teenager and she'd found some smelly old dog or stray cat or – or incontinent badger, and insisted on bringing it home and feeding it."

"That's the first time I've ever heard a malignant entity from another world compared to an incontinent badger. I suspect you of hyperbole."

"She never actually brought home an adult badger but she did keep a cub in the barn once, overnight, before we took it to the wildlife sanctuary. So I know what I'm talking about."

"And how is Mr Hound? Is she feeding him with a dropper?"

Bee rolled her eyes. "No. she goes and sits outside the field shelter. Not alone, Ver insists on going with her. Sam is not too happy about this but Luna can be very single minded when it comes to animals, even apparently animals who are not quite animals. She feels responsible for him. She's going to make a great mother."

"I'd like to talk to him, if I may."

"Hey, you're welcome. I was hoping you'd say that. You might be able to get more information out of him. Sam did try but he was unforthcoming. Simply stared, apparently. Although he wasn't actually rude. I find him scary."

"They are scary."

"But also faintly pathetic. Is he right, do you think, in that his soul will go to Hell if he renounces the Hunt? *Is* there a Hell?"

"Theologically, I am on somewhat shaky ground," said Nick. "I know what the Bible says, but let's say I have had a lot of conflicting reports."

"Stella asked Grandfather, and he either didn't know or wouldn't say. Same with Dark although I think he doesn't know. He's either in the past, or here. Ace, who is formally dead, apparently told Stella that he's never seen either Heaven or Hell, but his friend – William Blake, this just boggles me that someone I sort of know knows William Blake – has."

"I warn you that I am going to beg on my knees for an introduction to Blake when Ace gets here," Nick said.

"You and me both."

They left the floor repair team to do their work, Nick remarking that confronting a malign supernatural entity might on balance be less wearing on his nerves than dealing with the builders. When they reached Mooncote, Bee accompanied him down the field to the shelter. There was no sign of Luna, but Bee, remembering a note on the kitchen calendar, thought her sister might have an appointment with the midwife that day. Since the Hound's arrival Ver had moved into the spare bedroom by mutual arrangement, and she was not to be seen now either. But Dark was waiting for them. Bee slipped her hand into his as they made their way down the field.

The Hound, in canine form, lay on his bloody straw; he had refused to let Luna close enough to clear it out. He raised his head and gave Nick a long, cold stare. Nick held his ground and the Hound flickered into human shape.

"I have seen you before," the Hound said. He had a discernible accent, Bee noticed, but she could not quite place it. From the north, somewhere? He had mentioned that to Luna.

"We have crossed paths," Wratchall-Haynes said evenly. "I run a hunt of my own."

The Hound showed teeth. "But not like mine."

"No, not like yours. I want to talk to you about the man they call Aiken Drum."

"Once my master." There was a fleeting desolation in his face.

66

"Yes. Does the one who leads the Hunt – the Helwyr, is it? – become your master automatically, no matter who it might be?"

"It depends. If he wins the Hunt in fair fight, then yes. If by deception, perhaps not."

"You say 'he.' Is it always a man?"

The Hound's lip curled back. "A woman cannot lead the Hunt."

"No? And yet there are old German tales – the country over the water – in which the Wild Hunt is indeed led by a woman. You spoke to young Luna of challengers. I know and so must you that an ancient spirit of the deer kindred now walks free."

Dark said. "Noualen."

The Hound spat into the straw. "Deer are prey."

"Yet she is also a huntress. Slayer and slain, and now released from the chases of the old city and running free. Do you remember being a mortal man?"

"Gleams and snatches. Fighting. I remember that. And mud. And it was always cold."

"Was there a king or a lord?" Bee asked. "Someone for whom you fought?"

"Yes. I remember his eyes. Sometimes he looked at me. He had dark eyes."

The Hound fell silent.

"Nothing more?"

"Nothing." Then the Hound said, unwillingly, as though the words had been forced from him, "I believed that he loved me. But I don't remember more."

"Do you remember any women?"

"Women's love is worth nothing."

Well, that shut *her* up, Bee thought. How annoying, that despite having a really quite extensive coterie of men who actually did seem to treat women as equals, she was once again pussyfooting about trying not to make a man angry. But then, he wasn't really a man, more like a dangerous snapping dog.

Nick said, "You don't know what happened to him, this lord?"

"He went where I could not follow." For a moment, Bee had the image of a dog, head raised in howling, a dog whose master is never coming back. "And I took baser coin." He must mean Aiken Drum, or whoever led the Hunt before that. With attitudes like that, though, she couldn't see him responding well to Noualen. Probably Noualen wouldn't want to put up with it, either. Oh well.

"I want to ask you something. I broke my promise," Bee said, rather over-loudly to her own ears. "I was too late to stop my sister from freeing Noualen. Is that why Aiken is angry?"

"Yes. But it doesn't matter. Aiken is always angry. He did not truly expect you to succeed and the Feldfar, your mother, talked him from his anger for she is one of the few who can. I spoke of challengers: there are two. The deer spirit and another in the West, a wrecking man from a witch tribe. The sea challenges the land."

"Is that the man they call the Morlader?" Bee asked, dismayed.

"Yes."

"And how did you get hurt?" Nick said now.

"The deer woman is gathering followers. The green people, the wose, river spirits, oak folk, and others. She promises them much but can she deliver?" He had not answered Nick's question, Bee noted.

"Always the big problem with politicians," said Nick, smiling. "Do you know what she promised them?"

"Safety from the Hunt. We harry, always. We must dominate our lands; there are few enough of them and these small people," here he spat into the straw, "are in our way along the edge places. She says she will drive the Hunt north, away from here, and the others can live in peace. It will not be so."

"Why not?"

"She will bind them to her and they will harry us. It is always like this."

"Do you know that for certain? Has she said so?"

"Aiken Drum has said so," replied the Hound, with a certain respect.

"I see. Might Drum be lying? Why should you trust him, now that he has cast you out?"

But the Hound's head lolled onto the dirty straw.

"We should perhaps —" Nick hesitated. "Can we do anything for you?"

"Yes. You can leave me alone."

PART TWO
ILL MET BY MOONLIGHT

SERENA

"Mum! I do want to watch Ward's play and I promise I won't get into trouble, but can I go with Katie and Ghania?"

Serena looked up from her investigation of the picnic basket. "Go where, exactly, darling?"

Bella was almost hopping up and down. "Just over *there*." She pointed down the slope. The buttercup meadow ended in a stage, decked with fairy lights. Beyond, Serena could see caravans, many rows of tents like multicoloured mushrooms, and beyond that, a field or so away, the immense structure of the Pyramid Stage, awaiting the thousands who would, in a few days' time, be arriving for the Glastonbury Festival itself.

"I expect that's okay. Just remember you can't get onto the festival site itself. It's not open yet to punters and anyway you don't have a ticket."

"I *know* that, Mum!"

"All right. Off you go."

"Ghania's very sensible," Bee said. "Katie slightly less so, but she's a nice girl. They'll be fine. It's good for Bella to have some local friends."

"I do remember, at the same age, wanting to be with anyone less embarrassing than my own family."

"Same here. And yet here we all are, all four of us, sitting on a rug, with our various friends and relations. How are *you* coping?" Bee remarked to Ace.

"It's a bit green and cowy for my liking but I'll manage as valiantly as possible."

"Give him a beer," Stella said. "Make him feel at home."

"I must say, I am looking forward to experiencing some of your local hostelries in the fullness of time. Half timbered? Prints of eighteenth century hunting scenes? Ales on tap?"

"Check," Bee said. "All of the above. And there are no cows currently in this field – they're all over there."

"Marvellous! I did not, by the way, mean to sound churlish. It's exceptionally kind of you to not only bring me all the way to Somerset, but take me to see a play and put me up for a couple of nights."

"Not at all. And thank you for offering to help with the You-Know-What."

"I regard it as part of my job."

Earlier, Luna had taken Ace to see the Hound, having brought her visiting sisters up to date with events. But they had returned with the news that the field shelter was empty. Serena had been relieved: she had seen a Hound before, at close quarters, and it had not been a pleasant experience.

"Perhaps he's gone for good," she said, hopefully.

"No such luck," Ver told her.

"I don't think you should move back into the van until we're sure, Ver."

"I'd rather not, dear. It's not the van — it's the neighbours."

But the play was awaiting them. Bee and her sisters had found a suitable viewing spot, slightly high on the slope but quite close to the stage, and staked it out early. They had a couple of hours before the performance began and Bee and Luna had put together a substantial picnic basket. Ward was backstage.

"Are we expecting anyone else, Nick?" Bee asked. "I've lost track."

"The party from Amberley are bringing their own food, I gather. But if anyone's starving there are the vendors over there. I recommend the Thai one. I've had it before. If you like Thai." Bee confirmed that she did. "By the way," he added to Ace, "Talking about local hostelries, I would very much like to invite you out for a pint."

"Love to. I know no magician ever thinks that any other magician knows what they're doing, but you've obviously kept things together here in the countryside, as have you and Luna, Bee, and I would appreciate chewing the fat in a less public setting, although I don't suppose anyone can hear us here." Ace squinted into the evening sunlight. "The Elizabethan gent over there. Would that be your chap, Bee?"

"Ah, Ned! I wasn't sure if we'd be seeing you."

Introductions were made.

"He's definitely invited for a pint as well," Ace said. "If he can. I mean, *I* can so I don't see why a fellow ghost would not be able to."

"Yes, he's not infrequently down the pub."

"Outstanding."

"Luna, are you all right?" Her sister was shifting in her fold-up seat.

"Yes, thanks, Bee. Just a bit uncomfortable."

"She's past her due date – we were hoping for a Solstice baby – but you know what these things are like," Bee said.

"I wasn't sure if I should come along but Sam says he'll run me into Shepton if worse comes to worst – it's only a couple of miles down the road."

"I have a few tricks up my sleeve," Ver March said.

Ace smiled at her. "I'm sure you do!"

Serena did not want to bother Ward, who was by his own admission impossible just before a performance, and after devouring quiche, egg sandwiches and a glass of champagne, she went for a walk around the field. The site of the stage was adjacent to the festival fields themselves; essentially, this was the Glastonbury fringe, and soon the pastoral landscape would be a mass of bodies. Serena hoped it would not rain – the Festival was notorious either for mud or sunstroke – and she particularly hoped that the weather would hold off until later tonight. The air had a sultry, thundery feel to it and the glow of the western sky was marred by a few dark and gathering clouds. *Never mind*, Serena thought, *we are British*. They had brought plastic macs and two umbrellas, just in case.

At this point Serena, drifting through the buttercups and thinking about the weather, was hailed by distant shouts from the gate. She looked across to see Laura and Caro in the vanguard, waving, and went over to meet them.

"Serena, how lovely you look. All green and buttercuppy."

"Thank you, Caro. To be honest I did make this dress because I thought it would be summery and then it occurred to me that was a bit twee, to be honest, but I don't care."

"Serena," Laura said, giving her a hug, "Just quickly, Ben's with us. I hope that's okay."

"Yes, it's fine, as long as he's okay with it," Serena said, in her best breezy we're-all-grown-ups voice. She had not seen her ex since the winter and it was not only true to say that they had parted on bad terms, but that they had parted on weird ones. Still, she had done her best then to save his life and arguably had succeeded. She smiled at him as he approached, carrying a rucksack from which came the clink of bottles.

"Hi!"

"Hi!"

There were air kisses all round.

"We're over there," Serena said, "And you'd be welcome to join us, but it's got a bit busy since we sat down."

"We'll go a bit further up the slope," Richard Amberley said. "More room, but we will come and socialise."

"You'd be welcome. We've got friends down from London. And Nick's with us – Harris drove some of us over, actually. Great to be chauffeured."

"And how's Ward? Ready for his close up?"

Serena grinned. "Having a crisis. When I last saw him he told me to go away. I didn't take it personally. Maud will keep him sane. I hope."

"Did Bee tell you we were all glued to *Dragonholt*? Oh my God, it was so gory, but totally compulsive."

"She was rather magnificent, actually," Richard said.

"Richard may have been watching it for different reasons."

"Every woman I know perved over her co-star. Adrian Butterfield. Who is gay, by the way."

"Oh, is he? I thought he probably was. Oh well. A girl can dream. And he does *look* remarkably like a Viking."

Serena saw them settled on the slope and wandered on, congratulating herself on handling that in a civilised way. It felt, now, as though another person had gone out with Ben, had been made so unhappy by him, and yet a year ago she and Ben had come to the Festival where his band had been playing, had walked hand in hand in those fields in front of the Pyramid Stage in the baking sunshine. The scene was the same: the dark mass of the oaks on the opposite hillside, the sweet summery smell of hay, which the tedders had raked before baling. She stood still for a moment, thought of Ward, thought *right decision*. Give it time and she might be able to sit down with Ben and talk it through. But now it was still a little bit soon. She went back to where her sisters were sitting and waited for the play to begin.

LUNA

Luna thought that this was one of those evenings of which one should make a mental bookmark. *That was the time we went to the fringe to see Midsummer Night's Dream, and Stella's friend Ace came from London and we sat and had a picnic; that was the time when the Hound appeared. The night before, two days before, a week before I had my baby.* She imagined herself in eighteen years' time, sitting in this same field, saying to that son, that daughter, *this is where you were born, or nearly born, or just before you were born, when we came here to watch Ward in a play.* Luna caught her breath; for a moment, she could almost see someone, a person in their late teens with Sam's curly dark hair, their face turned away to the light in the west. An adult person, about to embark on adventures of their own, and Luna would worry and wish them well and worry some more. How short those years would seem, thought Luna, watching her life spool out before her.

Someone nudged her shoulder.

"You all right?"

"Yes. Yes, I am. Thanks, Ace. Just thinking about the future."

"I find it never does, to do that," the magician said, gloomily. "It'll take care of itself, my gran always said to me."

"Your gran was right," Nick Wratchall-Haynes remarked. "I was fifty two last week. How the hell did that happen? I thought."

"I remember being fifty-two. Bit of a shock to me, too. The whole thing. Then you die and find that there's fuck all difference."

"That could be depressing."

"No one I know who's dead seems to think that, though," Luna said.

"This is one of those occasions when I'm glad we're not in a crowded place."

"I know. I have to be really careful what I say these days," Luna confessed. "Mind you, you can say anything in Glastonbury."

"In Waitrose in Wells, for instance, not so much,"

"Precisely."

"Sure you're feeling okay, Luna?"

"Yes. Don't worry, Nick. If anything kicks off everyone will know because I shall be loud about it, even if it's in the middle of the play."

"They say that at every Glastonbury Festival, someone is born and someone dies."

"Well, let's go for the first option, eh?" Stella said.

"Wasn't some Tory MP found dead in the bogs one year?"

"Yes. What a way to go."

In the west, the sky was becoming suitably dramatic. A towering thunderhead was rivalling the light of the sinking sun, and she was grateful for the occasional breeze. In this sort of humidity, her hair and Bee's did not behave themselves and Luna experienced an unfamiliar pang of envy at Stella and Serena's straight locks. She felt fat, gravid, sweaty and frizzy. *Never mind!* she thought. *None of that matters and none of the people you are with will care.* She voiced this thought to Stella.

"Too right," her sister said. "No one gives a shit. As long as you're okay."

"I'm fine."

"I think they're starting." Stella gave a small wriggle of anticipation and Titania's retinue ran out from behind the stage. In the chancy light, in their wonderful costumes, they did indeed look like some fairy tribe. The nicer kind.

The fairies ran lightly through the maze of blankets, bodies and picnic baskets, nimbly dodging coolers of champagne as they scattered rose petals from baskets. With whoops and cries they vanished into the woodland at the top of the hill and the curtains were pulled aside. *A Midsummer Night's Dream* had begun.

By the time the interval was announced, Luna had forgotten her discomfort and become absorbed in the play.

"Ward's really good, isn't he?" she said to Serena.

"He really is. He's good about not rehearsing too much at home – he locks himself into his study when he learns his lines – but I still feel I know this thing by heart. I do love it, though. And the weather's holding off!"

"Not for long," Ver March said.

"You reckon?" Ver would know, Luna thought.

"Rain's on the wind. Never mind! If the heavens open we shall brave it out!"

"We've only got one half to go," Serena said.

Luna thought that she ought not to sit still for too long. She got up and walked down to the stage and back again. By now, the sun was low in the west, casting the humped form of the Tor into sharp relief. The little hill was small in comparison to the thunderhead, the black cloud's summit lit by golden fire. A strong breeze was driving across the land, tossing the hay and the crowns of the oaks. Luna was glad of it; she had been feeling too hot. But the storm was holding off.

By this point in the play, Oberon was hopelessly in love with Bottom, while Maud, as the fairy queen, strode about, declaiming her husband's lines. Luna thought that the gender exchange worked well: now Titania was the power of the fairy throne, and Oberon the victim of her manipulative magic. Luna did not know the name of the young actor who was playing Bottom; he was Black and very beautiful. Maud's girlfriend Jack, a Puck with full tattooed sleeves, was running about the audience when not on stage, scattering fairy dust.

"Reminds me of Hob," Luna overheard Stella remark to Serena.

"I know. Makes you wonder."

There was a distant mutter of thunder in the distance. Luna blinked, but there was no lightning flash. Out of the corner of her eye she saw something move and turned to see a girl crouching in the buttercups: her skin was faintly scaled, her eyes a serpent green. She wore a leather harness that left her breasts bare. She saw Luna looking, and winked. She must be a member of Titania's retinue, Luna thought, but then the girl was suddenly no longer there. She nudged Stella.

"Did you see anyone, just now? Where the basket is?"

"No. Why? Did you?"

"Yes, a girl, with scales like a snake."

"Shit," said Stella. "I hope things aren't kicking off again."

Ace leaned across.

"Stella, where's your friend Laura? She was here up until the intermission."

"I don't know –" but then Luna looked back up the slope. On the edge of the woodland stood a rider on a grey mare.

STELLA

Stella grabbed Ace by the sleeve.

"Come on!"

They made their way up the slope, sidestepping blankets and rapt playgoers. At least everyone's attention seemed to be fixed on the stage, where fairies on ropes were performing a kind of aerial dance. Serena had mentioned Maud and a trapeze... The rider remained motionless but Stella would have known her anywhere. The antlers were a bit of a clue. They had last met in London, where Davy Dearly had opened a door that released Noualen, ancient deer spirit, out into the world of men. The mare was the transformed Laura.

Noualen did not turn her head to look at Ace and Stella, toiling hastily up the slope. She was looking out over the fields towards the Tor. When Stella had last seen her, she had worn a green gown, but now she was in britches and a leather jerkin, all in shades of green and brown and fawn, like the land. Her flaming hair was braided beneath a small cap with a pheasant's feather in it.

Stella was about to hail her when she nudged the mare about and vanished into the woodland. Stella looked at Ace.

"I bet she knew we were here."

Ace, somewhat out of breath, nodded.

"Yeah, should think you're right. That was Noualen, yes? I've not seen her before."

"Yes, it was."

"Powerful presence."

"She makes me feel a bit spinny," Stella said. Ace laughed.

"Know what you mean. You've got to be firm, with these minor deities. And I should know."

"You can go first," said Stella, with feeling. "Want to follow her?"

"I don't think we should separate from everyone else right now. Also there's a case to be made for minding our own business."

"Good point. Let's be sensible for once," Stella said. But Ace's head jerked up.

"What was that?"

"Thunder, I think?"

"No, it was coming from the east."

Then someone ran out of the woods and down the slope. She moved so quickly that Stella only glimpsed her but she must have been the girl whom Luna had seen. Her green hair streamed behind her and her long legs gleamed.

"Who was that?" Ace snapped.

Stella grabbed him by the arm and pulled him out of the way behind a blackthorn bush. She could hear it now: not thunder, but the drumbeat of hooves. The Hunt exploded out of the woodland: a full complement of horses and hounds, fire-eyed and shadowy. They raced down the slope and Stella heard the eerie note of a horn, the summoning note to the pack. Horses, dogs, the bull-headed man and others ran through the audience, flickering in and out of sight. No one paid them any attention but Stella saw Bee, seated down the slope, start and throw her arms around Luna. Nick Wratchall-Haynes was already on his feet. But the Hunt rushed through them, through the stage and away, the only indication of its passage a path of firefly sparks across the twilight land.

Then another horse erupted from the woodland. A chestnut stallion, riding fast in the wake of the Hunt, with a ram-horned man on its back. He was urging the stallion on, wielding the reins. As he passed Ace and Stella he turned his head and she looked into his hot yellow eyes; it was like looking down into Hell. A single Hound ran behind him, in man form, mouth open in a shriek of dismay. No sound emerged but the Hound looked quite mad.

"Jesus Christ," Stella heard Ace say. Then they, too, were gone, but someone lay crumpled in the grass where they had run, not far away.

"Oh shit!" Stella said. "Shit!"

"What?"

"Ace, it's my mum."

79

BEE

Bee, Dark and Nick left Luna in the care of Sam and Ver and ran up the slope as quickly as they could; Stella was frantically beckoning.

"What's wrong?" Bee called, when they were not far away. Stella was on her knees beside something in the grass. Thankfully, there were no spectators up here; everyone was further down the field and no doubt wondering about the commotion. Some heads had turned in their wake.

"Bee!" Even in the chancy light, Stella looked pale and shocked. Then Bee saw why.

"Oh God!"

She dropped to the grass beside her sister.

"What happened?"

"The Hunt dropped her off."

"From a frigging height. She's not dead," Ace added quickly. "She's breathing but she's not conscious."

"I've just rung Harris and told him to bring the car up to the gate," Nick said. "Quicker to get her into A&E that way rather than call an ambulance out. They take bloody hours these days."

"Go for it," said Ace.

Blood was trickling from the side of Alys' mouth. Her eyes were open, but rolled back in her head, leaving only the whites. Bee found this particularly alarming. Then she was pushed aside. Serena had joined them.

"God! Mum? Bee, sorry – I was down by the stage. I saw the Hunt. I went back to Luna and she said you'd come up here. Where did she come *from*?"

But Bee was too busy directing operations. The Range Rover was now at the gate, with Nick's gardener at the wheel. Nick picked up the unconscious Alys with some effort, muttering about his knees, and carried her to the car. A burst of clapping from the field suggested that the play had ended, but it was drowned out by a sudden rumble overhead. The Tor was lit by a white-blue bolt of lightning.

"I'm not sure if we should even move her," Bee said.

"Fuck knows! It's not like she's been in a car crash. And it's about to piss down."

"I'll go with them to Shepton. Serena, you'd better wait here and speak to Ward – they're just finishing the play. Stella, you and Ace go back down and explain to Luna and Sam."

But Ver March, Sam and Luna were already coming up the slope in turn. It was a moment before Bee realised that the front of Luna's blue linen skirt was sopping wet. It was not yet raining.

"Oh no!"

"Oh yes!" Luna gasped.

The neon lights were very bright. Bee, sitting in the reception area of Shepton Hospital and nursing a plastic cup full of tepid vending machine tea, felt as though she had been wrenched violently from another age into the 21st century. Perhaps she had. Nick had disappeared to make a phone call and although Bee could see Dark, he was somewhat insubstantial and she did not want to speak to him in case the young receptionist thought she was a lunatic.

Sam and Ver were in a different part of the cottage hospital, wherever the maternity beds might be; Bee had lost track of them on the road, since Nick, taking over from Harris, had driven so fast, but a little later, looking out of the big plate glass windows of the main reception area, she had seen her own car, with Sam at the wheel, pulling into the car park. As soon as she knew how Alys was faring, she would follow Ace and Stella and go in search.

But just as this intention crossed her mind, Ace himself appeared in the doorway. In a tweed jacket that had seen better days and an open necked shirt, he looked most unspectral. Bee saw Dark smile.

"Bearing up, Bee?" Ace said.

"Just about. Thank you!"

"Any word?"

"Not yet. She was whisked in for a scan. How about Luna?"

"Says she's more or less comfortable. Stella's staying with her. I'm useless in this sort of situation."

Bee smiled. "I can't honestly see Stella being much better. Don't you have any old wives' remedies from days of yore to contribute to childbirth?"

"The old wives hung onto them. I tell you what," Ace said, sitting in the plastic seat next to her, "You wouldn't get this in the Smoke. You'd be stuck on a gurney in the corridor for the next nine and a half hours before getting a whiff of medical attention."

Bee nodded. "The NHS is a bit different in the countryside."

"You're telling me. The last time I had to go into A&E, not for myself, you understand, because obviously… anyway, it was for a chap who got knocked down by some arsehole on a bicycle opposite the Southwark Tavern. Someone called an ambulance and I went with him to St Thomas'. Saturday night and it was like a fucking warzone."

"I bet it was. The last time I was in an A&E was Yeovil when I'd broken my wrist and half the patients in there had been stabbed."

Ace eyed her with respect. "County town, eh?"

"A rough county town. And that was on a Thursday. But Shepton is a little cottage hospital, as you can see. This isn't even a proper A&E, it's the Minor Injuries Unit. They might insist on taking her to Taunton. Or Yeovil, actually. Or even Bristol if it's a serious head injury."

"Let's hope it's not."

"Did you see what happened?"

"No." Ace glanced around the reception area but the receptionist had gone, wheeling a woman into a room down the corridor. "I saw a bloke with horns on a massive horse and a Hound running behind him. I think that must be the remaining Lily White Boy and I assume the horned chap was Drum. Pity I didn't get a chance to speak to your house guest – be interesting to see if he shows up again. Then we saw your ma lying in the grass, but I don't know if Drum chucked her off the horse or if she fell off or what. I didn't see him shove her but it happened so bloody fast it was hard to tell."

"To be honest, I'm just relieved to know where she is," said Bee.

Dark said, "Now I know the heartache I caused my mother."

Ace laughed. "You and me both. It's like having an errant kid when your parent starts behaving like this. You know, Bee, this kind of swashbuckling can become addictive."

"Yes, it's struck me like that. As if she can't leave it alone. And the secretiveness is like an addict's, too."

Ace was about to reply but Bee saw the flick of a white coat at the door.

"Ms Fallow?"

"Yes!"

"Could I have a word?"

Her heart in her boots, Bee accompanied him to a side room. Alys was nowhere in sight. But the doctor – a Dr Mirza, she noted from his name badge – was very calm. As with most doctors now, he looked about twelve years old to Bee. He said, "Please don't worry. Your mother's had a bad knock to the head – fell off a straw bale pile, did you say?"

"Yes," said Bee with an inward wince. She hated lying. "At the Festival site. We were attending a play."

The doctor sighed. "She won't be the last I'll see from Pilton this week. However, unlike most of my future patients, your mother has no trace of drugs or alcohol in her system, is not suffering from sunstroke or dehydration, and frankly a simple concussion resulting from an accident is something that we can all be thankful for. There's nothing else wrong with her apart from bruised ribs. No signs of any internal damage."

"Oh, thank God!"

"I'm going to keep her in overnight for monitoring, but she should be well enough to come home tomorrow, all being well." The doctor paused. "She's dressed in a rather – unusual – manner. Do you come from Glastonbury?"

"No. She was dressed up Medieval style for the play," Bee said, once more lying frantically. "My sister's boyfriend is Ward Garner – he's starring in it. As Oberon. You might have heard of him. Ward, I mean, not Oberon."

"Oh, I see. Yes, I certainly have. I thought he was excellent in that police drama on Channel 4."

"I'll tell him. Glad you liked it."

"And your – sister, is it? Was also admitted earlier? To Maternity?"

"Yes. Luna Fallow."

"Your family are having a rather eventful evening, aren't they?"

"You could say that!"

"It might have been the shock of your mum's accident which sent her into labour – it's not unknown."

"Very likely. Can I see Mum?"

"Yes, I don't see why not, just for a couple of minutes. Sister is finding her a bed."

Bee followed him down a series of corridors until they came onto a small ward. The beds were occupied, with women reading or sleeping, or checking their phones. They looked up incuriously as Bee walked in. One of the beds was surrounded by green curtains; a nurse whisked them aside.

"Here we are, Mrs Fallow, here's your daughter come to see you!"

"Mum!" Bee sank to the side of the bed. Alys was as white as her sheets and her hair was damp. A great bruise was spreading down the side of her forehead. But her eyes were open and aware.

"You're going to have a spectacular shiner in the morning, Mum."

Alys grimaced. "Bring me some steak to put on it."

"How are you feeling?"

"Sore. A bit dizzy. What happened to me?"

"We think Aiken Drum threw you off his horse," Bee said, in a whisper. Alys looked at her blankly.

"Who's Aiken Drum?"

STELLA

Stella always thought of her youngest sister as being a strong young woman, but she hadn't realised she was quite this strong.

"Luna? Luna, I'm really sorry, but could you relax your grip a bit?"

"Sorry," Luna gasped. "Am I hurting your hand?"

"Yes!"

"Sorry!"

Stella had, perforce, become one of Luna's birth partners. Women were allowed two, and Sam was the other. Thank God there was a midwife in the room. Sometimes, when flying, Stella became a little nervous if the plane hit turbulence and she had developed a strategy for dealing with this. She would scan the faces of the flight crew and if they looked calm, Stella would tell herself that there was nothing to worry about. She thought, deep down, that this was probably not a very good strategy, because she suspected that flight crews were trained to not betray panic, but it was reassuring enough. Now, sitting by the side of Luna's bed in the dimly lit labour room, she applied this same approach to the midwife, a middle-aged Irish woman with bright hennaed hair, named Shirley Burns.

Shirley did indeed look very calm, and Stella ventured to ask if everything was all right.

"Oh yes, she's doing grand," the midwife said. "You're not a mum yourself, now?"

"No."

"I thought your friend said something to that effect. When your waters break, hopefully, you'll go into labour soon enough after that and she is."

"How long does it take? Or isn't it possible to say?" Sam was also in the room, sitting on the other side of Luna.

"No, it's not an exact science, but I will say that in my experience, which is considerable after twenty three years, it's longer with the first one. But it's not always the case and she's a good strong girl, aren't you, Luna?"

"I feel a bit feeble right now!"

"Ah, you're doing grand. Contractions still happening?"

"Yes. Bloody hell. Stella," Luna, gasping, looked up at her, "if you wanted to go and check on Mum or get a cup of tea or something, then don't feel you have to sit with me. I've got Sam and Shirley and Ver's not far away."

"Would you rather I wasn't here, Luna? I don't want to be in the way."

"No, no, I don't mind, but I am worried about Mum."

"What a terrible thing to have happen," said Shirley, who had also been given the fell-off-a-hay-bale story. "Still, what a tale you'll have to tell when it's all over."

"All right," said Stella, feeling guiltily relieved. She was, she found, squeamish about childbirth. "I'll go and see how she's getting on."

Outside, she found Ver reading a copy of *Hello*.

"What a load of tripe this is," said Ver.

"I know. Grim. I thought I saw a book swap shelf in the foyer. Would you like me to look?"

"Well, I wouldn't mind," said Ver. "I'll come with you and find a nice book. Seeing as I suspect we might be here for the long haul."

"Do you think?"

"It usually takes a while. Luna's always struck me as the sort who'd shoot 'em out like peas from a pod but it doesn't always follow."

"Serena said it was about eleven hours with Bella."

"I'd say that was pretty normal. I think the average is supposed to be about five. I don't think we all have to be here, if you wanted to go home. Sam and I will stay."

"As long as the staff don't mind us all taking up their hospital, I'd rather see it through. I can always kip on those seats. Legacy of gigs at festivals. I'm used to sleeping in odd places."

"Aren't we all, dear."

When Stella reached the other wing of the hospital, she found Dark, Ace and Bee deep in conversation.

"Oh, Stella!" Bee stood up. "How's Luna?"

"Contracting, apparently. She says she's okay, sort of, and the midwife is lovely."

"Do you want some tea?"

"No, their tea is foul, but I wouldn't mind a Fanta or something."
She went to the vending machine and juggled with it. "How can they
charge £2 for this?"

"Captive audience," said Ace.

"How is Mum?"

"Well," Bee said. "Could I have a quick word with you outside?"

They sheltered beneath the plastic roof of the foyer, since the rain
was now hammering down. Above, the sky flickered white and a
moment later, there was a rattling peal of thunder.

"I'm glad we didn't end up sitting out in this!" Bee shouted.

"A 'quiet word', eh?"

"Do you think this has anything to do with the you-know-what?"

"I don't know. It was building up before they appeared. But that
doesn't mean it's nothing to do with them."

"I have spoken to Alys. Asked her about Aiken. She didn't seem to
know who I was talking about."

"Shit," said Stella, "What does *that* mean?"

"I don't know. She has mild concussion."

"I'm assuming that could affect her memory?"

"Yes, the doctor says it can. He said it takes about a week to recover
and her memory should come back."

"What if it doesn't? What if she doesn't remember any of it?"

"She knows who I am. And when I said you were here, she knew
who you were. And she's concerned about Luna. She seems perfectly
lucid, just really tired. She's asleep now or I'd suggest you go in. Oh,
hang on, that's my phone." She rummaged in her bag. "Serena! Yes,
we're all fine." She delivered a quick update. "Nick suggested driving
me back, Ned will come too, obviously, under his own steam, but I'm
not sure about anyone else." She gave her sister an enquiring look.

"We don't all need to stay," Stella said. "Especially if Mum's asleep. I
said to Ver I'd stay with Luna but that's for me, really, not for Luna.
She's in good hands. Do *you* want to stay with her?"

"Theoretically, yes, but I don't want to get in the way – we can't all
be crowding round the bed, they won't let more than two people in,
and there's nothing I can do practically."

"Except yell 'Push!'"

"Not very helpful, possibly. Also I feel a bit bad that Ace has come
all this way and is now having to spend the night in a hospital and not

get any sleep. Even if he is, you know. *Dark* sleeps. I think we should take him home."

"Yes. Okay. Give me the phone," Stella said. "Serena, did you hear that? I think I'll crash out here and see Luna through, and Nick, or Harris, whatever, can drive Bee and Ace back. Ver will stay here, and Sam. Get the kettle on and I'll see you in the morning."

When they went back inside, Ace put up no resistance to this plan.

"I'm about as much use as a chocolate teapot when it comes to maternity matters. I didn't have any kids when I was, well…" Ace glanced at the receptionist and a disconsolate family whose child had broken his arm, "younger, let's say."

"Go back to Mooncote and give Nick a massive Scotch if Harris is driving – Harris doesn't drink."

"Sounds like a plan."

Released from half the family obligations, Stella wandered in and looked at her sleeping parent. Divested of her otherworldly skins, Alys looked not only her age, but older: evidently they did not have hairdressers in the other world and now her hair was completely white. For the first time, Stella realised what Serena would look like, when she was old, and perhaps her own self, too. Stella took a deep breath. Alys muttered something in her sleep – a name? The word made no sense. Uneasily, Stella left the ward and its occupants and went back to Maternity.

True to her word to Ver, she crashed out on the row of seats at the end of the reception area. She did not think she would sleep, but the day's events, and a late night the day before, caught up with her. They had been stuck in a queue on the A303, following an accident, and arrived at Mooncote too late for Bee to have her family dinner. Bee, ever, practical, had put the whole thing in the fridge. Stella, after a glass of wine and some scrambled egg on toast, had gone to bed, but that had been well past midnight. So now, sleep overtook her swiftly.

She woke with a start. Someone had screamed, was screaming. The reception area was empty. Stella, after a disoriented moment, hauled herself to her feet and ran into the room.

Luna was half sitting up and responsible for the screams.

"I'm all right!" she bellowed, when she saw her sister. "I'm just shouting! This really, really fucking hurts."

"Mum told me once she asked Gran to kill her when she was having Serena," Stella remarked. "Put her out of her misery."

"You hear that a lot," the midwife said. "Luna, you're a real little star. You shout if you want to!"

"Fucking hell!" Luna roared.

"You tell it," Stella said. "Do you want to hold my hand again?"

"No, I'll probably rip it off!"

"She's a lot calmer than some I've seen," Ver said.

"Isn't she doing great?" Shirley bestowed an approving smile upon the old lady. They had evidently formed a bond.

Stella tried to remember everything she knew about labour which wasn't a lot. "Shouldn't she have gas and air? What about epidurals?"

"You just leave all that to us," Shirley said, firmly but quite kindly.

"Stella, there is something you can do," Luna panted. "Take Sam to get some coffee."

"For him, presumably? Not you."

"No, I'm not sure if I'm allowed and anyway I'd just throw it out of the fucking window."

Stella went out of the room and found Sam with his head in his hands. She took him by the arm and led him from the room like a stubborn horse. Down by the vending machine, she made him sit down again; he had gone very pale.

"But hey," Stella told him, "Nearly everyone else in the family is laid up in here, why shouldn't you be? Put your head between your knees. Do you want milk?"

"No. Black. Thanks."

After a few sips his colour returned. He said, "I don't *think* I'm going to faint."

"Great! You'll be fine."

"It's really hard, seeing her hurting so much."

"When I get to the afterlife," Stella remarked, "assuming I'm not banged up as a dog or something, I'm going to find whoever's responsible and give them a piece of my mind about female biology."

"If you ask me," Ver said, appearing around the corner, "it's a really good case for there being a male God."

"So true."

"Have you considered having kids, Stella?" Ver asked, wrangling a tea out of the vending machine.

"No, I've never been in the right sort of relationship and to be honest, I think I'm a bit too freewheeling for it. Maybe I'll have some pups."

"At least you wouldn't have to pay for their education."

"Also true. Although I don't regret going to university."

"What did you study, Stella?"

"Music, but to be fair I mainly went clubbing. I got a 2:1, though."

"You could say that clubbing did you more good, since it's your career," Ver said.

"It's all good. Hey ho. I suppose we ought to go back up and see how poor old Luna's getting on."

SERENA

Serena found it hard to get to sleep. She kept rerunning the events of the evening, the delight of the play surmounted by the sequence of shocks. She kept telling herself that all would be well, the long ago words of Julian of Norwich echoing in her mind. Alys and Luna were in the safest place available; Bella and Ward were fine and back at Mooncote. Bella had not said much about the Hunt, only 'well, that was weird.' But she had seen them, and understood that her friends had not. She was more worried about her grandmother and her aunt.

"Do you think Luna will be all right?" she had said in the taxi going home, a small, scared voice.

"She'll be fine," Ward told her. "She's a big strapping girl."

"He's right," Serena said. "Don't worry."

"But things can go wrong with childbirth, can't they?"

"Yes. But think of all those generations of women before us who didn't have access to modern medicine. Lots of them still don't. It is scary – I was terrified – but actually it wasn't that bad. And look at the result!" Serena reached out and gently tugged Bella's trailing hair. "Positive thinking! Take all that energy you're spending on worrying and send it to Luna and Gran."

"All right," said Bella, sounding more sure of herself. "Okay, I'll do that. On it."

Now, however, Serena's brave words returned to haunt her. She lay awake, staring into the shadows and listening to Ward's quiet breathing. He had gone to sleep immediately, the result of a first night, although in Serena's experience this was unusual: he was more likely to stay up with the aftermath of adrenalin. She was glad of it, all the same; at least someone seemed set to have a good night's sleep.

Mooncote felt full of presences, as though the house itself was stirring. She half expected to see one of the Behenian stars coming to stand by the bed – this had happened before – but no one visited her. She started to drift off, then came awake with a start to the sound of voices. No one was there. Serena gritted her teeth, prepared for a night of insomnia, and promptly fell asleep.

When she woke, light was sneaking around the edges of the curtains. Ward had starfished the bed, on his back, and Serena found herself wedged against the bedside table. Smiling, she slipped out of bed, picked up her bag, visited the bathroom and went downstairs in her nightie. There was a text from Stella, around 2 a.m, three hours ago: *aok but no sign baby yet going 2 crash out spk l8r,* and nothing more. She liked having the house all to herself: the summer version of the night before Christmas, when all was still and quiet, but flooded with light and the mild air. An early morning feeling, before anyone else was up.

Something brushed against her knees, making Serena jump. Moth's long, anxious face stared up at her.

"Don't worry," Serena said, as she had said to Bella. "She'll be fine!" But the lurcher did not look reassured. Serena found a pair of wellington boots, the only footwear available, and opened the back door. "Come on. I expect you need a wee."

Moth raced out, but then stopped and looked back.

"I'm coming." She did not know where the spaniels were; perhaps upstairs with Bee. Moth cocked his leg on the drainpipe and waited for her to catch up. Serena, somewhat hampered by the wellingtons, stumped down the drive. Mindful of the Hound, she skirted Mooncote's own field just in case and clambered over the stile onto the footpath which crossed the adjacent land.

It was a beautiful morning. Somewhere, a thrush was singing. The hedges were filled with wild roses, the pale pink flowers that always reminded her of Elizabethan embroidery, and the tattered lacy remnants of elderflower. The grass was wet with dew, making Serena grateful for the wellingtons. Wasn't there a folk tale of washing your face with the dew on Midsummer Morning, to find your true love? But Serena thought on reflection that it might be May Morning instead, and her love lay in the house she was leaving behind her, hogging the bed. After his performance as Oberon, however, she thought he deserved it.

She turned to see the sun cresting in a burst of sudden flame over the chestnut trees that backed the church spire. The weathercock flashed gold. Moth whined and the world was filled with light; later, the sky would be a perfect unclouded blue. Dazzled, she swung away and found an oak wood where none had been before.

Oh.

"What do we do, Moth?" Serena asked aloud. But the lurcher had already answered: he was running lightly down the slope towards the wood. Cursing, Serena followed.

Within a few minutes, she was beneath the dappled shade of the trees. There were a number of oaks around Hornmoon, big mature trees, but not as densely wooded as this. Serena's boots crunched on acorns. The trees were not yet in their full summer darkness; the leaves had that vivid yellow glow of new growth. A sprig fell at Serena's feet as though the oak had cast it before her; she picked it up and tucked it into her nightdress. Being seen in her nightie was not likely to be a problem at this time of the morning and, anyway, Serena had bigger things to worry about.

Moth had paused. She could see his long form, poised and quivering. His tail was wagging, but uncertainly. Serena caught up with him and saw that he was standing on the edge of the woodland: not a glade, but the point where the wood actually ceased. A grassy slope led down to a bowl in the hills, downland rather than the farm country around Hornmoon. At the summit of the opposite slope she could see a ruined building, perhaps a church, like the one that stood on a neighbouring tump and where, at Christmas, she had experienced an odd slip of time. But it was not quite the same.

Serena caught hold of Moth's collar and paused. She would walk around the edge of the bowl, rather than approach the ruin itself. She did not want to risk being trapped in the building... Keeping to the edge of the trees, she made her way around the top of the slope, but then she heard hoofbeats. With Moth at her heels, she ducked behind a beech tree. The rider came fast from the wood, not far from where Serena had first found herself in this place. He was on a big horse, so black that it was almost indigo. Aiken Drum rode a chestnut: she had glimpsed him the night before. So who was this man? As if he had caught her thought, he turned his head and she saw his eyeless face beneath the brim of a hat. The man Stella and Luna had told her about; the pirate, the wrecker lord they called the Morlader.

He cantered down the slope then reined in the snorting horse. He slid from its back and looked around, as if searching for someone. For her? Serena kept very still. How could he see, out of those eyeless sockets? Streamers of faint darkness emanated from him, as though he was dissolving in the wind, and sparks flared briefly around his face.

A twig cracked behind her, not far away. Serena crouched instinctively down to the roots of the tree; a scrub of bramble would hopefully hide her. Minutes later a Hound strode past, his leather cloak swinging. He looked from neither right to left and he did not seem to see Serena holding her breath behind the bramble, although she could see him. His nostrils flared but he kept on walking, straight down the slope. He had a slight limp, Serena noticed.

Cautiously, Serena raised her head. She could see the two men talking. The Hound gestured, but he did not seem to be pointing directly at Serena herself. There was a taut desperation in his stance, his jaw thrust forward as he spoke. Putting forward an argument, perhaps? Luna had said that he was looking for a new master and had mentioned the Morlader, though not by name. Then she saw the Morlader nod. He slapped the Hound on the arm, mounted his horse and without a backwards glance kicked it into a gallop, down the slope and away. The Hound turned and loped back up the hill. Serena did not dare move. Halfway up the slope, he changed shape. Moth whined again.

"Shhh!" Serena hissed. She took hold of the dog's long snout and pressed it, but the Hound had either scented or heard them. The pale, red eared head cast about, moving from side to side. Then he headed straight for the beech tree. Serena knew she ought to get to her feet and run, but she was frozen to the spot. Moth looked down at her, puzzled, and it was a second before she realised that she wasn't human any more, either. The Hound was bounding up the slope, jaws scummed with froth. Serena felt herself picked up and lifted into the air; she squeaked. There was a strong, sudden scent of roses. Serena, turned on her back with her paws in the air, looked up into a tawny eyed face beneath a crown of roses. It was the woman they had sometimes seen walking in the orchard. She smiled absently down at Serena and then the sunlight changed, becoming dappled and uncertain. A curtain of wild rose concealed Serena, the woman and Moth, a screen of prickles and leaf and the little five petalled roses of the hedgerow.

With her hare's senses, Serena could feel the Hound scouting around the edges, snuffling, but the scent of the flowers was too strong. She heard him give a dog's grumble and then he moved away. Serena remained in the woman's arms, quite still, until the danger was past and the woman let her go. She slid to the ground in her human form. A tiny bead of blood welled up from the back of her hand and Serena dashed it away.

"Time to go home," the woman said.

"Thank you. Who *are* you?"

The woman smiled at her again. "Don't you know?" She held out her hand and in it rested an apple, rosy red like an apple in a fairy tale. Serena blinked. An image popped into her mind: a painting by Burne-Jones, a woman with a skirt full of apples. Pomona? Serena was about to speak the name but the woman and the woodland were gone. She was standing in the orchard of Mooncote, surrounded by the apple trees, with Moth by her side.

Her first thought was to get back inside the house; the house meant safety. Moth was inclined to cast about, following scents, but Serena took him by the collar and marched him firmly indoors. The kitchen was quiet: no sign of anyone. No dogs, either in or out of their baskets. The Aga was warm, but nothing stood on the stove. The kitchen table was tidy and on it sat a piece of paper. Stella went quickly over and picked it up. It was a list.

Picnic.
Waterproof blanket.
WINE.
Sunglasses.
DO NOT FORGET CHAMPAGNE 4 W.

And so on. Bee's list for the previous evening.

Serena checked her phone: it was five thirty in the morning and the right date. Back in the here and now. Thank God.

She dithered for a moment, worrying about the Hound. But he had been in the otherlands, not here. She did not want to lock the back door, in case anyone came home. Instead, she opened the door to the hall and went up the stairs, then leaped as a voice shouted in her ear.

"NOW!" it yelled.

Serena clutched at the bannister and found herself staring into the indignant face of Tut, peering down from the landing.

"For goodness' sake, cat!"

"NOW!"

"Tut, you've got food in the kitchen. I saw it."

But apparently that was not good enough. Tut bounced down the stairs, right between Serena's feet, and into the kitchen, still yelling. Sighing, Serena followed and opened a sachet of Whiskas. Silence fell. This never happened to Bilbo Baggins, Serena thought, or the heroes of other sagas. She left Tut to devour his breakfast and resumed her ascent. Her mother's bedroom was empty, the bed neatly made, the curtains half drawn, but the room felt stuffy. Stella flung them fully open, opened the window as well, and let in the sun. Alys should come home to an aired bedroom.

She turned to go but a man was standing in the doorway. She had seen him not long before. His face was white, his garb was black and the sockets of his eyes were empty. His mouth was open in a silent shout and firefly sparks shot all around him, fizzing and sizzling. He was wielding a long curved knife. Serena screamed. She stumbled backwards and caught the edge of the bed, sitting down abruptly. Then, just as suddenly, Ace was between them and Serena heard footsteps pounding up the stairs.

"Stay put, Serena," Ace ordered. He uttered a long string of syllables, nonsense words, but they couldn't have been that nonsensical, for the man began to dissolve, into the long tattered ribbons of shadow that Serena had seen before. A shaft of sunlight fell through the window, and the Morlader was gone. Dark stood in the doorway, with Nick Wratchell-Haynes at his shoulder, somewhat unshaven and dishevelled.

"What the hell?"

"Visitor," said Ace. He turned to Serena. "I don't suppose you'd like to stick the kettle on?"

BEE

Bee had thought that she wanted nothing more than her bed, but when they got home, around seven in the morning, she found that she was wide awake and twitchy. She was glad that so many people were already at the house, and awake. Serena, ethereal apart from a pair of rubber gloves, was washing the glasses.

"At least we always have a really clean house when there's a crisis," Bee said.

"I'll say," Serena said, with feeling. Bee frowned.

"Everything been okay here?"

"Not really. I'll tell you later. When I've washed up. The boys did offer to do it, by the way. But I thought it would take my mind off – well, anyway."

"It's probably better than drinking," Wratchall-Haynes said.

"Oh, I dunno. Pass me the wine, Nick."

Nick grinned. "Here you go, Ace."

Bee looked at Ward, who had just come into the kitchen, rather rumpled.

"'So apart from that, Mrs Lincoln – how was the play?'"

"Well, hell," Ward said. "Actually, apart from *that,* I thought it all went rather well. Even Jonathan muttered something grudging about 'better than the rehearsals'. The only dodgy moment was when I looked up from the stage and there was a load of fucking supernatural horsemen running towards me. Nearly dropped Bottom. Then I realised they were charging through people and then they were gone, so I thought, *well, that was bizarre* and got on with it."

"The show must go on."

"And did."

"I've actually only seen the Wild Hunt once before," Ace said. "And that was in Surrey – near Guildford, of all places. I don't think this was the same bunch."

"No, apparently it changes. I don't know what happens to the old ones."

"No idea. Everyone's very cagy on where you go after the afterlife. I just plain don't know."

"I've never had any straight answers," said Nick.

"I think I shall make some more tea," Serena said, divesting herself of the rubber gloves.

"Good idea. I ought to be ready for bed but I'm too wired."

"Go up if you need to, Bee."

"I'll see how I feel."

She sat quietly at the table, while Serena pottered about the kitchen and the man and the two ghosts talked, exchanging information, comparing notes. She found the experience to be dream-like, a night taken out of time, as perhaps Midsummer Eve should be. Although it was Midsummer Day now.

"You should talk to my grandfather," she said.

"He was an astronomer, right?"

"Yes. He's buried in Hornmoon churchyard. His spirit is sometimes there. He won't say where he is when he's not. But he's like a little blue light."

"Ah yes," said Ace. "I've known that happen. It's a bit like a screensaver."

This remark startled Bee so much that she fell silent again. The men's low voices were calming; she listened for a few minutes and then, to her surprise, awoke. She was in her bed. Ned Dark was standing by the window. The curtains were open and, beyond him, she could see the sky.

He said, "Bee? Your phone is ringing?"

Bee could hear its muted buzz. She reached out to the nightstand and picked it up, saw the time – nine in the morning – and the name.

"Stella?" she breathed. Her mouth was dry and she felt groggy. Stella, on the other hand, was as bouncy as a puppy.

"Hi, aunty Bee! Your niece Rosie wants to say hello. Well, she would if she could speak, I'm sure."

"Oh my God," Bee said, furrily. "Hang on." She groped for her glass of water and swigged it. "Sorry. That's better. Just woke up. How is Luna? How is Rosie? How is Mum?" She struggled upright against the pillows.

"Right. In order, Luna is fine. She actually gave birth half an hour ago – she's had a tough night, but she's absolutely okay. It took a while but no problems or anything. Rosie is also fine, the nurse did tell me how much she weighs but I've forgotten, sorry, anyway, she's got two eyes and stuff. Mum is still asleep, but I just spoke to the nurse and they said her vital signs are all right. She can probably come home later today."

"Fantastic!" Bee was now as wide awake as Stella, adrenalin burning off any vestige of a hangover. "Are they letting Luna come home as well?"

"Yes. She's having a kip now but they're going to kick her out later, I expect they need the beds, and if we can time it properly, Sam can drive everyone back."

"Right," Bee said. "I'm getting up."

Dark was smiling.

"All is well?"

"All is *very* well."

On her way downstairs, Bee could smell bacon frying. Downstairs, she found Ace and Nick still in the kitchen. The hunt master was cooking breakfast.

"I'm trying not to burn your pan."

"Don't look at me," Ace said. "I'm a shit cook."

"Have either of you had *any* sleep?"

"Yes. Nick crashed out for a couple of hours on your settee. I do sleep but I can do without at a pinch. Dark's probably the same. Ward's gone over to the hotel in Shepton to check up on his fellow thespians. Good morning, Bee, how are you?"

"I'm an aunty! Again!"

"Oh, what?" said Ace. "She's popped the sprog, then?"

"Yes. Rosie. Mum and daughter fine. Not an egg, apparently."

"Bit of a relief all round, I should think. How about your ma?"

"Asleep but basically okay and they're letting her out later."

"Great stuff."

As she had told her sister, Bee dealt with alarms and an early start by hoovering the dining room. When she went back into the kitchen, she found Serena.

"Bella's still in bed."

"When I came in, you sort of suggested there'd been a problem here?"

"I had a really weird experience this morning, but we'll tell you later. Can I do anything?"

"No, you cleaned the kitchen. Nick and Ace are taking a turn round the garden."

"I can see them," Serena said, peering through the French windows. "Nick seems to be explaining something to him."

"I'm not sure if it's reassuring to have two practicing magicians on the premises or not."

"Trust me, it's reassuring. Nick's really nice, isn't he?"

"Yes, he's a fine chap and all that. We've become good friends. I don't know if I'd describe Ace as 'nice', exactly, but I like him."

"Ace wants to talk to Alys, he told me."

"It's going to be awkward if she still can't remember anything."

"Or is pretending not to," said Serena.

"That's a good point. That hadn't occurred to me. As a way of dodging difficult questions, you mean?"

"Well, she certainly has some difficult questions to answer."

Nick Wratchall-Haynes went home for a shower and a change of clothes, but returned shortly before lunch. Just as he had sat down at the kitchen table there was the sound of a car in the drive and Stella, Sam, a tired and beaming Luna with a bundle, and Alys leaning on Ver March's arm, came through the door. The kitchen was suddenly full of people, all talking at once.

"Shut up!" Bee roared, like a quarter master. "I can't hear a thing. Sit down. Luna, you first. Oh my God, so this is Rosie. Hello, Rosie!"

The baby gazed at her from slightly unfocused blue eyes. Her face wrinkled.

"She's adorable," Serena said.

"They all look like the late Sidney James to me," Ward said.

"Howling oranges," Ace said.

"That's the one."

"Don't be so, so *bloke-y*! Luna, she's perfect. How are you feeling?"

"Yes," Luna said. "All right, actually. A bit sore. And knackered. But that's normal. I might go to bed this afternoon."

"Absolutely, just do what you feel you need to do."

"You must be Mrs Fallow," Ace said to Alys. "My name's Austin Spare. Friend of Stella's, from London."

"How nice to meet you." Alys extended a vague hand. Ver took Bee by the arm and guided her into the hall.

"She's still a bit on the hazy side."

"Serena thinks she might be faking it."

100

"Hmmm. It's possible. I'm not sure. Stella asked her some questions in the car and she didn't seem to know what Stella was talking about."

"Anyway, she's home. We can have a hopefully normal lunch and enjoy the baby."

"I remember normal," Ver said.

Alys ate lunch with them, making short work of a crab sandwich.

"Although I wasn't really in Shepton long enough to see what their food was like. Bee, do you mind if I disappear for a lie down? Must be getting old."

"Splendid idea, Mum."

"Sleep is the best doctor, my nan used to say," Ver remarked. "And how are you doing, Luna?"

Luna, bent over Rosie, stifled a yawn. "Actually…"

"I'll do dinner for seven o'clock," Bee said. "Until then, you might as well just crash out. I'm sure everyone can amuse themselves. You can have dinner in bed if you want."

"Why don't you take Mr Spare to see the church?" Alys said. "It's Arts and Crafts, you know."

"A lovely idea," Ace said. To Bee's secret amusement, he seemed to be projecting a somewhat professorial persona and his voice sounded plummier when he addressed Alys, although she had noticed that this was not the case when he spoke to Nick. "Most intriguing."

When Alys had gone upstairs, he said, "Christ, I actually *remember* Arts and Crafts."

"Not Ruskin et al?" Nick said.

"No, I'm not that old. But I met people like Voysey once or twice. It lasted until the twenties, remember. I wouldn't actually mind seeing the church."

"We've had a few encounters in it," Bee said. "Stella, why don't you go with Nick and Ace? Serena wants to go into Wells and get some stuff for the baby, now we know what it is."

"Not necessarily pink and girly," said Serena. "But there's a nice little shop which does baby clothes."

"All right. Nick, Ace, give me a couple of minutes to brush my hair and go to the loo and then we can head out."

Liz Williams

STELLA

She had, Stella reflected, met a wide variety of supernatural entities by now. Ghosts? *The new normal.* Demons? *Check.* Angels? *Same.* Star spirits? *Since I was a kid.* Rat girls with super-knowledge? *One of my besties.*

In fact, she *was* a supernatural entity. How many people can turn into an otter? Albeit not exactly of her own volition.

But she had already admitted to Ace that she was nervous about the possibility of meeting a Hound.

"Well, you might not," Ace said. "Let's hope he doesn't come back. Maybe Mr Morlader's adopted him now, from what Serena told me earlier."

"He needs a master. He told Bee and Luna there were two challengers, and Noualen was one of them and apparently the Morlader's the other."

"The Morlader's fucking terrifying. I don't like the idea of him showing up at the house."

"For what it's worth," Nick Wratchall-Haynes said, "He terrified me, the glimpse I got of him."

"That makes me feel a bit better. Because you must have met all sorts, Nick."

The hunt master looked grim. "You could certainly say that."

"He wasn't physically present," Ace said. "It was either a kind of projection, or he actually is a ghost. The guy's dead, by the way – I can tell you that much. And I should know. Anyway, old Vervain and myself put our heads together earlier on and we'll be upping the protections on your house, you'll be pleased to hear."

"Thanks! Is Serena all right? She seemed okay, if a bit quiet."

"Understandably," Nick said.

"So when did all this start for you?" Stella asked, stopping and turning to face Nick.

They were at the top of the field now, looking out over patterns of dense green, patches of woodland striping the land all the way to the hills. Across the valley, Amberley basked in the sunshine and the weathercock on Hornmoon church spire was still, untroubled by a breeze. The air felt languid and hot. Down in the field, the horses grazed on, seemingly unconcerned. Luna's van was all locked up. No smoke drifted from the field shelter.

"Oh, like you. When I was a kid. I've compared notes with Bee: she said you saw the Behenian stars from an early age. I grew up in a house full of ghosts. No one tried to hide it but I was never sure if my parents saw them or not, if they were just humouring me. My brother did, I know that, but if I try and allude to it now, he just looks blank. My younger sister remembers."

"Does she still see them?"

"I don't know. She's in hospital. In a mental institution. A private and very expensive one; a lot of my parents' inheritance went to fund it. She is sweet, she loses large tracts of time in a kind of fugue state, and she is very frightened of something."

"Christ, that's rough," Ace said. "Sorry to hear that."

"So am I," said Stella. She nearly added that she could understand ending up in the bin after exposure to all of this, but bit back her remark. Occasionally, she thought, she could be tactful.

"It's what it is. She's content enough, she says she feels safe. I have asked her if she wants to come and live here with me, she says not, it's too dangerous, but won't say why."

Stella felt a sudden pang for her own free-wheeling freedom. Best not take that too much for granted, then. She said, "Come on. Let's go and look at the church."

They walked down the lane, now white with elderflower and cow parsley and humming with bees.

"Ah, the English countryside," Ace remarked. "So peaceful, until it suddenly isn't."

Stella lifted the latch of the lych gate and they went through into the churchyard. Here, too, all was quiet. The verger had evidently not mowed for a week or so; daisies thronged the grass around the old gravestones.

"That bloke," Ace said, looking across the churchyard. "That wouldn't be your grandpa, by any chance?"

"What bloke?" But then Stella saw the blue spark that Abraham had become.

"Yes! How do you see him, Ace?"

"Elderly professor type?"

"I can see a little soul light," Nick informed her.

"Meet my grandfather!" Stella said. "Abraham Fallow."

"Hello, Starry," said her grandfather's voice. Introductions were made.

"Lots to tell you," Stella said, and did so, as concisely as possible. "I'm sure Luna would love to see you."

"We've spoken recently. I'm glad she's well and the baby, too. Tell her to bring Rosie to see me when she can."

"I will. What's the lie of the land, Granddad?"

"I see the Hunt is riding over Mooncote land these days. Bee explained why."

"Not recently, though."

"No, the Hunt is beset. It's harried and chased, and it faces a challenge in the west. Witch tribes from the coast, so rumour has it."

Nick frowned. "The Hunt doesn't really have much to do with the coast, as far as I'm aware. They keep inland, I thought. But someone does keep showing up. A ghost, of a man named the Morlader."

"I haven't heard that name," Abraham said. "But the moors of the west – Dartmoor, Bodmin, Exmoor – are the traditional lands of the Hunt and from what I hear, not that anyone tells me very much these days, there's a coastal clan who want the hunting rights on the moors, as well as the seas. Perhaps that's where this Morlader comes from."

"We're going to Cornwall in a few weeks," Stella said.

"Then you'd best be careful," her grandfather replied.

PART THREE
WATCH THE WALL,
MY DARLING

SERENA

Somerset and the events around Midsummer seemed ages ago, rather than only a week. The London residents had returned to the capital a couple of days after the play, leaving the household at Mooncote to settle down with its new addition and hopefully no further incursions or disruptions. Alys' memory had still not returned, and neither had the Hound, but Nick and Dark had introduced Ace to the Hornmoon Arms, with some success. Overall, Stella had remarked on the way back down the M3, she considered the visit to have been a good one, on the grounds that no one had actually either died or been abducted.

Now, they were in entirely different circumstances. Serena was watching her namesake, her hand to her mouth as Williams drove the ball across the Centre Court with ferocious concentration. This was Serena's birthday present from Ward: tickets for a day at Wimbledon, in the week before her natal day itself. Since Ward himself was unable to accompany her due to the play, Serena had given the second ticket to Stella.

"This is very kind of you. I'm not really very knowledgeable about tennis. Apart from fancying Roger Federer."

Serena told her that in her opinion this was compulsory. "However, you do know how to play because I remember you playing it at school. I also seem to remember you being quite good at it. Also, there will be strawberries and champagne, because Ward has given me a birthday budget."

"Excellent!"

A perfect day for it, too, Serena thought, as they set off. Since their return from Somerset, the weather had behaved itself: a classic English summer with only one thunderstorm.

"Also, it's Centre Court," Serena said. "So even if it does piss down, they can put the roof on." She was wearing a pale blue linen trouser suit, perhaps unwise if a strawberry got dropped down it, but Stella, in a sun dress, remarked that she looked elegant.

They took the crowded Tube to Wimbledon, emerging into a late sunlit morning. Serena, who had been several times before, knew the way and led her sister into the Long Bar.

"I'm not going to look at the prices," Stella told her. "I'm just going to sit here necking champers and repeating *Ward's budget, Ward's budget.*"

After a glass of champagne each and some lunch, they made their way to their seats and now the Ladies Singles was well underway, with Serena Williams battling a young Hungarian.

"Who's your pick?" Stella asked as the set was about to begin.

"Serena. Obviously."

Stella admitted that this made nominative sense.

"She's such a good player and also, she has such a sense of style. I love her clothes."

"It's amazing how varied they're able to make Wimbledon whites. I suppose it's like school uniform. You always made yours look stylish. I was always a scruff."

"Bee was very neat. Luna not so much."

"Luna and I were like Just William. Slow worms in our blazer pockets, twigs in our hair. Oh, they're starting, better shut up."

For the next hour, Serena's world consisted of cries of *love, fifteen!* and *out!* But Williams was doing well and after a tense final set, she won the match. Serena and Stella stood up and clapped.

"God, that was really exciting," Stella said.

"Don't sound so surprised! They're world class players."

Everyone was on their feet. Across the court, glimpsed for the first time, Serena saw someone she recognised. She clutched her sister's arm.

"Stella! That looks like Miranda!"

"Christ, you're right. Can't be, though. She's dead. I hope she's still dead!"

After Ward's ex-girlfriend's sticky end, "*Actress found dead in flat,*" the headlines had screamed, and a police investigation had followed. They had not got as far as interviewing Ward, however, despite Serena's fears, for a verdict of natural causes had been duly delivered and life had moved on, though not for Miranda. At least, not in her corporeal form. Stella and Davy Dearly both thought that Miranda's spirit might have been pressed into service in the great beyond.

"Anyway," Stella had said at the time, "it would have been outrageous if they'd suspected Ward of murdering her since he didn't have anything to do with her death."

"The police don't know that, though. And we can't tell them what really happened."

And now here was Miranda, large as life, standing on the other side of Centre Court. She was not, however, staring back at Serena and Stella, but chatting to an older man at her side.

"Are you sure it's her? It's not just someone who looks a bit like her, like a fan, maybe, who's gone for the same hair and make-up?"

Serena thought that this was a possibility. "I think she's shorter than Miranda, actually."

"Oh, they want us out. See if we can follow her."

Once outside in the throng, Serena thought that their chances of finding the Miranda-a-like were poor, but then she caught sight of the dark chignon and grey and white linen dress. The woman was with her companion. Chatting and laughing, she did not seem to be doing anything to avoid pursuit. Stella and Serena elbowed through the crowd in her wake.

At the exit, they became funnelled with the rest of the crowd.

"Damn," Serena said, when they were ejected from the Grounds. "No sign of her."

They looked up and down the road, but the woman had disappeared.

"All right," said Serena in defeat. "What do you want to do now?"

"Find a bar?"

"Champagne's worn off?"

"That was ages ago. But I was actually thinking of coffee. Unless we're still on Ward's budget, otherwise it will be a pornstar Martini for sure."

Serena laughed. "I think Ward's budget will stretch a bit further. There's a bar over there."

An awning half-hid the long plate glass windows. Potted palms stood beside the door.

"Looks classy," Stella said.

"Ward's budget style classy. Let's do it."

Someone was coming out as they entered. Stella and Serena stood aside to let them pass. But it was the woman in the grey and white dress.

"Hello," she said to Serena. Close to, it was evident that this was not Miranda, but the resemblance was still remarkable and she spoke to Serena as if she knew her. "Just as a heads up – *remember to watch the wall.*"

"The wall?" Serena repeated.

"Friend or foe?" asked Stella.

The woman gave a charming smile. "We'll just have to see how things go, won't we?"

"Who are you?" demanded Serena, but the woman was no longer there.

In the bar, Serena sent a text to Hob. "God knows when he'll pick it up," she said.

"Or in what century."

But to her surprise, ten minutes later, her phone pinged.

Whr r u now? the text read. Serena texted back.

"He's on his way," she said to Stella. "Says he'll be here shortly."

"Really? That was quick. I hope he's not stalking us."

"Perhaps he's doing a stint as a ball boy," Serena said.

Stella snorted. "You need focus and dedication for that, I thought. Mind you, he is quick and sneaky."

Shortly after this, the door opened and Hob was there, in a smart black shirt and jeans. But his sharp face seemed paler and more pointed to Serena and there were shadows beneath his grey eyes. His pallor made his hair look an even more fiery shade of red.

"Hi, Hob! How are you?"

"I haven't been too good, actually," Hob said. He sat down.

"Coffee? Something stronger? We're on the wine. We just came out of the tennis and we're debating the wisdom of having cocktails."

"A black coffee would be great."

"So what's up with you?" Stella said.

"I don't know. I ought to go to the doc but I'm nervous of medics. Always have been. Get white coat blood pressure and that sort of thing."

"Look, just go, if you're not right."

"I know. But then I think I'm just tired. I've been doing work for Bill, picture framing and that."

"Bill's still *working?*"

"Not really, although you'd be surprised – he does get the occasional customer. He thinks I ought to have a trade and, to be honest, picture framing hasn't changed all that much in two hundred years."

"I suppose not," Serena said. "It's still all wood and glue and glass, isn't it?"

"I quite like doing stuff with my hands."

"You were very quick to show up today." Stella was evidently reluctant to let him off the hook. "Hanging out in SW19? On Henman Hill?"

"No. I'm not a big fan of sports. Bill sent me over here on an errand. Before Wimbledon started – I don't mean the time it started today, either. When I came back, I saw your text." He forced a smile. "No such thing as coincidence."

"Apparently not." Serena told him about Miranda-who-wasn't. When she had come to the end of her story, Hob looked even paler.

"Shit. I don't like that."

"I texted you because Ward's busy and you probably knew her better than he did, anyway. Did she have any family that you know of?"

"She didn't mention it if she did. She told me that her parents were dead, killed in a car crash."

"Convenient," said Stella.

"I believed her at the time. I didn't see why she'd lie. And she said she was an only child."

"She told Ward the same thing," Serena said. "I thought it might be pretty awful for her parents to hear about their daughter's death, splashed all over the tabloids like that, but Ward said she'd told him she was an orphan. She made a big deal of it, he said."

"Yeah, she did."

"A single tear in the eye?" Stella said. "Pass the sick bag!"

"It was a bit like that," Hob admitted. "Because she wasn't really the sentimental sort, you see. But I felt sorry for her, coming from a bit of a fractured background myself. She said it was something we had in common. Went on about 'choosing your family'." He looked momentarily wistful.

Stella made vomiting noises.

"The one thing she did say – she was asked to do an episode of *Poldark* once, and that was really big at the time but she turned it down, and when I asked her why, she said it would mean filming in Cornwall and she hated Cornwall. I said, who hates Cornwall, it looks so lovely, I've never been and I've always wanted to go, and she said, like darkly, it was because of some of her relations. I did ask her about that since she'd never mentioned any other family before but she said she didn't want to talk about it and it was all in the past. I thought maybe they

111

were all toothless peasants or something and she was ashamed of them."

"The woman we just met had all her teeth," Stella informed him.

"And you said she looked a lot like Miranda?"

"Yes. I thought she *was* Miranda at first. Scared the hell out of me. And like I said, she seemed to know who we were. But when we met Miss Pa – this woman, a while back, she told us Miranda had family in Cornwall."

"I saw Ace a few days ago – he dropped by – and he said you're going to Cornwall soon."

"Yes, next couple of weeks. Family holiday."

"Better be careful," Hob said, echoing Abraham.

STELLA

On the road. Eventually.

It had been a chaotic morning. They had already had to revise their plans on the previous night, when Bella had returned home from a schoolfriend's house with the news that she had been invited to France.

"Only for a week. Sara is going and she's asked Lou Robbie as well. They didn't know I was going to Cornwall. But, they've got this old house in Brittany and it's near the beach, and…"

"And it will be exactly like Cornwall, if it's Brittany, only without your mother."

"I didn't say that!"

"Bet you were thinking it, though. We can probably wave to each other across the Channel. No worries, Bells, I was the same at your age and they are your besties, so yes, you can go. When is this for?"

"Monday."

"Stella and I are heading out tomorrow, as you know, so you'll have to stay with your dad. Have you asked him? Because he might have plans."

Bella was dispatched to phone her father while Serena, just in case, rang Sara's mother and checked that Bella had actually been invited and wasn't plotting some devious teenage scam.

"I don't want to seem untrusting," she said, putting the phone down. "But you never know."

"I was tricky as fuck at fourteen."

"So was I. And we were good kids. Imagine if we hadn't been."

"I could have been running a narcotics empire by now," Stella said.

Thus Bella had departed that morning to her father's house across London, Serena having been up half the night packing suitable clothes for France. When Bella had finally gone, Serena snatched some breakfast and broke a tooth.

"How in the name of God can you break a tooth on toast, Serena?"

"I don't know!' her sister wailed.

She managed to secure an emergency dental appointment while Stella, who had stayed at Serena's house that night, worked off her frustration by cleaning the kitchen. This did not come naturally, but it was not fair to leave a mess for Ward, now firmly embedded in the

London run of his play. Then she loaded the car, so that they would at least be ready for the off. At last Serena, somewhat lopsided and numb, returned, forced down a sandwich as it was now too late to stop for lunch on the way, and there followed a long crawl down the Great Western Road, since a bus up ahead had broken down.

"I can't wait to get out of this city," Serena said, indistinctly.

"Too right. Never mind, Serena. It's quite hot now, imagine what it will be like in Cornwall." Stella, who was driving, had been admiring the magnificent hanging baskets adorning the outsides of pubs and cafés.

"It'll be dark by the time we get there."

"No, it won't. It's twelve now, it's about a seven hour drive unless we get stuck – Google says five and a half but it's lying – so even if we got in at nine, it would still be light at this time of year. We're only just past the Solstice."

"That's true. I shouldn't be so pessimistic." They edged past the sick bus and speeded up fractionally. Then out through the sprawl, with one of Stella's summer mix tapes playing on the car stereo, through pretty Richmond, picking up the M3 and then the familiar road past Stonehenge, tiny as a toy in the vastness of the plain. The downs were bleached by the heat; the road shimmered before them. Once in Somerset, they waved to the road which led to Mooncote and sped on, heading for Exeter and the south west. Only at this point did Stella really feel she was on holiday. All the windows of the car were fully down, since Serena's air conditioning had stopped working.

"Pity this isn't a convertible," Stella said.

"Yes. Although it's a disaster for hair."

"I wouldn't care."

"Did you bring your wetsuit?"

"No. It's back at Mooncote. I didn't have room on the barge so I left it at home. I'll hire one. And a surfboard. I want to get some surfing in if possible. Come with me."

"I'll paddle," said Serena. "Surfing makes me nervous. Although I suppose the pressure's off with you, now."

"Otters, at least English ones, are more freshwater animals," Stella said, "though not all of them. Plenty of sea living otters up in Scotland and around the Welsh coast. So you have a point."

She could see the familiar wall of Dartmoor rising up ahead; it was now past five and the afternoon had a sultry, late-in-the-day feel. They skirted the moor, taking the fast dual carriageway further into Devon.

"Let me know if you want a wee," Serena said.

"Cheers, I'm fine. Are we nearly there yet?"

Serena consulted her phone. "About two hours. Yes, let's stop, but not just yet." Dartmoor was left behind and they crossed the river Tamar, cheering because that meant Cornwall at last, then headed up over Bodmin, suddenly quiet and still, with splashes of golden gorse across the reedy expanse of the moor.

Stella, after some debate, pulled off the main road at Jamaica Inn.

"I know it's cheesy. But we can afford a break." She stretched.

"Cheesy is fine. Do you want me to drive for a bit?"

"Only if you don't mind."

"I don't mind. We can swap again a bit later if you like."

They ordered a cream tea, since the sandwiches were now some way in the past, and ate it as far away from the tourist throng as possible, in a corner of the half-timbered dining room shared with a cardboard cartoon pirate. Jamaica Inn had been flying the Jolly Roger. Stella thought of the Morlader with a shudder.

"How's your mouth, Serena?"

"All right now. Bit sore. A scone will cure it."

"This is an excellent tea. However, I forgot that the entire population of Britain would also be on holiday now," said Stella. "With their screaming kids."

"I hope Bella has a nice time in France. I'm sure she will. She loves Lou and Sara."

"She'll have an epic time. Oh dear." A woman with a face like thunder was marching through the dining room, bearing a howling toddler. Serena and Stella finished their scones and beat a retreat to the car. As Serena pulled out of the car park, Stella found she had a text from Bee.

"Oh! They've already arrived. Mind you, they didn't have nearly so far to go. Bee says it's a lovely house. Wants to know if she's to book a table in the local pub for dinner."

"Yes, tell her. The cream tea might have worn off by then."

"It was only a scone," Stella said, texting away.

"Awesome. I wonder if it's another piratical pub?"

"It will be by definition if Dark's there. Although I could do without the Morlader."

"So could I. Dark can tell us about Cornwall in days of yore. Assuming he ever went there."

"I think he said he did."

The sun was sinking a little by the time they neared Penzance, cheering again at the first glimpse of the sea. The bay was golden in the falling light, with the little silhouette of St Michael's Mount a fairy castle in the gleam. The village of Mousehole was negotiated via a series of twisty instructions from the sat nav, and then they were heading on, up and then down a steep hill into the village of Tretorvic.

"Christ, this road is winding!" Stella said, teeth clenched, gripping the steering wheel.

"I know. And narrow."

They could have reached out and touched the white walls on either side.

"Pretty, though. Look at those geraniums!"

"Where am I going?" Stella said aloud and, as if answering, the sat nav said in its calm, annoying voice, "Turn right, at Looe Terrace. Turn left, onto Tregurnow Road."

"Penhallow is that big house up there on the headland," Serena said. "That yellow one. I recognise it from Google Earth."

"How do you get *into* it, though? Oh, here we are." Stella turned the car left between two columns crowned with stone pineapples into an overgrown drive and shortly they came out into a parking area, overlooking the wide sweep of the bay. Bee's Land Rover stood over to the right. They sat still for a moment, listening to the engine ticking down and looking up at the house: yellow as butter in the sunlight with a cupola perched on top. A golden galleon flew above it; bay windows along the front of the house looked out over the bay. It reminded Stella of a ship. Then Bee was running out towards the car.

"Hi! You made it! Where's Bella? Did you leave her on the motorway?"

"Yes. Had enough of motherhood. Actually, she's going to France on Monday instead. Short story. Stood me up, but she'll be here for the second week, Ward will bring her down. I forgot to tell you because we had a manic morning – I was up late last night packing for her because she decided she wanted different clothes for Brittany, even though it is almost *the same place,* and then I cracked a tooth and had to go to the dentist."

"Oh no!"

"She was lucky she got an appointment," Stella said.

"Is it all right now?"

"Yes, they filled it for me. It doesn't hurt. We had a cream tea."

"At Jamaica Inn," Stella said. 'We debated running away and becoming smugglers."

"Good idea, since we are in fact going to a pub called the Smugglers' Rest for dinner. I hope you're sort of hungry, though, because I booked a table for eight fifteen. And a taxi."

"Brilliant." Stella did not feel like wrestling with the narrow streets of Tretorvic in the dusk, before she had properly got her bearings, and neither did she feel like abstaining from alcohol. "Just enough time to have a shower."

Inside the house was a maze of smaller rooms, down steps and up steps, and one large dining area in a conservatory, looking south to the sea. Penhallow smelled old fashioned, of beeswax and salt air and lavender and roses, for a huge bowl of those, also yellow, stood on an old oak table. Stella, following Bee's instructions, made her way up a quiet staircase and along a landing with a polished floor, to a small door at the end which looked old, as though it had been carved from driftwood. Enchanted, she found a little low bedroom within, one white wall glowing with the sun. She unpacked her bags hastily, located the bathroom, jumped in a stuttering shower and pulled on fresh jeans and a striped sweatshirt which had, to her eye, a vaguely nautical appearance. Then she went back downstairs to find Serena looking remarkably elegant for someone who had just driven down from London, sitting with Bee, Dark, and Luna. Rosie lay in a basket at Luna's feet, fast asleep.

"Yay, a baby," said Stella. She kissed her sister. "How are you?"

"Good! How are you?"

"Also fine. Where's Sam?"

"Outside moving the Land Rover so the taxi has room to turn round. Ver's still upstairs doing her hair, she says."

"Taxi is on her way, according to my phone," Bee said.

"This is an amazing house. My bedroom door looks like someone purloined it from a shipwreck."

"They did," said Luna. "The Air B&B woman was telling us when we arrived. She said her friend's great grandfather was a sea captain but the doors and some of the panelling in the house are from wrecks."

"And there are a lot of those around these waters," said Dark.

"Shipwrecks?"

"Also wreckers."

"Not these days, surely?"

"Annette hinted that there might be," Bee said.

"She said it *darkly,*" Luna added.

At this point there was the sound of an engine and a people carrier with a taxi sign upon it pulled up with a cheerful woman at the wheel. They climbed inside, headed back into Tretorvic and were dropped at the harbour.

"Well," Bee said. "This really is stereotypically Cornish, isn't it?" The tide was out, leaving a smell of mud and weed behind it, and stranding a fleet of small fishing boats.

"I'm amazed there are any of those left after recent political events," Ver said to Stella.

"Yeah, tell me about it. I don't think we should mention Brexit in public."

"Very wise, dear."

"Annette did make a crack about people coming down here from London," Bee said, "And then hastily corrected herself when she remembered that you were some of those people. Said she meant second home owners."

"Well, it is a problem here, apparently."

The pub was not difficult to locate: a long, whitewashed building overlooking the harbour. Ace would approve, Stella thought. On a hanging sign, shady-looking men wrestled with a barrel. The pub looked settled into its position, the windows and doorway bright with flowers. Inside, it was shadowy and low-ceilinged, humming with conversation. The menu was extensive and seafood oriented; they chatted about ordinary things and watched the light die out to sea. When they got back to Penhallow it was fully dark, with only a scatter of lights to betray the opposite shore and the Mount. Stella undressed in her little room and opened the window to the cool, damp air, thinking of wreckers and, with some dread, of the Morlader. She hoped he would not find them there, and why was he interested in the

Fallows, anyway? Stella could not help thinking that it was all her fault, worrying that by going adventuring and poking about in that turret by the sea, she had left some kind of trail which he had followed. Yet he had pursued Luna and Serena, too. But what did he want? Stella came away from the window and got into bed.

When she closed her eyes, she saw the road, unscrolling before her. But no storm or squall disturbed her in the night and she woke to the screams of seagulls and the sun rising.

BEE

When Bee woke She knew, without listening or moving, that Dark was not there. This did not alarm her. She lay disoriented for a moment, before remembering that she was not in her own bed at Mooncote, but all the way down at the end of the country, in Cornwall. Through the open window she could hear the hush and crash of the sea, its rhythmic pulse against the foot of the headland, and she remembered the first sight of it as they came over the brow of the hill and onto the coast road. Serena had said the same.

"I am basically just a big kid."

"Well, it's that moment of excitement, isn't it? Like Proust's biscuits, or whatever they were. It was so special when we were kids that the feeling's imprinted on us."

Now, in the warm darkness, Bee felt another pulse of anticipation. On holiday. She was suddenly wide awake, too excited to sleep. She looked at the clock: it was 3 a.m., not long before dawn. Bee got up and went to the window, gripping the sill and leaning out into the blowy night. A breeze was coming off the water and although Tretorvic had its share of streetlights, her bedroom faced away from the little town and the stars hung, low and huge, over the western sea.

Bee found her flip flops and went downstairs in her nightie, as quietly as possible. The back door of the kitchen was unlocked and she let herself out, finding herself in the herb-scented garden. She brushed past rosemary and mint and peppery thyme, over the dew-damp grass to where a low wall delineated the end of the property. Then she took a breath. From here, she had a better view of those western stars: something very bright, probably Jupiter, hung amid a spangle of constellations. The moon must have already set; it had been hanging above the harbour when they had left the pub, a crescent on its back, holding the water in. The forecast had been for a heatwave and although Bee did not cope very well with heat, she thought it would be good to have some: proper summer holiday weather. She had brought a shady hat just in case. It was certainly warm now, in spite of the breeze. She watched the slow turn of the stars for a while, sitting on the low wall and enjoying the silence. There was a winking light on the horizon, star-like itself; a lighthouse or light ship, somewhere out to sea. As Bee watched, it flashed fiery and blinked out. A timer, perhaps, and it would cease when dawn was approaching? She did not know how these things worked, only that no lighthouse these days was permanently manned.

Then she realised that she could hear something. Voices? She stood, looking back towards the harbour. A ship was sailing out in the bay, a long craft with tall masts and a hazy globe at the stern. Her sails were furled; she was powered along by oars and it was the creak of these, and of the rigging, that Bee had heard.

She looked back towards Tretorvic and it was darker than it had been before. Bee took a breath, inhaling a rush of salt air. The wind had risen and when she glanced at the western sky only one star was visible, the clouds racing past it, thunderheads building until the star was abruptly blotted out.

"There's a storm coming," Dark said at her shoulder.

"When are we, Ned?"

"I'm not sure, but that's an old boat."

Bee nodded. She could hear the rising roar of the waves now, and spray spattered the headland, spume flung up by the wind. But the air around her was the same placid summer warmth.

"Look," Dark said. The garden had disappeared; Bee did not care to look back to see if Penhallow House, too, was gone. They stood amongst gorse bushes, at the top of a slope that led down to the edge of the cliff. A figure was running down the slope, sure footed as a goat, and then a light flared briefly up. The person was wearing skirts.

"She's lit a lamp," Dark said. Bee could see the gleam, swinging gently to and fro.

"Oh, my God. They're wreckers, aren't they?"

"Yes."

"Can't we stop them?"

"Bee, I think it's too late. It's already happened."

The boat was turning. It was difficult to see; though Bee could feel nothing on her skin except the summer night, the coast was now lashed with rain.

"No, don't!" she heard herself cry but the words were swallowed by the storm. Down at the edge, she could see the woman running along the cliff, bearing the false star of her lamp. Dark and Bee watched as the boat plunged out of sight, beneath the cliff, and tears came to her eyes as she heard the splintering wood, the cries of the men.

"It's a wicked thing," said Dark.

"It's a horrible thing to do."

"We are not really here, Bee." He took her hand. "Only witnessing through a window."

As he spoke, Bee found that she was, indeed, standing in front of her own bedroom window. The lights of Tretorvic marched up the coast road, reassuringly bright. The air was still warm and there was salt on the light breeze, a seaweedy smell. To the east, the sky was glowing lighter.

"Back again," Dark said. He put an arm around her shoulders, pulled her close.

Bee nodded. "Back again." And wondering why they had been granted such a vision.

STELLA

It was seven o'clock in the morning and the sea was calling. Stella rummaged in her bags, located one of several swimming costumes, threw on shorts and a t-shirt over one of them, and purloined a towel from the bathroom. Downstairs, she found Bee, preparing breakfast.

"What a lovely day! I'll have something later. Going to the beach. Sand between the toes and all that."

Bee gave her an elder sister look.

"No sand between *your* toes, young lady. Wear some shoes. Annette said three people this week have been carted off to casualty already. Weever fish. Remember Penmorth?"

"Oh God, I'd forgotten about that." But Bee was right. Years ago, not far from here, Luna had trodden on one of the little spined fish and it had, indeed, necessitated a trip to A&E. Luna's infant howls now echoed in memory's ears. "Beach shoes it is, then."

She found a pair in the boot cupboard and set out. Bee, debriefed by Annette, had given them an idea of the lie of the land on the previous evening, and Stella now headed out of the garden and towards the cliffs. Here, a path led between high valerian-fringed walls, the dark pink flowers nodding over the stones, and soon the garden was behind and Stella was out onto the shallow apron of land that was the cliff proper. The path was fringed with daisies and, a little further on, thrift. A narrow sand strewn track led down between the rocks in an erratic series of man-made steps. A smugglers' path, perhaps. Below, she could see the beach, a crescent of pale sand reaching around the headland. A Robinson Crusoe-like ribbon of footsteps danced across it and shortly, their maker came into view: the foreshortened figure of an elderly woman walking a little dog. Someone else had evidently decided to make the most of the morning. Stella approved. But then the path took her out of sight of the dog walker and she had the beach entirely to herself, save for a scatter of oystercatchers, running along the lacy edge of the water. Their faint squeaks drifted across the morning air.

Mindful of the weever fish, Stella took her beach shoes off for a moment, just to feel the sand beneath her bare feet. It was cool and slightly damp, but the day was warming fast. Then she stripped off to her bikini, slipped the beach shoes back on for a minute and ran down to the water and straight into the waves. The tide was coming in – she had looked at the tables last night. Evie's *How The Thames Behaves* lessons were standing her in good stead but Stella could feel the tide in her blood, the shift and swing of it. Her otter-self might prefer freshwater, but wild water was wild water. It was cold and Stella in her human skin felt the breath knocked out of her; she gasped and spluttered. There was a long shelf of sand and she was a long way out before she turned in the water and realised that she could not feel anything beneath her feet. She trod for a moment, then dived.

It was not very deep. The sea was clear, sunlight filtering down through the green water, and Stella could see glossy brown weed rolling along on the bottom. There was only a little pressure in her lungs and she surfaced, then struck out towards the rocky headland. Not too far: the waves churned and shattered against the granite jags and Stella did not fancy becoming a wreck herself. She had no way of knowing whether her otter nature would come to her rescue and it was stupid to take chances. But at this point, even if she got into trouble, the tide would carry her back to shore. She could feel no rips or eddies. A conversation with a young man at the bar last night had told her that the beach was safe enough, "but if you surf and you want smooth waves, you'll have to go further up the coast." There would be time for that. Now, she was enjoying the bay.

Nor was she the only one. Stella had company.

She sensed them before she saw them. She went under, saw their fat spotted forms streamlining along beside her, but much faster than she could swim. They doubled back. Stella broke the surface, treading water, and three heads joined her. Round dark eyes gazed at her, mild as cows.

"Oh!" said Stella. "Hello!"

The seals went under again with a flick of their tails. They swam together for a hundred yards or so, but Stella felt she was getting too close to the rocks. She could feel the pull of the surf. So she waved to the seals and swam back to safer water. The seal trio were hauling themselves laboriously onto a flat shelf of rock between the snags, perhaps their morning resting place. The water flashed in the sun and for a second Stella saw three women on the rock, not the slim tangled-haired selkies of legend, but big women, well covered, with short mops of grey-brown hair. Then they were gone and the seals lay on the shelf like beached torpedoes. A flipper languidly waved. Stella turned and let the tide bring her in.

The beach was still empty. Her beach shoes lay where she had left them, but the tide had come in further and they were perilously close to being carried out to sea. As a child, Stella had lost a shoe in this manner, and been told off. She retrieved her footwear, towelled herself hastily, did not bother to comb her hair, then took the cliff path back to Penhallow and breakfast.

She found her relations assembled in the conservatory.

"Help yourself to a croissant," Bee said. "Or several."

"Several, please. I'm ravenous."

"You've been swimming," Serena said. "Just call me Sherlock."

"I have. It was fab. I saw some seals. Actually, they swam with me."

"Wow, amazing!"

"I once read that a seal has a bite like a Rottweiler," Bee said.

Stella admitted that this was probably true. "They've got big powerful jaws. And you need sharp teeth if you're living off fish."

"Were there many people down on the shore?"

"No, it was very quiet, but I don't think it's going to be quiet for long. Height of the tourist season and all that."

"Yes," Bee said. "I and all the other emmets will be heading into Tretorvic this morning to go to the Co-op. Or the Waitrose, if they've got one."

"I doubt they'll have a Waitrose," Serena said.

"You're probably right. Well, whatever the Co-op can come up with, then. I brought breakfast down with us but not lunch. We can stock up on basics and mix and match that with the pub. Also Serena, you said you wanted to go to Rick Stein's?"

"I'd like to, yes, but I'll wait till Ward gets here. And do St Ives. Art and that. Lazy first week. Although Ward's put me in touch with a friend of his down here. He's got a boat, apparently. He sent me a text – I'm meeting him this afternoon."

"Great!"

"Do you want a hand with the shopping?" Stella asked, feeling obscurely guilty that she had gone for a swim while Bee laboured over breakfast, although there was no reason why Bee should not have gone for a swim of her own, and croissants were not difficult.

"Yes please! If anyone's forgotten their toothpaste, now is the time to tell me. I shall make a list."

They took Serena's little car, thinking it might be easier to park than the Land Rover, but there was still room in the main car park. A snicket led to the main street, occupied by two pubs, a hotel, an array of gift shops and the Co-op. It was, as predicted, already busy. Stella and Bee made their way through a horde of fellow tourists as the church bells rang ten o'clock. Stella and Bee shopped as quickly as possible, seizing milk, bread, butter and other necessaries.

"We've got wine," Bee shouted over the hubbub. "We brought it down in the car."

"So did we!"

"Nick gave us a case, as well."

"That was nice of him."

"What sort of cheese do you want?"

By the time they reached the counter, the shop had suddenly emptied, in one of those ebbs and flows of a crowd. The woman behind the counter was serving a single remaining customer: a tall man in shorts and boat shoes who had placed several bottles of water on the counter.

"Packet of Benson and Hedges, please." He pointed. "And these. Oh, and some winds, as well, if you've got them."

Was that a brand of cigarette? Stella wondered. Bee, who did not smoke, frowned. But the woman behind the counter said, "Yes, we've got a few. How many do you want?"

"Oh, I don't know. Three? Usual price?"

"Yes, he'll be in the Smugglers this evening, if you want to settle up then."

Bee and Stella were now openly curious. They watched as the woman took a piece of string from behind the counter, breathed gently out, and tied three firm knots into the string.

"There you go. That'll be twelve pounds and thirty pence for the rest, please."

"Do you take contactless?"

"Yes." The man held out his card and in a piece of financial magic, there was a faint beep.

"All gone through."

"Thanks," the tall man said. Bundling his bottled water into a bag, he thrust the cigarettes and the knotted string into his pocket, nodded politely to Stella and Bee, and ambled out.

Stella thought that this very definitely came into the category of 'stuff tourists probably shouldn't be noticing.' She hoped Bee felt the same, but as they approached the counter the woman said, "Don't often get asked for those nowadays, but there's a few as'll still do it."

"He wanted – winds?"

"Yes. I spoke to him yesterday; they came in the night before. From France. They're going over to Wexford later tonight."

"So how does the string work?" asked Stella. Bee nudged her, but she ignored it.

"You just undo one of the knots if the wind drops and you want more wind in your sails."

"But he didn't pay for it?"

"No, no, it's not a money thing, not directly. He'll buy my other half a pint or three at lunchtime. I should have told him to put them behind the bar but Tom's sensible enough. Mostly. Now, what can I do for you?"

Bee put the basket on the counter but Stella said, "Could I buy a wind?"

"Are you sailing, too?"

"Well, we don't have our own boat. We're staying up at Penhallow."

"Oh, the yellow house. Lovely place, that."

"But we're meeting some people this week and my sister's friend says he'll take us out in a boat. So a wind might come in handy," Stella said.

"No worries. I'll knot you one up. It'll cost you the price of a pint, same as the other gentleman. You can put one behind the bar in the Smuggler's if Tom's not there. Do you want a nice strong one? A westerly, maybe?"

"Sounds good!"

And after a moment, Stella was given her string, too.

"Buying a wind?" a voice said.

Stella turned. She saw a compact figure in a patterned white and grey sundress, with dark chignonned hair. It was the woman from Wimbledon. She smiled when she saw Stella.

"Oh, it's you," she said, without surprise.

"Someone you know, Stella?" Bee asked, intrigued.

"We met in Wimbledon, when the tennis was on."

"How's your sister?"

"Fine, thank you."

"Is she here with you?"

"Yes, she is," Stella said, conscious that she neither wanted to lie – too complicated – or give too much information to this Miranda-a-like.

Bee, whom Stella was reminded had not met Miranda, took charge. "Hello. I'm Bee Fallow. We're all staying up at Penhallow House for a couple of weeks. Are you local?"

"Yes. My name's Jane Thorn."

Stella felt cogs click into place. A cottage filled with shells and a kind elderly woman, saying, *"She claimed kinship with a family known to me, as if presenting her credentials, down near Penzance. Name of Thorn. But that would be in your day and age and when I spoke to them in mine, they had indeed heard of her, but did not care to press the acquaintance."*

Stella felt inside her bag. Deep within an inner pocket, was a spotted curl of a shell with a scrap of paper inside it. Those dear cousins would have lived two hundred years before. And yet...

"Would you like to grab a coffee?" she asked, handing over the shell.

Jane would.

LUNA

Sam had gone fishing. He also knew a bloke down here, he had said, with a boat. They had invited him out. Did Luna mind?

Luna did not mind. She was content to sit in the garden that afternoon, with Rosie in a basket at her feet and watching the bees bustle in the long beds of lavender. Ver had come to join her.

"Sometimes," Ver said, "it's nice just to have a sit down. I must be getting old."

"If you're getting old, Ver, then so am I."

"You've just had a baby. It's a lot of work."

"Six weeks ago, though, Ver. Women used to be back in the fields the next day."

"And died a lot younger than you're likely to. Anyway, you were up and about the next day. And you don't have fields. Well, you do. But not those sorts of fields. I always think, though, with a baby, it's good to be able to spend the time, especially with your first."

"I thought, I don't think I can go through that again. But I might change my mind. Now, it doesn't seem so bad. In hindsight."

"It's all those hormones," Ver said. "Lying to you."

"I haven't felt depressed or anything. I think I've got off lightly."

"Also, she's a very good baby."

For Rosie usually slept through the night, fed when hungry, did not scream much. Luna felt that she was, indeed, lucky ('wait till she starts teething,' Ver had said).

"And compared to what *you* were like, she's an angel," had been Alys' comment on the matter.

From here, beneath a lawn umbrella set into a round wooden table, Luna could hear the gush of the surf, the cries of gulls, and then, suddenly, Greensleeves, played at full jangling volume.

"That's an ice cream van," Ver said. "Would you like one, Luna? I shall run out and flag him down."

Well, why not? Luna thought. It was a baking hot day, they were at the seaside and on holiday. "Love one!" she said.

"I'll just find my bag." Ver disappeared.

Luna sat in the bee humming shade and waited for her to return. She looked down the terrace, across the lawn to a lilac hedge. The lilac flowers were long gone, the bushes retreating into their dark summer foliage. Beyond, the bay shimmered away to the distant horizon. She could hear voices: Bee talking to someone inside the house, then quiet.

But Luna and her baby were no longer alone. Someone was walking along the lilac hedge, strolling beneath a parasol, although no one had been there a minute before. The hedge was faintly visible through her long creamy skirts. Luna found herself on her feet, nearly banging her head on the umbrella. The woman turned. She was young, with hair upswept into a neat pile of dark curls. Her face lit up when she saw Luna and she waved with enthusiasm. Luna turned to see who was behind her, but there was no one there. And Penhallow, too, looked different: heavy brocade curtains now hung at the windows and there was the clatter of pans from inside.

She looked back. The woman was standing in front of her, although it was some distance from the lilac hedge to the table, and Luna had glanced away only for a moment.

"What a beautiful baby!" the woman said, and laughed.

Luna smiled, a little uncertainly. She had the sudden urge to snatch Rosie up. But, apart from the fact that the woman was evidently a ghost, though she looked entirely solid, presumably because they were back in her own day and age – there was nothing sinister about her, from her black curls to her rosebud sprigged gown and her fawn kid slippers. She wore a wedding ring.

"It is all right," the woman said, as if she had seen Luna's thoughts in her face. "I won't do you any harm. You are here for only a little time and we must make the most of it."

"What's your name?" Luna asked.

"I am Lucy. Born Lucy Thorn, if you know my people, although my married name is Hallow."

"My name is Luna Fallow," Luna said.

"Fallow and Hallow! We might be a firm of ironmongers." This time, Luna could not help smiling.

"Are your family witches too, Luna?"

"Not exactly."

"People tell me I don't look like a witch," Lucy Hallow said. "As if I were to wear a pointy hat and not darling M. Mesurier's finest concoctions. All my clothes come from Paris – Charles, my husband, is very generous."

She was very pretty, Luna thought, which possibly accounted for the generosity.

"And who of my relations do you know, Luna?"

"Well," Luna said. "I haven't met any of them, actually, although my sisters have met some people who know your family, I think. The Miss Parminters?"

"Ah, our dear friends! Of course. And darling Jane is in your day and age."

"I don't know Jane. So you are – a ghost?"

"Yes, I expect so. I shouldn't think I'll live to a hundred and forty although you never know. But we dot to and fro, not quite as we please, but as the task demands of us."

"What task is that?" Luna asked.

"We are coastguards." She looked very serious at this.

Luna could not stop herself saying, "You're not dressed for it!"

Lucy gave a peal of laughter. "Where's my sou-wester, you mean? But actually, you know, in my sprigged muslin I am *absolutely* dressed for it. You'll see. Oh, your companion is returning. I should go."

"No, she'll totally get it," Luna said, but there was now no one between herself and the lilac hedge.

"I got some 99s," Ver informed her. "I thought we could do with some chocolate. Here we are. Are you all right, dear? You look a bit pale."

"I've just had a visitor," Luna said, and brought her up to date.

BEE

The coffee shop was small and not branded, what Bee thought of as a tea room rather than a café. The walls were thick and white-plastered, making it a cooler, dimmer place within; salmon pink geraniums stood in tubs at the door. Stella ordered coffees for everyone. Bee felt she needed it, after an early start and a slight surprise.

Jane Thorn was evidently well known to the proprietress, who greeted her casually, suggesting that she was a regular visitor. Taking this cue, Bee said,

"So do you live here in Tretorvic?"

"Yes. We live on the other side of the harbour. You can see it from Penhallow – it's called Thornhold. The big pink house up the cliff."

"'We' being?" Stella asked.

"Myself, my aunts, my sisters, my cousins…"

"It *must* be a big house!"

Jane smiled. "We're not all there at the same time. And we have family connections with Penhallow, too. My great grandmother married a man who inherited it – he wasn't my great grandfather, long story, but her descendants still own it. You'll have spoken to one of them, I expect, if you're renting it."

"No, it was done through one of their friends – Annette? She said they were going up to Scotland for a month so they decided to Air BnB the place."

"That's right. They have connections up there," Jane said, reminding Bee vaguely of the mafia.

"But you are sometimes in London?" Stella probed.

"Yes. I have connections *there.*"

"One of whom's dead," said Stella.

"Stella, I –"

"It's all right, Bee. There was no love lost between my cousin Miranda and I. Nor indeed any of us. I sent the Searchers after her myself. When we heard she'd died? *Huge* relief." Jane Thorn took a victorious sip of her coffee. "I hope that doesn't shock you but frankly, I'm done with all that. She was a pain when she was alive and more than that. She stole something from me and sent my mother to an early grave. From which she has not yet returned."

Bee glanced uneasily about the coffee shop. Either everyone else was used to this sort of conversation or they simply had not heard. No one was giving Jane the side-eye, anyway.

"Obviously we didn't believe the tabloid reports. I'm assuming someone sent a fetch in her place? Or was it her actual body?"

"I've no idea," Stella said. "She fell foul of the Searchers and that was pretty much it."

"Well, I just hope she doesn't pop up in the non-mortal realm, because *really*... but since the Searchers took her I don't expect that's likely to happen. Fingers crossed, eh? Oh, hello, vicar!"

An elderly man in a dog collar had come to stand by the table. Smiling vaguely, he could not have fitted the stereotype of the country cleric more closely, Bee thought.

"Jane. Nice to see you. Having a coffee with friends? How lovely. I've got a jumble sale meeting in a moment, won't stop. I expect we'll see you in church tomorrow." A statement, not a question.

"Absolutely, Reverend," said Jane Thorn. "Good luck with the jumble sale. Don't let them bully you! Tell Julia Parsons I said so."

The vicar looked disturbed. "A challenging woman," he remarked.

"That's one way of putting it."

The vicar wandered away to his meeting.

"I expect you're surprised," Jane said. "But for a family of witches we believe in keeping on both sides of the religious fence. Just in case. Now." She finished her coffee and set the cup decisively on its saucer. "I want to tell you what's going on, but not here. Can I invite you to tea? All four of you, at the house? Will that be difficult?"

"We're here with relatives," Bee said. "Ver March – that's my sister Luna's boyfriend Sam's nan, sorry, but that's the only way to describe it – is very knowledgeable about this sort of thing. So I'd like her to come, and Sam, too, and my partner, Ned."

"All women are welcome," Jane said, "but not a man. That's not me being sexist, it's a thing with the house."

"Right."

"Sorry. It won't let men in. We could ask Sam and Ned to stand by the gate and shout, if you like."

"No, no, we'll leave them behind. Sam and Luna have just had a baby so he can be the child minder for the afternoon."

"Excellent. Then I would suggest tomorrow? After church and before Sunday dinner, if you have it in the evening. We do."

"Sounds good," Stella said. "We can leave Sam to cook. By the way, when we saw you in London, you told us to 'watch the wall'. What did you mean?"

Jane told her.

SERENA

Serena was flying. She leaned back into the spray as the *Iconoclast* veered around the buoy, skimming over the water. Up in the front of the boat – the prow? Serena knew few nautical terms – Adrian and Lily did rapid things with ropes.

Serena and Stella had met them down on the waterfront after lunch. Adrian had been to school with Ward. He was not an actor, but something in IT, working mainly from the farmhouse they had bought in Cornwall, 'escaping the insanity of Islington', Lily had said. From his hearty, upper middle class accent, Serena suspected family money, but she did not judge this: lucky Adrian, with his classy wife and posh boat. They both seemed relentlessly normal, which made a change. When they had picked Serena up and learned that Stella lived on a boat, albeit a currently stationary one moored on the Thames, Adrian's enthusiasm knew no bounds and he had invited her as well.

"Stella's better with boats than I am," Serena said hastily, after his introduction. "I can follow instructions. Sort of. Probably."

Adrian had taken this remark as evidence of greater nautical competence than Stella actually possessed and launched into a commentary which included, "J-slash-70s, IMOCA class, Cowes, Fastnet and a probable need for tacking given the breeze." Stella nodded along but then proceeded to manage some of his expectations, which slowed Adrian down somewhat, but only slightly. However, Serena thought that Stella might have rather underplayed her own capabilities, for she seemed to be leaping about and hauling on ropes and hanging over the side of *Iconoclast* with the best of them.

"Are you enjoying yourself?" she called to Stella, during a relative lull.

"Yes, are you?"

"Yes, it's fabulous, but I feel a bit useless. 'Sheets' are the sails, right?"

"No, sheets are ropes."

At this point Serena decided to give up trying to understand what was going on and just enjoy her time on the water.

"Anyway," Stella went on, "It's not a big boat. There's not a lot for everyone to do. Adrian and Lily usually go out on their own, or he goes out without her."

"Yes, he was saying. Kind of him to have landlubbers along."

"Look, you can see the house."

They were rounding the point on which, Stella had said, she had seen the seal women. Serena peered but the slabs of rock were partially submerged and empty. The cliff rose from the deep green water in a ragged column of rock, but past its summit she could see the houses along the coast road, including Penhallow. There was the umbrella in the garden, and then the little boat turned and they were speeding out into the bay. It glittered and glimmered in the afternoon sun; St Michael's Mount was swallowed by the light, rendered almost invisible. Another small craft shot across their bow, making Serena squeak: the crew were practically touching the water. Adrian laughed.

"Lily's dad tacked right across us once at Cowes. Lost us the eighth race."

"Yes, no G&T for him that evening," said Lily crisply. "I'm really quite competitive when I get going."

"Have you always sailed?"

"Yes, ever since I was a little kid. Horses and boats, that's my thing. My mother does a lot of dressage."

Lily was certainly fit, Serena thought: a lean, weatherbeaten girl with streaked blonde hair. The outdoors type. Nothing wrong with that.

"Watch it, Adrian! Bit close there!"

More incomprehensible rope and sail action. The bay was crowded, but it was the weekend, Serena thought, and holiday season, and a sunny day.

"This is all very Swallows and Amazons," Stella said, slightly out of breath.

"I thought that was the Lake District."

"No, Norfolk as well. Those books are all in my room at Penhallow. That's such an awesome room – it's like a childhood room. Maybe it actually *is* a child's room, I don't know."

"Assuming they read these days."

"Well, Bella reads. I might re-read them if we have a rainy day."

"Adrian said it might rain tomorrow," Serena said.

"It doesn't look like it now."

"No. But you know how quickly the weather can change on the coast. Anyway, we've got afternoon tea tomorrow, with the Misses Thorn." The pink house was visible, too, a distant rosy blob on the fast-receding shore.

"Talking of a change in the weather," Stella said uneasily, "wasn't it sunny a moment ago?"

Serena looked in the direction in which her sister was staring. A long line of black cloud had sprung up, covering the sun. A sudden wind stirred her hair.

"Adrian," she said, as he balanced his way along the deck, "It looks like we might be heading into bad weather."

"What? No, lovely sunny day! Don't worry!" He made his way back to Lily.

"Serena," her sister said, "I don't think we're in Kansas any more."

"I don't, either. But I think Adrian and Lily might be…"

In Serena's version of reality, the little boat had now begun to heave up and down on a churning sea. She was doused with water. Spluttering, she felt under the edge of her life jacket to the skirt of her sundress. It was quite dry.

"I think we'd better hang on, all the same," Stella hissed in her ear.

It was now growing dark. The clouds had devoured the sun and Serena saw a splintering bolt of lightning, far away to the south. They had been sailing far out in the bay but the cliff rose up ahead of them, coming in fast.

"There's a light!" Stella said. Serena could see it, high on the cliff, steady at first then wavering for a second. Lily was steering directly for it.

"Lily!" Serena shouted. "*Lily!*" But their steerswoman did not seem to hear.

They were nearly on the rocks. Serena crouched, pulling Stella down next to her. But just as she made her move, she saw a woman standing on the rocks. She was naked, stout and glistening; her skin was a mottled grey but as Serena stared, it paled. Her lips were pursed. Serena heard a thin whirring whistle, over-riding the roar of the wind. The woman was staring up at the cliff. The whistle rose in pitch. Serena covered her ears. Then all was sunlit and the boat was turning, far out in the spangled waters of the bay. The cliff and Penhallow House were sharp and distant against the blue summer sky.

"Serena, you okay?" Adrian's face was concerned.

"Bit queasy. Sorry!"

"She gets sick on the dock," Stella lied.

"I'm all right now. I'm not going to throw up. Promise" She stood, unsteadily.

"Sometimes it's just the way the boat moves," Lily shouted back. "Keep your eyes on the horizon."

"No, really, I'm all right."

"Great! Well, we're heading back, anyway. Fancy a drink? The Yacht Club's got a great bar!

"Sounds fantastic," Serena said faintly.

"To be honest, I could do with a stiff G&T after all that," she said to Serena, in the Ladies.

"Christ, you're not wrong. I thought we were going to capsize. Sorry to throw you under the bus with the seasick thing. It was the most logical explanation at the time."

"No, you're fine. I don't mind a bit of humiliation in a good cause." Serena repaired her lipstick and they went out onto the balcony, where Adrian was ensconced.

"Had fun?"

"Absolutely. Thanks so much for taking us out."

"And you're feeling better, Serena?"

"I'm fine, thanks, Lily. Just caught me off balance for a moment."

"We had one day off the Needles where the entire crew threw up. Including Adrian. It happens."

"It was nearly a Force Eight, though, Lily. Shouldn't have been out but it came up suddenly."

"Sometimes I'm okay and sometimes I'm not," Serena said, lying again. "But it was lovely today."

"Adrian has to go up to town for a couple of days, but we'll be out again in the week. An evening sail, this time. Want to come?"

"Yes, we'd love to," Stella said, before her sister could demur. But from her slightly calculating expression, Serena thought Stella might have a plan. She had to admit that, away from the rigours of the sea, this was a pleasant place to sit. The Yacht Club overlooked the local marina, and the sound of rigging clonking gently in the sea breeze was soothing. She could see the Thorns' pink house from here, and it occurred to her that there must be few places on the immediate stretch of coastline that it did not overlook. In silence, Stella placed before her a second stiff gin.

BEE

In the morning, it rained. The French Riviera guise of the bay was wiped out by a blot of very English rain and cloud.

"Look at it," Ver March said, staring out at the turbulent grey expanse. "It might as well be the middle of November."

"That's Cornwall for you. The Beeb says it will be fine again tomorrow. The papers are talking about a heatwave, in fact."

"Great," Stella said. "I shall get some rays in."

"Are you likely to go surfing?"

"I plan to. Adrian's going to lend me a board. He and Lily surf, so he says he'll take me down to Portleath at some point – tomorrow, perhaps, if this clears up. Show me the lie of the land. Or the breakers. But I'm obviously not going to go surfing in this."

"I should think not."

"It's a great day for tea and cake, though," Ver said. "Sam's going to be left holding the baby."

Her grandson grinned. "I don't mind."

"He's fallen in love," Bee said.

"Well, who wouldn't?" But Ver, too, was smiling. Sam was besotted with his new daughter. This had slightly surprised Bee, but when she saw Sam with dogs or cats or horses, perhaps it wasn't so surprising. Luna, too, was devoted, but in a more practical way, as if constantly wondering if she was doing motherhood right. Bee could not blame her. They split the care, but Sam seemed more relaxed about it. She was not worried. Luna must do as she saw fit. She had not expressed undue concerns about leaving Rosie with her dad, and they'd had a dry run a week or so before, when Luna had gone to Bristol for the night to see a friend, without the baby.

"Mind you, I was a nervous wreck."

"But she's fine! They're fine! They had a nice peaceful evening."

"So did I," said Luna.

Now, Luna seemed set on the meeting with the Thorns. She had asked a lot of questions, being the only Fallow sister not to have met Jane. Serena was nervous about it, Bee knew.

"It's just that they've asked all of us. What if it's some sort of trap?"

139

"We'll have Ver with us and Sam knows where we're going. So does Dark. He's going to come too, but not come into the house. I think they'd know if he did."

"She looks so like Miranda," Serena said.

"Have you mentioned it to Ward?"

"No, he's got his play to think about and I don't want to freak him out before he gets here. Stella's keeping Ace appraised, though. Via the pub, on the phone."

"And what did Ace say?"

"Said we might as well check it out and meanwhile he was going to do some digging at his end."

"Good," said Bee.

She had hoped the weather might clear up, but by lunchtime it was obvious that the rain had set in for the afternoon and it worsened as the day grew on. It was thrashing the coast, intermittently hitting the conservatory windows like a handful of thrown pebbles. Luna was walking up and down, holding Rosie, and the baby stared unblinkingly out at the weather, as though assessing it.

"I've put her blanket in the basket," Luna said.

"You've already told me that." Sam's voice was mild.

"Oh, sorry, did I? I should shut up, shouldn't I, and go."

"I'm actually ready," Stella announced, swathed in a yachting jacket that was rather too large.

"Where did you find that?"

"In the cupboard. I think it's a man's."

"Very elegant," Serena said, straight faced.

"I know Jane's all Miss Paris Catwalk, but I just want to stay dry on my trip to and from the car. I notice, Serena, that you are in a *designer* raincoat. Or what looks like one."

"It's Lululemon. Luna, are you coming?"

Bee drove, taking them steadily down one hill and up the other side. Once the white houses of the old town were behind them, the road closed in: more like a shrouded Dartmoor lane than a main road leading into a seaside resort.

"Sorry," Bee said, crashing the gears.

"I feel like we ought to be leaning forwards."

"Stella, that is not helpful! Do you think this is their drive? I don't fancy backing out of it."

"It's a real witches' drive," Stella said, hopping out to look at the name plate. "Yes, this is it. Thornhold."

As she drove down the drive, between the narrow hedges of laurel, Bee was relieved to see, from the corner of her eye, the figure of Dark at the gate, briefly in the rearview mirror.

The pink house stood tall on the cliff: its walls were a wild rose colour rather than the somewhat violent pink that Bee knew from south Somerset and Dorset. Like Penhallow, it was Georgian in style, but Bee thought that more recent eras had added some features. Also like Penhallow, it sported a cupola and here, too, the drive opened out onto an apron of land set into the side of the cliff. The view, which must be spectacular on a fine day, was an ocean of cloud and spray. Bee locked the car while her sisters and Ver ran for the door. It opened immediately.

"Come in! Isn't it foul!" Jane Thorn, in pristine white jeans and a nautically striped charcoal sweater, ushered them inside. Bee found herself in a long hallway, Victorian tiled and scented with polish. It was not remotely sinister and neither was the comfortably conventional living room into which Jane ushered them. Did witches hire interior designers? Bee wondered, impressed. These ones evidently had.

Serena, of course, was used to this sort of thing.

"What a lovely room! Those lamps are gorgeous. I love that coral design. And I love your curtains."

"My sister, Louisa, trained at St Martins. Went to work for Nina Campbell."

Behind Jane's back, Luna mouthed, "Who?" But Serena seemed to know exactly who Jane was talking about.

"Oh, I love her stuff!"

"I mean, it's a bit pulled together? All this blue and white and the sea themes. Louisa wondered if it was a bit of a cliché, but I don't care. It suits the house and the room."

"Beautiful," Bee said politely, admiring a porcelain lamp stencilled with indigo coral. She meant it, too.

"Do find somewhere to sit. Move those magazines, Stella. I'll bring the tea things in."

"This is terribly civilised," Ver said.

"We try."

"Well, it makes a change, is all I can say."

"Cheers," Stella said, accepting a cup of tea. "I feel like something out of a nautical Jane Austen."

"I know this must seem a bit freaky. Thanks for coming. I did wonder if you might get cold feet with all this magic stuff. Then I thought, probably you wouldn't,"

"By the way, if you see the ghost of an Elizabethan pirate at the end of your driveway, that's my boyfriend."

Jane did not bat an eyelid.

"That's fine. Louisa's been out for a swim, she's just getting changed. She'll come and join us in a minute. Have a biscuit."

Stella looked out of the window. "She's been swimming in *this*? Or do you have a pool?"

Serena said, "We had a bit of an insight, let's say, into how rough this coast can be. Yesterday."

Bee half expected Jane to say 'but the weather was so nice then!'. Instead, she said, "Yes, I know. Louisa saw you."

A movement at the door. Bee looked up to see an older woman with bobbed hair, linen trousers and a wrap top of the same pale grey shade: heavily built and elegant.

"Oh!" and "It's *you*," Serena and Stella said simultaneously. For it was the seal woman.

"Hello. Louisa Thorn." Her voice was gruff, but not unfriendly. "Yes, I saw you yesterday. You were out on that boat."

"When Louisa told me about that," Jane said, "I knew I'd done the right thing in asking you to tea. If the wreckers have targeted you, you can't be with them, you see. And we had rather wondered."

"The wreckers?"

"Jane, would you pour me a cup? Thank you." Louisa Thorn sank ponderously into an armchair. Bee was reminded of members of the Bloomsbury group; with her Bohemian linen and bobbed hair, Louisa was more like someone from the pre-war period. "We knew you were involved in Miranda's death. But we didn't know quite where your affiliations lie, since your mother is known to ride with the Hunt."

"About that," Stella said.

"Yes, she didn't tell us she was going off with them. We've been very worried." Despite a developing rapport, Bee did not like to confess that

142

they had wondered if it had actually been Alys herself who had returned from the otherworld, or something else.

"I'm not surprised."

"In London," Stella said, "in the spring, Miranda made some sort of pact with the Hunt. They asked her to do something but she fucked it up. The Hunt don't often come into the city, I gather, and this was like a one-off? But anyway, she didn't seal the deal – Bee did."

"I negotiated for the Hunt to have access to some of our land," Bee explained.

"In exchange for what?"

"Our lives."

"Oh," Jane said. "I see."

"I didn't just go – hey, give me a load of fairy gold and you can use our back field. We were desperate."

Serena snorted. "They say fairy gold turns to leaves, anyway."

"Then Mum was hurt," Luna added. "At Midsummer. The leader of the Hunt threw her off his horse and she hit her head and lost her memory."

"Oh no! Has it come back?"

"Not yet. This was a few weeks ago. She's staying with her friend Caro while we're down here. She's okay, just can't remember anything magical. Or pretends she can't."

"Can I ask a question?" Bee said. "What did Miranda steal from you? Was it your shape?"

There was a short silence. Then Louisa said, "I can see you all, you know. Hare and wren, otter and swarm. It's as though the images are superimposed – not all the time, but sometimes. And you have seen me, Serena and Stella, in my seal guise."

"You're a selkie," Stella said.

"In fact, technically I'm not. A selkie needs a sealskin to change from human to animal."

"I couldn't change into an otter, we think, without a skin. I had one. It disappeared. I think I sort of absorbed it." Stella made vague retching noises. "I don't like that bit. Vegetarian, you see."

Louisa smiled. "So you are the selkie, not I. In my case, it's a spell laid on this part of the family, long ago. We can choose, but it must be a sea creature, since we are sea witches, and we can't go far from the coast."

"But like a seal or a – a dolphin, right?" Stella said. "Not a whelk or something?"

"No, not a whelk," Jane Thorn said, rather faintly. Bee thought she might be struggling not to laugh. "Louisa is seal. Our sister Helena, whom you haven't yet met, is oystercatcher. I was gull, but that was what Miranda stole from me. She stole the key to my part of the family spell and took it for herself."

"Bitch!" Serena said.

"I wasn't exactly pleased. You know about the Searchers. I tried to get my shape back but I couldn't find it. I think she left it somewhere in the past."

"So you can't now – change shape?"

"No, I'm stuck as a human and it really pisses me off."

"For the record, she was a pretty crappy seagull. I realise that probably doesn't help."

"Not really but thanks for saying it. Anyway, I haven't given up hope but it's been like looking for a needle in a haystack and we have bigger things to worry about."

"Such as?" Bee did not mean to sound quite so nervous.

"We have a job to do. We're supposed to guard the coast. Louisa volunteers on the local lifeboat and Helena's a nurse – that's why she's not here right now. She's working. I volunteer at the museum in Tretorvic, which isn't really 'guarding' but we get some odd stuff brought in from time to time and I can usually neutralise it if it's nasty. When I had my shape changing ability I could do a bit more – look out for local sailors, for instance. I've guided more than one fishing smack through a gale. And you've already met some of the people we're here to guard against."

"The wreckers?" Luna said.

"Yes. I really hate it when people romanticise the past. All those stories about kindly, roguish old smugglers tricking the horrid excise men, and pirates with a twinkle in their eye, and the poor folk scraping a living by rescuing the odd bottle of rum from a grounded ship. Smugglers, pirates and wreckers were usually just criminals. People got killed."

"Sir Cloudesley Shovell," Bee said.

"Oh, you know about that?"

"What was that?" Serena asked.

"There was a piece in a history of Cornwall I was reading last night – it was in a bookcase at Penhallow. Got wrecked off the Scillies and when he was washed up, a woman murdered him for his emerald ring. She confessed on her deathbed years later."

"He probably actually died in the shipwreck," Louisa said, "deathbed confessions not always being accurate and a lack of supporting evidence. But that folk were willing enough to believe it tells its own story. I know for a fact that some victims were murdered."

"But wrecking now, right? Does it still go on? I mean, I know it happened in the past. I saw it." Bee related her night time vision. "But I've seen those massive container ships going up and down the Bristol Channel – they don't try and lure *those* onto the rocks, do they?"

"Well, smuggling certainly does – it's drugs these days, of course. They found £80 million worth of cocaine on one trawler off Falmouth. As for wrecking, the locals will swear blind it doesn't happen these days, but I know of one incident in the last twenty years involving a freighter. Not round here, though – further up the coast. But the wreckers we're talking about aren't interested in rum or boxes of radios. They lure ships onto the rocks for a different cargo."

"And what cargo is that?" Ver asked, into the silence.

"Human souls."

On the way home, Bee suggested a pre-prandial drink at the Smuggler's Rest. They found that in some unrevealed way Dark had realised this and got there before them. He was sitting alone, at a table overlooking the harbour, with a tankard.

"You must have put everyone else off," Bee told him. "I've never seen a pub look so empty."

"Rain's done that," the barman said, though she did not think he could see Dark. Perhaps he thought she was talking to one of the women. "Although you'd think there'd be a few stragglers still in here. We were rammed at lunchtime."

"Are you serving Sunday dinner?"

"Sunday lunch and Sunday dinner. Food orders start at six. That table all right for you?"

Bee looked at the clock. Half past five. "Fine," she said. "We can have a drink first – I'll drive back – and you can phone Sam, Luna. Tell him to jump in a cab with Rosie. We can do that chicken tomorrow night instead, Serena."

Her sisters approved of this plan. Bee felt a need for a fire in the grate and shelter against the storm. And for somebody else to do the cooking.

Sam arrived shortly afterwards, with Rosie in her basket and Moth on a lead. The baby was fast asleep.

"Any problems?" Bee could tell that Luna was trying not to look too anxious.

"No. Good as gold."

"We bought you a pint."

"Outstanding. How did it go?"

"It was interesting. Dark, did you overhear any of this?"

Ned laughed. "No. That house is very well protected. Something old guarding it. I did not go too close."

"What sort of something?"

"I don't know."

Bee had a vision of a dragon, scaled, beneath the Thorn's residence. She said, "They were quite honest, I think. As far as I could tell."

"I liked them," Serena said.

"They said that they're sea witches, their job is to guard the coast, and the local equivalent of the Hunt is a group known as the wreckers, led by the Morlader, who lure ships of all times and types onto the rocks and steal people's souls. Then Jane went on to say that the Hunt don't ride here, they ride up on Bodmin and Dartmoor, but they don't come down to the coast. That's the wreckers' territory, but she thinks that there's been some recent contact between the two groups. Something their younger sister overheard, but she didn't say when or where. She doesn't like it."

"Grandfather said there were rumours of some sort of dispute, between the Hunt and the witch tribes, over territory," Stella said. "Remember?"

"I told them that. Basically Jane said that Cornwall's got its own magical scene and we don't want to get too involved but we might not have a choice. She said we should be careful."

"If we can," Serena said.

STELLA

The rain had swept out into the Channel, leaving a clear, calm morning in its wake. Stella, despite a mild hangover, woke early and went downstairs in search of coffee. Having made this, she took it out into the dripping garden, towelled off one of the plastic chairs and sat down to recharge with caffeine. The bay was flatly well behaved. *I don't trust you*, Stella said to it. She watched a bright scarlet sail tack across the water, catching the slight breeze.

"Morning."

"Hello, Bee! How are you?"

"Fine. How are you?"

"I can tell I had a drink last night. But only a little bit."

"You didn't drink that much," her sister said. Dressing-gown clad, she put her tea on the table and took the other chair. "I think we've all been rather well behaved so far. What are your plans for the day?"

"Well. Adrian and Lily texted me last night and we're going surfing. I mentioned that to you, didn't I? Up the coast to Portleath."

"Sounds good!"

"It should be great, actually. I've surfed there before but not for a long while."

"And you've got a gig," Bee said.

The barman in the Smuggler's Arms had got chatting to Stella and found out what she did for a living. He had promptly asked her to do a turn at a little festival, later in the week. Coastival, it was called.

"I thought that was folk?" Stella said. "I don't know any shanties."

Nate had laughed. "You don't have to. It's not really folk, it's all sorts. Pirate themed."

"I don't know that they were really into electronica. It not having been invented then."

"They would have been if it had," Nate said, with what Stella considered to be extremely shaky logic. "We'll pay you, obviously."

"Sure. Well, I'm happy to give it a go."

"Great," said Nate. "You'll be on the boat, by the way."

"Even better."

She said now to Bee, "Whatever else happens, it's turning into a proper Famous Five holiday."

"Ward's coming down on Friday night and bringing Bella. We can tell him to go straight to Coastival. Where is it again?"

"Penroth. It's about five miles down the coast."

"Easy enough."

Stella drank more coffee, accepted Bee's offer of toast, then went back in for a shower. She reached the end of the driveway just as Adrian and Lily pulled up in a 4x4.

"You're ready! Great!"

"Looking forward to it," Stella said. "Although we were rather late back from the pub last night."

"A day on the board will soon set you up. We've got some kit for you."

The drive to Portleath took longer than Stella had expected.

"This is why we picked you up early," Adrian said over his shoulder, as they inched down a hill in a queue of traffic. "Emmets."

"I'm an emmet, though, aren't I? And from London, even worse."

"You're an emmet who is known to me, though, so that's different. At least you're not a second home owner."

"I gather that's a bit of an issue."

"Cornwall's really poor," Lily said. "By national standards. Only about twelve percent of the economy is based on tourism but they just take over in the summer. And so many people buy holiday homes or properties for Air BnB that young people can't get a foot on the housing ladder. There are weeny little cottages going in Mousehole for nearly seven hundred grand."

Stella, still feeling slightly guilty about her tourist status, agreed that this was a problem.

"And then there's the parking."

Adrian did, however, manage to find a spot in the overflow car park looking out across the beach. Stella squeezed into her borrowed wetsuit and they carried their gear down to the sands. Portreath was big: a classic expanse of pale yellow sand between two low headlands.

"Tide's on the turn," Adrian said. "We might as well get started. I hope you'll be okay, Stella. I hope that board's all right."

"What he's too much of a delicate flower to say," Lily said, "is that we didn't get you a rash vest."

"No worries! It doesn't feel like it's going to chafe and I'm happy with the hybrid. Sea's looking good!"

The beach was already beginning to get crowded. Stella could see a surf school a little way along the sands.

"Lifeguards are obviously out," Adrian said. "You can see the flags."

Stella, to stop him worrying, got going. She could hardly say, "Don't worry – if I get into trouble I'll turn into an otter." In fact, her own main concern was that she suddenly might. How embarrassing would that be...? She ran into the surf, straight into a strong onshore wind. The swell looked about four to five feet, quite manageable. It was some time since Stella had been on a board and, not normally self-conscious, she was aware that Adrian and Lily might be watching critically. *So let's not fuck this up*. Like actually getting up on her board and not clutching it all the way into shore. She swam out, felt the first big breaker pick her up and flipped onto the board without, thank you God, falling ignominiously into the sea. She rode the wave down and bounced into shore, exhilarated. And then she did it all over again.

Adrian suggested heading home around five o'clock. By then, Stella had almost had all the sun, sea swell and sand that she wanted, and despite a perfectly adequate packed lunch, found that she was ready for something more than sandwiches. She said so.

"Completely agree," Adrian said. "And it's gin o'clock, in my opinion. But I think we should head somewhere else – I passed a couple of pubs when I went up to the cashpoint and they were rammed."

"Also I don't fancy sitting in a traffic jam for an hour," Lily told him. "So why don't we take the back road up through Trelso and have dinner in the Hand and Bundle?"

Stella thought she might store this up to tell Ace, in what was a growing collection of odd pub names. "Sounds good to me," she said.

"It's up on the moors. It's not very far and is on the way back to Tretorvic, but it's far enough away from the coast not to be inundated by tourists."

Stella took advantage of the outdoor showers further along the beach to wash the salt off, reasoning that it was still so warm that her hair would be at least half dry by the time they reached the pub. Then she tucked the board under her arm and accompanied Adrian and Lily back to the car, conscious of that slightly wistful leaving-the-beach sensation so familiar from childhood.

Never mind, Alys had said to them, that old comforting mantra. *It will still be here tomorrow.* But of course they had, at the end of each holiday, come to the point where the beach might have been there, but they had not: packing everything into the car, Grandfather waiting patiently in the driving seat before heading east again, to Mooncote but also to school. Stella had always liked coming back to the house, to the quiet orderliness which awaited them, clean sheets with no sand in them and lots of hot water, and ghosts and stars, but then term had begun again and education had loomed. Never mind. Out of that now, and Stella was content to be grown up. She put the board in the car and fastened her seatbelt, but as the 4x4 pulled up the hill out of town she could not resist that last look back, to the emptying beach and the sea glittering under the sun.

Adrian pulled off onto a second fork in the road and headed inland.

"We said it was away from the coast," he said, over his shoulder. "But we're so far west that you can see the north shore as well once we get up onto the heights." The land changed as he drove, a long rolling expanse of fields and stretches of bracken, still quite green, but Stella knew that it would not be too long before autumn would beckon it to russet. Rosebay willowherb, herald of late summer, was starting to frond the verges; Stella could see the hills rise and fall through its purple light. At length, Adrian pulled into a car park and she saw that they had reached the pub: a low whitewashed building hunkered down against the weather. Hard to imagine on this peaceful, sunlit evening, with the shadows racing away from the stone walls, but Stella had been down here in winter and even without their strange experience of the other day, she knew how quickly the gales could lash the coast. The little hawthorn trees, all pointing in one direction, told their own story of the winds that blew.

The pub had a painted sign: a hand grasping a white bundle. What was in it, wondered Stella. A baby? Sausages? The sign was too faded to offer many clues. She ducked under the low lintel and found herself in a surprisingly dark room, but perhaps it was only in contrast to the bright evening outside. There was certainly nothing sinister about the smiling young woman who showed them to a table and asked them if they wanted to order drinks before seeing the menu. Stella glanced out at a garden filled with fuchsias and the rolling land beyond. A gleaming line betrayed the presence of the sea.

"What would you like to drink, Stella?"

"I'll have a medium Sauv Blanc, please. But you must let me pay for myself."

Brief wrangling ensued resulting in a compromise. Stella would pay for the drinks, Adrian and Lily for the food. But before the drinks arrived, Stella realised that responsible rehydration over the course of the afternoon was having its inevitable effect.

"Where's your loo, please?" she asked the waitress.

"Through that door, across the courtyard and out the back. You'll see a sign."

The toilets looked as though they had once been a cattle shed, with white walls and a slate floor. Long after their original purpose, they had been handsomely renovated with brass basins and an air diffuser. Stella noted in the mirror that her hair had, in fact, dried, a testament to the warmth of the day.

But when she went back outside, the warmth had gone. She stepped into thick mist.

"Shit," thought Stella. That had come quickly, without warning. Too quickly. She couldn't even see the back wall of the pub, a handful of yards away. She backed up, searching for the door to the lavatory, but that was no longer there, either. She looked down. No flagstones under her feet, only cropped grass, a scattering of rabbit droppings, a clump of rushes. Typical moorland, in fact, like the landscape of Bodmin over which they had driven a few days before, but this part of the county was farm country. Stella tried not to panic. This had happened before, a lot. There was no immediate danger. From somewhere off to her left, she could hear a rhythmic tapping, metal on stone.

Okay, thought Stella. She took a careful step in the direction of the sound, then another. A wall loomed up in front of her, waist height, roughly mortared. Then a face, appearing suddenly out of the swirling mists. Stella yipped. But it was only a donkey, mild eyed and curious.

"Oh," Stella said, aloud. The donkey's head went up, the whites of its eyes flashed. It turned clumsily and fled into the fog. "Hey, I'm friendly," Stella said, but the sudden drum of hoofbeats made her turn sharply. The rider came out of the cloud, face hooded. She had time to see a spotted horse, as big as a shire, feet feathered and thundering, and then she was grabbed by the collar of her sweatshirt and hauled over its withers. The fog closed over their wake.

SERENA

When Stella had still not come home at eleven o clock, Serena was not too concerned: probably they had found a pub somewhere and were carousing. By half past eleven, she asked Bee if she thought they should text Adrian. Luna, Ver and Sam had already gone to bed.

"Yes, it wouldn't be a bad idea. Maybe not wind him up. Ask him if they had a nice evening."

Serena did this and shortly after this a text arrived back.

Yes thx Hand&Bundle awesome as usual hope Stella not too hungover 2moz! I might be LOL. Dropped her in yr lane told her not to fall in ditch! Soz we did not come in was bit late.

LOL! texted Serena in return. Some pubs were open until quite late… she googled the number and phoned the Hand and Bundle.

"Hi! Was my sister there earlier this evening? Tall-ish girl, light blondish brown hair, stripy sweatshirt? She thinks she might have dropped her phone."

But the voice on the other end, professionally helpful, said that she remembered Stella and her friends, they had left about seven thirty, and she would go and look. Serena felt guilty about this and even more so when the phone, obviously, failed to be found. She thanked the staff member and hung up. Then she went to find Bee.

"Christ," said her sister, clutching her dressing gown around her. "Maybe she *did* fall in the ditch!"

"We'd better go and look."

"Let me put some clothes on."

They found torches and went up the drive. It was a mild, clear night, star strewn. Serena could hear the distant gush of the surf at the base of the cliff, but the sea was calm. They searched up and down the lane, once having to flatten against the hedge as a car went past, but there was no sign of Stella.

"Who are you seeking?" Serena jumped and clutched at a handful of hawthorn before realising that it was only Ned Dark.

"Stella. She went out with our friends and they said they'd dropped her off, but she's not here now."

"Where did they set her down?"

"In the lane, they said. I'm presuming at the gate."

"I have been in the garden all evening. No car slowed down."

"Shit," said Serena. "Maybe they just *think* they dropped her off."

"Can they be trusted?"

"I think so. They seemed like perfectly ordinary nice people. I mean, you never know, but…"

"You don't think she might have gone off the cliff?" Bee said, wide-eyed with sudden fright.

"Oh God. But even if she was pissed, Stella can handle her drink, and she doesn't actually drink that much anyway. Usually."

"We'd better look."

They went back down the drive and through the garden.

"I will look," Dark said. "It doesn't matter if I fall off the edge."

"Cheers, Ned. I was in fact about to tell you to be careful."

Serena half-hoped he might hover, but he didn't. He simply went to the edge and looked down, holding Bee's torch.

"Anything?"

"No. What was she wearing?"

"A navy and white sweatshirt and light coloured jeans."

To Serena's relief, he shook his head. "No, there's nothing white down there. I can see a ledge. Only the surf."

"Could she have been taken by the waves?"

"No, the tide's not high enough yet. Come and see."

Ghost or no, Bee gripped his arm quite firmly while Serena held her breath. "See? If anyone had fallen, they would be on that rock, it is so flat and wide."

"Yes, I see," Bee said. She stepped back. "I don't know what to suggest."

"I think we should go up to the Hand and Bundle," Serena said. "That's my feeling."

"They'll be shut by now."

"I know, but we could look around. And not get arrested for snooping."

"No, let's not get arrested. And didn't they say Stella had left?"

"Yes, but I keep thinking of your episode at the racetrack in the spring. When something truly weird happened but it just drained out of everyone's memory."

"That's a very good point," Bee said. "Do you think that happened with Adrian and Lily?"

"I don't know but at least we're doing *something*." She did not want to rattle Adrian's cage any further. He might, of course, turn out to be a psychopath and Stella taken by the couple in a prosaic abduction and murder (oh God, no), but given recent events, Serena thought it far more likely that forces unknown were at work. And she had a hard time seeing jolly, hearty Adrian as a serial killer, although one could never be certain.

Serena found the pub on her phone and they set off, angling through the dark, narrow lanes. Away from the street lights of the coast, with only an occasional hamlet or house appearing, Serena realised how dark it actually was. She was not deeply perturbed, being used to this in the depths of Somerset, but she remarked on it to Bee.

"London's always so bright. Too much light pollution."

"You told me once you missed the stars."

"I do. But they're very bright tonight." If it hadn't been for her worries over Stella, she would have enjoyed the drive. It was warm enough to wind the window down and the land smelled of mown hay. A blowy, blowsy night, thought Serena.

"Serena, do you know which way?" They had come to a T-junction. Serena consulted her phone.

"Left."

She could see that they were climbing now, up onto open moorland. Serena had not realised that Bodmin extended so far, or perhaps this was another moor. Then she noticed something else: no lights. Bee suddenly braked.

"What?"

"We've run out of road," Bee said.

It was true. The tarmac had disappeared.

"This happened to Granddad once, in Ireland. They'd taken up the tarmac to get at someone's peat cutting. They told him they were going to put it back..."

"I don't think this is someone's peat cutting," Bee said.

Serena opened the door and got out. In the headlights, she could just see a faint, double grooved track like a cart track, running off into the distance. She looked back. Thank God, the tarmac road was still there, stretching behind them. She studied the reassuring light of the phone. A small red dot showed up. So did Ned Dark, materialising from the night.

"Are we anywhere near that pub?" Bee asked, somewhat raggedly.

"Well, yes. It's supposed to be right here."

"I can see a – a house?"

It was not a house, more like a byre. Stout walled with a tiled roof.

"Do you think we should go and look?" Bee said.

"I don't want to leave the car. But I don't want to split up, either."

"No, definitely not. If we go, we all go."

After a moment's deliberation, they all went. The track did not lead to the byre, but up over the hill. As they came closer, Serena could see a light inside, a faint dim flame.

"Is that a candle?"

"I'm not sure. It doesn't look bright enough."

It sat in an open glassless window and as they came nearer, Serena could see that it was a rush light, a tiny flame in a little clay lamp.

"Is anyone there?" Bee said, loudly. No answer came. They went to the door and looked in. A single room, almost empty: a bed of bracken lay along one wall with a rough piece of material, more like a sack than anything else, upon it. There was a blackened hearth with a cast iron pot, a tin plate and nothing else. The little lamp flickered, making their shadows jump huge along the wall. Then something big moved at the end of the room. Serena clutched Bee's arm but it was only an old ewe. She did not look as though she had been shorn for a year or more, a bundle of grubby wool. She gave a petulant bleat at being disturbed and collapsed down again into the hay.

"God, that was a shock," Bee said, breathing out.

"What's that?" Dark said.

"What?"

But Serena had also seen something on the window sill, by the light. She went in and picked it up: a piece of plastic, about the length of her hand. When she turned it over, she saw a familiar jaunty figure on the back: the Pink Panther.

"It's Stella's phone," she said.

STELLA

The most annoying thing was being wet. Good job it wasn't cold as well, but that might depend on how long she was in here.

And then there was the matter of the dress.

Sea spray was regularly flung in through the window of this round room, which had no glass; it spattered the stone floor and the walls. The only place out of its reach – and this might change with a higher sea – was opposite the window. Stella had managed to drag the settle over to the far wall, which at least gave her something to sit on. She had, after some debate, put the dress on the settle as well. She had considered hanging it over the sill to get thoroughly soaked, purely to annoy Aiken Drum, but then it occurred to her that she might need a covering at night. The dress, which was as blue as the sky and made of velvet, was not the ideal quilt, because it was covered with thick gold embroidery and semi-precious stones, making it uncomfortable on which to lie. Stella, after some thought, had turned it inside out.

She had not grown up with a father; Abraham had taken that role. They had clashed a few times, but her grandfather's approach had always been the iron bar of logic. He was so *reasonable*. At the time, when Stella had reached her teens, this had been infuriating. He had explained, with a patience tinged very faintly with disappointment, why it had been wrong for Stella to tell her mother that she was spending the weekend with a friend and then go alone to a rave in Derbyshire instead. Stella had been impulsive, but she did possess a conscience and a vestigial sense of social responsibility, and her grandfather had known it. All too well.

So to be confronted with her mother's current boyfriend in the role of outraged parent, at her age, was really a bit much.

"I'm not wearing a bloody frock," Stella had told him.

"What's the matter with it? It's a beautiful frock! I can't present you at court in those – those britches."

"Did I ask you to present me at court? Coming out balls stopped in the Seventies. I'm not your daughter!" *As far as I know.* "Did I ask, in fact, for your henchman to snatch me off my feet and throw me over a horse and abduct me? Kidnapping is a crime." She had been brought here an hour or so before, after a wild ride over moorland with no trace of habitation and a moon rising in a storm of cloud. Stella had struggled, and once managed to fall off the horse entirely, fortunately into a bed of heather, but the rider had simply scooped her up again. She had kicked, squirmed, tried to change to otter and bite him, but to no avail. Finally they had reached a pair of iron studded gates and been brought inside this fortress, where Stella learned who had initiated her abduction. When passed into Drum's dubious custody, she had seen the face of the Huntsman who had taken her: a man missing an eye. Despite his ruffianly appearance, he looked slightly relieved as he left the room; Stella hoped she had given him a great deal of trouble.

Aiken Drum, horned and goat-eyed, wearing a long leather coat and boots, plus a brace of flintlock pistols, was intimidating, but Stella had been too furious to care. They stood, facing one another, in a high stone turret overlooking a turbulent sea. Stella had no idea where they were, although the coast did have a Cornish look about it: a great granite cliff fell sharply away beneath the open window. She could see the gold of gorse halfway down.

"Anyway, why me? Serena's much prettier. Not that I'm suggesting you abduct *her*," Stella amended hastily.

At this, Drum appeared faintly embarrassed. "It's not because of your looks, girl, or lack of them. It's because of your – other nature."

For a moment, Stella couldn't think what he meant, but then she realised. "What, you mean my animal nature?"

"Yes. Work it out. A riddle for you. What forms do your sisters take?"

"What?" Stella pondered the question. Bee: a swarm of her namesake. Luna: a wren: Serena: a hare. Two could fly, one could run. But – the sea slapped and hissed again below the window.

"I'm the only one of Alys' children who can properly swim?"

"Exactly."

"And why," Stella asked, "the fuck would *that* be important?"

Aiken Drum turned away from her and went to the window, where he placed his gloved hands on the sill and looked out.

"I'm in a difficult position," he confided.

"Like I give a shit!"

"You're very confrontational, Stella."

"Which I consider to be reasonable behaviour under the circumstances!"

157

Drum laughed at that. "You have a point. I'm not your enemy, though. Not really."

"We're not going to be great mates, Drum. Seriously, not. You might be my mum's dodgy boyfriend but that's it. Your huntsmen have come after me, you forced a really iffy deal on my sister, and you chucked my mother off your horse."

"Oh Stella," Drum said. "I didn't throw her from my horse out of malice. I threw her off to save her life. You didn't see what was coming after us." He grimaced.

"What *was* coming after you?"

But Drum did not answer. It did not bode well, Stella thought, that there was someone who scared the Wild Hunt.

"You haven't even asked me how Mum is. We had to take her into hospital. She had concussion."

"I haven't asked you how she is because I already know. I went to see her, several times, and the most recent was the night before last. But she couldn't see me."

"What do you mean? She wouldn't see you?" Hardly surprising."

"No, I mean she couldn't. I could walk through a supermarket in Penzance, Stella, with my yellow eyes and my horned skull, and perhaps one in a hundred might notice me, but no more than that. I am unseen in the haunts of men. But your mother has always been able to see me, until now."

"So," Stella said. She was not uninterested in this discussion. She went across to the oak settle and sat down. "People literally can't see you. I kind of realise that this works, but I don't know how."

"No, neither do I."

"Don't you? I'd sort of assumed that you would."

"No."

"And you are what, exactly? You're not human. You're not a ghost, I don't think. So what are you?"

"I was human, a long time ago. I was a highwayman. After the Lord Protector's day was done, I took to the road, a masterless man. I was taken and hanged on a gibbet, and all was black and I thought I was done, too, but then I woke with a noose light around my neck and I took it off and climbed down and went free. I thought they had believed me hanged, and left me to rot. But the land into which I walked was not my England, for I had truly died, and yet risen, like

Christ himself. Well," he added, catching Stella's look, "maybe not exactly like Christ, I must admit. My pride is speaking there. Someone came to me, an antlered man, and said that the manner of my life and death made me suited for the Hunt and would I ride with them, for coin and for adventure? I knew then that my soul belonged to Hell, my horns already grown and my eyes aflame, and I had no choice. The leader of the Hunt was different then, but later he was slain and I took control, as I had wanted long to do."

"Right. So when he was slain, if you're actually also dead, and in a sort of afterlife, where did he go?"

"I don't know. To Hell?"

"Do you know whether Hell actually exists?"

"I confess I do not. But I do believe in it. It is always at my back. I see its flames in my dreams."

This did not sound like fun, Stella thought. But she wasn't about to fall into the trap of feeling sorry for him.

"And what about Mum? Do you – love her?"

"As much as I can love anyone. But love is not in my nature, I think. I would not willingly hurt her. Perhaps you should be asking whether she loves me."

"That's going to be a bit tricky, given that she can't even see you at the moment, according to you, let alone remember who you are."

"It might be better that way." He gave her a sidelong glance. "It is not like me to be unselfish."

"Yeah, I got that. And what about me? What's with the swimming thing?"

"First, the court."

And then they were back to the dress, which Stella, on principle, refused to wear.

BEE

Bee and Serena had got back to Penhallow about two in the morning. They had been relieved to return to the car and find it not only still there, but with the tarmacked road running once more before it. Neither of them felt like searching the area for the person who had taken Stella's phone, but what if Stella herself was there, perhaps hurt or unconscious, in the gorse bushes? So Bee and Serena had searched, remaining in sight all the time, while Dark kept watch. They had found nothing and no one. Eventually Bee suggested going back to the car and, feeling rather downcast and guilty that they had not done all they could, drove home without further incident.

Bee had gone straight to bed and slept dreamlessly, knowing that Dark was there. She woke to sunlight at half past eight and hurried downstairs to find that Serena, looking exhausted, had got up before her and told their story to the others.

"Her bed hasn't been slept in," Ver said. "I went up to check."

Luna said, "I think we ought to speak to the Thorns."

"Yes, I think so, too. I feel that they are allies. I might be wrong."

"At least they know the territory," Sam said.

Bee made toast and at nine, phoned Jane Thorn.

"Shit," was the first thing that Jane said, when Bee had finished her story.

"Yes, that's more or less what I said."

"I know the Hand and Bundle," Jane told her. "And I know the story behind it. I'll come up to Penhallow now."

Bee felt a little better after this, as though things were moving forwards.

"Don't worry," Serena said. "We'll find her. And Stella's tough as old boots."

Bee admitted that this was true, but after Alys' disappearance, then Ben's, this additional vanishing was proving ragged on the nerves, since by now she had a better idea of where Stella might have gone and who she might have met. Or even worse, what.

"Have you contacted Ace?" Luna said to Serena. Her sister's hand flew to her mouth.

"Christ! No, I haven't, and he ought to have been the first person I thought of."

"Well, you couldn't have phoned him last night, anyway. Stella told me he doesn't have a mobile and you can only get hold of him via the pub, which would have been shut. Still will be, actually, unless they've taken to opening the doors at nine o clock in the morning in London."

Serena informed her that it was still usually a respectable eleven a.m.

"I'll ring them as soon as they open."

"What about her friend Davy? And her landlady? On the boat?"

"Yes, of course!"

Serena went out onto the terrace and shortly could be seen talking into her phone. Just as she came back in, Jane Thorn's little Mini pulled into the drive.

"Right," Serena said, when they were assembled in the dining room. "I've made my phone calls. Davy's going down to Southwark now; says she's taken a few days off anyway. Evie's alerted but sitting tight. There's not really anything they can do until Ace gets on the case."

"Who is Ace?" Jane asked. "Oh, your friend in London. Good thinking."

"Thanks for coming over, Jane."

"I know the Hand and Bundle. It's not the first time there's been trouble up there but it's not a hot spot or anything, otherwise I would have mentioned it."

"Don't ee go out on the moor!" Sam said, sepulchrally.

"It's not far from some Roman ruins: there was a whole village up there at one point. But by 'trouble' I mean stuff like hauntings, not actual abductions."

"Why is it called the Hand and Bundle, though?"

"There's an old folk tale that a woman around these parts was forced by the Devil to give up her baby. A sort of reverse changeling. And there's lots of stories about the knockers and the fogous."

"What's a 'foo-goo'? And what did she do with the baby?"

"A fogou is a shaft in the earth, possibly prehistoric. The story says that she put the baby in a bundle and took him to the Mount, and didn't bring him back."

"What happened to him?"

"The story doesn't say."

"Stories never do," said Luna.

"I'm wondering if the 'Devil' was the Morlader. But I also wonder if one of the Hounds might be Hob's father? Stella said that Hob reminded her of them."

"Maybe. I suppose some stories do tell you. People end up dead, though, or blinded because they've seen something they shouldn't have seen. Sorry. That was pretty tactless."

"Don't worry. What do you think we should do?" Bee asked.

"I think we should go up to the Bundle in daylight."

In the event, Bee and Ver went up with her, in Jane's car. It was tacitly understood that Dark would join them there. Serena and Luna would hold the fort back at the house, with Serena on the other end of the phone to field any calls, since Jane said that reception was erratic up in the countryside. It was a very different journey to the one that they had made at midnight. Cornwall was at its summer best, the light pouring down onto the land as if from an upturned cup, leaching the fields and hills into a sequence of faded green and tawny and mauve, with the sea silver in the distance. Jane rolled down the windows to catch the breeze. She parked outside the Hand and Bundle with ease, since the pub was still closed.

"We can't really go poking about the pub," Bee said.

"We could pretend to be foreign," Ver remarked.

"I don't think my acting skills are up to it. We need Ward."

"We can take a look at the cottage, though," said Jane.

Bee led them down the slope to the place where they had found Stella's phone. The byre was still there, but only just. Unlike the previous night, when it had sported a roof and walls, however rudimentary, it was now only a low outline of stone in the long grass. Sheep and rabbit droppings were liberally scattered about.

"It wasn't like this last night," Bee explained. "And there was a rush light in the window."

She followed Jane into the empty space. No furniture remained, only harebells in the lee of the wall. She could hear a lark high above, the song pouring down the air, the bird itself a dot against the blue of the sky. Inside the byre, it was very quiet, save for the song of the lark. Bee broke the silence.

"There's clearly nothing here. Can you –?" She hesitated. How to put it? Sense something? Feel something?

"I'm no psychic," Jane said, as though she had caught the thought, and given the lie to her words. "It just feels like an abandoned ruined byre to me."

"Same here. Ver?" Sam's gran had joined them, picking her way through the stones. But the old woman shook her head.

"Not a peep, lovey."

And Dark echoed the same. "No ghosts."

They scouted around, hoping to locate further clues in daylight, but there was nothing to be found. On returning to the car, they found the landlady of the Bundle, clad in jeans and a pinny, washing the step.

"Morning! Oh, it's you, Jane. You're a bit early for a pint."

"I rang you last night," Bee said. "Looking for my sister's phone. We thought we'd come up and see if she'd dropped it in the car park."

"You're welcome to look. I had a good search last night in the bar but I couldn't find anything. Mind you, we had a lot of covers last night, a lot of kids from out of the county, so I wouldn't mind betting someone picked it up." She pushed a strand of russet hair back into her scrunchie. "No harm intended, I'm sure, but you know what teenagers are like."

"Too right," said Ver.

"I had a look in the loo, as well. Hope she finds it. It's a nightmare, losing your phone."

The landlady was clearly busy, so they did not linger. Once they were back on the road and heading back to Penhallow, Jane said, "I've had an idea."

SERENA

To try to take her mind off Stella's disappearance, Serena went up the stairs to the cupola with a sketchpad and her phone, hoping to jot down some drawings. The nautical styling of the Thorn's house had given her some ideas. She did not expect to be able to concentrate properly, what with worry and lack of sleep, but sketching was a calming pastime and could be put down and taken up without difficulty. As it was, once ensconced on the comfortable cushions of the window seat, she found her gaze drifting out to sea.

From here, the view was panoramic. She could see down into the garden, where Luna was strolling amongst the lavender with Rosie in her arms, and then the edge of the cliff. The glitter from the morning water had almost swallowed the Mount, bars of shadow appearing across the bay, but the sun was nowhere near its noonday peak. Serena opened the window catch and the faintest stir of air crept in. She dropped her gaze from the shimmering horizon and began to draw.

A gull cried suddenly, a wailing mew. Serena blinked, glanced at her phone. Half an hour had gone by, as she had sketched the frothy gown that was occupying her mind's eye. But she had not drawn the gown at all, only thought she had. A ship in full sail raced across the sketchpad, wings unfurled, charcoal-dark. Her figurehead was a rotting skeleton, a moon rode the shoulder of her sails. Serena gaped at the illustration. She did not know enough about sailing ships to draw one; had she consciously tried, a child's boat would have surely occupied the page, a semicircle, a line for the mast, a triangle for the sail. But this ship looked alive. Serena sought the horizon again; all was calm and blue. Her phone shrilled. She grabbed at it, saw an unfamiliar number, answered anyway.

"Serena, that you? I'm in a phone booth," Ace's voice said.

"I didn't think there were any left! I thought they were all Little Libraries and defibrillator units!"

"I have spent all of 60p," said Ace, "And I expect to get my money's worth. I've just seen Davy Dearly. Says Stella's gone AWOL. I sent Davy round to Blake's. I'm waiting for her now. The pub's not open yet, which I consider to be a gross oversight on the part of society. When I was a young nipper, some boozers never shut."

"I think it was the war," Serena said vaguely.

"Yes, you're right; I remember that. Wanted everyone to rise and shine nice and early so they could put in a hard day down the munition factories. Anyway. We'll hear what Bill's got to say but Davy has some ideas. She's coming to see you. *We're* coming to see you, in fact."

"Really? Fantastic!" The prospect of reinforcements cheered Serena up no end. "Is she driving? Because you can get a train from Paddington straight through to Penzance."

"We won't be coming by train," Ace said.

Serena went back down the stairs to find Jane's car pulling into the drive. Once assembled in the kitchen, she told Bee about the phone call.

"Okay, great. The more the merrier. I'm relieved, I must say. Ace will know what to do. I've left a message for Nick, as well, to keep an eye out back in Somerset."

"It's a few hours' drive from London, obviously," Jane said.

"I think Ace and Davy had other travel options in mind."

"Oh! Right, how stupid of me." Jane rubbed her eyes. "Sorry, I'm not thinking straight."

Bee said, "I had an idea about contacting Jane's friend, in case she's heard anything. Also named Jane."

"Miss Parminter," Jane Thorn said. "At A La Ronde. That's a good idea."

"She did, after all, make the initial introductions."

"And she has a better idea than I do of the lie of the land," Jane added. "But I have a feeling, from what you've told me, that Mr Spare and Ms Dearly might get there first."

"Best if Serena and I do it," Bee said, briskly, but from the corner of her eye Serena caught sight of Luna's face. Luna's expression of disappointment was fleeting, but it was enough.

"Luna," Serena said. "Would *you* like to do it? I don't want you to feel left out, like *she's a mum and so she has to sit it out now.* Do you know what I mean?"

"I'm sorry, Luna," Bee said. "I think that was at the back of my mind. But I can stay with Rosie. In fact, it'll be lovely."

"All right," said Luna, with a deep breath. "Part of me does want to stay. But part of me wants to see A La Ronde, too."

"Then you and I will go," Serena said. And they did. All the way up the stairs, as it turned out.

"Da – someone we know has a map," Luna said, as they went up to the cupola. "Of the entry ways in London."

"We know some of the coastlines," Jane said. "I don't mean 'the line of the actual coast.' I mean the points by which you can travel. Like leylines, but by sea."

It had not occurred to Serena that leylines might be international, but she supposed it made sense. They were not very far from France, after all. But perhaps there were leys which only ran across the sea?

"You can sit on the window seat before we try and contact A La Ronde," Jane said. "Take a look."

"I've spent a bit of time up here already. It's lovely." But she remembered her drawing of the ship and something inside her shrank a little.

Jane smiled. "Look again."

Serena did so, leaning her forehead against the glass and looking towards the south. At first she could see nothing, but then there was a shimmering change. A masted ship, full sailed, rode at anchor, under a crescent moon. The sky was green and so was the sea. A warm wind touched Serena's brow and she smelled spice, cinnamon-strong, and other, unknown odours.

"The tropics?" she said aloud.

"Yes. The Windwards, I think. Try the western window."

Serena moved around the clock of the cupola. To the west: a wild sunset coast, a surging sea against granite cliffs. To the north: an iceberg floated, serene in a pink and blue sea and she shivered with remembered cold. To the east: unfamiliar islands, a red-sailed junk rode a warm wind.

"Can I have a go?" asked Luna.

"Yes, of course." Serena relinquished the window seat to her sister.

"I can see a ship," Luna said after a moment, looking south. "An old fashioned one. And there's an island behind it. And a star."

"I saw the ship, too," Serena said.

"Do you know which ship it is?" Luna said to Jane Thorn.

"It's probably my umpteenth great grandfather's ship, the *Stargazy*. But I can't be sure. If you try to look through a telescope, all you see is the bay."

"Did he sail from here?" Serena said. "From Tretorvic, I mean."

"Yes, long ago. She is a merchant ship. We have an old box that smells of spice. He brought it back as a present for my great grandmother, full of cinnamon and cloves."

"What happened to the *Stargazy*?" said Luna.

"She was wrecked in a storm. Great grandfather survived, though. Family legend says he clung to a reef with the first mate for three days until they were rescued. They were lucky. And he came back to Cornwall on a Navy ship and never went to sea again, because his leg had been crushed in the wreck. I suppose he could have had a wooden one, like a pirate."

"And a parrot," Luna said.

"Yes, and a parrot. I say he never went to sea again. I meant, when he was alive. After he died, that was a different matter. He and the *Stargazy* seem to have been reunited. He loved her so, after all."

There was a moment of silence.

"But what does it mean, that we both saw all those places, and your grandfather's ship?" Serena asked.

"It means that the sea roads are open. And that the *Stargazy* is coming home."

BEE

Bee, left downstairs with Ver and Sam minding the baby, was trying to clean the house to take her mind off things. It wasn't really working, because Penhallow's mistress had left it spotless, and they hadn't been there for long. Having tidied the kitchen, Bee went up to the bedrooms and hoovered the trail of sand that Stella had left across the rug. She tried to force the thought from her mind that this might be all that was left of Stella.

"Don't think like that," Dark said, from the window seat.

Bee jumped. "God! That was sudden. And what are you – suddenly telepathic?"

"It showed upon your face," he said.

"I don't think she's dead. I think I'd know."

Dark smiled. "I think I would know, too, because the first thing that your sister would do would be to come back and berate me."

Bee stared at him. "Yes, that's true, of course. You're still here, and Grandfather. But when Mum went missing, neither you nor Abraham could tell us if she had died or not."

"No, we did not know. Nor did we know where she had gone, for she left no trace and covered her tracks. But she had not in fact died. And Stella's disappearance is a different matter."

"I do feel sure that she was taken, though. Stolen away. She wouldn't have just disappeared on her own initiative in the middle of an evening with friends unless something very urgent had happened or someone had abducted her. And she wouldn't have left her phone. She's not a tidy person but she's not that careless with her possessions and her phone's really important to her."

"And the friends seemed to remember bringing her back," Dark said. "Do you want to go down to the cliff, to see if there's anything to be seen? To see if anything changes?"

Bee found that she did. It was a lovely morning, even if any holiday feelings had, for the moment, fled. With Dark, she went down to the bottom of the garden to the edge of the thrift-decked rocks, the pink fuzzy heads of the flowers tossed in the sea wind over the shining bay and the marguerites nodding over the waves. Gulls screamed and mewed above their heads as they stood looking out across the water.

"If I knew where she had gone," Dark said, unhappy, "You know that I would follow her."

"I know. I remember the *Golden Hind*. And Drake."

"I may try to call upon him again," Dark said. "If she does not come home. Perhaps, since we are on the coast, there's been word across the sea roads."

Bee reached out and took his hand. "Thank you, Ned."

STELLA

After the argument about the dress, Drum had left Stella alone for a day or so. She kept an eye on the sun, a bright silvery disc chasing its course through the clouds, just in case time decided to skip and hop. But the sun remained constant, sinking down into its fiery bed amid a mass of black cloud that heralded a storm. Stella was exceptionally bored. She tried to sleep, and succeeded to some degree. She ate the food that was provided: bread and cheese, with an earthenware mug of milk, and a chunk of meat that she decided was probably mutton. Stella, having been a vegetarian since childhood, hated herself for this but there was no point in starving. The food was brought to the door along with a rough woolly blanket: that was a plus, thought summer-clad Stella, and both were shoved through a grille by the one-eyed huntsman. He looked sour, but also terrified, and she thought that was a good thing.

"When's Drum coming back?" she demanded, but he mutely shook his head and hastened away. All she could see through the grille was the opposite stone wall. She made a thorough investigation of the room – it couldn't really be called a cell – but there was no means of exit except the window, which was a slit too narrow to crawl through. Stella had fallen off a high building into a river before now, but she couldn't entirely control suddenly becoming an otter and what if she didn't? Even in murine form, the fall might well kill her. And unlike her previous journey, no little door suddenly appeared.

There was a tiny side chamber, containing a hole in the floor for purposes which were olfactorily obvious. Stella, holding her breath, tried to peer down the hole, but there was no sign of light and even if there had been, she thought that the shaft almost certainly opened out above the sea, presenting her with the same issue as the window.

She stood at the window, watching the last of the light die. A single star hung low over the sea. It had become very cold and Stella was grateful for the blanket. There was the crack and rumble of thunder in the distance. She had been right about the storm. The sound died away and she did not hear the door open, but suddenly Drum was there.

"You're not wearing your pretty dress, Stella."

"Too freaking right. I'd prefer one of your pistols. You don't need two, surely?"

"In fact," Drum hesitated. "I actually do. They don't respond well to sea air. There's a weak spark in the damp."

"I see!"

"Don't test that, Stella."

"Okay. But I'm still not wearing that frock."

Drum gave a barely audible sigh. "All right. You win. On the question of the dress, at least. I implore you to wear this, however." He held out a hooded cloak, midnight blue velvet, spangled with the sequin of constellations. The hood was framed with soft, dense fur.

"That had better not be otter," Stella said.

Drum bit back a smile. "I think it's mink."

"Fine," Stella said, though it wasn't. "All right. Purely for the sake of warmth, you understand, I'll wear it."

"Thank you, Stella."

Stella wrapped herself in the cloak, fighting the urge to put the hood up. *You cannot hide, Stella, in a hood.* It fell beyond her ankles, which purely from the point of view of style was a good thing; cloaks and Converse do not really sit well together.

"After you," Aiken Drum said, with a gallant bow.

Stella, feeling oddly grand in her borrowed cloak, swept through the door ahead of him. She could ditch the cloak and take off – but a Hound was waiting outside in the passage. He gave her a nasty grin and Stella was suddenly glad that Drum was right behind her. The Hound said nothing. He turned and began to walk away, so that Stella was sandwiched between the two men. She wondered if Drum knew that the Hound's twin had sought out the Morlader but thought twice about mentioning the fact: it might make him angry and, anyway, perhaps it was best to keep back that piece of information in case it proved useful later.

The passage was stone, its buttresses ornamented with carved faces. They looked Medieval; Stella was reminded of the cloisters of a cathedral. Unlikely that Drum would have set foot in a cathedral, though – perhaps he would burst into flames on holy ground? They came to the head of a flight of winding stone steps and Stella was again reminded of churches: the chapter house in Wells had a similar flight. She was thankful to be wearing sensible footwear. Drum indicated that she was to go down, so, picking up the hem of the long cloak, Stella followed the Hound and at length found herself in a large hall.

This, too, was stone, and not even the immense fire blazing in the grate at the far end of the room could do much to dispense the dampness and chill. The fireplace was big enough for a man to stand upright in, and the walls were covered with weaponry: axes and huge swords which Stella supposed to be broadswords. She made a mental note of some smaller swords for future reference. The prospect of running the Hound through was appealing. A banqueting table, carved from dark oak, ran the length of the room.

"Are we meeting someone in here?" she asked Drum.

"No. We're going somewhere else." He smiled, not without malice. "Your coach awaits, my lady."

"Seriously? Let's hope it's not a pumpkin." But his blank look told her that he did not understand the reference.

"You ride ahead," Drum said to the Hound, who went to an enormous, iron studded door and wrenched it open, letting in a blast of cold salty air.

Outside, Stella saw that there was indeed a coach, a rickety looking contraption drawn by two restless black horses. It looked like the sort of thing one associated with ghosts and headless horsemen, but Stella thought it best not to say so. She also risked a quick look behind her: not a cathedral, but an extremely large, fort-like house. A grim place. A shadowy turret, perched on the sea ward side, gave her a clue as to the location of her imprisonment. Iron gates creaked, then clanged open.

"Hurry up," said Aiken Drum. "We don't want to be late."

172

LUNA

Luna did not know what it would mean for the *Stargazy* to come home. She was about to ask Jane Thorn that question when Jane raised her hand and placed it on the door. The air inside the cupola shimmered and shivered and they were somewhere else. Luna blinked. She could still see the cupola, but the wall behind her was covered in shells.

"Oh!" said Luna.

"Jane, my dear, I see you have guests," said an elderly lady. In a long grey dress and white mob cap, she should have looked severe, but her face was a kindly one, Luna thought. "Are you Miss Stella Fallow's sisters, perhaps?"

"Yes, that's right," Serena said.

"I have met her, and her young friend Davy. A boy's name, surely? Well, never mind. And Mr Spare was with them. Why, we are almost old friends by now. As you perhaps know, they came to my house," Miss Parminter said. "Where, in fact, you see me now."

"It's full of shells," Luna said.

"Yes. My doing, and that of my cousin, with whom I live. We chose to make the house in the form of a folly, but of course it is more than a house. It is a crossroads, for the sea ways."

Jane picked up a shell that had been sitting on the desk in front of Miss Parminter. Luna could see the opposite window of the cupola through her form, very faintly. But it was not so much that Miss Parminter was transparent, ghostly, as that the two places had become superimposed upon one another. "You gave one of these to Stella, Jane."

"Yes. A letter of introduction. I thought it might be of use, since the Misses Fallow were coming to Cornwall, and sadly it seems that I was right. Louisa has told me that Stella has gone missing."

"Yes. Last night, with no word. And we don't know where she's gone, except we fear that she's been abducted."

"Has the ship been spotted?" Miss Parminter said. Luna assumed that she meant the *Stargazy*, but perhaps not, for Jane Thorn answered,

"No. Not since the winter."

"Then it is surely due, though I have heard no word."

Miss Parminter turned to Luna and Serena.

"When folk go missing, from these coasts, under unusual circumstances, it is often because they have seen or interrupted something that they should not have done."

"You mean, like smugglers?" Luna said, thinking of the pub. "You mentioned that when we visited you."

"Yes, smuggling or wrecking have traditionally been the two drivers of the Cornish economy, unfortunately, along with fishing and farming. The same people, sometimes," Jane added.

"But how would Stella have stumbled across anything like that in broad daylight in the middle of having a meal in a pub?"

"I don't know. But I fear the Morlader's involvement."

Jane Thorn said, smiling. "But I'm very pleased to see *you*, Miss Parminter. I'm bringing the girls to you, to see if you had heard anything. They have just looked through the glass, and glimpsed the *Stargazy*."

"Then surely that, too, is a sign that the ship is due," Miss Parminter said.

"I would think so."

"Which ship are you talking about?" asked Luna. "I thought at first you meant the *Stargazy*, but you didn't, did you?"

"No," Miss Parminter said. "We mean another ship."

Miss Parminter had signed off, with mutual good wishes. The shell-lined room had faded as gracefully as it had arrived, leaving them alone in the cupola. But Luna found that the day was later along than it should have been, and the sky was darkening – not with the onset of twilight, but with storm. A bank of cloud was building out to sea that had not been there that morning. She said as much to Jane.

"Storms can come in quickly here on the coast," Jane said.

It was not yet raining but a sudden gust of wind rattled the windows of the cupola.

"Does the weather often change so fast here, though?" Luna said. "I don't remember summers here being so wild."

"Oh, I do, Luna," Serena said. "There was one week where we never saw the sun and it poured every day. You might have been too little to remember that, though."

"Maybe. I remember a year where we played a lot of board games."

174

"That was a couple of years later. The weather wasn't quite so foul that year, but nearly. We taught you to play Monopoly, didn't we?"

"Early exposure to the evils of capitalism," Luna said.

Fat spatters of rain were starring the windscreen and the sea was a distant murk. The wind was tearing through the laurels below, thrashing the leaves. Serena stepped back from the window.

"I don't want to alarm anyone," she said, "but that castle on the island, on the Mount, is all lit up. Is that normal?"

STELLA

Stella had not realised, prior to now, how uncomfortable stagecoach travel could be. She suspected that the roads weren't up to much, either. Perhaps belting down the M5 in this contraption might be smoother. She was forced to clutch a strap on the side of the seat in order to avoid being flung from it, being equally averse to clutching Aiken Drum.

"I know it's bumpy," said the latter.

"You're not wrong. Jesus! These things must have overturned for a pastime."

"They were easy to stop," Drum said, then gave her an uneasy glance from his goat's eyes, as though he might have put his foot in it. But Stella did not need reminding that her travelling companion had been a highwayman. She said, "Did they have highwaywomen, as well?"

Drum laughed.

"Why yes. The Wicked Lady of Markyate Cell, and more. Gentlewoman impoverished after Cromwell's time and others."

"Excellent."

"You are of an equality-loving frame of mind, Stella." Now the yellow gaze had become appraising. "Perhaps *you* would care to join us?"

Stella was horrified to find that, for a second, this was almost enticing.

"My mum would kill me," she said, to squash that thought.

"True, true." He seemed to accept this as a viable objection, somewhat to Stella's relief.

It would have been easier, perhaps, if she had been able to see out, but there were shades drawn down against the windows of the coach. Stella had heard of people who had been kidnapped taking note of the sounds along their route, but all she could hear was the howl of the wind slamming against the side of the coach and occasionally making it teeter alarmingly, and the drumming of the horses' hooves. Impossible to tell where they were going, since she didn't know where she was in the first place.

At least she didn't get travel sick. Had the coachmen of old been obliged to keep stopping to let passengers throw up?

Then, at last, the coach began to slow down and eventually it rattled to a halt. Stella could still hear the wind, but it was muffled and the buffeting had stopped.

"Okay," said Stella. "Are we here?"

"Not quite yet." Aiken Drum opened the carriage door and jumped down. "Allow me to assist."

"Cheers, but I'm fine," Stella said. She gripped the side of the coach and swung down the steps. It was not far and she did not want to touch Drum: on the occasions that she had done so, she had felt mildly and unpleasantly invaded, not in a physical sense, but a psychic one. A bristly, hairy, strong-smelling sense from which Stella flinched. She suspected it might be intentional, too, but she was determined not to let him see her revulsion. "Right, where are we?"

Her question was rapidly answered. The rumble and rush of a great wave breaking over the nearby sea wall nearly doused her. Drum grabbed her arm and dragged her back. They were standing at the landside end of the causeway to St Michael's Mount, but the causeway itself lay under water.

"We're not going across that," stated Stella, shaking her arm free.

"Not in the coach, no. We're waiting for the boat."

"The boat? In this?" The sea was a grey flecked churn under the flying moon. "You've got to be kidding me. It looks like a washing machine."

Drum laughed. "It's not so bad tonight. I've seen worse."

"I hope it's a massive boat with an engine."

"Wrong day and age. And you couldn't put up a sail on a night like this. It will be a rowing boat."

Stella was about to say, again, that he must be joking, but at this point the castle on the Mount flared into brightness. Stella gasped. She had seen the Mount lit up before at night, but by floodlights: glowing steadily across the dark water of the bay. This light was pale green and flickering, witch-fire, bale-fire, flying ragged pennants from the turrets into the storm.

"What the hell is that?" Stella whispered.

Drum's eyes flared gold. "It means her Ladyship's at home."

Ten minutes later, Stella was wishing she hadn't asked about the boat. It had appeared, seemingly out of nowhere, grinding up onto the beach, but the sea was so rough it could simply have been that Stella hadn't noticed it. Otterhood meant that the likelihood of drowning was probably somewhat reduced even in a violent sea; let's see how goats handle *that*, Stella thought vindictively of Aiken Drum. She briefly considered flinging herself over the side and making her escape, but the same logic held as at the tower: she could not guarantee physical transformation and she wouldn't last long in such a sea in human form. So she crouched in the bottom of the rowing boat, clinging to the gunwales alongside Drum, the Hound, and the rower: a huge man with a bushy beard, wearing oilskins. Any potential resemblance to Cap'n Birdseye was negated by the grimness of his expression. No sign of a smile in *that* beard, but maybe he was simply intent on the job in hand and hadn't wanted to pitch out on a night like this in the first place. Stella gave him a hopeful smile all the same, but did not receive so much as a flicker of acknowledgement, let alone any softening. Oh well.

Despite his grimness, however, the boatman rowed strongly. Stella could not see how he was even managing to keep it on course, but Adrian's comment about seas looking rougher than they appeared came to mind. Perhaps the skipper was used to it? The boat rode the waves like a roller coaster. It was hard to see anything through the incessant showers of spray – Stella's new cloak was soon soaked through and so was she – but occasionally a flicker of green fire shone and she thought they were getting closer. Like one of those nightmares, however, the journey seemed unending, until suddenly the boat rocked and jolted and ground up on what turned out to be a tiny fingernail of shingle beach. Stella was thrown forward, narrowly missing the boatman's lap. Drum hauled her back up.

"Out you get."

Stella was only too pleased to scramble onto the shore. Drum followed, and in the chancy light, Stella though he was looking paler.

"Seasick?" she asked, sarcastically. Rather to her surprise, Drum admitted, "I am not so good upon the waves as on land."

"That was super rough, though."

"And you, little otter?"

"I feel fine. Shaken but not stirred." It occurred to her that Drum probably didn't know who James Bond was.

"That's good. Off we go."

The Hound, who appeared completely unaffected by their short voyage, was striding up a flight of rough, foam-flecked steps which joined the top of the causeway. Stella and Drum followed and found themselves in front of an enormous door. The Hound hammered on it. Stella had visions of Boris Karloff, but the door swung soundlessly open and a small girl of perhaps thirteen or so appeared behind it, dressed in yellow muslin.

"Oh," she said without enthusiasm, when she saw who was standing there. "It's you."

"And good evening to *you*, too," Drum said.

"I suppose you'd better come in. We've been expecting you."

"Hi," Stella said, as they passed through into a courtyard. "I'm Stella. What's your name."

To her surprise, the girl gave her a sunny smile. "Stella. That's a pretty name, like a star. My name is Snipe."

"And are you one?" Stella asked, caught offguard, but the girl just said, "You're very wet. Would you like to stand by the fire for a while?"

"I'd bloody love to." To Drum, she said, "That's all right, isn't it? Good thing I didn't wear that lovely frock, isn't it? It would have been completely trashed by now."

"You have a point," Drum said, surprising her yet again. "Yes, we will both go. I do not care to appear before the court looking as though I have been shipwrecked."

To the Hound, he said, "Stay here."

Snipe led them in to a cavernous room, clearly part of the kitchens. A fire, of normal hue, was roaring away in the grate, which was as large as that in Drum's abode. A spit, currently unoccupied, ran along it.

"Come and stand as close as you can," Snipe said.

"We're gonna steam," Stella told her. But the heat was bliss, even if it did make Drum smell more strongly of goat. Since there had been no provision for washing back at the turret, Stella thought, an involuntary bath, even a salty one, had perhaps been no bad thing. Now that it seemed that Drum had a purpose for her – and was being not entirely unreasonable – and they were out of the boat, Stella felt that she might relax for a moment. Only a moment, mind. She didn't know what Drum's purpose was, or who she was about to meet, and the uncertainty gnawed away at her. Who was 'Her Ladyship'? She was about to ask Drum, but Snipe, who had left them by the fire, returned.

"She's ready for you now."

179

SERENA

"The castle's often floodlit," Jane said.

"Surely not at this time of day, though? And surely not green?"

Serena thought that Luna had a point, but Jane Thorn, staring out across the bay, said absently, "No, they sometimes do light it green. Not quite like that, though."

A towering thunderhead of cloud rose above the Mount, which flickered emerald above a frothing sea.

"What's happening?" Serena asked.

"I don't know. You can't go to the Mount at such times; the causeway's always underwater. I know there are people who live on the island, obviously, but they never talk about it. There are all kinds of rumours – that devils are haunting it, that a faery court is in residence, that the ghosts of drowned sailors come for a night on land... all sorts of stories. But even as we are: knowing this place, coming from it ancestrally, even we don't know for sure."

"You said your great grandfather's boat is coming back. The *Stargazy?*"

"Yes, that's right, Serena."

"What was his name?" Luna asked.

"Henry Thorn."

"I wonder if Dark has heard of him," Luna said.

"He would have sailed quite a long time after Dark's day. But I know time gets blurred and mixed up, so... The *Stargazy* was sailing in the eighteenth and nineteenth centuries. She wasn't a pirate ship. But Henry – my great plus grandfather – became obsessed with the legend of another ship, a bit like the captain in *Moby Dick* who's got a bee in his bonnet about hunting down the white whale. A ship called the *Balefire,* owned by the Morlader."

Serena recalled Jane saying that smugglers on these coasts sometimes smuggled more than lace and brandy; they also smuggled souls. They were in league with the wreckers and pirates, in league with the Morlader.

Now Jane said, "The Morlader's ship comes twice a year. It takes on a cargo of souls and transports them, then comes back with a – no pun intended – skeleton crew."

"Where does it take those souls?" Luna asked, wide-eyed.

"No one knows. The *Stargazy* is in pursuit; there are sometimes battles. At the end of the winter and at harvest-tide. And it's not far from harvest-tide now."

STELLA

Stella felt rumpled and salt-stained, but definitely warmer. It was easier to think, now; the chill had numbed her sufficiently for moment by moment survival to have been the main thing on her mind. But now Stella was contemplating escape. Or at least appeal. Perhaps she could throw herself on the mercy of Her Ladyship, whoever she was. Unless Drum had meant Elizabeth, of course. Stella quailed at the prospect of seeing that particular monarch again, but surely he would have said 'Her Majesty,' in that case. Fingers crossed it was someone else.

But what if it was somebody worse?

Telling herself that they would cross that bridge when they came to it, Stella followed Drum and Snipe into the upper reaches of the castle. It looked more recent than Drum's own grim stone house, with a tiled hallway and stained glass windows overlooking a twisting, polished staircase. There was still a faint odour of damp, however. When did the Mount date from? Stella had a vague idea that it had originally been Medieval and that parts of the current building might be Victorian, but she was not certain. Perhaps this place, like so many others, belonged to all times and none.

Snipe ran lightly up the stairs. They came out onto a broad landing. Through the coloured windows, Stella could see flickering fire; it cast patterns on the polished boards of the floor. Two great oak doors, studded with nails, stood before them and behind the doors Stella could hear a great throng of voices, all talking at once. Laughter rang out. How bad could this be?

The voices and the laughter ceased, as abruptly as a flock of starlings do, in that odd silent pause before they take flight. Then a voice began to sing. It was very high and sweet and something about it reminded Stella of the Behenian stars. The song snaked around herself and Aiken Drum and Snipe and caught them in their tracks, held them captive. Stella felt as though it was snaking into her brain, running through her veins, replacing her blood. It spoke to her of the sea, of the deep green ocean, the wild wave. The air was filled with the smell of salt. She took a breath, was back for a second on the summer shore of Tretorvic with the beach and the day stretching ahead of her, filled with promise and joy. Then the winter wind snatched the memory up and blew it away;

she was out on the deck of the strange sea fort, the Maunsell Fort where for a time, earlier in the year, she had stood and watched the searchlights and heard the siren which warned of enemy aircraft, the bombers sweeping in from Germany. Then that, too, was gone and the white sails of a ship roared above her head, catching the wind and sending the spray flying past her. The song stopped, as swiftly as it had begun.

"Wait," Snipe instructed them. She went to the doors and knocked, hard, three times. The doors swung open. "In you go," Snipe said.

Drum hung back, so that they could go in together. He did not offer Stella his arm, for which she was grateful. God forbid anyone should mistake them for a couple. She stepped through the door and saw an enormous hall, which must run the entire length of the castle. More stained glass, casting glints of green and gold onto the assembly below. People filled both sides of the room, seated in tiers rather like the theatre. Stella had, back in the winter, found herself in an amphitheatre beneath a building in London: the seating here was in two multiple rows, but the effect was the same. She stole a look at the left hand crowd. She saw beautiful faces, male and female and indeterminate, a tapestry of colours and textures, owl's eyes, cat's eyes, faces which flickered between bird and animal and human. Their sudden attention made Stella feel faint and hot; it rested upon her like a weight and it was difficult to bear. She took a deep breath. A woman in a long gown of silver and blue announced:

"Hunt Master Aiken Drum and Miss Stella Fallow."

There was a susurrus of interest. Straight ahead, at the end of the long clear passage between the two tiers of seats, Stella saw a throne. How odd: she could have sworn that it had not been there when they came in. On it sat a woman, and to Stella's relief, although she was wearing a crown, it was immediately obvious that it was not Elizabeth. Her hair was white, for a start, glinting with icy silver and spilling over her shoulders to the floor; her skin was a pale azure. Her gown was the colour of the sea, all blue and green and sprays of lace and fronds of tatters which perhaps actually were seaweed: they looked like it. The gown spread around the woman's feet and down the steps of the throne and to the floor. Stella frowned for a moment, as it looked as though the edges of the gown were moving, tidally in and out. She blinked; surely an optical illusion. The woman reminded her of someone but her head was still rather muzzy, mazed with the song.

"This is our Lady of the Island," a nearby man said to Stella, in quite a kindly fashion.

Stella managed a curtsey and the woman smiled.

"Come closer!" she called. Her voice was high and clear and sweet and Stella now knew who had been singing. She beckoned Stella forwards. "No, not you, Mr Drum."

Stella walked up to the throne, stopping a few feet away.

"You'll have to forgive me, your Ladyship," she said. "I'm not used to meeting the aristocracy."

"We are not formal here," the woman said, smiling, although Stella thought this was somewhat belied by the sumptuous surroundings. "Do you know who I am?"

"No, madam, I do not."

"I am the lady of this castle in this time. My name – well, you may call me Azenor." Her gaze flickered past Stella, to where Aiken Drum stood. "So. You are the Hunt Master's choice?"

"To be quite honest, Az – your Ladyship, I haven't the faintest idea what's going on. I've been kidnapped, held prisoner, and now brought here. How about just letting me go?"

Azenor gave Stella a look of extreme irritation, but Stella did not think that this was aimed at her.

"I was afraid that might be the case. I am sorry, Stella." She sounded sincere, but Stella was finding it hard to look into her eyes: they were summer morning blue and like the green eyes of Noualen the deer goddess, it was difficult to meet that gaze without feeling that you were falling into it. "All claimants have a right to choose a champion, and Aiken Drum chose you."

"Whatever for? And don't I get a say in the matter?"

"Unfortunately not."

"You're kidding me," Stella said, adding rather hastily, "Your Ladyship. Sorry."

"No, I understand. As for why he chose you, I presume he thought you were the best person for the job."

"Jesus, I don't have to *fight* someone, do I? Because I must say, if that's the case, Drum's made a really crap choice."

"No, you don't have to fight someone. You have to *find* someone."

184

Not again. "Story of my life," Stella said.

They were no longer in the big courtroom, but in a side chamber with a cold wind blowing straight off the sea through the open window. At some point – Stella could not have said when – dawn had come, but the light that now streamed in was an afternoon light, with a bright brassy sky. Yet she had been on the Mount, surely, for no more than a couple of hours. And she had no recollection of actually going to the chamber, either, or of seeing Azenor stand up. She took a quick peek under the table. Azenor's gown was definitely moving, like the rush of foam as the tide comes in, but more slowly.

Drum was also in the room, staring moodily out of the window.

"Who am I supposed to look for?" Stella said.

At this point, Azenor looked more human than she had done so far. Her face creased with worry. "It is my mother," she said. "I have had word that she is in danger, and Drum has already asked me for preference, so he must earn it. The two tasks can be conjoined."

"So if I succeed, in finding your mother, Drum – what? Gains your favour?"

"Yes."

"Preference over whom?"

"Over the sea challenger."

"Do you mean the Morlader?"

"He indeed. He has challenged the Hunt for land rights."

"He can't have them," Drum said, harshly.

"Could you unpack – I mean, could you explain that?" Stella said.

"Kernow – this country – is divided between the Hunt on the moors and the wrecking witch tribes of the coast. The Morlader wants his soul-hunting rights extended onto the moor. He has challenged Drum here, for them."

Drum made a disgusted sound and went to stand by the window, looking out.

Jane had given Stella the background to this. "The wreckers are like the Wild Hunt of the sea, right?"

Drum snorted, but Azenor said, "Yes, the wreckers and knockers, with the Gentlemen dealing with both. Each hunts souls. Both have asked me for my favour. I have thus set them a task: to set a champion to find my mother, since I cannot leave this castle, here at the edge of Lyonesse."

Stella did not think it politic to ask why Azenor was apparently confined here just yet.

"And if I succeed, you'll look favourably on Drum and uphold his claim, right?"

"Yes. But that depends how the Morlader's champion performs."

"And if I refuse?"

Azenor's eyes were sad. "Then I must leave you to the hands of the Hunt."

Stella, furious, turned to Drum.

"What would you do? Lock me up again? Kill me?"

"That's not what she meant."

"Then what did she mean?"

"Will you refuse, then?"

"I'll need a bit of time to think about it."

Aiken Drum bowed to her with a flourish.

"Take all the time you need. As long as it's less than an hour. The tide's on the turn."

BEE

The rain had not held off for long. By the time Serena and Luna had come down from the cupola, the clouds were once more building out across the Channel, the day casting a steely, stormy light. They held a council of war in the conservatory.

"Before we came downstairs," Serena said, while Jane was visiting the loo, "We discussed what to do. Jane thinks we ought to sit tight, here in the house. Hold the fort while they try and find out what's happening on the Mount."

"They are local, after all," Bee said. "They know the scene better than we do."

"Yes. It's not our fight, except for Stella. And I want to help the Thorns if we can. I like them. I think they're good women and we already have some history because of Miranda. But we don't really know what's going on."

"I don't care about the Hunt *or* the Morlader," Luna said. She was sitting in the big armchair, with Rosie on her lap.

"No, sod the lot of them. I don't really care who wins, as long as we're all right and the Thorns are all right, and no one else gets caught up in it if they're innocent. It's like being in the middle of a gangland turf war. You see enough of that in London. Though perhaps not where I live."

"That's basically what it is, Serena. Ancient gangs and tribes."

"I felt a bit sorry for the cast-out Hound," Luna said. "I know I shouldn't have but I did."

"I actually felt a tiny bit sorry for Drum," Bee said. "Even if he's a bastard. I suppose it's the great British impulse to take the side of the underdog."

"Yeah – literally in the case of the Hound. Who seems to have gone off with the Morlader anyway, according to what you saw, Serena."

"All the people in the otherlands seem so marginalised. Scraping together bits and pieces of territory to live in."

"Not just the otherlands," Serena said. "If you walk along Regent's Canal, bang smack in the middle of the city, you'll see people living in benders and tents."

"Well, there are plenty of them round our way," Bee said.

"Yes," said Luna. "Or in decrepit old vans. Hey, I'm one of them. But I'm just pretending, really. I could live at Mooncote if Bee would put up with me. Sam's the real deal. So is Ver."

"You're not pretending," Sam said, quietly.

"I don't judge anyone on where they live," Ver said. "I've known plenty of scumbags who lived in benders and caravans and plenty of lovely folk who lived in big posh houses – look at Nick. And the other way round. I just reckon it's people being people and leave it at that. I can see the Hunt's point of view but they're still also scumbags as far as I'm concerned."

"So do we do as Jane suggests?" Bee said. "Sit tight?"

"I think we should do what Jane says," said Ver.

If only, Bee thought much later, they'd been able to.

Bee was the last one to bed that night. The wind howled and raged around the house, but when Bee took Moth outside for a final pee in the garden, she found that it was not all that wet. The rain sounded worse from inside Penhallow than it actually was. She looked across to the Mount and saw that it now lay in darkness. The sea was running high, driven before this big south westerly and the wind was strong enough that Bee did not care to go too close to the edge of the cliff. She wondered how safe Penhallow was, up here on this headland: there had been plenty of cases around the south coast of houses losing chunks of their garden, or even sliding down the cliff. Penhallow's cliff seemed solid enough, and the garden was a long one, but it was a disquieting thought. Bee had a moment's gratitude for Mooncote, safe in its vale. Mind you, they'd had floods and with the possibility of the sea rising due to climate change, perhaps nowhere was entirely safe... Maybe, like Luna, she ought to listen to the Shipping Forecast more regularly. With this thought at the forefront of her mind, Bee ushered Moth inside and firmly closed the door.

The radio was on. Hadn't Bee just been thinking about the forecast? She thought she'd switched it off, not wanting to disturb those who had gone to bed. But the calm voice recited the litany:

"*Shannon... Rockall... Malin... Hebrides...*"

Bee washed the glasses and put the cups into the dishwasher. She heard Moth's claws clicking on the flagstones, then up the stairs as the lurcher sought his rest with his people.

"...visibility, poor... Fastnet... Scilly... Lyonesse..."

Bee frowned. Was there a weather station called Lyonesse, after the old drowned lands off the end of the Cornish coast? She didn't remember hearing that name in the Shipping Forecast before. She tugged at the blind to draw it down over the window. Something flared in the garden, a tiny light. Was someone out there lighting a cigarette? Bee peered through the window. More sparks joined the first, flashing through the wet night. Bee stood frozen for a moment, then leaped as something touched her shoulder.

"Bee? It's me." Dark spoke softly. "There's someone in the garden. Pretend you haven't seen."

"Do you know who?" Bee breathed. "Is it the Morlader?"

"I think so." Reflected in the darkness beyond the window, Bee could only see herself in the glass, not Dark.

Forcing herself to act normally, Bee reached out and tugged the blind halfway down. She turned, but she could hear voices now, speaking low and urgently outside. She went to the kitchen door and, once out of sight of the window, ran as fast as she could up the stairs and into Sam and Luna's bedroom.

"Sam! Luna, wake up —" But the bedroom was empty, the bed unmade. Moth was nowhere to be seen. Bee went into Serena's room at the end of the corridor. No one, and Ver, too, had gone.

Shit, shit, shit, thought Bee. She went back down the stairs, avoiding the kitchen, and into the conservatory, which lay in darkness. But there was a figure standing by the glass door at the end. Bee froze again, but as her eyes adjusted she saw that it was not the man with sparks around his head, but Louisa Thorn. Louisa was beckoning. Bee ran to the door and opened it as quietly as she could.

"Bee, sorry to turn up in the middle of the night, but the wreckers are here."

"Everyone else has gone!"

"What? Where?"

"I don't know!" Bee whispered.

"Come with me, both of you."

Bee turned and saw that Dark was once again at her shoulder.

"You can't fight them here, Bee. The *Stargazy* is on her way – you'll be safe there."

"Bee, let's go," Dark said urgently. "If no one else is in the house, it doesn't matter if the wreckers come." She could hear someone knocking on the front door, a tiny sound that nonetheless sent a chill through her bones.

"But where *is* everyone?"

"Penhallow has its own methods of defence," Louisa said. "Perhaps it's split you up and sent you in different directions, away from your enemies."

In the kitchen, the Shipping Forecast droned on.

"Wind, northeasterly... visibility, very poor..."

"All right," Bee said, and stepped through the door.

They set off down the cliff path, the steep, zigzagging route that took them down the cliff to the little bay below. Out in the bay, the Mount was once more flickering with fire. Behind the island, the sky was black with storm cloud under an edge of moonlight.

"I don't like this weather," Louisa Thorn said, gruffly, as if she did not care to admit it.

"No," Bee agreed. "It feels wrong."

Dark turned. He had gone in front, traversing the path with a sailor's sure footed ease. Occasionally Bee glimpsed the gorse through his sleeve or the flick of his coat.

"Don't worry. We won't be out in it for long." Louisa said. "I hope."

Soon, they came down onto the shore. At lower tide, this led around to the main beach but now the sea was racing in, scouring the sand with a frothy lace and snatching it back again. It would not be long, Bee thought, before the sand was entirely covered.

Louisa reached out a hand. "Bee." She took it: a strong, short fingered hand, cold in her clasp, then reached out with her other hand to take Dark's.

"What do we do now?" Bee asked.

"Just wait."

Bee looked down at the froth around her feet and hoped that the wait would not be a long one. The Mount looked at once very big, towering over them, and then suddenly very far away. She blinked and shivered. The wind was rising, swinging due south, chasing the big breakers out on the bay. Bee tasted spray. *...visibility, poor,* said a voice... She looked up, water blinded, and saw a great white billow above, the wave immense. She hung onto Dark's hand as tightly as she could but the wave was coming, curling, thundering down... Louisa was calling something: it made no sense. Bee shouted out.

Then spat sea water over the rail. Hard boards plunged beneath her; she staggered, but Dark pulled her upright and hauled her onto a bench. The white billow was a sail, huge, one of many, driving the ship forward into the spray. Sunlight flared up, dazzling.

"Oh wow," Bee said.

"I would not let you drown," said Dark, fiercely.

"Ned, where are we?" Bee turned to him. "This isn't the *Hind*."

"No," Louisa Thorn pointed at the carved winged figurehead, mounted on the prow and visible as the ship reared up. An angel, with a crown of stars. "It's the *Stargazy*. My great great grandfather's ship."

STELLA

The boat took a long time to arrive. Perhaps Boatman Grim was wrestling with the tide. Stella wished she could have waited in Snipe's warm kitchen: she was getting cold again. Then, suddenly, the boat was there. She had not seen it approach.

In the end, she had taken her hour, but she had agreed to be Drum's champion. She did not care about Drum or the Morlader, or who won their contest, but she did not like to think about what might happen – not only to herself, but to her sisters and her mother and her friends – if she did not agree. After all, she had already assisted one supernatural being, Noualen, in a quest, with some success. Perhaps she could become some sort of consultant? If she survived.

Aiken Drum helped her into the boat, with an ostentatious gallantry that Stella did not feel was needed.

"Are we going back to your house?" she asked. Drum did not reply. The boatman pushed off and they were once more out in the bay. Stella hung onto the gunwhale; it was impossible to avoid a second drenching. She looked back at the Mount. The fire had gone, perhaps swallowed by the lowering sky. Any brightness about the day had vanished. Impossible, too, to keep track of time. The sun was not high, but it had dropped beneath a heavy bank of cloud. Only a livid yellow gleam betrayed its passage.

"What is that?" Aiken Drum said, suddenly, sharply.

"What's what?" Stella squinted into the churning spray.

She couldn't see a thing, but the boatman grunted, "Marshfire."

"I see it," Drum said. This time his voice was uncertain. And Stella could see it, too: an icy blue flicker just above the waves, like captive lightning. The boatman turned, the oars snapped up and they were heading directly into the blue glint. Then it was all around, just as the green flames had licked about the Mount. It was not dazzling, but a coldly gentle light. It sapped Stella's will and strength; she released her hold on the gunwhale before realising that she had done so. Aiken Drum turned towards her and spoke but she did not hear what he said: his lips moved as if under water. Stella looked up and saw swirls of colour overhead. They were mesmerising. Dark, vertical lines drifted across them. Stella frowned. Then, all of a sudden, they made sense.

They were reeds, very tall, and ending in fluffing bulrush heads. But reeds did not grow far out to sea. Stella looked over the side of the boat and saw that they had entered a narrow channel of water, brackish and oily with cold. She glanced up to mention this to Drum and the boatman and saw that they were becoming transparent. She could see the reeds through Drum's body. Drum and the boatman began to withdraw. As if in a dream, Stella watched as they and the boat separated from the boat in which she sat, as though someone had overlain a tracing of two men and a boat over a drawing of Stella and her own vessel. Something had divided it into two boats. They sailed away through the reeds and were lost. There was a sudden golden glint, a flare of the last light of the sun before it sank below the horizon, leaving Stella with the marshfire lightning flickering before her, leading the boat on.

It seemed to Stella that the task itself had taken her in hand, outside of her own volition. The task, her quest, was a living thing, the marshfire embodied it. Its azure fire reminded her of her grandfather's spirit in the churchyard of Hornmoon, but when she spoke to it – *"Who are you?"* – it did not respond.

Stella now felt wide awake, the lassitude had passed. She looked for oars, a tiller – but the boat was bare of these. It followed the dancing fire obediently through the channels and runnels, redolent of rotting vegetation and salt water. The great reeds were so tall that Stella could not see where they were going. The channels curved, a watery maze. Stella closed her eyes, pursed her lips and tried to think otter. She'd be better off as beast than woman in this liminal environment. She could feel her otter self, far inside, a seed, but she could not bring it to fruition. She gave a sigh of frustration and opened her eyes to see that they had come to the heart of the maze, a round eye of open glassy water.

Across this inner lake, a hut perched on stout wooden stilts. The boat headed directly for it, despite Stella's efforts to grasp the prow and divert it. At the foot of a rough flight of steps, not high, the boat finally stopped. The message was clear: *out you get*. Stella stood, rocking the boat ominously, and hopped onto the lower step, steadying herself as best she could: there was no railing. To her consternation, the boat moved backwards as she did so. She grabbed at it but it slid out of reach.

"Shit!" said Stella. The boat seemed to have a life of its own. It glided backwards and was soon lost among the reeds. She looked up to see a bluelight glitter, hovering above the closed door of the hut. Stella climbed the steps and pushed it open.

BEE

Dark, as a sailor, knew the etiquette of being passengers on someone else's vessel.

"Don't get in the way. They're busy. Someone will speak to us soon."

Bee nodded. On the *Hind*, even with the water placid as milk below, the boat had seemed very flimsy to her, a fragile protection against the might of the sea. And this boat, though bigger, seemed equally vulnerable: a boast of man in the face of the waves. She told herself that she could always fly, that if the *Stargazy* should founder, she could take flight, but she did not fancy the chances of a swarm of bees out here in this world of water and driving wind. The sunlight had given way to a misty spray through which the star-crowned angel plunged.

She could not see the coast, but Dark told her that it was there.

"The spray is hiding it. You'll get glimpses."

"But we were in the bay," Bee said.

"Not any more. But not far out, in fact. I've just seen Land's End. We'll be in proper sight of the bay again soon."

"It's nearly dark."

At this point, Louisa rose to her feet. She smiled. A man was approaching them across the rolling deck, walking with practised ease. A tall man, his grey hair pulled back into a queue, wearing a brass buttoned naval coat and boots. He gripped Louisa by the arms.

"Louisa! So it's you, my many times grand-daughter. I thought I heard a spell for aid. And are these folk your friends?"

"Yes. Beatrice Fallow and Ned Dark."

Henry Thorn smiled.

"Ah, I think you are a seaman also, my good sir?"

Dark smiled back. "From an earlier age."

"Perhaps a greater age. Though an age of some ill practice, from what I know of it."

"He sailed with Drake," Bee said. Dark looked slightly embarrassed at this, as though Bee was name dropping.

"For a time," he murmured.

"The *Hind* is a legend, of course, as is her captain."

"Everyone, this is my umpteenth grandfather, Henry Thorn."

"Welcome to the *Stargazy,*" Captain Thorn said, with a bow.

"Thank you for rescuing us," Bee told him. "I'm afraid you see before you an absolute landlubber who doesn't know one end of a boat from the other."

Captain Thorn roared with laughter. "You won't be the first such on board this ship. We will take good care of you. Would you come below?"

Dark and Bee followed Louisa and her relative down a narrow flight of steps into the depths of the ship. It smelled of tar and tobacco and a faint air of men's changing rooms, but the chamber into which Captain Thorn led them along a passageway was surprisingly cosy, and clearly his own cabin. Bee looked admiringly at the oak panelled walls and sturdy table. The slanting maritime light cast a gleam from silver and glassware: surely risky, on a sailing ship?

Captain Thorn went to the table and unrolled a map.

"We think we know where we are," Bee said.

He laughed. "Well, then, take a look at the map and let us see if you have your bearings."

Bee looked down at the Cornish coast, finding familiar landmarks.

"Dark thought we weren't far off Land's End," she said.

"That is right. We are here." He indicated a point not far from the coast. "We have a swift wind behind us; we will soon be in sight of our home, Louisa."

"Excellent. We think we might have a problem with the Mount, though. A visitation."

"We ourselves are in pursuit of another vessel," Captain Thorn said to Bee and Dark. "Perhaps Louisa has explained. A bloody-sailed ship with a smuggler's crew, a privateer owned by the Morlader and sailed by his current captain, Portobello Jones. Her name is the *Balefire.* We caught up with her last night, fire was exchanged, but she slipped into the mist. She will be heading towards Tretorvic, and the Mount."

"What happens when you catch her?" Bee asked.

"We aim to sink her."

"Will that – well, will that work?"

Captain Thorn laughed. "Maybe. For are we all not dead and gone in your day and age, Louisa? And yet we go on. And on."

"Do you mind?" Bee asked, hesitant.

"To sail the seven seas forever? No. It was for this that I was born and made."

"Do you never set foot on shore?"

"Not on shore, no. Not since my death. But you see, when alive I was forced to retire from the sea, through injury, as my granddaughters may have told you. When I died, and found myself confined upon the waves, I rejoiced. We are permitted onto the Mount, sometimes."

There was a knock on the door and the Captain went to answer it, disappearing into the passage. Bee heard the sound of voices, exchanging nautical details.

"*Does* he mind, do you think?" Bee said to Louisa. "He seems not to, but – it seems a hard fate, somehow."

"I think he has adventures along the way," Louisa said. "As an afterlife, it seems interesting enough."

"As is my own," Dark told her, with a smile.

The door opened once more. "We're coming alongside the coast," Captain Thorn said. "The *Balefire* is in sight."

LUNA

Luna woke, her heart hammering. Downstairs, someone was knocking on the door. She reached over and shook Sam by the shoulder.

"Sam! Wake up!"

But he did not even stir. The knocking went on: not loud, but insistent and somehow insidious, as though it was coming from inside her. She could feel its thump like her own heart. In alarm, Luna swung her legs over the side of the bed and found her slippers. From the cot came a little cry: Rosie was awake, at least. In the corner of the room, Moth whined.

"Sam!" Luna said, more loudly. But Sam was not only sleeping, she saw as she snatched the baby from her cot. He was fading. Luna watched in open mouthed fright as Sam, the bed, and then the room grew faint upon the air and then started to slide gently away, leaving her standing on the bare boards and taking Moth with it as well. The last thing she saw was the lurcher's long, puzzled face staring up at her. Holding Rosie tight, in case she, too, vanished, Luna ran to the door and onto the landing.

"Ver! Serena!"

No reply.

"Bee!" She shoved Bee's bedroom door open but there was no sign of her sister or Dark and the bed looked unslept in. The knocking on the door continued, making Luna cold with fright. Rosie wailed. But now Penhallow itself was growing dim around her. The knocking went on. Luna bolted for the stairs, thinking that perhaps she might make it to the back door. As she did so, a figure stepped suddenly into her path. Luna choked back a scream as she realised it was Ver, wrapped in an ancient dressing gown.

"Oh, thank God! Ver, Sam's gone! He just faded away and so did the dog!"

"Oh Christ! I think we'd better get out of here," Ver said. Luna agreed. Clutching Ver with one hand and the baby with the other, she bolted down the stairs to the hall. The noise had increased from that original soft, sinister knocking: it was now so loud that it seemed as though the front door might splinter. Luna and Ver ran for the kitchen. Luna jumped as the radio sprang into life, at full volume.

"Biscay... Trafalgar... FitzRoy... Sole... Lundy..."

The announcer's voice was as measured as ever but behind it Luna heard again that wailing seagull cry. Rosie gave a fretful squeak that heralded, so Luna now knew from experience, an ear splitting scream.

Another baby was crying, not far away. And it was definitely human, not the plaintive gull's cry that had occasionally startled Luna as she sat in the garden or walked along the harbour front, or the sound in the Shipping Forecast. It sounded as though it was coming from inside the house.

"What's that?" Ver said. "That wasn't here before."

A little door stood open in the white washed wall: made of driftwood, like so much of the house, gnarled and sea-bleached. She could see the old nails which studded it, their heads blackened, then they shone and for a moment it was as though a constellation starred the door. The hammering sound abruptly stopped, followed by men's voices.

"In!" Ver snapped. She reached out for the round iron ring and wrenched it, then pushed Luna and the baby through the door.

They were on a high hillside, surrounded by gorse bushes. The pursed yolk yellow flowers seemed to hold their own light. There was a strong wind blowing and Luna could taste the salt on its breath. When she turned, she saw the full moon riding low over the sea and the waves were wild, huge breakers rolling into the shore and smashing against the rocks. There was no sign of the house or the town; this did not look like the cliff on which Penhallow stood, but the high moor, with its tors and outcrops. The grass was sheep-cropped short between the gorse and rocks. A mass of clouds had built out over the sea and the moon swung between them like the pendulum of a clock, riding the wind. Luna held Rosie as tightly as she could, appalled, and took a deep cold breath, fighting down panic.

"Ver!"

"We'll be all right, Luna. We'll be all right." But Ver did not sound sure.

Some distance away lay a track, the sort of path that has been made by a cart: there was a strip of grass down the middle. It shone faintly. From experience – the corpse path of the lych way, the leys – Luna did not want to take this track, but she did want to see where it led, for it was heading purposefully up over the brow of the headland.

"If we follow alongside it?"

"Might as well keep on the move, dear. I'm not sure what might be coming after us."

Keeping well clear, among the prickly maze of the gorse bushes, Luna and Ver followed the track. Then they heard voices.

They ducked down into the gorse, peering through a spiny spray of flowers, Luna praying that Rosie would keep quiet. The heat of panic thundered in her head as she heard a baby's cry but it was the same cry that had led her here, plaintive as a kittiwake. What would a baby be doing, out here in this wild land?

"Look!" Ver hissed.

Someone was running up the track. Luna knew she was a ghost, for she could see the outline of the hill, the uneven shrine of rocks, through the woman's silvery body. She wore long skirts and a shawl; her hair was loose and flying behind her. Her face was filled with a terrible distress. She carried a lamp: a guttering tallow candle in a small glass box.

"Baby!" she cried, "Oh, Baby! Where are you?"

She paused, a few feet away from Luna, and span around. She was young, Luna saw now, but her face was already lined, the cheeks sunken with a lack of teeth. In the moonlight, Luna thought her hair might be red, but it was difficult to tell.

"Baby!"

Luna longed to run and help her, try to comfort, but the thought of her own child held her back. Ver seemed to read her mind, for she put a restraining hand on Luna's arm. Rosie stared up solemnly at her mother, her earlier yell aborted. The woman ran on, up over the lip of the headland. Luna gasped. Had she plunged into the sea?

"I have to see!" she told Ver.

"All right. Be careful. I'm coming with you."

Luna pushed through the gorse, ignoring the prickles but keeping Rosie clasped against her breasts. The baby was so quiet that, frightened, she took a quick look down, but Rosie was still staring wide-eyed, up at her.

"Our first adventure together, Rosie-posie," Luna mouthed. *Let's hope it's not our last.*

The gorse soon came to an end in a thick wall of spines, with one small gap. Luna could see that they were on the edge of the cliff, a grassy slope overlooking the immensity of the sea. She could see the dark rim of the coast, but no lights anywhere. On the faint silver trackway cast by the moon, Luna glimpsed a ship: narrow hulled, full sailed. She was turning. The stars raced overhead and the moon dipped to the horizon's line. The ghost was running along the cliff, to and fro, holding the little light high. The light blazed out, dazzling Luna. The ship's sails caught the wind, driving her into the coast. For a second Luna heard the rattle of the rigging and the crack and billow of the sails above her head, felt the ship plunge down into a trough of sea. The light flashed, fire-quick. She was back on the top of the cliff, clutching Rosie, as the wind roared overhead and the ship came onwards.

Someone was running past the gorse bushes, a man in leggings and a dark coat. More followed him. Luna counted nine. As the last man raced by he turned and looked at Luna: his eyes burned silver-empty in his face. They all went over the cliff, as if leaping into space. The ghost fled along the cliff, her light bobbing. Luna and Ver hastened to the edge and looked down: a narrow path led to the cove below, with nine black figures pouring down it. The ship was almost on the rocks, trying to turn, but it was too late. Its prow hit the upended slabs of granite at the corner of the cove but instead of an anticipated splintering crash, the boat glided on. Luna saw the men – the wreckers, surely – leap on board. One of them grabbed the wheel and steered the boat through the rock of the cliff and out of sight. Like the vision that Bee and Dark had told them about, when they first arrived.

Over Luna's head, the sky was a shadowy bowl. In the west, Arcturus hung low over the sea.

"What now, Luna?"

"I don't know." She took a deep breath. "But we know which direction we're facing, so the sea will be south and west. Maybe we should go inland away from the wreckers?"

"Might be a good idea to put some distance between us. They didn't seem that interested in us, mind you."

"I wondered if they could actually see us. And who was that poor woman?"

"That lamp she held," Ver said, "it was that light that lured that ship in, like Bee told us. Not the wreckers themselves."

"Maybe that's how they do it? To draw souls. Use some poor frightened ghost?"

"I don't know. You might be right." Ver shivered. "Stella thinks it's her mate Hob's mum. But she might not be the only one."

"I wish we could help her," Luna said.

"So do I. Do you think we ought to try? I must say, dear, I wish I was wearing something other than my dressing gown!"

"You've got plenty of layers underneath it, Ver! You're decent."

"You know what I mean."

Luna did. Her own nightwear was a set of tracksuit bottoms and a sweatshirt, practical enough, but not ideal. The land smelled like summer up here but the night was cold. "Let's get going," she said.

STELLA

Inside the hut, it was dark, but a square of fainter grey occupied one wall: a window. As Stella hesitated on the lintel, waiting for her eyes to adjust, someone moved. Stella stepped quickly back, nearly falling down the steps. A light flared up. Someone had lit a candle – no, it was marshfire, a willo' the wisp.

"Don't fear me," the person behind it said.

Stella relaxed, if only a little, when she realised that the person was female.

"Sorry to intrude," she said.

"You're not intruding." The voice was peaceable, with a trace of an accent that Stella could not place. "The boat brought you here, I saw it."

"I'm looking for someone."

"You've found me. Come, sit down."

Stella perched on a small wooden stool. Another light glowed up, allowing Stella to see that the woman was very dirty, her face smudged. She was dressed in scraps of fur and feathers, all white and grey. She was also somewhat familiar.

"I think I've met your – sister?" Stella said. It was hard to tell how old the woman was, because of the grime. "Snipe?"

"My daughter." The woman laughed. "She went into service at the great house, not wanting to live out her life in a swamp with her old ma."

"That's young people for you these days," Stella said. "I'm Stella, by the way."

"My name is Hraga." The woman rose in a jostle of tatters and went to the window. She drew a hide across it, blotting out the twilight, and secured it with a wooden peg.

"Is that a bird, too?"

"Heron, in your language. We are the marsh dwellers, the half kindred, people who live on the edges."

"I suppose an island counts too," Stella said, thinking of Snipe. She blinked. For a moment, a tall bird stood before her: she saw its fierce yellow eye, the long stabbing beak. A dinosaur's child. Then Hraga was back, crouched on the bare boards. "Can you help me, with my quest, then, Hraga? I'm looking for Snipe's mistress' mother." What did Heron think of Azenor? No way of telling what local politics might be.

"When morning comes," the heron woman said, "we'll have to see."

The hut was damp, cold, lacking in comfort and smelling of fish. Stella, curling up on an old piece of sacking, was determined not to sigh. This was a somewhat trying adventure, thus far. The cloak had to be discarded for the night as it was much too wet. Hraga hung the sodden mass up on the door. Stella did not expect to sleep, but it claimed her all the same. She dreamed of swimming, flicking through the waterworld of reeds, sunlight sparkling down from above. She woke to find the real sun streaming in through the little window and flexed a paw, stretching.

Ah. Stella sat up, feeling her otter form slip away with the last of the dream. Heron, slicing a large flat fish with a little knife, smiled at her. Beyond the window, Stella heard a curlew's plaintive cry.

"Was I an otter all night, then?"

"Yes. You changed once you'd gone to sleep. I expect your inner self thought it would be more comfortable that way. This place is a bit primitive for ordinary humans, I admit."

"I can't change at will, you see."

"Some can, some can't. I daresay your inner self knows best."

"Hope so."

"Want some fish? It won't be cooked. There's no fire here – no need."

"It's fine. I'm veggie but I have actually tried sashimi," Stella told her. And the fish was sustaining enough, although Stella suspected she would have enjoyed breakfast more had she remained in her animal form. Hraga looked blank at her remark, so Stella added, "Raw fish."

"Just as well. We have no means to make bread, no need of it. The marsh is a generous place in which to live – eggs, birds, fish and frogs. Samphire and sea buckthorn and dulse."

Like living in Aldi, Stella thought, but did not say. When she had finished her breakfast, she said, "I suppose I ought to be on my way, but I'm not sure how. Will the boat come back?"

"I don't know. How did you get here? By boat all the way?"

Stella told her. Hraga said, "Your story has begun, then. It will take you on the next step of your journey."

"If I let it?"

203

"Whether you let it or not. Aiken Drum," and here her face registered distaste, "has signed you up and your quest has started. It will carry you through to the end, whatever that end might be."

"I don't like that," Stella said, indignant. "Can't I do anything to change it?"

"I don't know."

They stared at each other.

"Oh," said Stella. "What if I just – sat here? Not that I'm going to do that, in your house and at your inconvenience."

"As you 'just sat' in the boat?" But Hraga did not seem unsympathetic.

"Yeah, look what happened there. All right. I'll go outside and see what happens. I need a wee, anyway."

The question of interactions between animal and human form had caused Stella, earlier in the spring, to engage in some speedy and intense research. In this, she had been greatly aided by Davy Dearly who had, after all, been doing it for longer. Stella had a lot of questions.

Are otters allergic to anything? Like dogs with chocolate?

Do they menstruate? Is changing form going to fuck up your menstrual cycle?

What if – *really not planning this one, Okay* – I got pregnant as an otter?

Davy had managed to supply some answers, but rats and otters are different and in the end, Google was their friend.

"After all," Davy said. "It's not like human women don't go through changes and transitions of their own. Puberty. Menopause."

"Yeah, but you don't actually turn into a different being when you're menstruating, do you?"

"Speak for yourself," Davy said.

Stella did not feel, even yet, that she had all the answers, but she had a few, and that would have to do.

Outside, she found that a watery sun had come up, glimmering over the marsh and sparkling fire off the wet reeds. She could see the bottom of the water, a pebbled speckle; it was about thigh deep. She could wade to the nearest bank of reeds, but forcing her way through… Behind her, Hraga spoke, but the words were indistinct. Stella turned, frowning, but the hut was becoming transparent, just as Drum and the boatman had done, a sketch upon the air. Stella felt herself seized by a powerful compulsion, an inner wrench and turn. The steps fell out from under her, she was falling through the air, to land with a splash. She kicked out, swimming, otter once more, and arrowed into the maze of the marsh.

Time seemed different for animals, like a long dream. But Stella knew by the taste of the water that her environment was changing. A greater sweetness, a freshness after muddy salt. The channel through which she swam was broader and she shot out into a river. She surfaced, bobbing about in the current, and looked about her. Colours were also different to the eyes of otters, the human part of her mind observed; she had noticed this before. The reed beds seemed to have greater texture and depth, the water told her more than it did in her human form. She knew this river ran roughly northwest to southeast, and that it was partly tidal, but not as brackish as the salt marsh.

"Where to now?" Stella asked the air. But the tidal current was already pulling her along, in the direction of the sea. Stella dived and swam with it, loving the swiftness, the freedom. The river ended in a great burst of light: the coast and open water. Stella rode a wave onto a little muddy beach, also flanked by reeds, and stood up, shaking off her otter skin like a crumpled cloak.

Okay. Now what?

She pushed through the reeds and climbed up onto a low bank. The sea stretched before her, with the flat bulk of an island dimly visible through a sparkling mist. It was bright, but she could not see the sun. The air was mild, knifed with a little breeze which ruffled the sea, but it was a summer warmth. The saltmarsh stretched behind her, a vast expanse of loops and channels. A flock of redshanks pottered about on the mud. Beyond the marsh, very faint, she could see low hills. Along the coast, a long promontory of land stretched out into the waves and on it was a small building. A familiar building: Stella had been here before, in the unwelcome company of an enemy, a man – if one could call him such – named Tam Stare. The building was a chapel.

SERENA

Serena had spent some of the evening writing a long email to Ward, then deleting it. She did not want to worry him. And Bella had sent her a text, expressing a great deal of enthusiasm for Brittany: no need to worry about her daughter, at least. It was raining, the wind strong, and when she looked outside Serena could see neither stars nor moon. She made herself a cup of tea, said goodnight to Bee, and took the cup up to bed with a book: an old copy of an Elizabeth Goudge novel she had found in the bookcase in the hall. Ver, Sam and Luna had already turned in for the night.

She did not know what woke her. The bedside lamp was still on, forming a small rosy pool of light. The novel lay splayed on the duvet. Serena lay blinking, adjusting, then realised that the door was stealthily opening. Oh God, please don't let it be that horrible man again – she sat up straight in bed, looking wildly around for something to throw. But to her surprise and relief, it was not the Morlader, but Sam, with Moth's long nose edging around the door.

"What –?"

He was pale and flustered.

"Sorry to barge in," he said in a whisper, "but Luna's disappeared, and Rosie. Gran's not in her room, either."

"How?" said Serena, feeling stupid.

"I heard a noise, downstairs. Someone's knocking on the door. I tried to wake Luna, but she wouldn't wake up – and she and Rosie just – just faded away."

"Oh *shit*," Serena said. "Sam, turn your back while I put some clothes on." She struggled into her jeans and found a pair of shoes. "I can't hear anything now." But as she spoke, she did hear something: someone was indeed knocking on the front door, a soft persistent sound that made her shiver.

Serena twitched the curtain aside and looked down into the garden: her room overlooked the front door. There were shadows below, low to the ground; when one looked up, Serena saw two sparks in the oval of its face. A man strode down the path; she recognised the broad brimmed hat, the sweeping coat. Then she heard the front door creak open.

Sam and Serena leaped for the door, out onto the landing, and up the attic stairs, running for the cupola. On the face of it, this was not a sensible choice: how easy, to trap someone in that little room. But they could not go down the stairs. Perhaps Miss Parminter could be contacted?

When they reached the top, Serena realised that things had changed again. The sky, which had been obscured by storm clouds, was the same twilight green that she had seen before. Far out to sea, the evening star hung over the horizon and as Serena watched, a light flicked out, echoing it. A light house, with its regular wink and dark.

Sam came in after her, ushering Moth ahead of him, and bolted the little door shut. It was an old door, driftwood and not strong, and the latch did not fit properly. She peered out of the window to the garden below. She could see sparks, fireflies in the hedge, dancing specks of azure and green and gold, but all of a sudden they winked out. With Sam silent by her side, she crouched on the window seat, waiting. A shadow pushed its way through the hedge, followed by others. Men, wearing stocking caps and sea boots, made their way swiftly over the lawn and disappeared.

"Where have they gone?" Sam said, into her ear.

"I don't know." They checked the other windows, but could see no one. Then, down by the side of the house, Serena caught sight of a dim shape. A light bobbed and wove, then vanished.

"Hang on a minute," she said. The light reappeared: a lantern, bearing a green flame. She did not know if the flame itself was green, or the glass of the lantern. The little light mirrored the sky, seemed to hold it. It was a star, Serena thought, green Venus captured. There was no difference, she suddenly knew, between the sea and the sky: they were all one, with the stars shimmering water deep, drifting between the seaweed fronds. Fathoms deep she glimpsed the moon, shimmering like a pearl on the sea bed, and at the back of her mind she remembered the old story of the moonrakers, telling the excise men that they were fishing for the satellite, not their smuggled goods beneath the surface of a Bodmin pond, and she knew that the moonrakers had not lied, that if you only reached down deep enough you would find the moon waiting for you. Water lapped around the four windows of the cupola. A huge fish, silver eyed, mouth gaping, came up to see Serena and was gone with a flick of its tail. Serena could see the moon, waiting for her, and she dived –

– and was pulled back. She hit the floorboards with a painful thud and the shock jolted her back to reality.

"Serena!" whispered Sam, shocked. "What were you *doing?*"

"I –" she swallowed hard.

"Moonstruck. Gran's told me about it. Drawing your soul out of your body – I could see it on the air, like a mist. Don't fret, Serena. You're not the first to fall for an old trick like that and you won't be the last, but it's not everyone as can do it and it's not all who can withstand it, either, though some can. Maybe it's a hare thing," he added. But Serena could hear footsteps.

"They're coming up the stairs," Serena said.

STELLA

Stella contemplated the chapel. It was a squat stone building, a solid little place that nonetheless seemed in keeping with its surroundings, as though it had grown out of the saltmarsh, that coil of reed and mud and water. No stone, unless you counted the occasional patch of shingle; someone had gone to some trouble to erect this building. Unless it had simply grown there by itself. She looked away, to see if she could glimpse it from the corner of her eye, but when she did so, the whole scene looked different: a black, smoking wasteland. Hastily, Stella looked directly at the chapel once more. She preferred the marsh.

"All right. Where to next?" But nothing happened. She stayed human; the chapel remained on its neck of land. Stella took a breath and plodded towards it.

But the chapel was coy. It was visible, but Stella could not reach it. Whenever she thought she was drawing closer to the promontory, it shifted, and she found herself on yet another stretch of reed fringed mud.

"This is getting boring!" Stella said aloud. Perhaps she should wait and see if the chapel came to her? She sat down, on the least egregiously muddy tussock that she could see, and folded her arms around her knees, but nothing happened. She rose, and wandered until the light became golden around her, then a deep green. A star came out, very faint as if seen through mist. A pair of swans flew overhead; she could hear the great soft pulse of their wings. By now Stella had lost track of time and, apparently, she was going to have to spend the night on the marsh. How annoying was that? And alarming. She had seen enough of this country before to suspect that some unpleasant things might be in residence here. She remembered her flight through the window of the chapel, the sinister dragging noise that had suggested something large and malign moving deep inside it.

The starlight strengthened; the light died. Stella, close to dozing, was jerked into full wakefulness by a sudden sound.

WHOIIIIIING! it went.

"What the fuck?" said Stella. She stood up. The sound was all around, booming from different directions across the reed beds. Stella's Somerset-mind took brisk control of her city head. Either she had wandered into an outdoor didgeridoo convention or – there was a rattle in the reeds and Stella ducked as a brindled shape shot out of them and over her head. Stella just had time to glimpse its pterodactyl beak and mad yellow eye. Bitterns, rare in her own day, but evidently still common here. What else might be lurking in the marsh? Stella thought with unease of Medieval accounts of wild boar, of wolves. She shivered, felt a shudder run through her, and shook herself with vigour, the damp droplets of mist flying from her fur. Well, then. She'd rather spend the night as otter than woman; the chill was starting to creep into her bones, but now her sleek pelt, designed for the cold and the damp, kept it at bay. She found a suitable patch of mud among the reeds and curled up in it. Without her own holt, any hollow would do. Apparently otters were much less fussy than humans – and with that thought, Stella slept.

She woke to find the dawn coming up over the marsh. The sky had brightened to a pale gold and the marsh was filled with fire, sparkles of light struck from the rippling water. Stella, who usually took a fair amount of time to wake up properly, found herself on her paws and raring to go. She was out of the reeds and into the water without a second thought. Diving down into the brackish, mud-swirling water, she glimpsed something ahead: a small carp. It was not a carp for long; Stella tore through it, and then another, gulping them down on a slope of mud. Having breakfasted, she paused, sat up, felt herself elongate in the growing light of the sun and was human again. Fortunately, a dry one. The question of where your clothes went was not a new one to Stella, who had discussed it extensively with Davy and her sisters, but it was not a more pressing question than where your hair disappeared to or where your tail came from. There was a rather fishy taste in her mouth, which made Stella pull a face, but she was neither hungry nor thirsty, at least. It was time to have another crack at the chapel.

It had occurred to Stella, late into her long wait on the previous night, that perhaps she needed to speak directly to the chapel itself. Something about this land, and White Horse Country, and the other realms through which she had passed, suggested to Stella that everything here was alive in some way, not just the people and animals whom she met. Perhaps this went for buildings, too. She stood to face it, and asked.

"Will you let me come to you?"

Nothing happened. All right, Stella thought, and started walking in the direction of the promontory. Movement caught her eye and she turned, quickly, to see a man running through the reeds, some distance over the marsh. He wore a pipe-shaped hood and was bundled in a rough brown cape. His head was down and Stella hoped he had not seen her. She crouched in the reeds, all the same, not wanting to attract his attention. Soon he was gone into a grove of alder, and out of sight.

Stella did not like this. There might be all sorts of people, with who knew what intent, roaming about the landscape, as well as animals, and hadn't Azenor said something about the Morlader having a champion, as well? She waited for a few minutes but the man did not reappear and, uneasily, Stella emerged from her hiding place and went on her way. She held her breath as she drew nearer to the chapel, but perhaps her plea had been heard after all, for the neck of land remained directly ahead and soon Stella was stepping onto it. She walked quickly, in case it disappeared on her again, but the chapel was up ahead, quite solid. Stella could see its familiar small door. Then she was standing before it. She took a last look back over the saltmarsh, but the maze of reeds and channels seemed empty and peaceful enough. Stella put a hand to the door and it swung open.

BEE

Bee had enjoyed her voyage on the *Golden Hind* and she was enjoying this voyage, too, if rather guiltily. She said as much to Dark.

"Although, admittedly, I have not been out in a storm and obliged to shin up to the crow's nest."

"I have done my share of that and more," Dark said, watching a small, agile boy whom Bee estimated to be no more than twelve, clamber up the mast.

"Health and safety would have a fit."

Dark grinned. "A different day and age."

"Is that boy looking for the *Balefire*, Captain Thorn?"

"He is looking to see what may be seen. Look, you can see our quarry for yourself. Against the shore."

After a moment, Bee realised that the lines and squares were sails against the field patterns. Perhaps she was not really cut out for a life on the ocean wave after all. She said as much.

Captain Thorn handed her a telescope. "Here."

Bee's vision adjusted to the telescope and she was able to see the black bulk of the *Balefire*, scudding along, towed by a skeleton figurehead, following the coast and leaving a white wake behind. The wind was clearly in her sails and she was moving fast. Too far for the *Stargazy* to catch her? They did not seem to be moving very quickly. But Bee did not think that the intent was to continue all the way up the English Channel. A race to the Mount, then? Spray spattered over the deck and Bee clutched Dark's arm to steady herself.

"Where's she going?" she asked. "Is it to the island?"

"Perhaps. But we think her captain has another plan in mind. She's sailing under Portobello Jones; I've spotted him on deck. I will wager that soon she will weigh anchor."

"What happens then? Do we catch her up?"

"No. We wait. Until night."

Bee did not understand why they were to wait but Captain Thorn invited them below once more and said he would explain. He had instructions to give, he said, so Bee went back down below with Louisa.

"Do you want something to eat, Bee?" the seal woman said, gruffly.

"Captain Thorn mentioned something about provisions. I hope, not hard tack."

Louisa laughed. "They don't live entirely off ship's biscuit, I know that."

"Good. I'm quite hungry."

"They take on food and drink from the villages and farms along the coast."

"Surely not in our time?"

Louisa smiled. "You'd be surprised."

"What's happening up above?" asked Bee.

"You may as well eat, since we have to wait till night."

"Why night? I meant to ask but your great grandad's got enough on his plate without answering stupid questions, so…"

"Because that's when the *Balefire* will take on her cargo," Louisa said. "If they confront her now, it won't help the cargo, because they'll have been taken but they're not on board yet. The *Balefire* is a soul trafficker, remember. If the *Stargazy* tackles them once they're loaded up, or loading, then they have a chance of freeing the folk."

"That's ghastly," Bee said, indignant. "Bad enough to die but then to be taken prisoner and loaded up onto some people-smuggling ship! What do they *do* with the souls? Where do they go?"

"No one knows."

"Can they be intercepted when they're still on shore?"

"That's sometimes our job," said Louisa.

SERENA

"Oh great," said Sam. The knocking had resumed. It was a soft sound, a gentle, one which nonetheless made the little door shudder as though it was being hammered and which thudded through Serena's body like a great beating drum. Weren't there creatures called the knockers, in Cornish folklore, she remembered?

"Shit," she whispered. "What do we do?"

"We open the door," Sam said, firmly.

"*What?*"

"We open the door." Sam took a quick stride across the room and seized the doorknob. Serena stared, appalled. She knew that the door opened inwards into the cupola, but Sam was clearly pushing it the other way.

"Sam, what are you –?"

"Come on!" The door had suddenly given way, opening out into shadows. Serena hesitated, then followed. It was part of the network, after all – maybe they would find themselves in A La Ronde? Oh please…

But Serena could see nothing except a faint blue glow up ahead. Sam was already marching into it. She looked over her shoulder. No door, just a grey darkness. Moth nudged her; the lurcher's message was clear. *Go on.*

Serena did not like this but it was better than facing whatever had come up the stairs. The glow intensified. They turned a corner and Sam stopped, suddenly.

"Shh!"

Ahead, Serena could hear the murmur of voices. They were in a low passage, with rough stone walls that dripped with damp. The floor was stone, too, made of big square flags. She looked at Sam, who mouthed,

"*We can't go back.*"

Serena agreed. She heard a footstep. Sam crept forwards. Serena hoped he had some trick up his sleeve as neither of them were carrying anything resembling a weapon. She did not feel very brave, but once she had taken on a minotaur, Serena told herself, and won. Sort of. She could hear someone creeping along the passage.

Sam stopped. Serena gripped his shoulder, letting him know that she was right behind. A figure came around the corner. In a sudden surge of dog, Moth rushed past them and flung himself onto it.

"Jesus fucking Christ!" the figure shouted.

Serena nearly collapsed with relief.

"Ace!" She hurled herself into his arms, rather as the dog had done.

"Oh, hello, Mr Spare!" said Sam, as if he'd run into him on a walk to the shops.

"God almighty. You nearly gave me a heart attack. Good thing it's not technically beating."

Something dropped down from the ceiling behind him. Serena glimpsed beady eyes and a long tail, and then Davy Dearly was standing there.

"Serena! We were coming to find you."

"I don't think we should stand here nattering," Sam said. "Someone's right behind us, someone not very nice. I just hope you're not in the same position."

"Actually, no." Ace said. "Follow me."

Serena and Sam pursued them down the passage, emerging into a candlelit, shell filled gallery.

"Oh!" Serena exclaimed, her artist's eye caught at once. "A La Ronde! Thank God! And how pretty!"

"Thank you, dear," said Jane Parminter, emerging into the hall. "We've spent a lot of work on the gallery. Would you like some tea?"

"More like a stiff brandy," Ace murmured, but *sotto voce*, possibly in case, Serena thought, he might shock Miss Parminter, who looked the picture of teetotal rectitude.

"Miss Parminter, I'm so pleased to see you properly, in person. Tea would be lovely," she said, as demurely as she could. "I'm really glad to be here. It feels safe."

"Well, dear, it is not entirely safe – we have had –" here Miss Parminter paused, then pronounced, "Moments. But we have taken precautions this evening, with the aid of Mr Spare here."

"So, Serena," Ace said, "What the h- what happened to you?"

In Miss Parminter's sitting room, Serena brought Ace and Davy up to date.

"Chri – I mean, this does not sound good, Serena," Ace said through a mouthful of cake.

"It was really frightening."

"Do you know who the men were?"

"I think they must have been the wreckers. Or knockers. I'm not sure what those are."

"Spirits of the ancient dead, pressganged into service," Miss Parminter said, adding reflectively, "The Morlader is on the move. Is his ship in? The *Balefire*?"

"I think it was coming in. I think Captain Thorn's ship is, too."

"The *Stargazy*?"

"Yes, that's the one. Could the wreckers follow us here?" There had been something peculiarly horrible about being attacked in Penhallow, which had seemed such a peaceful place, and being cornered in the cupola, and she knew that the Morlader had already made an advance on A La Ronde when Stella had visited it before.

"Basically, yes," Ace said. "Which is why I want to move on. Where's Bella, Serena? Is she still in France?" He replaced his plate on the table with some care, as if nervous of dropping it. Serena understood: the shell house was lovely, but the furniture was a little old maid-ish and rather fragile.

"Yes. She's not due down in Cornwall for another few days and I'm actually going to call her friend's mum and ask if she can stay on with them. I'll say we've all got food poisoning or something. I can tell Bella the truth. She's seen enough."

"What about Ward? He's a big boy," Davy Dearly said.

"I don't want him dragged into this. I will tell him what's been going on, though, when I can." She finished her tea and glanced out of the window. It had been sunny when they arrived, with the scent of wallflowers drifting in through the open window, but now Serena could see clouds gathering over the distant shore. She rose and went to the window to join Davy. A dark mist was rising from the estuary, a pall of shadow.

"Weather's changing," Davy said.

"That might not be the weather." Ace turned to Miss Parminter. "Thank you, again, for your hospitality. Time to go."

They would be sent to the point nearest to Tretorvic, Miss Parminter told them as she led the way to the centre of the shell-encrusted house. *Eau de nil* walls reminded Serena again of being underwater.

"Not to Penhallow, just in case of who might be lurking there."

"To Thornhold, then?"

"Not to Thornhold, no. Unless you wish to split up?"

"What?" Ace said.

"Oh, no, she's right. I'd forgotten. The Thorns' house doesn't like men," Serena remembered.

"Helpful."

"Don't blame me for its prejudices!"

"I shall send you to the Lizard," Miss Parminter said firmly. "To the lighthouse. From there, you may need to take a carriage, or hire horses."

"There's probably a bus," Davy said, sotto voce.

"Thank you, Miss Parminter!" Serena clasped her hand. "I hope we see you again. I hope you stay safe, and that we haven't brought too much trouble to your door." She had not liked the look of that rising mist.

"We are hardly unaccustomed to it, my dear."

Serena and Sam took Ace and Davy's hands and looked up to the gallery, with Moth huddling at their heels. In the height of the house, set into the ceiling, was a spiral of shells – perhaps the pivot around which A La Ronde revolved. Miss Parminter took a small brass bell from a table in the hallway, and struck it, once. The sound reverberated throughout the hall, growing stronger and stronger, ripples of the clear bell-note and the spiral of shells began to turn and spin. Serena saw Miss Parminter's stately figure whisked away, vanishing through time. An impression of other places, as though she leafed through a sequence of slides: the passage through which they had first come, a stone room looking out to sea, a panelled library with a fire burning cheerily at one end, a church with an arched stained glass window casting coloured light over plastered walls… and then time slowed and stopped. Serena found flagstone beneath her feet. But all she could see was mist.

STELLA

The chapel was damp and quiet. Stella stood uncertainly in the doorway, wondering whether it was wise to go in. But she had struggled to get to the chapel: she ought to check it out. She pushed the door to, but did not close it, and went inside. On that previous occasion, back in the autumn, she and Tam Stare had found the captive star, Nephele, on the other side of the room, partially encased in stone and unable to free herself. Stella had helped her. But the star was not there now; the chapel was empty. Did this mean that Stella had arrived before or after the star's imprisonment? It seemed likely that this was in the past, given the wildlife in the marsh. Either the southern counties had seen a miraculous level of environmental restoration, or this was before the depredations of the industrial revolution had begun. She wandered about the chapel, trailing fingertips over the old, rough stone.

It was very quiet. Did no one else ever come to these places? But just as this thought occurred to her, Stella heard a noise. She froze. It was a stealthy sort of sound, from the back of the chapel. That the place from which, on her previous visit, she had heard the noise of something large moving about.

She looked back at the door. Was something coming out? She could run for it... But then a thin voice called out.

"Help me!"

Great, thought Stella. She said, loudly, "Who's there?"

There was no reply.

"Who is that?"

Nothing.

Stella, significantly doubting the wisdom of her actions, went to the opening of the chamber and looked in.

The star Nephele lay on the floor of the chamber. Her eyes were closed and one hand was flung towards Stella, as if the star was reaching out. Her long dress, all seaweed tatters, trailed away from her body – or perhaps it actually *was* part of her body? – into the corner of the room which, Stella now saw, was occupied by a pool of black water. A hole set low in the wall betrayed a gleam: the chapel was open to the sea. And that dress – now Stella knew who Azenor had reminded her of. Was Nephele-the-star Azenor's mother?

"Fuck," said Stella. She went over to the star and knelt beside her. "Wake up, Nephele!" The star did not respond. Stella touched her shoulder, tentatively: it felt as hard and cold as stone. When she took her hand away, her fingertips were blue and smeared with frost.

There was, from outside the chapel, a sudden loud bang. Stella jumped. A voice said something, urgently, in a language Stella did not recognise, but a moment later, she realised that it had made sense after all.

"Have you got the cage?" the voice had said.

There was a window set high in the wall. Stella ran over to it, hauled herself up and peered through. The window looked out over the sea, which was lapping right up to the wall of the chapel. It had been dawn when she first set foot in the place, not very long ago, but now the sun was going down in a sullen smear of light. A ship rode at anchor, some distance out. It was a squat, dark craft, a lugger with a single crimson-brown sail. Craning her neck, she saw the stern of a rowing boat disappearing behind the chapel wall.

Stella ran back to the main door and shut it as quietly as she could. Then she ran back to the star.

Nephele was still unconscious. Stella did not think she could be dead. Did stars die? Presumably so: even the great suns to which they were connected burned out. But Stella had heard of no recent supernovae and, besides, she was still convinced that they were in the past. She shook the star's shoulder again, but there was no response. Out of the corner of her eye, however, Stella could see movement. She turned. Something was coming through the hole in the wall. It was black and glistening, like a long wet twig with a large bud on one end. Then the bud unfurled into a hand, with thin, groping fingers tipped with claws. Stella nearly screamed, but managed to button it. The hand reached the edge of the pool – how long was the thing's arm, she thought? The pool was at least three feet wide. The black, shiny claws gripped the hem of the star's gown and began to tug.

"Oh no you don't!" Stella shouted. She seized Nephele by the shoulders and pulled, but the star was not only cold but very heavy. She reminded Stella of a ship's figurehead, beached. Stella hauled away but the star barely moved. Stella gave up and ran to the hand instead. She stamped at it, but it evaded her, whisking briskly back into the pool. Then it grabbed her by the ankle. Stella hit the floor. Now it was her turn to grab the star's gown. She clutched it as she was pulled backwards, trying to climb up the star's prone form. The little hand was horribly strong; she was already half into the pool.

The sunlight was blotted out. She heard the rattle of wings and a bird arrowed in through the window. Stella saw the fierce golden eye as it hit the pool and struck.

"Hraga! That you?"

The heron's beak went straight through the thing's wrist, narrowly missing Stella's foot. There was a high, whistling shriek. The hand's grip came away from Stella's ankle and she rolled free and felt herself change.

Now, the pool had become a more natural element. Stella dived. Down, down, down, past walls of stone: this was more like a sea well than a pool. The water was murky but otter's eyes granted her a wider range of vision than human ones. Something shot past her, something big. A fish? It had been man sized: a porpoise or dolphin. Stella swam after it and cornered it in the depths of the well. She did not know how long otters could hold their breath but it seemed that she was about to find out: not very long. The thing turned and Stella saw an arrowing shape, legs and arms pressed closely together, huge eyes like sunken moons, a bald scaled scalp and a great many sharp teeth. It snapped at her. Stella kicked, soaring up the well and breaking the surface with a snort.

By the side of the pool, the heron, hunting, stabbed again and again. A coil of smoke snaked out of the pool from an oily seep of blood. Then the heron tossed her head upwards and a long branch shot out of the pool and hit the opposite wall. It fell with a wet smack and lay still. Stella dived again, through the pool and out into the sea which lapped at the rocks on the far side of the chapel. Surfacing briefly, she saw the lugger riding at anchor, not far away. She thought of Louisa, crewing for the local lifeboat. She thought of seals. Stella arrowed towards the boat, churning through saltwater, took a breath and ducked beneath it. *Yes!* The anchor was secured by a rope, not a chain. Stella bit. Her sharp teeth made short work of the rope; it frayed and broke. Stella turned and swam swiftly back through the pool and flopped onto the flagstones where the heron was standing. There was no sign of the thing she had met in the well.

Hraga hauled Stella to her feet, human suddenly.

"Quickly!"

The heron woman seized the star by the arms and dragged her towards the door; she must be exceptionally strong, Stella thought, because this time the star did move. She helped as best she could but that wasn't a lot. From beyond the chapel there came a cry of rage.

"Keep going!" she panted to Hraga, who gave a nod.

Stella ran into the main chapel, hauled a chair to the narrow window which faced the sea and looked out. Out to sea, under the rising moon, the old-blood sail of the lugger was flying erratically away, whisked on the tide. Stella heard someone shout in a wail of dismay,

"The boat! The boat!"

But the lugger was free from its anchor and heading out into a thundering sea. Below, Stella could see the rowing boat, caught in the wind's teeth and swirling after the ship. Its oars followed it, flimsy as matchsticks. As the rowing boat shot past the window she saw two heads looking up: white and bald as stones, with sharp teeth and round grey eyes. One of them was nursing the bloodstained stump of its arm. Stella did not know what they were and did not want to. She dropped down from the window and ran back to help Hraga.

The star's gown was now free of the pool and Hraga was dragging Nephele along the floor. Her sodden, heavy garment slithered and Stella recognised the sound that she had heard, nearly a year ago in this same place.

"Hang on!" she hissed to Hraga again. She pushed past her into the main body of the chapel and saw the heel of a Converse sneaker vanishing through the window.

"Wait!" Stella shouted, but Stella-in-the-autumn had gone.

"What is it?" Hraga called.

Stella turned to explain, but the doorway had become blurred, the walls of the chapel had doubled, then tripled, like a series of transparencies overlain on one another. Stella's head swam as though she was suddenly tripping. Her brain was trying to make sense of it, and failing. Something knocked into her, sending her off balance: Hraga, stumbling.

"What's happening?" Stella thought she heard Hraga say.

"I —"

The only thing she could see clearly was the star. Nephele's eyes opened and they shone. She lay still for a moment, then began to rise up, seemingly without effort. Her hands did not move; she simply became vertical. She towered over Hraga and Stella, then sank slowly to the floor. Her gown spread out, rippling and running like water, seeping into the flagstones, and froze. The blue light that was emanating from her faded and Stella could see properly again.

"Are you all right?" Stella said.

The star looked at her. Stella remembered that marshfire gaze, all too well. It made her head spin all over again. Her daughter had inherited it.

"Azenor sent me. Your daughter?"

"My daughter? It was good of her to care," the star said, wonderingly, as if Azenor should not.

"She sent me to find you."

"Tell her I am safe now. I shall stay here," said the star. "I shall rest."

"She might not believe me," said Stella.

"I will tell her," Hraga said. "And of my own part in this. She trusts me. She knows I never lie."

"Will she be cross that you helped me, Hraga? I'm assuming she wants her mum to be safe, but this is a test as well, isn't it?"

"I don't think she will be angry," said Hraga.

"You should be rewarded," Nephele said to Stella. "I'll send you where you need to go."

"Back to my own world?"

But the bluegreen water fire of the star's eyes died, leaving them black and blank. Slowly, her eyelids closed.

"Okaaaay," Stella said.

"Why did you run out of the room?" Hraga asked.

Stella explained. "I think these sorts of places overlap in time. In the future, I rescue her. I thought – I will think – God, this is a mind fuck – that a man named Tam Stare might have imprisoned her, but we never really got to the bottom of it. But now it looks as though she imprisoned herself. Sort of. She told me she was a 'captured star'."

"She was," Hraga said. "The lugger came in yesterday, from the sea. I know the people who sail it. They are not good people; they are enemies of the bird clans, and others. I followed the boat. I could tell someone else was on board – the marshfire was drawn to it, there was a glow in the hold. Then, a short while ago, the star broke free. She fled across the water. She must have sought sanctuary here."

"But they came after her," Stella said. She remembered that Nephele had been able to walk on water.

"Yes, they came after her. I did not know you were here. I was going to send word to Azenor but there wasn't time."

"I'm glad you rocked up, anyway. We know that she'll be all right here," Stella said, looking at the column of the star. She did not look remotely human now, more like a statue. "But I don't like to just leave her."

"We will watch the chapel," Hraga said.

"I wonder, what's happened to those – people?"

"The scucca. What did you do, Stella, to send their boat away?"

"I chewed through the anchor rope."

"I'll send a message to the court. Azenor might hunt them down."

"Mission accomplished?"

Hraga frowned for a moment, not quite comprehending, then she nodded.

"I don't know what to do now," Stella said. She and Hraga stared at one another. Then Hraga said,

"Look."

The flagstones at the edge of Nepehele's gown were glistening, and after a moment they sparked. Marshfire snaked out, bright gold, green and azure, softening to silver and deep blue.

"Someone is waiting for you," Nephele said.

"Who?"

"Go and see."

Cautiously, Stella went to the door of the chapel. In the autumn, Tam Stare had bolted the door from the outside, but now it opened easily enough. She looked out. On the sward of grass between the chapel and the shore, sat a woman on a moon grey mare.

"Hello, Stella," her mother said.

LUNA

Luna and Ver had made their way up onto the moor, but this could hardly be said to have taken them away from the coast. Both the Channel and the Atlantic were visible from this high point, which Luna thought must be the neck of land lying roughly between Penzance in the south and St Ives on the north shore. It was sparse ground, with ancient field boundaries marked by boulders which gleamed in the moonlight. Occasionally they disturbed a sheep, who would rise with a grumble of protest from the thin grass and lumber away. Luna did not know if they were in her own day or another – or perhaps, like the otherlands of Somerset, this was a patchwork, idealised Cornwall. But she could see no lights on either coast.

At least the air was still. The great wind which had whipped around Penhallow that evening had dropped and the moon rode free. They could see the Milky Way, dropping down towards the ocean. Luna's arms were growing tired; Rosie was a heavy baby, but she held her close all the same. Perhaps it showed in her stance, however, for Ver said, "Do you want me to take her for a bit? Give you a rest?"

"Would you mind? I should have brought her sling," Luna said.

"You didn't know we'd be leaving the house, lovey."

"I hope everyone else is all right," Luna said, handing over the baby. "It's really worrying."

"I know. But it's happened before and all worked out. I can't say as how something's looking after us, but I hope there is. I'm worried too but you mustn't dwell on it: it won't do any good. At least you can feed her."

Luna nodded. "Yes, I've got a couple of containers with me at the right temperature."

"Exactly, dear!"

"Let's see what's at the top of this rise." Luna took a few steps ahead and the world fell away, everything went black.

"Luna! *Luna!*"

Luna had never heard Ver sound really frightened before. She lay looking up. A single bright star shone down the tunnel of stone; Luna marvelled at its changing, sparkling brilliance.

"Luna, answer me! Are you all right?"

Carefully, Luna sat up. Her tiny claws scrabbled in earth but then she was wren no longer. She moved her arms and legs, rotated her head. "I think so, Ver!" She stood up. She had fallen – fluttered – onto a soft bed of earth. Above her head, about eight feet up, Ver's alarmed face appeared in a halo of sky.

"You just – disappeared!"

"I fell down a hole, Ver." Suddenly it struck Luna as funny. She gave a hiccupping laugh. "Sorry." In Ver's grasp, Rosie chuckled in return, sounding like a contented hen.

"You certainly did. Can you climb back up, do you think?"

Luna looked. The shaft of the tunnel was rough and contained outcrops.

"I think so. Maybe I can fly. Just let me take a look around."

"Surely you can't see anything down there, Luna? It's pitch black."

"Yes, I can. But I don't know how." There was a faint, bluish luminescence.

Luna saw that she was in a small square chamber. She could see something across the room, a pallid shape resting on the floor. The luminescence was coming from it.

"Hang on a mo, Ver." She went across and squatted down, reached out to touch the thing then snatched her hand back. It was a human skull. "Shit."

"What is it?"

"I think this might be someone's grave."

"Get out of there, Luna. Here." Luna saw a strip of fabric appear halfway down the shaft. "Dressing gown cord!" said Ver. But in the event, Luna did not need it. She considered trying to change shape again, but her inner self was not co-operating. So she scrambled up the shaft, balancing on the little ledges of rock, and soon fell out onto the grass. She lay there for a moment, breathing hard, with relief as much as with exertion.

"Oh, Luna," Ver said. She sank down onto a nearby granite boulder, still clutching Rosie. "You did give me a fright."

Luna gave a shaky laugh. "I gave myself a fright. Sorry. I'll be more careful from now on."

"You're sure you're all right?"

"Yes."

"I think that must be one of them fogous," Ver said. "They might be Bronze Age, someone told me once. Maybe storage shafts."

"Maybe graves," Luna said. She told Ver about the skull.

"Perhaps that was someone who *couldn't* get out. I'd say being more careful is definitely a good choice from now on."

They rested for a few minutes, until Luna had got her breath back, and then continued. This part of the landscape had been worked by man, Luna realised: the field boundaries, the cairns, the ring of standing stones which they had passed a little while ago, the fogous... She took Rosie back from Ver and they walked on. It felt almost dreamlike and not unpleasant, with nothing but the mild air and the stars above them, the great gleaming path of the Milky Way. They went across a gap in a low stone wall, down a boggy field, winding between tussocks of reeds, skirting a ruined byre.

"Luna!" whispered Ver. She stopped, suddenly, and put a hand on Luna's arm, breaking her reverie.

"What?"

"Someone's coming."

BEE

They ate in the Captain's chambers: not hard tack, but cold beef and bread and cheese. Dark put in a brief visit, accepted what to Bee looked like an entire pint of wine (but then, he was dead and didn't have to worry about the ill effects of alcohol), and said that he had been helping the crew.

"She is a marvellous ship. Seafaring has truly come on since my day."

"She's old fashioned now, Ned. Steam put her out of business."

"But now sail is coming back, so I see in your newspapers."

"To an extent," said Louisa. "Ocean racing's obviously a big thing, but they're talking about using sail again for some cargo. More environmentally sound."

"You couldn't replace those massive cargo ships with sail, though, surely? I see them ploughing up and down the Bristol Channel sometimes, the big car carriers? And that boat that got stuck in the Suez Canal..."

"No, I don't think you'd replace those with sail, that's true." Louisa turned in response to a knock on the door. Her great grandfather came in.

"It's dusk. We're closing in."

Back on deck, Bee could see a faint sullen light hanging over the western horizon, but otherwise the bay and the Mount, now unlit, were snared in a hazy twilight. A low mist was hanging over the sea; Bee did not know enough about sailing to wonder if that was a good thing, for concealment, or a bad one, for the danger. Presumably both Captain Thorn and Louisa knew the rocks of the coast, but when were they? She could see no lights on the shore where Tretorvic should be and this coast was prone to change, hammered as it was by the equinoctial gales, the great smashing winter seas.

The ship shivered, gliding forwards. Dark came to stand at Bee's shoulder.

"We're moving," she said, unnecessarily.

"So we are. So are they."

"Ned, how can you possibly see?"

"I know what to look for," he said, softly. Bee squinted into the murk.

"I can't see a damn thing."

"Fortunately Captain Thorn can. She will run without lights. So will the *Balefire*. Up to a point."

Bee was about to ask him what he meant when she saw a light of her own, a little flare and then a dim distant glow along the coast.

"There's one."

"Yes. That is, I think, a wrecking lamp, seeking to lure ships in. Remember the one we saw, when we first came to Penhallow?"

"It won't work on the *Stargazy*, surely."

"No. Nor are they trying to lure her. They seek ghost ships, the little lost boats that might bob up on time's tide. Draw them in, then pounce like a cat at a mouse hole. No pun intended," he added, for the village of that name was not far away.

Bee looked at the dark line of the coast and shivered. The mist was rising faster now, the *Stargazy* gliding through it with barely a ripple. There was no wind, and she could not see how the ship was being powered. Oars? Magic? She turned to whisper her question to Dark but he had disappeared. Louisa had also gone somewhere out of sight, but just as Bee noticed this, she reappeared, marching along the deck.

"All right?"

"Yes. We were just thinking we might be in the way."

"You won't be in the way," Louisa said. She turned, grasped the rail, and vaulted over it. There was a faint splash. Bee gasped and ran to the side of the ship. Through the mist, a round grey head thrust briefly up through the water. Bee thought it might have winked.

SERENA

"Ace?" Serena whispered. "Guys, where are you?" No reply. She cursed under her breath and took a step forward. The flagstones were uneven and old, faintly slimy. Was that seaweed? Serena wondered. She could not see much through the mist, which wreathed about her in smeared coils, but she could hear and smell. A sea cave? It smelled brackish, that cold musty odour that some caves have. Serena did not like caves. A long ago school trip to Cheddar had been quite enough and those caves were dry and full of interesting rock formations. This was simply dank. Miss Parminter had said that she was sending them to the Lizard: was this it, or had something gone wrong? Surely something must have done, or they would still be together. Uneasily, Serena thought of that dark seeping mist. Some spell spanner in the works, interfering with Miss Parminter's wholesome, friendly magic?

She put out a hand, reaching for the wall, and touched something clammy that wasn't rock. Serena snatched her hand back. But nothing happened and, steeling her nerves, she reached out and touched it again. Damp wood, she thought. Her fingers traced its curve. A barrel?

To Serena, this suggested smugglers. Shit. Where smugglers were to be found, were wreckers far behind? She put her hand on the top of the barrel and stepped forwards: there was a row of the things, and she used the barrels as her guide. She counted eight, and then there was a door. Serena listened but could not hear anything beyond it. Fumbling, she found an iron ring and turned it. The door opened with a creak. Serena held her breath, but no one was there, and the mist was lighter here. An oil lamp burned high on the wall. She followed the passage, which curved around a wall of rough rock. Where were Ace and Davy and Sam? *Come on*, Serena told herself. *Buck up*. But then she heard voices.

Serena looked down the passage. The voices were coming from up ahead and now she could hear footsteps. She ran back along the passage, passing the door and following the curve. Then she came to a dead end. There was no door. The passage simply ended in a wall of damp rock.

The voices were coming closer. At least two men, perhaps more. They were grumbling, Serena could tell that much, and their accents were West Country thick, difficult to understand even for someone brought up in Somerset. They might even have been speaking Cornish and not English at all. In a moment, they would be around the curve and the door was far behind, no chance of running back and nipping through it. Then Serena remembered what Jane had said to her, when they'd first met at Wimbledon, an age away. She had forgotten it, in the panicking moments in the cupola and beyond, but she remembered it now.

"Remember to watch the wall."

Later, at Thornhold, Serena had asked Jane what she'd meant and Jane had told her.

"If you're in trouble, anywhere along the coast, turn your face to the wall."

"What good will that do, Jane?" Serena was curious and a little unsettled: it was an old country way of saying that someone had given up living, was preparing for death.

"Remember your Kipling?" Jane laughed. "If they still teach him in GCSE English these days – probably not politically correct, I must say. He was a bit of an old colonialist."

Serena agreed but she did know what Jane meant: Grandfather had been an admirer of the writer and had once taken Serena and Bee to see his house at Rottingdean, during a family holiday in Sussex. She recited:

"If you wake at midnight, and hear a horse's feet,
Don't go drawing back the blind, or looking in the street,
Them that ask no questions isn't told a lie.
Watch the wall, my darling, while the Gentlemen go by."

"Well done!" Jane had said. "That's the one. It's an old code of the coast. Kipling knew more than he was letting on, I reckon."

Now, Serena took a deep breath and turned to watch the wall, standing stock still. Her spine crawled as she waited for the men to come along the passage, and she hoped Jane was right…

STELLA

Stella ran across the grass to where the grey mare stood. The mare bent her head and, with a knowing eye, flicked her nose across Stella's shoulder. But it still took Stella a moment to recognise her.

"Laura?"

Alys laughed.

"She's very kindly agreed to carry me. You'll have your own mount. Don't worry – I haven't borrowed it from the Hunt."

"If you recall, Mum, I'm not the greatest horsewoman on the face of the planet."

"Don't worry, Stella," a familiar voice said. Nick Wratchell-Haynes came around the side of the chapel, leading his big hunter and another, smaller, grey. He looked as though he'd come straight from the County Showground. "This is your pony. He'll look after you."

Stella grinned at him. "Been told that before. Usually just before they bolted. Good to see you, by the way. Is he one of yours?"

Nick smiled back at her. "No, when I said he was 'your' pony, I meant it, Stella."

"What? I've never had a pony. Serena used to ride a bit but she borrowed one of the Amberley's if she fancied a hack."

"Don't you know him? You probably last saw him in the spare bedroom."

The pony turned and fixed Stella with a limpid, knowing eye. Somehow, she had the sense that the animal was amused. What on Earth was Nick talking about – and then she realised.

"Nick, you're kidding me. That's never the rocking horse?"

"Well, if *Laura* can turn into a horse…!"

"Fair point!" Stella took another look at the pony and decided to move on. "So, where are we going? Are you coming too? And Mum, it hasn't escaped my notice that you seem to have got your memory back."

Alys grimaced. "I never lost it. Sorry to worry you all, though. I needed to buy myself some time."

"Hmmmm," was all that Stella could trust herself to say. "So where are we going on this fine moonlit night?"

"We don't actually know. Captain Coral does, though."

"Who? Oh, that man Bee and Luna met in the spring. The one who helped them."

"He's gone on ahead. Our scout. Quite a bit has been happening since the rest of you left for Cornwall," Nick said. "To fill you in, as quickly as possible, your mother came to see me on the night you left and explained a few things."

"*Did* she. Can I have a word with you in private?" Stella said to him.

"Yes. I think Alys wants to get going, though."

"Okay, just for a moment."

When they were around the side of the chapel, Stella hissed, "I can't trust her, actually."

"No, I realise that. But you can trust me, I assure you, and you can trust Coral – he doesn't have any reason to think well of your mother, unfortunately, since she pretty much sold him out to Drum last time they met. But he's a realist. He knows the lie of the land and he's used to making temporary alliances. I don't know if he's been tailing you or if he'd heard something on the grapevine – he was cagy on that point – but he came to me earlier when I was at Mooncote and told me where you were. He'd already spoken to Alys."

"You see," Stella said, "I can't throw stones. I'm on a quest for Drum – well, not for him, exactly, for some sort of local minor deity. Again."

"A quest? To find what?"

"Her mother."

"Which 'local minor deity'? Not Noualen this time, I presume?'"

"Called Azenor. Ring any bells?"

"Ah," Nick said. An expression of enlightenment spread across his face. "Yes, I know who that is. Come on. We ought to get going. We can discuss this on the way."

"Are you coming with us?" Stella was rather hoping that the answer would be *yes*.

He nodded. "For part of the way. Coral will take you the rest. I'll need to keep an eye on things in Somerset."

"Okay. Better get on with it, then."

"I'll give you a leg up." The hunt master boosted her into the saddle. Stella had ridden before, but she was not good at it. The saddle felt, as always, unnatural and uncomfortable. She grasped the reins and tried to let muscle memory, assuming there was any, take over. But the little grey plodded forwards at a slight touch of her heel.

"Let's hope he's bomb proof," Nick said.

"Up hill and down dale? Or just on the flat?"

"You'll be fine." Nick patted the rocking horse's backside and mounted up on the chestnut.

"Hope so. Fingers crossed, eh?"

"We'll be heading west," Alys said over her shoulder.

Stella did not like to look back at the chapel. She was afraid of what she might see and she needed to focus on the act of staying on horseback. She followed Alys and Laura along the neck of land that led back to the marsh, with Nick bringing up the rear.

As they rode, the night faded away to the shining sky of pre-dawn and soon the sun came up, streaming over the countryside. Stella looked across to the blue haze where, in her own world, the New Forest would begin. She started as a female blackbird shot out from a stand of alder, sounding her loud alarm cry, but the grey seemed unperturbed. Alys was picking up the pace. Stella hoped they would not fall into a trot; she was prone to bouncing around like a sack of potatoes until she found the rhythm. If she found it, which had not always been the case.

"Take it easy, Mum."

"If Laura's in agreement, and I can't see why she wouldn't be, we can swap if you find the pony too challenging. Laura obviously understands humans."

"She can't speak, though, right?"

Although it seemed she could understand, for Laura turned her head and rolled an eye.

"Sorry," Stella said to her. "I always thought it would be really cool to go to Narnia and have a talking animal as a friend. And now I've not only got several, I bloody *am* one."

"What?" her mother said, squinting back into the sun.

"No one's told you," Stella said. "Otter, apparently."

"Oh Stella, how lovely." Alys sounded as though Stella had given her a particularly nice present. Perhaps she had.

"Might be the time to ask you about good old dad," Stella said.

"Well, he wasn't anything to do with *Ring of Bright Water*, I can tell you that. I can't tell you his name because I never did find it out."

"I see. One night stand?"

"He was a musician," Alys said. "Blame cider."

"Folk night?"

"I thought you might prefer not to know that. It's not exactly your sort of tune."

"I like *some* folk music," Stella said. "I expect I'll live it down eventually."

"I don't know where to find him and he never knew."

"Whatever. Where *are* we going?"

For the landscape around them was now giving way to a denser woodland.

"We're heading into the edges of White Horse Country, and other places. We need to catch up with Coral – he left us by the gibbet and went on ahead."

"The gibbet. That does not sound promising."

"He knows the way," Alys said. A rough track, heavily overgrown, led through the trees: mainly beech, if the stone grey trunks and the litter of mast beneath were anything to go by. It was summer here, too, with a bronze green canopy hiding the sun. Stella was wary. She was nervous about controlling her mount, although the pony did indeed seem pretty amenable, and wanted to concentrate on that without, say, some eldritch horror hurtling out of the undergrowth.

They passed the gibbet, which to Stella's great relief was unoccupied, and out onto a wide slope of hillside. They headed down the slope, Stella being jolted at every step.

"I hope we're not going to ride all the way to fucking Cornwall," she complained.

"This is a shortcut. We're heading to the river. There'll be a boat waiting. If everything has gone to plan."

Stella estimated that the river, if by this Alys meant the Severn estuary, was a long way away, at least in her own day and age.

"By *shortcut*, do you mean: it's not far?"

Alys smiled. "'Are we nearly there yet?'"

"Well, soz, but I'm not used to a life in the saddle. The ocean wave, maybe."

"It really isn't very far. Unless the lie of the land has changed."

Stella sighed. "Which we know it does." But she was becoming a little more accustomed to the pony's motion, now, a tiny bit more confident in the saddle.

"I've been here before. See that steeple? I met Bee there, with Ver, in the spring. But it was closer to Somerset then."

"So what *about* Drum, Mum? Boyfriend?"

It was Alys' turn to sigh. "Lover, in fact. He's not an entirely bad man. I know how to handle him."

"Or you think you do."

That remark sparked a flash of anger in Alys' eyes but then she sighed again. "You might be right, Stella. God knows I've made mistakes before."

"Haven't we all. I can't talk. Do you actually love him?"

"I don't really know. We've had our moments. But I think, if I'm honest, it's more what he represents."

"And what is that?"

"Adventure. Mystery. Freedom. Well, maybe not that, because this world has its own traps, as I know all too well. But how many people get the chance to do something truly original?"

"Did you know this other world was here, when we were growing up?"

"Not really. I knew about the ghosts and the stars, but not about White Horse Country or the other places. To the Saxons, Stella, there was no such thing as the supernatural. Did you know that? I didn't. They believed in devils and spirits, and ghosts, but they thought those things were just part of our world, and I think they were right. There's no such thing as supernature, just nature, but nature's bigger than we think."

Stella thought of the scucca, and gave a sombre nod.

They were now moving through a crest of oak. Through the trees, the landscape looked more like the South Downs rather than Hampshire. She caught sight of a winding, snaking river, the kind that, eventually, formed oxbow lakes (thank you, GCSE Geography). As was often the case, when she tried to look at it directly, it disappeared. A shallow oval further down the hill looked like one of the dewponds that you found on the downs, and the high bright light in the south betrayed a coastal sky. She saw another church, a squat Saxon tower, and mentioned it to Alys.

"They come and go," her mother said.

"This looks like Sussex."

"I agree, it does. But I know we're not far from the river. Can you smell the salt on the air?"

"No."

She was wondering about the layout of the landscape when Laura whickered and shied.

"Laura, what is it?" Alys said.

"Smell that," Nick said. Stella noted a rank, earthy odour.

"Badgers?"

"Wights."

"Which means?"

"There's a nest," Alys whispered. "There, under that bank. Don't say anything more, Stella. Follow me."

The grey mare stepped delicately along the track, with Stella behind and Nick following. Stella studied the bank with some nervousness as they passed, but it looked like an ordinary ridge of earth, crowned with the nodding purple-pink of willowherb. She stole a glance over her shoulder as they passed and saw that the bank was crested with actual flames. Willowherb was known as fireweed, she remembered. Then only the wind-stirred flowers were back.

They rode for a couple of hours, coming out onto the bare flank of the downs, then over a ridge, and now the landscape had changed around them. The downs and the wooded ridges were no longer visible. Stella saw a maze of reedbeds ahead, channels of dark water, and for a moment thought she was back in the salt marsh where the chapel lay. Then Nick said, "Know where you are now?"

And suddenly Stella did.

"It's the Levels." Mooncote lay on the edges of the Levels: Somerset's fen country, brackish to the sea.

"The Summer Country," her mother said.

So called because in winter, as they knew all too well, the land flooded; it was viable for pasturing only in the warmer, drier months. How many times had Stella glimpsed the Tor, surrounded by a sheet of mirroring water that had perhaps given the land its old name, Ynys Witrin, the Isle of Glass?

"Feels like summer to me," Stella said. The air was mild, the light golden and soft upon the land. The reedbeds were dense with vegetation and filled with bubbling, chattering cries. She did not remember the Levels being so *loud.*

"I know this place," Nick said, with a reassuring degree of confidence. Dismounting, he helped Stella down from the pony.

"Just as well," Stella told him. "Because I don't. Not even in my own day and age and I don't think this is it."

"No, you're right there, Stella. This is a lot longer ago than that." He put his fingers to his lips and gave, not the expected whistle, but a long warbling cry that merged with the bird calls, both familiar and unfamiliar, around them. "We'll need to get going before the clouds come at dusk."

"Good idea," Stella said. "We don't want to get caught in the rain." Her mother gave her a curious glance, as if about to say something. "What?"

"Nothing," Alys said. She turned to the grey mare and put her hand on her neck. "Laura?"

The mare was gone; Laura stood before them in jods and riding boots, and a long sleeved sweatshirt.

"Hello!" she said to Stella, and gave her a hug. "I was so pleased to see you, back there. Couldn't exactly say so, though. Look."

Stella turned to see where she was pointing and saw a long, narrow shape gliding between the reeds. A boat, roughly hewn like a dug out canoe and with no apparent means of motion.

"Was that what you called for, Nick?"

"It was."

"Like a sort of early marshland uber," Stella mused. "No, never mind. What about the horses?"

Nick spoke into the ear of the chestnut, and with the grey pony behind, the big horse wheeled away and headed into the marsh.

"They'll catch us up later. They know where to go."

The boat rocked a little as they stepped into it, moving gingerly across the thick mud at the base of the reeds. Then it set off, as mysteriously as it had come.

Stella heard once more the hollow boom of a bittern, but she did not recognise half the bird calls around them. The boat took them through the channels between the reeds, the water black with peat, and then out into a more open channel past a drowned stand of alder. Definitely summer: the alder's broad, serrated leaves were in full growth, faintly tinged with yellow. Stella clutched the side of the boat as a flock of birds lifted up in alarm, sailing on huge wings above their heads.

"Cranes," her mother said. "They're trying to reintroduce them, in our day."

"I can hear cows!"

"There are cattle in some of the pastures. But those aren't cows that you can hear." Nick pointed. Stella saw a second flock of enormous birds, white and yellow beaked, gliding over the water.

"Are those *pelicans?*"

"Yes. Dalmatian pelicans, to be precise."

"We're not in Dalmatia!"

Nick smiled. "They used to live here in large numbers, but they're not part of the British landscape now. Like a lot of things."

"Is that smoke?" Laura said.

"Yes."

"They're all right," Nick said. "Those people. But I'm not going to bother them." He touched the prow of the boat and it veered to the right. Away over the marshes, Stella could see a collection of large hats. After a moment, she identified them as roundhouses. There were still a few on the Levels, constructed several thousand years after their original day for educational purposes. Smoke was rising from their centres.

"To be honest," Alys said in a low voice, "this place is quite heavily populated. You tend to think of the marshes as empty, but they're great places to live – lots of food. As long as you don't mind dying at thirty five raddled by fever and rheumatism."

"Sounds great." She remembered her conversation with Hraga. "What do they live off? Frogs?"

"Fish, frogs, birds, eggs, plants."

The boat now took them through a narrowing series of channels and eventually the reeds took over, growing too thickly for the boat to continue further.

"Dead end?" Laura asked, worried.

"Not at all," Alys said. She stood up and jumped out of the boat. Stella saw that she was standing on a low wooden platform, held up by logs tied in the shape of an X.

"I know what that is," she said. "The Sweet Track, or one like it."

"I'm glad school taught you something," her mother remarked, as Stella scrambled out of the boat.

"We went to that museum, out near Shapwick, where they've reconstructed some of it. A four thousand year old motorway."

Wide enough for one person, anyway. Stella wondered, as they pushed through the overgrowth of the reeds, what you would do if you met someone else. Got up close and personal, or would one of you have to jump down into the reeds? But perhaps the marshes had not been as densely inhabited as all that. The track was sturdy enough and she could only imagine the long, wet effort that the people who had made it must have undertaken, in order to set this passage through the marshlands. The wood was alder, some of it newly cut and still red as fire. Apart from the local flora, Stella had forgotten how mosquito-ridden the Levels were in summer and she was not thrilled to be reminded. She had already had several bites. Clouds of midges swarmed over the reeds and there were places where the marsh was thick with dragonflies, from tiny darting needles of neon blue, to the shadow-winged demoiselles, to the big blue and green banded monsters that resembled miniature helicopters.

"Where does this go to?" she called to Alys, who was up ahead.

"One of the villages. They're friendly. Sun's going down – I want to get there before dusk."

Stella remembered that Nick had said something about it clouding up, but the sky looked clear enough, with only a few pink wisps to the west. It had that brassy tone that suggested that sunset was not far away. But only a little breeze sighed through the reeds and the last of the day still held its warmth. Given how unkind these other lands could be in winter, Stella was relieved that the seasons seemed to be running in parallel. She said as much to Laura.

"It's been really hot in Somerset. How was Cornwall?"

Stella explained, as briefly as possible. By the time she finished, they had covered perhaps a quarter of a mile of the trackway. It ran onto a long spit of soil, which might have been an island, and resumed on the other side. This section of the track looked older, more weathered. By now the sky was bronze to the west, and in the east it was overlain by that shadow that starts to come across the sky close to summer dusk. Nick turned and said, "We should be at the village in a bit. If I tell you to run, you run."

"Why?" Stella asked.

"Because you'll need to run. Watch the sky, if you can do that while still minding your footing. If you see so much as a willow warbler, let me know."

Uneasily, Stella did as he told her.

"There are some more pelicans," Laura said. Nick regarded them for a moment. The dying sun stained their milky wings to pink.

"That's all right," he said.

"It would help if we knew what we were looking out for," Stella said.

Nick was looking beyond her, facing east.

"That," he said. Stella turned. A huge smoky comma was rising out of the distant reeds. It flexed, squirmed and grew. She knew exactly what that was. A murmuration.

"Starlings," she said. "You see them all the time out here."

"Except," Nick Wratchall-Haynes replied, "those aren't starlings."

LUNA

Luna and Ver ducked behind the wall of the ruined byre, crouching down. The stones would not provide a great deal of protection, but hopefully they had not been spotted. The moonlight was so bright that Luna had little difficulty in seeing the small procession that was now making its way across the moor, and the path on which they walked gleamed, too, with its own hazy light. There were six men, wearing breeches and stocking caps, carrying a coffin. They sang as they walked, just under their breath, a mocking, repetitive chant. Luna did not like the sound of it. Shadows flicked and flitted around their heels, like the spirits of some small animal. At their head walked a tall figure with a lamp held high on a pole, wearing a broad brimmed hat. To Luna he had a vaguely clerical air. His head, with a long jaw like the Hounds, swung from side to side and she caught a glimpse of his eyes: bright as copper pennies, and perhaps they were, set in his eye sockets in payment for the dead. He moved jerkily. Luna had seen men like him once before, in White Horse Country; they haunted the lych paths. As he drew level with the byre, he halted. Luna held her breath, praying that Rosie would not cry out, but it was Luna herself who nearly squeaked when someone plucked at her sleeve. She stifled it just in time.

There was a young woman crouching beside her. Luna saw a straggle of hair, possibly red, and a desperate face. She recognised her immediately: this was the girl they had seen running along the cliff, crying for her baby, the girl who was perhaps Hob's mother. And into Luna's mind, too, popped the memory of the skull, down in the fogou. Perhaps this had been where the girl had died? The old stones of the byre were visible through her body. She whispered, "Come with me."

"Wait here," Luna heard the tall man say. A reedy, whistling voice like a draft under a door. She preferred the ghost. The girl disappeared into the byre. Ver and Luna followed, and found themselves underground. There had been no drop, no steps, but the girl drew Luna into a dark chamber. From the rustling behind her, Ver had followed.

"Hush."

They kept very still. Luna could hear the man moving about overhead.

"Where have they gone? I know someone is here." A thin, unpleasant voice. Further away, a man said, "Perhaps it was just a sheep, master. Moor's full o' they."

More scrabbling sounds. But then the man said, nastily, "It would not be like you to be right, Branock. Yet perhaps the moon will turn blue, and you are correct."

Luna heard him moving away. She held her breath.

"Wait," the ghost breathed. Luna could not see her, but she had the sense of someone leaving. A moment later, the girl was back.

"They've gone. Away down the coffin path with the Gentleman and the knockers. They won't pass back tonight. But we'll keep to the tunnels."

"Why, where are you taking us?" Luna asked.

"To Prussia Cove. I know you've come to help me find my baby. I called, and it was you who answered." She sounded absolutely certain, though Luna remembered doing no such thing. But perhaps the girl had called, in some magical fashion: that baby's cry in the spell of the Shipping Forecast, that seagull squeal. Luna had heard it and perhaps that was enough.

"What do you think, Ver?" she said into the darkness.

"Well, at least she knows where she's going. Which is more than we do."

To Luna's relief, the tunnel was not very long, perhaps three quarters of a mile or so. The girl conjured a faint flame from somewhere, a glow like the one Luna had seen in the fogou, so they could at least see the rough stone walls and rutted floor.

"What's your name?" Luna asked as they walked. "I'm Luna. This is Vervain. My grandmother. Well, sort of."

"I'm happy to adopt you, dear!"

"Thanks, Ver! My baby's name is Rosie."

"My name is Elowen," the ghost murmured.

The tunnel began to slope downwards, at quite a sharp gradient which then changed into uneven steps. Still carrying Rosie, Luna concentrated on her footing, but then realised that she could hear something: a great resounding voice which reverberated through the tunnel. The sea.

"We must be quiet," Elowen cautioned. "In case someone is waiting."

Luna did not like the sound of this, but she tried to tread softly. The phosphorescent light went abruptly out and she blinked, but she could still see. The walls of the tunnel were roughly cut and streamed with water, making its way downwards through the rock. The stone floor was slippery and Luna had to concentrate in order to keep from slipping.

There was lamplight up ahead, and a familiar pattering sound which, after a moment, Luna identified as rain. The tunnel widened into a cave, partly filled with barrels. A lamp hung at the entrance and Luna could see the downpour catching the light, the streaks and slashes in the air, with the bars of the breakers beyond. There was no one there. Elowen led them to the mouth of the cave and onto a small shingle beach. A harbour lay beyond. Luna saw a huddle of cottages, all in darkness, but the rain was easing off, no more than a sea squall, and the full moon sailed out from behind the clouds. She had no more than a minute to take in her surroundings, however, because Ver seized her arm and dragged her back inside the cave.

"Wait! I can hear something!"

Luna once more held her breath. There were voices. A man ran lightly, barefoot across the shingle and vanished into the air with a leap. Another followed and Luna thought she recognised him: surely he had been one of the men on the coffin path, following the Gentleman. A wrecker, or a knocker. He, too, ran across the shingle and disappeared, as if leaping through a door in the air. This seemed strange to Luna. If they wrecked ships for a living, wouldn't they rely on a pitchblack night and a chancy light? Smugglers might, too. But the full moon illuminated everything.

A third man followed, but he did not disappear. Instead, he turned to face the cave.

"Well, girl? What have you brought for me?"

Oh no, thought Luna, recognising the jutting beard and the sparks which flew restlessly around him. Like the Gentleman, he wore a long coat and high boots, but his eyes were empty sockets. The Morlader.

"Have you brought me the baby?"

"I have done what you asked me to do!" Elowen cried. "Hold to your promise and release me! Where is *my* baby, whom you stole from me?"

"Who gives a damn about your brat?" The man – the Morlader – strode forwards. Behind him, the wreckers ran into the air, one by one, taking no notice of what was happening in the cave.

"Oh Christ," Ver said. Luna turned, intending to run back into the cave with Rosie but there was a man behind her: wild faced. There was a glint of gold at his ears. He grinned, and then he tore Rosie from Luna's arms and threw her into the air.

SERENA

Serena waited. The voices were right behind her now and she did not recognise the language: she suspected it must be Cornish. She expected a hand on her shoulder, waited to be grabbed and pulled roughly around, or perhaps a knife – Serena quaked inwardly but she remembered not only her Kipling, but also the story of Orpheus and Eurydice: of a love lost and a life lost because a man disobeyed instructions and looked back. Serena had no intention of disobeying Jane's instructions. She remained resolutely watching the wall.

Then she felt something brush against her arm. She flinched, but it passed: the wall had vanished, and the men, too, had gone by. From the corner of her eye she could see their backs: two sturdy forms in linen shirts and breeches. They were so similar that they could have been brothers and perhaps they were. Beyond them lay a long low-beamed room. An oil lamp stood on the table and on one side of the room was a tea chest and a rope ladder. The men went to a door in the end and disappeared through it.

Serena released a long, shaky breath and went into the room. On the wall opposite the tea chest was a square of sackcloth – a window? She pulled the sacking aside and looked out onto the sea. A pale line of light ran out to the horizon: too constant for the intermittent flash of a lighthouse light, perhaps the moon. The waves rolled calmly away, clockwork regular. It was a quiet night, with barely a breath of wind through the glassless window, but the opening looked out onto jagged rocks and the tide was high. Serena withdrew from the window and went over to the rope ladder. This was not simply hung on the wall for convenience, she realised – it actually led somewhere.

That somewhere, however, was distinctly unappealing. The rope ladder vanished into a black hole in the ceiling. Serena took a moment to think. She could go back and try the room with the door again, but she could not be sure that she would find whatever other entrance it contained. The window was out of the question, and she did not want to open the door at the far end of the room, on the heels of the men. That left the ladder. She could see a faint gleam, high up. It must lead somewhere... Serena took hold of the wobbly ladder and began to climb.

The ladder took her up through a narrow funnel of rock. She could not tell if this was manmade, a smuggler's escape, or a natural feature. When she hauled herself over the entrance, however, in trepidation for what might be waiting, she saw that she was on the top of a cliff, a headland. The sea lay on either side and up ahead was the lighthouse. Serena had been to the Lizard once before, as a child, and had a distant memory of a large and very white building. This lighthouse, though, was a funny top-heavy wooden structure, looking far too flimsy for a promontory beset by gales. There was a dim gleam within. Serena could not see it being of any great use as an aid to shipping.

Beside the lighthouse itself was a huddle of old thatched cottages. A candle flickered in a window; best avoid that one. Serena skirted the lighthouse and explored the clifftop, also trying to avoid holes in the ground. It seemed that the shaft she had just climbed up was the only one, but she also knew that she wouldn't be the only person to use it. She kept an eye on it, therefore. The clifftop was exposed.

On the western side, a rough set of steps had been cut into the rock. Serena could not see where they led, for the cliff fell away too steeply. She went back towards the cottages. Just as she was walking around the base of the lighthouse, which creaked and groaned in even this light wind like the rigging of a ship, someone gave a shout.

"You! What are you doing there?"

A man was running across the cliff, with the glint of metal in his hand. Serena turned and bolted, scrambling over the close cropped grass.

"Stop!"

Serena came to a depression in the cliff, caught her foot in a rabbit burrow and fell, rolling down the slope. She landed as hare and instinct took over. She fled into the long grass as the man, bewildered, teetered on the edge of the slope. Through the grass, Serena could see him peering about. Then he muttered something in disgust and marched away. Serena crept up the slope to see where he had gone. She did not fancy ending up in someone's cooking pot. Jugged hare, indeed.

The man was marching back to the lighthouse. Serena followed, at a distance. As the man reached the cottages, a woman in a long skirt and a headscarf came out of the door, holding a lantern. Serena, crouching by the side of the lighthouse, could now hear them.

"Who was it, Will?"

"A boy." Serena was reminded that she had been wearing jeans. "Didn't know him. He ran from me. Then he – just vanished."

"Where did he go?"

"I can't rightly say. I think he must a'gone over the cliff, but I heard nothing."

"I don't like the thought of someone prowling about."

"No more do I, especially when we've got company."

At this point Serena saw something move in the shadows by the cottage door. It was very small and it had a long, thin tail. As she watched, it ran along the wall, unseen by the man or the woman, and vanished around the side of the cottage.

Rats were commonplace throughout both ports and the countryside – commonplace everywhere. But Serena thought that this might be just a bit too coincidental.

Then the woman said, "This champion, of the Captain's – it wasn't him, was it? He's no more than a boy, if you ask me, for all that the Capn' says he's spriggan born."

"No, this one had fair hair."

"Well, come inside, Will. It won't do to leave our guests unattended. Jowan's sent word to the *Balefire*. We'd best stay up till morning."

They went back inside the cottage. Serena followed the rat.

STELLA

The wooden track had been easy enough to walk along, if a little precarious. Running was another matter. Stella and Laura pounded after Alys with Nick bringing up the rear, but Stella was a faster runner than her mother and had to keep checking herself in case she barged into Alys and knocked her into the marsh. Also, what the fuck were they running from? What were those things, if not starlings? Vampire bats?

She risked a glance over her shoulder. The murmuration was colossal: Stella knew that a million starlings could make up one of these mega-flocks, so whatever those things might be, there were a lot of them. They were not far behind. In another minute – then Alys stumbled. She went down on her knees on the track.

"Shit!"

Laura and Stella took an arm each and unceremoniously dragged her to her feet, but they had lost time. Stella, shoving her mother along, was dimly aware of Nick shouting and then someone was running along the track from the opposite direction. She caught a brief glimpse of dappled cowhide, of someone jumping down into the marsh to make way for them. Then something boomed, like a bittern, but a longer note. Stella and Alys fell out onto an expanse of turf in front of a crescent of roundhouses.

"Stella!" Laura shouted. She scrambled off the end of the track, but Stella was watching the girl who had gone past her. She was tall, dark skinned and wore a cowhide cape, mottled chestnut and white. Her fair hair, the shade of straw, straggled down her back. In one hand was a bow. She took an arrow from the hide quiver slung over her shoulder, notched an arrow with efficiency and no haste, and fired it into the heart of the murmuration. As she did so, the sound boomed out again: it came from a man, holding a huge bronze horn. The reverberation seemed to lend speed to the arrow. It caught the light, glowing red gold, and there was a spark at its tip. The murmuration fell apart, thousands of flying things parting into separate flocks and dispersing across the marsh.

The man lowered the horn just as the girl lowered her bow.

"You were lucky," he said sombrely to Nick.

"I know. My thanks to you."

The man briefly bowed his head. "It is of no account. A return for what you did for my son, nine moons ago."

"And that in turn is what any man might have done," Nick said.

"Might have, and did not. Only you."

Nick smiled at him. "Well then, we are equal now."

The girl was coming quickly back along the track. When she reached the end, she stepped down onto the turf, turned back to face the track, held up her hand and spoke a word. A firefly sparked in the air and the marsh was lost to shadow.

"It's closed for the night," she said.

"Then that's done. You'll eat with us." He and the girl spoke with an accent that Stella could not identify. Their eyes were a pale bright blue. They reminded her of the Berber, some of whom she had met on a visit to Morocco but their faces were broader, their hair fair.

"What are your names?" Stella asked, adding, "If you can tell me. I don't mean to be rude."

But it seemed there was no taboo, at least not over this.

"I am Scaup. This is Curlew," he said, pointing to the girl. Further introductions were made.

"I've now met several people named after birds," Stella said as they walked to the largest roundhouse.

"It is common."

"What does Scaup mean?"

"I think it's a kind of duck," her mother said. "A diver."

"I really ought to join the RSPB. If I survive. What *were* those things?"

Curlew overheard her. She turned, reached into the folds of the hide, and said, "One of these."

Stella looked down at the blotch of shadow in her hand. The light was fading quickly now but she saw a comma of darkness, the glassy glint of an eye.

"What *is* that?"

"The old shaman of the shore people says they are scraps of night, some say they are the shades of birds. Our priestess believes they are the souls of the dead who have not in past years, when folk were ignorant, been burned over the inner lake as our people decently are, but rather left to rot on the platforms of the hill of the dead." She pointed to the east. Stella wondered whether she was referring to Glastonbury Tor.

"What happens if they catch up with you?"

"You would be dismembered in an instant. I've seen it happen. The young people are sent out at twilight, once a year, with the word and the bow and the name. Not all of them come back. But they have to learn."

"You came back, though," Stella told her.

Curlew smiled. "I came back, yes. And now it is my purpose to be the twilight guardian. But the murmuration does not usually come so close." She held aside the hide that concealed the roundhouse door. A skull rested above it, in a nook. A human skull, but then Stella blinked. A horse's long bare skull was there instead, and then in the next moment it was human again. Stella wondered if Laura had seen this and rather hoped she hadn't. She ducked under the hide and stepped into the roundhouse.

It was almost dark outside and not much lighter within. It took a minute for Stella's eyes to adjust. A red fire burned in the middle of the roundhouse with a figure bent over it. Rough benches were set around it and beyond, at the edges, she could dimly see beds of skins and furs. The atmosphere was smoky and fusty, halfway between campfire and school changing room. Curlew and Scaup had seemed remarkably clean given the circumstances; perhaps bathing among the reeds was a thing.

"Sit," Scaup said, hospitably. Stella perched on one of the benches, which was somewhat wobbly. Laura's weight steadied the bench a little. They were close to the fire and it was too hot, but Stella knew how cold Somerset could get even on a summer's evening and the sky had been cloudless and clear when they entered the roundhouse. Other people trickled in one by one: the tribe gathering from the night. Alys stood a little apart, talking to Nick.

"This is so weird," Laura said in an undertone.

"You can talk."

"I know, but – time travel? Assuming we have. It's interesting, though. Did those – those shadow things exist thousands of years ago?"

"I'm a bit more freaked out by the possibility that they exist in our day and age and we've just never seen them. I used to like watching those big flocks of starlings go over and settle in the trees, all shouty and squabbling." She told Laura about the Saxon view of the supernatural.

"I can't feel that I'm a supernatural creature," Laura said. "I mean, it's really just the horse thing."

"Same. Otter thing. I don't think I'm some kind of chosen one or anything. I seem to have no magical properties apart from the obvious."

"Neither do I. But you *were* chosen, Stella – you were chosen for a quest."

"I don't think that's because I'm special, though. I think it was because I could swim. That's why Drum abducted me and not my sisters. And I think Drum might have been a bit desperate, to be honest."

"But did Drum know about Nephele, then?"

"I don't know but I think maybe Azenor simply told him to choose a champion who could swim, just in case. Perhaps she had an inkling about her mother."

"I don't suppose stars can swim," said Laura.

"Not in that dress."

"So if you've found Nephele, and if Hraga's told Azenor that you did, does this mean that Drum has won and the Hunt gain supremacy in the west?"

"I don't know. The Morlader had a champion too, but I don't know where they went. I might have seen them – I saw someone running through the marsh near the chapel – but I'm not sure. It could have been anyone. I hope Drum chooses someone a bit more capable if it comes to some sort of actual battle. Curlew might be his girl. I can't see myself on a horse in a suit of armour, or hurling spells. I don't know any spells."

"Maybe he'll find someone else if it does come to that," Laura said, comfortingly.

"I might resign."

"If you can."

It occurred to Stella then that Laura was presumably partisan, being Noualen's steed. Noualen sought to lead the Hunt, after all. She said so.

"She doesn't talk to me all that much. She's been visiting different groups. I don't remember a whole lot when I'm a horse, you know, Stella. I've thought this before, but there often isn't a whole lot going on in the average horse's head. Talking of which, did you see the skull over the door?"

"I did. I kind of hoped you hadn't."

"There might be others like me" Laura said. "But I'm not sure I want to meet them."

"You'll be fine. Horsy types always have something in common, after all."

"Yeah, but it doesn't mean they'll get on. You didn't grow up going to gymkhanas," Laura added gloomily.

"Never mind. You're a long way from the pony club now."

Laura gazed around the hut, which was now full of people. Horn beakers were being handed around. To Stella, it had the jovial air of a pre-prandial drinks party, end of day, when people could finally kick back and socialise. A group of women with small children at their feet and babies at the breast sat talking quietly, but Stella saw Curlew chatting to two young men, their arms decorated with spiralling tattoos or perhaps scars, and from the look of it she was talking tactics. In their leather trews and jerkins, the men would not have looked out of place walking down Glastonbury High Street. It made Stella wonder about reincarnation. Someone thrust a beaker into her hand.

"Be welcome!"

"Slainte!" Stella said. She tasted strong honey and apple, the underbite of alcohol. "Probably shouldn't drink too much of this stuff," she said to Laura.

"No, me neither." But in the end, they did.

Stella woke and it was very quiet. She lay still for a moment, wondering where she was. A large and sensible beaker of spring water just before going to her allotted heap of skins had taken the edge off the considerable amount of booze which she had imbibed, but hey, she'd completed a quest and survived a number of perilous journeys. Celebration was required. And indeed she felt remarkably clear headed. Perhaps this was the natural nature of the alcohol, untroubled by modern sulphites and chemicals. She hoped she had not done anything too embarrassing. She remembered most of it. Dancing with one of the lads with tats, at one point. Oh well. Hopefully this did not mean they were engaged.

There was a long, whining yawn nearby: one of the dogs. Used to sleeping with animals in childhood, Stella was not troubled by this, but the roundhouse seemed quiet given the number of people who had bedded down in it. Stella had done quite a bit of yurt-sharing at festivals. You would expect a certain amount of snoring, farting, and possibly loud sex, but the roundhouse was as still as the night before Christmas. Stella sat up. Laura's pale hair spilled on the skins beside her and on the other side, Alys was bundled up in a hide like a rolled cigar. Someone muttered in their sleep and she saw Nick huddled on the other side of the roundhouse. But no one else.

As carefully as she could, Stella got to her feet. She had not bothered to undress, and her clothes had suffered somewhat from a trip to the Levels C. 4000 B.C. and elsewhere. Good choice of original clothing, though: a strappy top would not have kept out the ravages of the local mozzies.

She crept to the door, wondering as she did so who she was afraid of waking, and lifted the hide. Outside, the immensity of the stars nearly knocked her off her feet. The whole sky was ablaze, the full moon was riding over the southern horizon, and the night was bright.

Stella looked around her. The little huts stood silent, with a drift of smoke rising from a couple of the chimney holes into the starscape. Presumably other people occupied the roundhouses and not everyone slept communally in the big hut, but Stella had no idea how this society worked. Without her phone, she had no idea of the time: it felt like the small hours of the morning. Indeed, if they had entered the roundhouse at dusk and been drinking and dancing for, well, rather a long time, this made sense. But Stella felt wide awake.

She did not want to poke about too much, but she did need a wee. Once that had been taken care of in some conveniently nearby bushes, Stella fully intended to go back into the roundhouse and try to get some sleep. She did not, however, do so. Movement caught her eye: someone small running quickly and furtively along the edge of the trees. Stella, cautiously, followed. Surely that person was either very short or a child, and as she came out around the side of a hut, she saw that the runner was in fact a little girl, one of the kids she'd seen earlier. The child ran down the slope of grass on the other side of the village and a shifting huddle behind one of the huts showed Stella how they kept the grass so closely cropped. Sheep, or perhaps goats. They were small, too, and wild-eyed, kept in a wooden pen for the night. Wisely, perhaps: a fox barked somewhere out in the marsh and Stella jumped at a shadow passing overhead. A barn owl; she saw its moonwhite face, the great wings softly outspread. Something gave a whirring call – nightjar?

The villagers were gathered by the edge of the water. Stella realised, in the bright starry light, that it was a sizeable lake in the middle of the marsh. A spit of land reached out into the water and two men, perhaps her fellow dancer of the earlier evening and his friend – Crane and Crake, the terrible twins, as Stella now thought of them. They carried long poles with a mesh of net on the end and they were fishing.

Stella frowned. The lads were not fishing with any pretence at stealth or skill. They cast the nets wildly, with exaggerated movements. Stella could see no sign of rising fish and otter sense suggested, with a curious unfamiliarity to human woman, that there were no fish there: they were all gliding on the other side of the marsh, lost in fishy sleep. The only thing visible in the water was the round fractured reflection of the moon.

A hand stole into Stella's. She jerked, jumping again, but when she looked down she saw the little girl.

"Hey! Warbler, isn't it?"

A shy nod. "Do you want to see?"

"Am I allowed?"

"Oh yes. Everyone is invited. But we did not want to wake you, you are our guests." She said this with great pride. Stella wondered how many guests they actually had. But this did not feel remotely sinister.

"Okay. Yes, love to. Lead on, MacDuff."

"It's Warbler," the little girl said.

"Sorry, thinking of something else!"

Warbler tugged her hand. "Come on or we'll miss it!"

Stella went down towards the crowd and they parted to let her through. She found herself standing by Curlew.

"Hey, Stella! We didn't want to wake you up."

"If this is something – secret…"

"Not at all."

"What are they fishing for? Can you fish at night? God, I'm so ignorant." For an otter.

"Oh yes, Pike on moonlit nights, such as this. Carp on darker nights. But now of course they fish for the moon."

"For the –?" But Curlew's words were clear enough. The moon, huge and harvest, the colour of butter, hung low overhead and her reflection was clear, too. Stella remembered those old Wiltshire folk tales of the moonrakers, who claimed to be fishing for the moon where in fact they were fishing for casks of smuggled brandy. Wiltshire people were known as moonrakers to this day, this day which now lay far far in the future.

Stella did not think she should ask what Crane and Crake were actually fishing for: not smuggled booze, presumably, but then she looked up. She saw, with a shiver of shock, that the full moon was no longer riding overhead. The starscape was still vivid: Stella saw a shooting star blaze across the sky, an emerald portent like a dragon. The crowd gave a collective gasp. Warbler's hand tightened on Stella's.

"It's all right," Stella said, feeling that atavistic moment of maternal reassurance. But Warbler just gave a nod. The young men danced and wove, the nets dipped in and out. A great round light lifted up, balanced on the poles, the crowd cried out in a word that Stella did not understand but which made her give a single convulsive shiver, and the world of the marsh was full of light, spilling cream and gold from the net and released to float upwards.

The stars winked. The full moon once more rode the sky, but the water of the marsh was black and unmoving.

Crake ran up.

"Did you see?" he exclaimed to Stella. "Did you see?"

"Yeah, awesome!" She had no idea what she'd just watched.

This was evidently the right thing to say. Crake seized Stella and kissed her; she returned it with enthusiasm. He tasted of honey and apples and smoke. She saw dark water and the full moon in his eyes and then he released her.

"It was easy," he said. "I have been so afraid – and yet it was easy!"

"Great when that happens," Stella said.

Curlew said. "It's good. We must rest."

They filed back to the roundhouse. Stella had a sense of completion: you wake up, you go out, you see weird stuff, and so to bed. Hand in hand with Crake she reached the hide door of the roundhouse: they clasped hands tighter, smiled at one another, and parted. Stella burrowed into the piles of skins beside her just-stirring mother and sought sleep. It was not long in visiting her.

LUNA

Luna was cold, soaked through with spray and confined in a damp, foul smelling hold with a collection of ghosts. She did not care about any of this, however, for Rosie had been tossed to another man who, thank God, had caught her, and then he had scooped up the shouting Luna and thrown her over his shoulder. He bore her out onto the shingle shore where the ship rode at anchor, waiting. Rosie had been handed back to her mother as soon as they were on board. She suspected that the wrecker did not want the trouble of a baby – or did the Morlader want her, as he had suggested, for some sinister purpose unknown? – but at least he had not simply chucked Rosie over the side. Ver sat on the pallet beside her.

"Where do you think we're going?" Luna asked.

"I've no idea. I don't know where trafficked souls might end up. I can't imagine it's anywhere nice," Ver said.

"Do _you_ know?" Luna asked Elowen. But the ghost merely looked blank. She was a wisp of a thing, Luna thought. It occurred to her that this was no more than a scrap of Elowen as she had been in life, reduced to a shade with a single-minded obsession. She looked so pale and thin. Luna could not find it in her heart to blame her for what she had done. And the Morlader had thrust her down here with the people she had betrayed, presumably because she was no longer useful.

Covertly, Luna studied the other ghosts. They ranged from a young man in jeans and a leather jacket, under which a Motorhead t-shirt was dimly visible, to two sailors – brothers? – in old fashioned oil skins, and an old woman in drenched skirts, mumbling to herself. The wreckers must sweep up stray souls from time to time, and perhaps there were many of them, stranded on this cruel coast where such a large number of ships had gone down over the centuries.

Maybe this ship was even one of them. It seemed solid enough, but the creaks and groans that it made were alarming. It was not a large craft – Luna had caught a glimpse of it when carried on board, of its single mast and dark sail. There had been shouts as the anchor had gone up, and then the ship was away, heading out of the harbour. Luna had caught sight of the cave and the shore, receding quickly, and then she was hauled below.

She had thought about trying to change shape, but what about Rosie? She mentioned this to Ver, keeping her voice as low as possible, and not alluding to the matter directly.

"This ship's thick with spells," Ver said. "Probably all that's holding the old tub together. I can't do much either, and we can't leave the baby. Anyway, we'd better pipe down. The door's opening."

The Morlader came through it, striding along the narrow gap between the pallets. The ghosts looked at him in sullen alarm.

"Well, well," the Morlader said. His voice was reedy, whistling thin, like the voice of the Gentleman. "Rare to have the privilege of flesh and blood on board."

"Stay there, Luna," instructed Ver. She stood to face him. "Aren't there laws, against taking the living?"

He grinned. Yet he was strangely expressionless, Luna thought, as though nothing really animated the white face and blank eyes. A hollow man, with the sea wind whistling through. "Not so you'd notice."

"What are you going to do with us?" Ver asked.

"Strikes me as you might be useful. Since that one's sister is Hunt's champion." He nodded at Luna.

"What?" Luna almost said *don't you mean my mother*, but stopped herself just in time.

"The otter girl. She's been helping Drum, and I have an old grudge agin him. You're the only ones I've got hold of, but you'll do. You and your baby and the old 'un here."

"What do you mean?" Luna said.

"Let's see what happens, eh?" the Morlader said, and grinned again.

SERENA

Behind the cottage lay a byre and Serena, still hare, sensed movement from within. She doubted it was human; probably sheep or the family cow. What had the man meant by 'guests'? Prisoners? She still felt sure that the rat had been Davy. She loped across to the byre, keeping close to the dense shadows of the wall. Clouds had swallowed the moon, a further reassurance, though the wind was getting up. For a hare, its stiff salt breath was much stronger than it would have been in Serena's human form.

At the entrance to the byre, she paused. The half door was closed, but it would be easy enough to get over. Serena took a breath, twitched her whiskers and made a great leap, vaulting the half door entirely and landing in the byre. Immediately something started towards her, growling. Serena jumped back. Her small heart pounded, everything spoke of danger, of teeth from the night, of the sudden snap of her neck, and deep within a voice that had never been human said *it is the red death.* Her jump had taken her against bales of hay, arranged in steps: Serena scrambled up, taking full advantage. She looked down into a long narrow head filled with teeth, instantly recognisable as Moth. He was staring up at her, puzzled now rather than predatory. His tail gave a dog's wag of uncertainty, half bewilderment, half apology. He was tied by a long length of rope.

"Moth," Serena tried to say, but all that emerged was a bizarre sound like a child's squeaky toy. Behind her, came a plop. She turned to see that a rat had dropped down from the ceiling and was sprawling in the straw. A moment later, Davy Dearly was scrambling onto hands and knees.

"Serena! Thank Christ."

"Oh, Davy!" Serena said. She, too, was human again. She threw her arms around Davy. "I'm so pleased to see you."

"Me too, but keep your voice down. There's a bloke roaming about and I don't know where he's gone."

"He went into the cottage," Serena whispered. "Unless there are more than one. There are men in the caves under the headland."

"I know. They nobbled us; they had pistols. Magic I might have been able to handle, guns not so much. Not sure how much damage it would have done to Ace but Sam and I aren't immortal and I'd kind of like to wait a bit before I hit that stage, if you know what I mean?"

Serena, with some feeling, said she did.

"They took us to the cottage and stashed us in an upstairs room. The bloke's the lighthouse keeper and the woman, Jen, is his sister. I get the impression that lighthouse keeping isn't his only job, either. I don't think his sis approves of all these shenanigans – she was decent enough, actually. Gave us a loaf and some milk. They took the dog away. Glad he's all right. Sam was worried they might have stiffed him, but he's probably a bit too useful for that. The bloke – I didn't catch his name – was a lot wary of the dog at first, said something about shucks. So they have some magical experience, as you might expect."

With care, she climbed down from the bale and released Moth from the iron ring to which he was tied. "I'll keep hold of the rope in case he runs off."

"Good idea," Serena said, following her down to the ground.

"What happened to you?"

Serena told her, adding, "So what now?"

"Well, we didn't exactly have much of a plan. I did the rat thing, obvs – that cottage is like a leaky sieve. But the lads are pretty tightly held although they're not tied up. Between us, Ace and I might have affected some kind of escape but we didn't know where you were and we didn't want to leave Sam."

"What happened, then?" Serena asked. "We were all together when we left A La Ronde."

"Yeah, I think that mist derailed us. We ended up in a room full of people."

"Shit!"

"That's what quite a few of them said."

"Was the Morlader there?"

"No, but one of the Gentlemen was. Do you know who they are?"

"I think so. They haunt the coffin paths, right? Is the Morlader a Gentleman?"

"I'm not sure, but he's certainly similar. His champion is here as well – I don't know who that is."

"The lighthouse keeper was talking to Jen about the champion. Said he wasn't much more than a boy, or something like that."

"He wasn't in the room when we were, because someone mentioned him and asked if he was to be told, but the Gentleman said there was no need because the Morlader would be here soon."

"Oh great."

"Anyway, at least I've found you and the dog," Davy said. "All we have to do now is rescue Ace and Sam."

STELLA

Stella woke to sunlight. The hide skin at the doorway was pulled back and secured and all around people were going about their business. She could hear a rhythmic, unfamiliar noise, a discussion about arrows, someone admonishing a child. When she made her way to the door and looked out, the odd sound turned out to be made by a woman working a quern of grain. She looked up when she saw Stella and smiled. Curlew.

"There's bread for you. Is your mother awake?"

"She's gone out. My friends are still asleep."

"Let them. Want some milk? Warbler's just done the goats."

"Cheers," said Stella. She accepted a beaker of milk and swigged it back. No objections to goat's milk. It was buttery and strong. "Bread, you say?"

"Over by the oven."

It was flatbread, similar to the bread that Stella had eaten in Morocco, charred and smoke-tasty and made in the same way, slapped on the side of a clay oven. Even better, someone handed her a hard boiled egg, quite big, in a shell that was the colour of an evening sky. It was a little fishy, but Stella was grateful. Thinking of Hraga, she hoped that it wasn't a heron's egg.[1] But birds raided other bird's nests…

There was movement by her side and Alys squatted on her haunches, feet flat.

"Stella. How're you doing this morning?"

"Awesome, cheers, Mum. How are you?"

"I slept well," said Alys, blinking. "That was some party."

"It certainly was. I had a –" Stella hesitated. To tell her, or not? She explained about the moon.

"I don't know what that was. Whether it was some sort of hallucination, or a mass delusion caused by ritual, or a real thing in some way…"

"You have to wonder about some of these folk tales," Alys said, swallowing a mouthful of bread. "Whether something very ancient got

---

[1] *Reader, it was.*

passed down over the generations, or whether stories just float about the stratosphere or wherever and settle on people, or what."

"Do you think that might have been what happened to you? Snared by a floating story?"

Alys gave a rather hollow laugh. "I *know* that's what happened to me."

"Do you mind? Did you try to change things?"

"Yes and yes. And no and no. I will, however, have a few things to say to Mr Drum when I see him again." She reached out a hand and grasped Stella's. "We'll be moving on today."

"I'm kind of sorry. It's very chilled out here. They seem to have a really good vibe. I hope I'll see them again."

"If you want to," Alys said. "I'm sure you will."

Curlew went with them for part of the way, which reassured Stella. She strode along the track, swinging her bow.

"Are we likely to be attacked again, by anything else?" Stella asked Nick.

"I don't know. There's all sorts, in these parts," he replied, dourly. But the morning seemed sunny and untroubled enough. After what Stella estimated to be a mile or so's journey through the reeds, Curlew turned, balancing on bare feet.

"We're nearly at the edge of the Lake People's territory. I'll leave you here. I hope you travel safely, from now on."

"Thank you," Alys said. "Where will we be going now?"

"The marshlands will end soon. You might find yourself on the shore for a bit, near the great river, but the hunting grounds are not far away. You'll need to take care."

"Whose hunting grounds are those?" Stella asked. "Do you mean the Wild Hunt?"

"Sometimes, but their territory has been shrinking of late, as I discussed with your mother. No, these are the great parks, many years ahead of our time. We do not care to go there ourselves."

"I know where she means," Alys said.

"This does not sound good."

"It's a dangerous place. We'll just have to take it cautiously."

They thanked Curlew, who vanished into the reeds. Soon, only a faint stirring of the great bulrushes betrayed her presence and then not even that. Stella was sorry to see her go. Alys pointed to a grove of trees.

"We'll try through there."

But as the chapel had done, the grove seemed to elude them. It lay always up ahead, at the same distance, no matter how they tried. The land was different here, still boggy and wet, but alder and elder had taken over again from the reedbeds and apart from a narrow badger track, the spindly trees were surrounded by bramble, impenetrably thick. They had to take care not to step into the deep, peaty pools which encroached upon the path. It was summer still, though: the trees were in full leaf and wild roses climbed up them. A flock of long tailed tits, like animated lollipops, took up residence in one of the alders, chattering away as they bounced up and down. The day was still mild, but the sky was overcast and once Stella thought she heard a distant rumble of thunder. Alys' head went up.

"Did you hear that?"

"Yes."

"It feels like a storm. I always get a headache."

Stella remembered her mother complaining of this in the past, but Alys was right: the air had a muggy thickness and the wind was rising, stirring the tops of the trees. She could no longer see the grove from this angle; the alder was obscuring it. Just as she was wondering whether a storm might hit, the first fat drops of rain spattered onto the leaves. A moment later, the sky darkened to a livid yellow grey and the downpour was upon them.

There was no choice but to endure it. Stella and her companions were soon soaked, but at least, Stella thought, it was a summer rain: heavy and penetrating but not cold. Ruefully, she thought she could probably do with a shower. Then her mother turned.

"I think I know where we are."

"How could you possibly distinguish one alder thicket from another, Mum?"

"I know what she's seen," Nick said. He pointed. On a small islet in the bog, one of the trees was decked with strips of white and red ribbons. When Stella looked more closely, she saw that they were not ribbons as such, just strips of torn rag, such as might come from old clothing.

"A clootie tree," she said.

"This way." Alys and Nick, to Stella's consternation, led them from the path and into the bog. But Alys had evidently been right. Soon, Stella was out of the mire and plodding uphill. It was still raining, but at least she was now traipsing through leafmould and not mud. Nick put out a hand and gripped her arm. Stella squeaked.

"Shhh."

"What?" Stella breathed. Nick dragged her down behind a bramble thicket, Laura and Alys following suit. A short distance away, on the opposite hillside, Stella saw what he had seen. A man, riding a white stag with immense, tined antlers. There was a golden chain around the stag's neck and its antlers also glinted with gold. The man wore a leather cloak and as he turned, Stella recognised him. He must be the other Lily White Boy, the companion of the cast out, disgraced Hound. Unless he *was* that outcast Hound… but what would that mean, if he was?

"Stay still," someone hissed into her ear. Stella jumped. The face that looked into hers was male and grubby beneath a fantastically decorated bonnet. It gave her a gap-toothed grin and saluted.

"Meet Kit Coral," Nick whispered.

Stella gave a fractional nod. The Hound was looking for something, she could tell. His head swung from side to side and then he raised it and sniffed the air. Dogs' noses were, Stella knew, sensitive, and they were not a very fragrant group by now. But she could also smell roses, an overpowering scent. Serena had spoken of her encounter at Midsummer… After casting about for a few minutes, the stag turned and the Hound rode away.

It was still raining hard, somewhat muted by the canopy above. They were now into woodland of beech and oak, with the occasional stand of holly. Then they came out into a clearing and there was another chapel: not the same as the one on the shore, but possibly the one familiar to Luna and Bee, Stella thought.

"I know where this is," Laura said. She looked uneasy. "It's Hunt lands, but we knew that anyway because of the Hound."

"It's raining harder," said Stella.

"Inside," Alys said.

"Will it be safe?" Things lurked in chapels, as Stella knew all too well.

"The Hound won't come in here."

But how long might the Hound wait, if he knew they were hiding in it?

Inside, the chapel smelled of damp and Stella could see patches of green mould high on the plaster walls. She had the impression that no one had been here for a very long time; the place felt deserted. Alys went immediately to the stone block that presumably served as an altar, its carvings worn away with age,

"What's she looking for?" Laura drew Stella to one side.

"No idea."

"Your mother's very mysterious, isn't she?"

"Yes, Laura, she is. Escalatingly so. I don't know whether to envy you Caro or not."

"Well, it's been a bit of a problem keeping stuff from my mum, but she seems to waft through life deliberately failing to notice things unless her nose is absolutely rubbed in them, for instance, my brother's disappearance."

"She is remarkably normal, though. I'm beginning to think that's a good thing."

"What was that?"

"What?"

Laura wheeled around. "Someone's outside."

"Shit. The Hound."

And with that, the door of the chapel began to open.

LUNA

Luna had been trying to sleep, but could only manage a fitful doze. At last she handed Rosie to Ver saying, "I'm going to see if I can explore."

"I don't think that's very wise, dear."

"Not as a human," Luna whispered. "And I won't be long." She was not sure if it would work this time, but she shut her eyes and tried anyway.

Wren, tiny and brown, a mouse of a bird. She concentrated on the feeling of weightlessness, of being caught by the wind, high tossed, a little spark of spirit. The spells which wove around the old ship pressed heavily upon it, but Luna focused on the cracks, the chinks and creaks, on slipping through...

She opened her eyes. Two giants sat in front of her. Rosie's face was the size of the moon; Ver was enormous. Luna gave a chirp of reassurance and spread her wings.

The door of the hold was bolted from the outside, but this ship was too ancient to be truly watertight. Ver had been right: a spell was holding it together but the magic, too, had cracks, just as the boards did. Luna squeezed through a knothole and was free within the ship.

She flew down a passage toward the sound of voices. Luna perched on the rafters and put an apple-seed eye to a crack. The room was dimly lit but she could see that the Morlader was within, surrounded by a half dozen of his uneasy human crew. Their disquiet was palpable. And one of the Gentlemen was there, too, and the silver-eyed ghost sailors whom Luna had seen running along the tideline. From the corner of her eye she glimpsed one, a skeleton, but when she looked directly he was solid once again.

The Gentleman said, in his breath-of-wind voice, "Why are you keeping so close to the coast? You have your cargo. Should you not be setting out for windward's back?"

"Patience. I'm not short of enemies," the Morlader said, querulously. "We keep to the coast to avoid a certain vessel, which patrols the Channel even now. I'm waiting for true dark to give him the slip."

"True dark will be days away," one of the crew grumbled. "Moon's as full as a guinea gold piece."

"Be silent. I don't mean the dark of the moon."

But he did not explain what he *did* mean, rather to Luna's frustration.

"And we have a port to make before we head out into the black to meet the Ship of Souls and unload the cargo."

"Very well," the Gentleman said, in a more conciliatory tone. "You are the Captain, after all. Where is this port?"

"The Lizard first, for I've had word there might be someone there of use to me, and I don't just mean my own champion. I have a bone to pick with him; he's failed me once already. But that's by the by. Then back to the Mount. I have an ace up my sleeve and maybe more than one by the time we return. You see," and here the Morlader's voice became laced with sly cunning, "Not all who lie in the hold are dead."

"The girl with the baby?"

"The girl, indeed. The old woman has some magic, too, I reckon – I can smell it." He gave a snuffling, sniffing laugh which made Luna inwardly recoil. "But it's the baby I'm most interested in."

At this Luna's little twig legs stiffened and she felt her feathers ruffle. She swung upside down from her perch, then righted, forcing herself to look through the crack once more.

"You have plans for the child?"

"I told you. The mother's sister's Hunt's Champion."

"A hostage?"

"Girl might risk her sister's life. But her sister's child, an infant? Not likely."

"Drum won't give a damn about that, though."

"All the more reason to get to the island afore him, then. But I'll have to give old Thorn the slip before that. Or take the battle to him."

He went to the door and opened it. Luna remained still, perched high in the ceiling. But the Morlader did not look up. She looked down briefly onto the crown of his hat as he proceeded down the passage, his gait rolling with the movement of the ship. She should get back; if he were to go into the hold and find her gone… She followed him down the passage. He was heading for the hold, but to Luna's relief he turned for a moment, to squint through a hatch and speak to the man within. Luna did not wait to hear what he said. She shot past him, back through the knothole, and dropped into her own form in the place where Ver was waiting.

She relayed what she had overheard. Ver bristled with anger.

"Hostage, indeed! He'll have to get past me first."

"And me." But Luna was conscious of a frustrated despair. She might be able to tackle one man, but there were at least six on board, not to mention the mist sailors, the Gentleman and the Morlader himself. She looked down at her baby's sleeping face.

"Oh, Rosie," she breathed. Ver squeezed her arm in silent sympathy. Then Ver's head snapped up.

"What was that?"

Shouts echoed outside the hold. Luna ran to the door and put her ear to it.

"*The Stargazy, the Stargazy!*" someone cried. And then, "To the cannons!"

BEE

Despite the bread and cheese that Bee had eaten at the Captain's table, she felt light and empty as the *Stargazy* sped along, almost weightless. It was an unusual feeling, so much so that Bee looked down at herself, checking that she had not suddenly changed to her namesakes. But her own sturdy human form told her that she had not. The mist had thickened now and it was difficult to see ahead, or even as far as the lamp that hung from the mast, although that had been doused to dark some minutes before. The mist was cold and salty on her skin and the ship made barely a sound as it cut through the still water. She wondered how far they might be from shore. She hoped her sisters were not in too much trouble.

She focused on the mist ahead, willing thoughts of family from her mind. Dark touched her arm and mouthed, *are you all right?*

Bee nodded. She could hear a distant hush, familiar and yet hard to place. After a moment, she realised what it was: the sound of the waves hitting the foot of the cliff, gentle now in this oily calm rather than the crash and boom of the big breakers when the swell was up. Peering through the mist, she thought she could see the granite crags rising and hoped that the *Stargazy* would not run aground. She had confidence in Captain Thorn, however: he had been sailing this coast for hundreds of years, so surely he must know it? Yet the coast did change, as she knew.

Dark said, into her ear, "We are nearly there. Do you want to go below?"

But Bee shook her head. She'd had her share of adventures, acquitted herself well enough. She would do so again, she told herself, willing herself to be brave. A moment later, there was a tremendous bang and the whole ship rocked from side to side. Dark and Bee were doused with spray.

"What the –?" Bee shouted.

"Firing on us! Missed!" Dark answered. He grabbed Bee and pushed her against one of the masts.

"Hold on tight!"

"What was that?" shouted Bee. "Cannonball?"

"Yes."

Shouts accompanied the aftermath of the blast. Men came running along the deck. They were silent, black capped, wearing grey clothes which streamed out behind them, as though they were made of mist themselves. But their eyes were silvery fire. Abruptly, Bee let go of the mast. One of the silent men was before her, a dagger drawn. Something within her buzzed and hummed and Bee, in the form of a swarm, was away. She shot upwards into the rigging, and was lost to the deck.

Once up on the struts, she made her way to the end so that she could see past the sails. It was hard to adjust to the swarm's vision, but she was able to make out the deck below: more a pattern in her mind than in her eye. Dark and Captain Thorn were grappling with two of the shadow crew; Bee rocketed down to help, past other sailors similarly engaged. She hummed across a mist sailor's flaming gaze, bothering him, harrying him, trying to sting and failing. He gave a muffled shout of annoyance, stumbled, and Dark shoved him over the side. Bee heard a splash and nothing more. Dark ran to help the Captain. Bee tried the same trick with his assailant, but the sailor brushed her aside. Bee hit the deck, human again, and for a second, lay stunned. The sailor's boot caught her and sent her sliding down the deck, following the man whom Dark had pushed overboard. Bee, gasping, let herself go over but just before she hit the waves, she swarmed again and flew. She came back up over the side of the *Stargazy* as another shot exploded close to her, knocking her off balance. She buzzed up into the rigging again to recover.

The mist was now filled with smoke and fire. But below, the Captain's assailant lay still on the bloodstained deck. As Bee watched, the blood itself changed to smoke and drifted away, a crimson smear against the mist. The sailor's body faded and was gone. Ahead, she could see the *Balefire*, her sails in tatters, a gun aflame. She looked like an old ship, a wreck, like the *Dutchman* – then the wreck winked out and Bee saw the *Balefire* intact and whole. The fiery mist came down and swallowed her up. Captain Thorn shouted to the steersman and the *Stargazy* glided forwards, moving fast.

"We're heading straight for her!" Dark said. Bee dropped down onto the deck in her human form. "He's not going to stop!"

A minute later the *Balefire* appeared again, straight ahead. This time, she was listing badly to one side. Her crew were scrambling to safety but the *Balefire* was surely going down. The *Stargazy* hit her amidships with a splintering crash. The impact knocked Bee off her feet; she found herself tumbling in mid-air, over and over until she righted herself. Below, sliding down the deck of the *Balefire*, she saw the shadowy figure of an old woman. Her long skirts were hitched up, her mouth was open in horror. Bee cried out, her scream lost in the sudden roar of the sea, but there was nothing she could do. She watched, aghast, but as the old woman slid over the side of the ship, a door opened in the air, just a crack, but through it she glimpsed, most incongruously, a kitchen, with a fire in the stove and a cat on the chair. Then the crack closed and the old woman was nowhere to be seen.

"Did you see that?" Dark cried.

"Yes, what was it? Where's she gone?"

"I think perhaps that was her heaven," Dark said. Bee hoped he was right. Below them, the *Stargazy* seemed undamaged. She had passed right through the *Balefire*, and along her sides Thorn's crew were hauling stray souls onto the deck. The *Stargazy* sailed triumphantly on and behind them, the *Balefire* went down. The mist grew ragged and thin and filled with light. Two forms emerged from it, one holding a bundle. Bee put her hand to her eyes, peering through the haze.

"Bee!" the person with the bundle shouted.

"Oh my God, Luna!" She ran forward and flung her arms around her sister. "And Ver! I'm so glad to see you!"

"I have to say," Ver remarked, "that in my opinion, a life on the ocean wave is considerably overrated."

SERENA

Together, Serena and Davy slunk around the side of the cottage. It seemed riskier in human form, but Serena could not change her shape so readily as Davy could, so had no choice. Her night sight was not as good either and she was grateful for the lighthouse, but illumination came with added risk. Davy had worked out the lie of the land, however. After some debate, they had decided to bring Moth with them.

"He's not a stupid dog," Serena said. "He'll know when to keep quiet." And Moth trotted along beside them, without making a sound, until they came to the side of the cottage. Above their heads, under the eaves, was a window, grimy with salt spray.

"In there," Davy mouthed.

"Will it open?"

"Yeah, but it's too small for a person to fit through." Serena peered up and thought she saw the pale shadow of a face: Ace or Sam, looking down. One of the foursquare panes opened. A moment later, something struck the ground at Serena's feet and she snatched it up before Moth could get at it. It was an apple core. Message received: they'd been spotted.

"There's fuck all else in the room," Davy breathed. "Couple of chairs and a bed. Nothing small or useful."

"Could they take the whole window out?"

"Not without making a racket."

Then a voice said, alarmingly close by,

"Have you had word?"

"Yes. He is coming, but delayed. Trouble in the Channel."

"And you've told the champion?"

"Yes, he knows. They're bringing him down from the village now."

Both, again, were men, but Serena did not recognise the voices. She did not know if watching the wall would work out here in the open, but drew a breath to tell Davy to try. However, the voices were moving away.

"And what are we to do?"

"We must wait, down on the shore. Tell the keeper to ready the prisoners. We'll all board together when the *Balefire* comes."

Serena and Davy looked at each other. Davy gave a hopeful thumbs up in the direction of the window and they retreated to a place behind the cottage wall, heavily studded with fronds of pink valerian. Moving along the wall, and looking through the valerian, they could see the front door of the cottage without being seen. Or so Serena devoutly hoped.

The men were nowhere in sight, but it seemed that they had gone into the cottage, because after a few minutes the door opened and two men came out, in the company of the lighthouse keeper. They were not the same as the men whom Serena had seen in the caves, but their dress was similar. Both were bearded. Serena heard Jen say, "All right, boys, off you go, and take your cargo with you."

"Where's the lass?" one of the men said, sharply.

"I'll be keeping the girl here," Jen said. "Tell the Morlader he owes me for last time. He'll know what I'm talking about. I could do with a hand about the house and it's no place for a maid, with a rough lot of sailors."

"I could disagree with you there."

"Watch your tongue," Jen snapped. She must have known that Davy had escaped, Serena thought. Was she trying to help them? Davy had said she'd had the impression that Jen disapproved of her brother's actions. Or was it simply that she knew they'd get into trouble if the men found there was a prisoner missing?

"What about the dog?" the second man said.

"And *I'll* be keeping *him*, for my trouble," the lighthouse keeper, whom Jen had called Will, told him. "Not much use for a gazehound on a ship, is there, but plenty of coneys for him to chase up here and bring back to the pot."

"I'll allow as how he's a fine looking hound. Can't be blaming you there."

Serena held her breath and a moment later Ace and Sam, looking somewhat dusty but not the worse for wear, emerged. Their hands had been bound with rope and they looked straight ahead, not scanning for their companions. Davy and Serena kept quiet behind the valerian, watching as Sam and Ace were marched towards the steps which led down the cliff. The lighthouse keeper went with them; Jen went back into the cottage and banged the door in a manner indicative of displeasure.

Serena and Davy waited until the little group had almost reached the steps, then ran after them. Again, this was open ground. Serena hoped that no one was watching from the cottage, but perhaps Jen had sensibly sought her bed. No shout went up behind them, and they dropped behind a stand of gorse in time to see Ace and Sam being led down the steps. Faintly, beneath them, the ground shuddered.

"What was that?" Serena whispered in alarm.

"Horses." Davy indicated towards the lighthouse. A group of horsemen broke out from the ground between the cottage and the lighthouse: three horses, one carrying two men. The lighthouse keeper turned at the head of the steps.

"Who's there?"

"It's me, Gowan. We've brought the champion. Capn's orders!"

The horses trotted by. Serena saw a black haired man on a tall grey, with a passenger riding pillion and clinging to his waist. As they passed the stand of gorse, the passenger turned his head.

"Oh!" Davy gasped.

If that was the Morlader's champion, Serena thought, then he was hardly a stranger to them. It was Hob.

BEE

Turning into a swarm of insects was migraine inducing. Bee had only changed form a couple of times before, did not remember much about it, and had been disconcerted to find that she had done it yet again. It was as though her consciousness had been splintered into a myriad fragments, yet still was one. She recalled only fragments, too: seeing Dark fighting, and the blind urge to attack the men below, which she did not like to remember too closely. Bee was accustomed to irritation and annoyance, but not to murderous fury. Now Bee was human again; a human with a headache.

"Sit down," Dark said. "It might pass in a minute."

Bee nodded. She was experiencing the customary light show of a visual migraine, along with the beginnings of tightness around the skull, but sitting still on a bench and concentrating on the sea did eventually help. Captain Thorn was leaning over the side of the *Stargazy:* speaking to someone below. Someone in a boat? But then the person slid up over the side. It was Louisa.

Bee stood up to greet her and found that the headache was fading.

"Well done," Louisa said to her. "The Captain's told me what you did."

"And well done to you, great grand-daughter," Captain Thorn added.

Louisa looked grimly pleased. "Managed to hole the *Balefire.*"

"I wondered why she suddenly listed to one side," Luna said. "Has she sunk?"

"Let's hope so. But for now, she is gone and we have work to do. The Morlader is still at large and the *Balefire* is not his only vessel."

Bee, Ver and Luna followed him along the deck. At the end, in the high stern of the ship, a small group of ragged people were gathered. They were mainly male, and dressed in an array of garments: a haggard faced man in a seaman's jersey and knotted handkerchief, another in ordinary denim jeans. A crack of light appeared on the deck: each one stepped through it and was gone. But the final person in the little queue was a woman. One of Captain Thorn's men was trying to help her to her feet, but she was having none of it.

"I won't go!" she cried. "I won't! Not without my boy!"

Bee could see the water through her body; like Dark, she was a shade. And when she had lived, Bee thought, she would almost certainly have been poor. Her face had the sunken cheeks that accompanied a lack of teeth and her red hair straggled across her shoulders. She wore a grubby brown woollen dress.

"She won't go," the sailor said to the Captain, unnecessarily. Bee caught the glance that Thorn shot in her direction and hid a grin. She did not need to know the Captain well to understand that plea. *It's a woman's problem.*

"Her name's Elowen," Luna said. "She won't go without her baby."

The ghost wrung her hands.

"My baby was taken from me. I had no choice, I was made to give him up, into the fire. The Queen wanted him, they said, but what would such a woman want with a child of mine?"

"The Queen?" Bee said. For a moment, she thought of a dumpy figure in pearls with a pair of corgis, but obviously, this woman came from a different age. And it seemed more and more likely, from what Stella had said, that this was Hob's mother.

"Elizabeth," the woman whispered, as if the name burned her tongue.

Bee looked up at Dark. "Ned here is from your own day. Perhaps he can help us?"

But Elowen looked fearfully up at Dark and whispered, "Oh no. He would not have any mercy for the likes of me. He is a gentleman."

"First time anyone's called me that!" said Dark.

"I don't know. You do look rather dashing."

"I'll go and talk to Thorn," Dark said.

Bee had noticed before that there were sections of Dark's memory that were missing, or about which he was vague. She wondered whether this was a ghost thing, for it seemed from the ensuing conversation that Elowen, too, could tell them little about her life. Bee would have to ask Ace, when she next saw him. Yet maybe Elowen did not care to remember. From what she said, it had been grim enough: a hovel somewhere up on the moor which was probably the byre that they had seen near the Hand and Bundle, a clue if ever Bee had heard one; the baby the result of a chance encounter which sounded more like rape than seduction. She did not want to press Elowen on the subject, for the ghost was by now weeping. But one thing on which Elowen was clear was that the baby's father had not been human.

"A spriggan," she whispered. "A devil."

Bee, thinking of the Hounds, questioned Elowen as to what her attacker had looked like, but Elowen either didn't remember or was too distressed to say. Nor had she seen him after the assault. When she realised she was pregnant, her mother had been first tight lipped and angry, then resigned, and it sounded from what Elowen had said that a similar thing – a rape – had happened to her mother as well. It was not likely that Elowen had much of a chance on the marriage market even before her pregnancy. Talking to her now, Bee began to realise that Elowen probably wasn't very old, younger than Luna was now, most probably. And it was also clear that she had loved her baby. "More than anything in the world," Elowen wept. Enough not to flee into whatever otherworld awaited her when she died, which had not been long after the loss of her child, but to wait, and to be used by the wreckers, for all this time as she searched the moors for her child, even surely knowing that he was not there.

"Can I have a word, Bee?" her sister asked.

She handed Rosie to Ver and Bee followed her along the deck. Luna had that stubborn, concerned expression that Bee knew all too well.

"She did give us into the hands of the Morlader," Luna said, and explained. "And she helped the wreckers, I think, but she might not have meant to. Her lamp was one of the ones that lured ships onto the rocks – I think she must have been the woman you and Dark saw – but she was really only looking for her baby. I just feel very sorry for her."

Bee found herself stumped. There was a big missing piece of the jigsaw. If Elowen's baby was Hob (whom Bee had never met), which seemed more and more probable, what on earth was he doing in twenty first century London, hanging out with the dubious Miranda and living the life of a young gay man about town? Also, he seemed to have *had* a mother. What had happened between baby Hob being carried off with Elizabeth's retinue, and grown up Hob causing minor havoc in contemporary London? That was an awful lot of time and story to account for, Bee thought.

She said, "What was her baby called?"

But Luna explained that Elowen had said that she had never named the child, he was unchristened. She had never known the name of her

277

own father, and if she herself had been the product of a rape, why should she? And she could not think of another name that she liked.

"She told me she always thought of him as Baby."

"If her rapist was a Hound," Bee said, "How does that work? I thought they were grown from teeth."

"Some of them are. But maybe human/Hound interbreeding is different. And the Hound seems to have come from a very long time ago. And he said that women's love is worth nothing," Luna added indignantly. "So she was just something to be used and then thrown away."

"Could you wait here with her?" Bee asked. She made her way down the deck to the prow, where Louisa and Dark were talking to Captain Thorn. "Bit of a problem," said Bee.

"She's obviously very upset," Louisa said. "Do you know why?"

"Yes. Her baby was taken from her and sent via magical means to, we think, Queen Elizabeth. The first one."

Louisa gaped at her. "How in the world do you know that?"

"Because my sister Stella watched it happen." Bee elaborated. "But the thing is, we don't *know* it was Hob. And we don't really know that it was Elowen's baby. For all I know, this might have happened more than once."

"An annual sacrifice?" Louisa mused.

"Do you know of this, Ned?" Captain Thorn asked. "Were there rumours, in your day?" Good question, thought Bee, for Dark had once seen the Queen himself, when alive. But Dark laughed.

"A great parcel and muddle of rumours, all the time. But who was ever to know for certain, beyond the great men and ladies of the court? I saw her once, a sovereign moment, you might say. I knew I would remember it always. But as for stealing children through the fireplaces of the land, no, I never did hear that."

"I think," Bee said, "that it might be worth proceeding on the assumption that Elowen is Hob's mum and that he was the child whom Stella saw. In that case, we could potentially reunite them, if the *Stargazy* can reunite *us* with our day and age?" Might be tricky, to say the least, as Stella was still missing. But Ace, if he had turned up by now, would know how to get in touch with Blake and Hob. Who did not know who his true mother was... Well, they would have to cross that bridge when they came to it.

Captain Thorn nodded. "I'll do my best."

STELLA

Motioning for quiet, Nick pushed a loose block of stone to block the door. Alys spread her hands over the altar. Stella saw her close her eyes. The back of the chapel shimmered and faded; the woodland lay beyond.

Nick mouthed, "Run! Split up."

Stella clasped Laura's hand and they fled through the vanished wall. The stag belled behind them as they ran headlong down the slope. Stella caught her foot in a skein of bramble, let go of Laura's hand, and fell, rolling before she was able to scramble upright by the edges of a little stream.

"Laura!" she yelled. "Horse it! Get out of here!"

She could not yet see the stag and his rider but she knew they were there. Laura gave her a look of agonised indecision.

"Do it!" Stella roared and the grey mare leaped away, sure footed along the stream. Stella ran in the opposite direction; no use in making it easy for the bastard. Then a blur of white caught her eye and she glanced up to see the Hound above her on the ridge. He was staring down at her, his face filled with cold calculation.

"Shit." Stella stumbled back but someone caught her arm.

Kit Coral was standing beside her. Stella looked down. He held out a hand and in it was something curious: a little fuzzy ball of crimson and brown. It took Stella a moment to recognise it: a robin's pincushion, a wasp gall of the kind that you found on wild roses. Coral grinned. He drew back his arm and threw the gall upwards. It was surely too light to travel far, but the gall sailed through the air, trailing crimson tendrils, and as it flew, it grew. It hit the ground near the stag's hooves, bursting into rosy flame, and the stag reared in alarm, nearly unseating the Hound, who gave a shout of fury. He fought to control the stag, which gave a great leap off to the right, but a coiling wall of wild roses had sprung up. Stella watched with a repelled fascination as the roses twined swiftly up the legs of the stag, up the body of the Hound, and into the mount's antlers. Soon, all that was visible was a statue of a man astride a deer, made of roses. Their faint, sweet fragrance drifted across.

"Like Sleeping Beauty!" said Laura, human again and coming downstream with the others.

"Quite right, Laura. However, I doubt it will hold them for as long as a hundred years," Alys said. "Unfortunately."

They made their way as quickly as they could, up the hill. Stella's skin prickled as they passed the motionless stag and his rider.

"How long is that likely to last?" she asked Nick.

"An hour or so. If we're lucky. Summer magic, soon gone."

At the bottom of the slope, Stella halted.

"Wait! What was that?"

It was a thin, reedy little voice. It said, "This way!"

"Who's that?" Stella said.

"I can't hear anything," Nick told her.

"Here!" Now she could see that the speaker was an elder tree, a spindly wisp of a thing, past flowering. She could see the berries starting to form. She glanced back.

"Here!" the elder said and a dark hole opened up at Stella's feet. She hesitated.

"Go!" her mother said. She dropped down the hole, landing with a thud. They followed.

It was very quiet down here, not cold. Stella landed awkwardly; Laura and Nick helped her to her feet. She stood to find a small green light in front of her. It was not a bright spark, like her grandfather's spirit, but a diffuse dim glow.

"Hello?" Stella said.

"Stella?" said the spark.

That was a surprise.

"How do you know my name? Who are you?"

"It's Aln. Do you remember me?"

"No way!" Of course Stella remembered her. A green skinned girl, wose-kin, whose brother had become a tree. "Aln, what are you doing here?"

"These are wose lands," Aln said, out of the air.

"So you *did* get home again!"

"Yes, and my brother, too. We've had many adventures."

"Know the feeling," Stella said.

"Follow the light."

Stella did not entirely trust this – what if it was someone pretending to be Aln? But she thought that if this were the case, the person would feign being someone whom Stella knew more closely, and what choice did she have, after all?

"Keep talking," she instructed Aln. "Tell me about your adventures."

As the little light led us through the darkness, Aln did so, speaking through its faint glow, telling Stella about her journey down the great river, about the clan of root witches who had helped her free her brother, about returning home just as the spring had come and the primroses were out.

"We had word of you, Stella, and of your sisters. Of your kindness to the strangers who were some of my people, of your struggles with the gull witch."

"Word travels fast," Stella said, impressed. She could see now that they were walking through a passageway of earth, like a badger's burrow, but big enough to stand upright. Then it came out into chamber where a green fire blazed on a hearth and Aln herself was sitting on a large tussock of something that looked like moss.

"Stella!" she said, jumping up. She held out her hand and the green glow flashed bright and fell into the flames. "And our friends!"

"Aln, hi!" Hugs all round.

"How did you know we were here?" Stella asked her.

"A sparrow brought the news," Aln said, "when you entered our land of the green sun. You're right on the edge here. I had to travel a day to find you all."

"A Lily White Boy was after us, riding a stag," said Stella.

"I know. He will not find you here. Why is he after you?"

"His master might not be very pleased with Nick here. Or Mum, for that matter."

"My brother's on his way; we will take you further. Would you like some beans?"

"Why not? Breakfast was a while ago."

Aln gave everyone a bowl. The beans were cold and rather sloppy, but Stella thought this was no time to be fussy. At least they seemed meat free. She ate them all and handed back the bowl.

"When Hob gets here, we can make a plan to take you through the land," Aln said.

This remark gave Stella a moment's pause, before she remembered that Aln's brother and Blake's apprentice shared a name. She mentioned this. Her Hob had said it was a common name. Like Dave, Hob had said.

Aln laughed. "Oh, he's right. there are dozens of people called Hob. It means the Bright One, Shining Fame, in one of the old tongues. I suppose people like it because it sounds grand, even if you're not."

And perhaps this was yet another clue that red-haired Hob's origins were not exactly earthly.

On request, Aln gave her a bowl of water with which to wash and Stella had just completed her sketchy ablutions when she heard a voice, calling Aln's name.

"Come outside," said Aln. Stella did so, through a round door in the side of the hill. The light outside was dimmer and greener than it had been, and although the trees here were also in full leaf, Stella did not recognise some of them. A boy was standing there, of perhaps sixteen, with Aln's greenish skin. He had not looked like this when Luna had known him; she had told Stella about Aln's brother, how he had the face of an otter (Christ, maybe they were related?), but sometimes resembled just a bundle of sticks. Then he had become a tree. He looked more or less human now and he was smiling as he held the horses: Nick's big chestnut and the moon grey rocking horse. Evidently the root witches, whoever they were, had done a good job.

"We have a favour to repay," Aln said.

"Well, not really. We helped you back in the winter, but you helped us as well. And Hob became a tree as a result."

"As you said, we're both all right now."

She went to speak to her brother.

"Have you been here before, Nick?" Alys asked.

"I've been to the edges before, but not deeper. It's not really a place for ordinary humans – they're different here. As you'll have noticed!"

"Bee mentioned the Green Children of Woolpit when all that kicked off at Christmas. I'm assuming this is where they came from?"

"Probably. The boy died but the story goes that girl lived and lost her green colour. Probably a dietary thing."

"Or, like, a magical thing?"

Alys grinned. "Or that."

Aln came back. "We should get going. We're taking you deeper into the green world – the Hunt are less likely to follow but they do raid our country, so keep your eyes open. We won't be here for long – we'll show you to the edge and then you'll have to venture on."

"Where will that take us?" Alys asked.

"The chase."

Alys nodded. "All right. I do know that part a bit."

"As in 'hunting chase?'" Laura asked.

"Yes, that's right."

"And what would be hunted there, Mum?"

"Well. Let's hope it's not us."

SERENA

Hob did not look happy, Serena thought. He slid down from the horse's back with a palpable grimace of relief and dusted off his jeans. He was dressed much as usual. Then he looked across to the top of the steps and saw Ace. Serena saw his face light up, but before he could speak, Ace snapped,

"Who the hell's he? Another one of your pirate crew?"

Hob took the hint; thankfully, Serena reflected, he was quick on the uptake. He said nothing but the lighthouse keeper remarked, sourly,

"That's Captain's champion. Come all the way from the capital to lend a hand."

"I told you," Hob said, "I don't know who you are. I don't want anything to do with any of this." His voice had the ring of conviction. Serena believed him. The lighthouse keeper laughed.

"What you want or don't want has nothing to do with it. If the Captain pipes, we all dance to his tune or take a spell with the Gentlemen."

Hob was silent. Serena didn't know if he knew who the Gentlemen were, but she thought he probably did.

"Champion? He's just a lad," Ace said scornfully.

"He's spriggan born, though, and that's enough for the Captain."

"What?" Hob said, but the lighthouse keeper added,

"Right, enough chatter from the lot of you. Down the steps."

Hob was nudged after them, by a tall man who glanced warily back as he departed over the lip of the cliff. But Serena and Davy were well hidden by the gorse. As soon as they had gone Davy said,

"Okay, I think I've got a plan. You said you came up a rope ladder. I'm gonna go down the same way."

"What if someone's in the room below? And what are we going to do with Moth?"

"What if they are? All they'll see is a rat. If there's no one there, you can follow me down. The dog can stay here and wait for us – he's smart enough. Aren't you, boy?"

"All right," Serena said. They crossed to the hole from which Serena had earlier emerged and Davy slipped down the ladder. She was quickly back.

"Not a peep. You ready? I'll go down first again – if someone comes in the room, I'll nip your heel. Just don't squeak."

"I'll be quiet," Serena promised. "Moth, stay here." But the room was empty.

"I know where we are," Davy muttered when they were both underground. "We were taken through here. There's a chamber at the end, beyond that door, which leads out onto the shore. Bet the lads are down there by now."

Cautiously, they tried the door. It was locked.

"Well, drat," Davy said. "Wait here."

Serena watched anxiously as the little rat squeezed under it. There was silence, followed by a metallic chink and rattle. A moment later, a key appeared beneath the door, shoved from the other side. Serena snatched it up and unlocked the door.

"Thanks!" Davy said. "I was just going to check out the lie of the land but then I spotted the key. Luck is on our side," she added optimistically.

"Let's hope so. Do you know how extensive these caves are?"

"Not very. Have you been to the Lizard before?"

"Yes, we went to Kynance Cove once when we were kids and there were caves in the cliffs there, but I don't really remember how big they were. Not very big, I don't think. And there are mine workings throughout Cornwall but I don't think there are any here."

"Depends if this is the past or the actual otherworld, though, coz that's often different. My vibe is that it's the past."

"Same here," Serena said. She pocketed the key, just in case.

The chamber was open to the sea: they could see the long lines of the waves beyond. But halfway down was another door, set into the rock. Serena tried the key and opened it. Rough cut steps led upwards.

"We might do better as animals, Serena."

"I'm scared," Serena admitted, "But not scared enough to change."

"Okay. Well, let's see how it goes."

The steps curved up into the cliff. Serena jumped as a voice said, suddenly, close by, "We don't know where the you-know-who have got to, either."

"Ace!" hissed Serena.

"Serena! Where are you?"

"Where are *you*?"

"On the other side of the wall, from the sound of it."

"So where's the door?"

"We were dropped in from above. Hob's ricked his ankle. Sam and I are all right."

"Serena, where's Moth?" Sam's voice said.

"I don't know!"

"We'll keep going up," Davy said. "See if we can find you."

The stairs led out onto a platform of rock, around six feet in width and thus easy to walk along, but Serena noticed with unease a substantial drop on the other side and the surf scudded and rumbled beneath.

"Look," Davy said. A short distance along the platform was a wooden hatch. "Bet they got put in there."

They hastened to the hatch and pulled it up. Three wan faces peered up at them.

"Get on my shoulders, Ace," Sam said. "Then you pull me up and we'll pull Hob up last."

With some scuffling and cursing, this was achieved. Hob flopped onto the platform, white in the face and panting with pain.

"Sorry."

"No, don't apologise."

"Do you think you've broken it?" Serena said.

"I don't think so, but it bloody hurts."

"Put your arm round my shoulders," Sam said, as he and Ace hauled Hob to his feet.

"Better start calling you Hobble, mate," said Davy.

"That's not funny!"

Davy grinned. "Let's get going."

Serena hoped that they would not need to try the wall watching trick again, but although they heard voices, and halted, the sound receded into the passages. It was not until they found their way back to the rope ladder that they met opposition.

BEE

Bee had taken Elowen down to the captain's cabin, and put her to bed. The ghost went with her obediently enough; even if dead, she must be worn out. She had become a little more solid. Bee was used to this, with Dark, who looked and felt perfectly mortal most of the time, but who was prone to occasional transparency. Once the ghost was settled, Bee went back up on deck and found that they were somewhere else entirely.

The sea was now as calm as glass, the shore a shadow. Ver and Luna were sitting on a bench nearby, heads bent over the baby. Dark came to stand by her side.

"It's so quiet," Bee said.

He smiled. "Quiet as Paradise."

Bee said, "I read somewhere that some sailors had a sparrow tattooed on their arms because even a fallen sparrow is allowed into Heaven. And that's why the chap in that movie is called Jack Sparrow. But you have no sparrow on your arm, Ned, only a swallow among your other tattoos." Mention of the fallen sparrow reminded her of William Blake.

He grinned at her. "Maybe I didn't fancy actual paradise. Maybe I just wanted to go home."

"Good forward planning!"

"I've rarely been accused of that. How's Elowen?"

"She looks done in. I've put her to bed. Hope she can sleep. Oh, Captain Thorn!"

"We'll pull out in the morning, head for the Mount at first light and seek help– the folk there have been good to me and to this ship. The men need a rest after the battle. There's drink waiting, Mistress Bee. Will you join us?"

"A tot of grog?"

He laughed. "You can have grog if you want but we have recently taken on a decent barrel of wine."

"How civilised!" Bee said, and went to join him.

Elowen was not the only one who was exhausted. Bee, staving off yawns, had a glass of wine and then joined her in the Captain's cabin. She, along with Ver, Luna and the baby had been given bunks to sleep

287

on; Bee had a hammock. She hoped the calm weather would prevail as she did not fancy being pitched out onto hard floorboards. She had a brief battle with the hammock and, feeling too nervous to move, lay in it staring up at the rafters, as the ship gently, imperceptibly rocked and creaked – and then she was asleep.

She was woken by Dark. "Thought you'd like to know. Cap'n says we're underway."

It was dark up on deck, but the eastern sky was growing paler. A full moon hung low over the water and there was one bright star, which Bee thought must be Venus. The *Stargazy* sailed on into the light, chasing the dawn. Bee hunched and rolled her shoulders. "This shape changing stuff really takes it out of you. I was hungry last night. Come to think of it, I still am." She looked hopefully at Dark. He laughed.

"I'll find you some bread and honey. That's what I had."

In the east, the light grew. A moment later, the sun roared up, banishing the deep green hue of the morning sea and casting everything into gold. Bee gasped and shielded her eyes, and when she got her vision back, she saw the Mount up ahead. No sign of Tretorvic, no pink house or yellow house upon the cliffs, but a huddle of white fishing cottages strung along the shore. The Cornish wind caught the sails of the *Stargazy* and she ploughed on through a rougher swell, towards the island.

Bee watched for a little while as the Mount grew bigger. She could see the castle clearly now, its turrets picked out by the morning light. There was a dock far below and Bee thought she could see a figure standing on it, to welcome them. Or so she hoped. She went below again, to check on Elowen before the *Stargazy* cast anchor.

The ghost was sitting on the edge of the bunk. Luna was already up and feeding Rosie. Bee could see the panelling through the ghost's body. She wondered whether ghosts became more transparent depending on their mood, or state of mind; she must remember to ask Dark.

"Where are you taking me?" Elowen asked.

"To St Michael's Mount?"

Elowen looked at her in alarm.

"The island? No! That's where *she* is! That's where she made me give up my baby!"

"Who do you mean, Elowen? Who is 'she'?" Ver asked. Bee was conscious of a growing dismay: what if they had made some terrible mistake and they were delivering Elowen to her enemies?

"Bersaba. The eel witch, the Morlader's witch. She was the nurse at the castle. She made me put my child in the fire –" And Elowen began to weep again, at the horror of it.

"Wait here," Bee told her. She ran back up on deck to find Captain Thorn or Louisa, but when she got there she found that the *Stargazy* had already weighed anchor and that the boat was being made ready.

"Hang on!" Bee commanded. The Captain gave her an enquiring look. She explained.

"They won't be there now," Louisa said.

"Well, she seems very sure," Bee said, "And I don't imagine you'd forget a thing like that."

"No, you have a point. I have heard of eel witches. Mainly over the other side of the country, though, in the Fen lands. I don't know of any here."

"I think," Bee said, "that even if the Captain does think they're friendly, we'd better see exactly who's waiting for us at the castle before Elowen disembarks."

STELLA

Stella would not have even considered riding the grey pony if Aln had not accompanied them. The green world here was composed of woodland, mainly ancient oak, with thick undergrowth between. Deep pools lay in the hollows, and without Aln they would never have found the track. It reminded Stella of things she had read about Medieval forests, too thick and impenetrable for all but the most adventurous hunters, and just as this occurred to her they came out into a small glade filled with a pungent, scorched smell. A small conical hut, rather like that of the lake people, stood in its centre and a stack of beech logs by its door.

"Charcoal burners," Alys informed them. Then they were through the glade and back on the badger track, the horses plodding along. Kit, on foot, was more adept at dodging the brambles. Stella was starting to lose any sense of time and was relieved when they came out onto the bank of a small, fast flowing river.

"We'll follow the river," Aln said. "It flows into the chase. It's the border."

"I'm leaving you here, as we agreed, Alys," Nick said.

"Fine. I'd rather you held the fort back home," said Alys. "And you've come further than we originally planned. Hope you get back safely."

"You'll be in good hands with Kit."

To Stella it seemed that the light that filtered through the canopy was a little more golden here. She looked back as Nick led the chestnut away and saw the green world disappearing into the mist, but before the wood was swallowed completely she glimpsed the round central tower of a castle, with a wooden walkway around it. There had been no sign of this previously, yet they must have ridden straight past it. The stones were massive and moss covered, and there was a pennant drooping above it, bearing a green sun. Then it was gone into the mist. Stella mentioned it to Aln.

"It's the farthest most watchtower on the western border," Aln said.

"Is that where you live, Aln?"

Aln laughed. "No, I am no watchman." She spoke as if it was a special kind of profession. Maybe it was. "I come from a village, much further in. Your sun is very bright to me, Stella. Too bright."

"It must have been good to come back home."

"Yes, it was. I'll return there tonight, once I've seen you into the chase. I'll make sure Nick travels safely through our lands."

"Is it far now?"

"No, not very." The light was growing, a summer noon. Stella saw butterflies, a host of Red Admirals feeding on the flowers of the ivy that grew up one of the trunks. They splashed up from the river onto softer grass.

"I'll leave you now," Aln said, parting with their thanks. Stella had one last glimpse of her as she made her way back along the river but then the mist took her as it had taken Nick, and Aln was gone.

"A relief, frankly," said Alys. "I don't want to drag other people into this as long as I can help it."

"Yeah, I kind of feel she's been through enough. Is this the chase?"

"Yes, this is Beaudesert."

"That's its name?"

"Yes. There's a place called that in our England, up near Cannock Chase, but this is different. I think it's like a title, or a name that was often granted to the lands set aside for hunting."

"Beautiful desert, right? Why am I not encouraged?"

"It is a bit sinister, I agree."

"The vegetation's more familiar, though. I've seen that stuff that's all over the ground before. I don't know what it is, mind you."

"Dog's mercury," Kit Coral said. "Poisonous."

"Nice."

"It's an indicator species for ancient woodland," said Alys. "So's that." She pointed to a small pink flower.

"I know what that is," Stella said, keen not to seem totally ignorant. "Herb Robert."

"That's right. And you can see how much lichen is on those trees — that's a sign that the air quality is good. Not that you'd expect a lot of acid rain or industrial pollution."

"Is it all trees?" Stella asked, but a moment later she realised that it was not. The oak woods came to an abrupt halt. They were in open ground, at the top of a slope, looking down onto parkland. A long ride, close cropped, led away into the distance and for a second Stella glimpsed a house, a Palladian-fronted mansion similar to Nick Wratchall-Haynes' place. The windows caught the sun and blazed like fire, but then all Stella could see was the distant blue hills.

"Right," Alys said, reining in Laura. "I know this looks peaceful, but looks are deceptive. I don't want to head straight out into the open, although we'll have to do so eventually. So I suggest we skirt the wood for as far as we can."

"Fine with me. Can I ask who, exactly, we're likely to meet?"

"Hunters," Kit Coral said. He spat into the nettles.

"The Wild Hunt? I should think that might be in some disarray. What about that Hound? He's probably broken free by now."

"The Hound's a worry, yes, although he might not venture in here on his own even if he's made it round the edge of the green world by now. I mean different human hunts, through time."

"I saw Henry once, hunting deer. The Eighth."

"Lucky you," said Alys.

"Yeah, right. But that was in London."

"A lot of London was parkland or hunting chase."

"Windsor, too. We had a bit of an adventure in the great park."

Alys looked interested. "Meet Herne?"

"Yes, as a matter of fact."

"Rather Herne than Henry."

"Fewer murdered wives, for starters. As far as I know. He helped me."

"There seems to have been a lot going on to which I have not been made privy," Alys said.

"Tit for tat, Mum."

"Fair enough. Do you trust me, Stella?"

Stella looked at her mother. She had, over the last day or so, become increasingly convinced that Alys actually was Alys, at least. She hadn't done anything particularly out of character – her new character, at least. And she hadn't, as far as Stella knew, done anything to help Aiken Drum, who even now might be pounding towards them across the hinterland, flintlocks cocked.

Stella said, "I sort of trust you."

"You don't have to be polite."

"No, I'm not just being polite. I sort of trust you."

"Coral doesn't."

Kit Coral gave a shrug. "I don't trust many."

"I don't have much choice," said Stella. "Either that or Laura and I strike out on our own and I don't know if Laura knows where we are or which way to go. I certainly don't."

"I'll get you through if I can."

"Fair enough," Stella echoed.

By now, they were some distance around the edge of the wood. The grey mare stepped with delicacy and precision; the pony followed her lead, with Coral bringing up the rear. But then they ran out of wood. The stand of beech which they were skirting ended halfway along the hillside. Beyond, the largest trees were thorn, no higher than Stella's knees and interspersed with harebells.

"We're going to have to risk it," Alys said.

"I can't see anyone down there."

"Unfortunately, that doesn't mean a thing. We're going to make a run for that big oak – see it? Once there, we'll aim for the woods on the opposite side."

"What about that house?"

"What house, Stella?"

"I saw a socking great mansion, but then it disappeared."

Alys said nothing but she did not look happy.

"Go as fast as you can," she said. Coral sprang up behind her. Her heels touched Laura's sides and the grey mare sprang down the slope, cantering fast and then into a gallop as they hit the shorter grass and flatter land of the park itself.

"Oh Christ," Stella said. She kicked the pony into a trot. The rocking horse did not have Laura's speed but he did his best and by the time they hit the park, he was galloping. Stella did not have the skill or the time to find a rhythm and she simply hung on, having lost the stirrups some distance down the slope. Perhaps, she thought, she might have tried to change form herself but otters weren't that speedy on land. She found herself slipping in the saddle. At this rate she'd arrive at the oak with her arms wrapped round the pony's neck, if she arrived at all. Amid the effort of staying on the grey's back, she was dimly aware of shouts.

What the hell was happening now? Out of the corner of her eye she saw a white blur. She turned her head. A greyhound. It wore a thick, studded collar and soon it was joined by others, brown and black and pale. They chivvied and herded the grey so that, shying, he veered off track.

"Stella!" That was her mother, off to the right somewhere.

"I can't do anything!"

Then she lost her grip altogether and fell off. She hit the ground in a mass of dogs. Winded, wheezing, she made it as far as getting up on her hands and knees and looked back. The hounds were the outliers; they had ringed her now. They did not look as though they were about to attack but their tails weren't wagging, either. Behind them, heading fast across the parkland, came a group of men, women and horses. They were colourful, dressed in silks as vivid as parrots, and at the front, on a white palfrey, rode a woman all in green, with a green hat. Oh no, Stella thought, because she had seen that cold white face before and she had hoped not to see it again. Not since the last time when Elizabeth, the Queen, had snatched a living child from the midnight fire.

SERENA

Sam and Ace had gone up the rope ladder first, using it to haul up the injured Hob while Davy and Serena kept watch. Then the ladder dropped down again with a rustle and Serena was just about to set foot on it when the shadow came. It descended like a curtain. Serena opened her mouth to call out but it was filled with the taste of mist and rot. It blotted out her sight and filled her ears with cotton wool. It was, she knew instinctively, the same power that had split them up and sent them astray from A La Ronde. It also sent her into hare: she dropped to the floor on all fours and found herself beneath the mist, but she could see it above her, blotting out the room, and she knew what it was made of: the souls of men, crying out in fear, but with an animating force behind it.

She bolted, fleeing through the passages. There was a man, he gave a startled shout, but Serena was jinking away, streaking by, and no human was swift enough to catch her. She had forgotten Davy, left behind in the chamber, forgotten Sam and Ace and Hob. She knew only the run and her nose and ears took her towards the fresh winds of the clifftop and the soft grass and the starfilled sky. She shot out of an opening and saw the space ahead of her. She raced for it, avoiding the figures who stood on the cliff, avoiding the huge, bewildering buildings, running for open country – but there was a rustle and a scuffle in the gorse and something struck her amidships and bowled her over.

Serena sat up, human and winded, clutching Moth. The dog was ecstatic to see her: tail whirling like a propellor, long tongue rasping her face. The others were running towards her over the grass.

"Quick!" Ace said. He clasped her by the arm and they ran on.

"Davy! Sorry I left you!" Serena was now horrified at herself.

"Nah, it's all right. I get it. I did the same but I was a bit more compos mentis, that's all, Wits about me. More practice."

"What was that thing?"

"I think that 'thing' was a knocker," Ace said. They had made it round the back of the lighthouse and paused for breath.

"I always thought they were sort of cute leprechauns. We saw some in a gift shop in Tretorvic. Like gnomes."

"That was nothing like a gnome," Davy said.

"Gran said they're the spirits of men killed in the mines," Sam told her. "But some say as how they're the ancient dead. Maybe they're both."

"They felt like that," Serena said. She found the thought horrible and sad: difficult lives, awful deaths. Davy was more pragmatic.

"Anyway, let's hope it's not coming after us. There's an entrance around here, I can feel it. We know there's one here – Miss P said so, that's why she sent us here, and I thought I got a whiff of it when we were in the cottage."

"Escape route, Davy?" Ace said.

"Yeah, I think so. Follow me." And following Davy, they stepped around the curving side of the lighthouse, into sudden brightness.

A round room, sunlight washing in and the blue of the sea beyond. Then Serena's phone chimed, followed by Davy's and Hob's

"Good to be back in the here and now," Davy said, looking at her screen. "We're a day after we left."

"Yes." Serena did a rapid calculation. "We've lost a few hours."

"Maybe one day we'll catch up. Like Daylight Savings Time."

"I feel as though the last few months have put years on me," Serena said. She went to the leaded windows of the modern lighthouse and looked out. She could see the line of the coast, running away to the west, and the steep granite cliffs of the Lizard itself. A gull swooped overhead, crying out. Sea and sky and light, far from the smugglers' haunt of a few hundred years ago.

"I wonder if the light still works," Davy said, looking up at the huge glass optics.

"It does," Sam told her. "I read an article by some bloke who has to go around fixing these. Floats in a bath of mercury, apparently. The light, not the bloke."

"There aren't actual lighthouse keepers?" Serena said.

"Not any more. Which is probably just as well for us." Ace went to the door and opened it. "Unlocked, thank God."

They crept down a spiral flight of stairs, with Hob holding tightly to the handrail. At the bottom, rooms led from a hallway and Serena saw a list of rules, marked "Air BnB." The lighthouse owner – presumably Trinity House – must be renting out the adjoining cottage. The front door opened onto a long stretch of grass and a paved walkway. A road led north. In silent agreement, Ace and Serena and Davy took it, and within ten minutes or so, found themselves in the village.

Here, they hit a snag. There was a bus to Tretorvic, but it took three hours.

"You're kidding me!" Ace said, when Serena, after checking both the timetable and Google maps, reported this unhappy fact. "It's what, thirty miles away?"

"You're not in London any more, mate," Sam said, studying the map. "Bus goes up through Redruth."

"What about that thing – what's it called? I never use it. Uber?"

"Doesn't exist in Cornwall," Serena told him.

"Jesus. Well, there's nothing else for it. We'll just have to find a pub."

"Great choice of name," Davy said, as they sat in the pub called the Witchball, nursing drinks. Serena felt distinctly disoriented. It wasn't the lost hours so much as being whisked halfway across the south west in a matter of seconds. She sipped her white wine gratefully and tried to focus on the old walls and beams of the pub. Davy and Ace, who had made a quicker recovery – perhaps they were used to it? – were discussing options in low voices. Sam was making a fuss of Moth. In a low voice, Hob said, "Serena, I just wanted to say thanks, for getting me out of there."

"You should thank Davy, really. I didn't do much more than freak out and run away."

"I don't know what the fuck's going on. I didn't want to be anyone's champion. Champion of what?"

"What exactly happened to you?"

"I was walking back to Blake's. Along the river. I could see this mist coming in over the Thames and I thought, I don't like the look of that, and then suddenly this man, this *thing*, was standing in front of me and he said he'd chosen me as his champion because wasn't I spriggan kin, and I was just about to say that I didn't know what he was talking about when suddenly it was night and we were on this boat in a cove at the bottom of some cliffs. And I felt terribly weak. I couldn't focus. It was like he was draining all the power out of me. Then he took me to some island – I think it was St Michael's Mount but I'm not sure. It felt – *familiar*, like I'd been there before, but I've never been to Cornwall. I told you that, didn't I, when we met in that bar? He introduced me to this woman as his champion – I think she was a woman but she might have been a mermaid, come to think of it."

"Surely you'd have *noticed*, Hob?"

"It was all really weird. It was like a dream. Maybe it *was* a dream."

But Serena did not think so. Hob went on,

"She set me this task, of finding her mother, but I didn't know where to start. I told Him that and he didn't like it. Went on and on about my heritage and didn't I know where I was, and eventually I told him to fuck off and he locked me up in this tower somewhere. Then eventually he had me taken on that sodding horse to wherever we are now – the Lizard, isn't it? I've never been so glad to see anyone as I was to see Ace," he ended pathetically. "So what happened to you?"

"Well," she said. "It's all a bit complicated. We've had a few problems because Stella's gone missing and this man, or ghost, whatever he is – the Morlader, anyway, he…"

She brought Hob up to speed as rapidly as possible.

"I just hope no one's followed us here," she finished. But the pub felt safe enough.

Serena wandered over to the Ladies, used the facilities and washed her face in the basin. After this she felt fresher, if not prettier. The mirror revealed wide, startled eyes: Alice fallen down the rabbit hole. Alice changing into rabbit? Serena dried her face on a paper towel and went back out into the bar. As she did so, she nearly cannoned into a large man making his way across the room. She squeaked, but her alarm was misplaced.

"Serena, my darling!" the man bellowed. "Fantastic to see you. How are you?"

"Adrian! Just here with some friends. Down from London," Serena added, since it was no more than the truth.

"Awesome. So am I – just got back, not a bad drive but the A303 was a bit hellish, as per bloody usual. I thought I'd swing by to see old Jeremy and pick up a surf board he's got for me."

"You're driving, then, Adrian?"

"Yes, I've got the car – had to take some stuff up to town. Think I told you that."

Serena mildly hated herself for putting on her most pleading expression, but she did it anyway. "I don't suppose, if we squeeze in, you could give us a lift?" she said.

Adrian had come up trumps, taking them all the way to Penhallow. Good thing he had an enormous car; even so, Sam had to sit in the boot, illegally, with Moth and the surfboard. Serena had made up a story about a bus to that went to the Lizard, but not back: it was half true, anyway. As they came into Tretorvic she braced herself for what they might find, but despite these legitimate fears the yellow house stood in sunlight and peace. She was afraid that Adrian might want to come in, but pleading stuff to do, he dropped them at the gate and accepted Serena's offer of dinner later in the week. Hopefully, that would actually come to pass.

The front door showed no signs of damage, but the house itself was empty. Serena ran from room to room, calling people's names. No one. Penhallow was like the Marie Celeste, with beds unmade and clothes dropped on floorboards. She went up to the cupola, which now looked out onto the sunny bay. The Mount lay in silver shining water. She waited, holding her breath, but nothing untoward befell her and the four windows showed only the sea, the sky, and the Cornish coast.

Serena went slowly back downstairs. The others were sitting in the conservatory. As she went in, her phone pinged and she saw that there had been a response to the text that she had sent Jane, from the Witchball. Serena called her back.

"I'm very glad you're all right." Jane sounded distracted with worry. "Louisa is with Bee. They're fine, so are Ver and Luna and the baby. But I'm afraid no one's seen Stella yet."

Serena sank onto the couch. "Okay, thanks so much for letting me know. Most of us are accounted for, at least."

"My great grandfather's ship is on its way. He sent me a message, by kittiwake. They're nearly here."

"Do you want us to meet it?"

"You'll probably see the *Stargazy* in the bay." Jane gave a rather hollow laugh. "I'm not sure anyone else will, mind you. They'll send a boat for you – meet them on the shore beneath the house."

"All right, we'll keep an eye out," Serena said.

STELLA

The Queen slowed when she saw Stella, who by now had got to her feet. She felt as though someone had punched her in the ribs. But she met Elizabeth's dark eyes all the same.

"Your Majesty," she said.

"Well, well, well. We meet again, little otter. I never forget a face." She strode around the perimeter of hounds, chiding them away. A man with a ruddy face and a salt and pepper beard rode up, fast, and whistled the dogs off with quick professionalism. They cringed around his feet. The Royal Hunt Master, Stella assumed. The Queen stared at her, tapping a fan against the opposite hand. Stella nearly said that she had not meant to trespass but since this was precisely what she had intended, there seemed little point.

"What are you doing here?" the Queen said at last.

"Fleeing, your Majesty."

At this, Elizabeth gave a very faint smile. "Fleeing from me? Or someone else?"

"Fleeing from the Wild Hunt, mainly. W – I didn't know you were here." She did not dare look round to see what had become of the others.

"And what have you done to upset the Hunt?" Elizabeth asked, in what must have been quite a kindly tone, for her.

"Lots."

Elizabeth stared at her for a long moment and then she burst out laughing.

"Why," she said, "for some reason that is the funniest thing I've heard all day. Did you hear that, Master Gregory?"

The ruddy faced man nodded. "No more than they deserve, your Majesty."

"I would say so. Well, I think this does call for some celebration. Take her to the house. But bind her hands."

SERENA

Halfway down the cliff path, Serena realised that they were in the past once more. The thrift which nodded above the rocks, the gulls screaming and wheeling overhead, and the sunlit beach below were the same, but the little yachts which had been flitting about the bay had gone, and Tretorvic itself was smaller, no longer strung out along the bay but just a handful of white houses above the harbour. Serena could not see Thornhold. But there was a ship at anchor in the bay: white sailed, with a colourful, star-crowned figurehead on its prow. A rowing boat was proceeding from it towards the beach, stroke by stroke. There were figures clustered on the deck of the ship, but Serena could not see who they were. High in the gorse, she heard an angry machine-gun ticking: a wren, hiding among the needles. She smiled. Perhaps Luna had come to guide them in.

She stepped from the last of the rocky ledges onto the sand. A few yards away it was wet: the tide was going out, stranding the limp rags of weed and a poor starfish, which Serena picked gingerly up by one arm and dropped into a rock pool.

"The boat's here," Ace said. "Let's hope it's the right one."

STELLA

She was doing more socialising on this trip through the otherworlds than she had ever done before, but unlike her time with the Lake villagers, Stella could not be sure that she was making friends, let alone influencing people. With her hands tied, she had been led back to the Queen's hunting lodge, a tall, oddly imbalanced building with narrow windows, plastered white and brown beamed. It looked strange, and nothing like the classic Georgian mansion she had glimpsed from the ridge, although she estimated that this must be in much the same place. Perhaps that had, in the mundane world, replaced this older building, somewhere.

Inside, the lodge was a curious mix of roughness and luxury: a lot of skins and furs and tapestries, but with uneven wooden boards on the floor and damp stone walls instead of panelling. The ground floor consisted of a single big hall with a fireplace at one end, not unlike Aiken Drum's house (if it had been his house. Stella could not rid herself of the conviction, baseless though it may be, that Drum had somehow borrowed someone else's place, possibly without their knowledge). Weaponry and the heads of slain animals decorated the walls. As a vegetarian, Stella did not like this and as an occasional otter, she liked it even less. She still remembered that crack the Queen had made back in the spring, about someone seeking a bow.

However, it was obviously wise to say nothing. She was keeping her ears open, trying to find out what was going on and, more specifically, what had happened to her mother and the others. She did not want to ask, just in case they had somehow escaped the Court's notice. But all the chatter was of the deer that had been slain that day, the performance of the hawks, fierce and golden of eye, that rode upon several of the ladies' wrists. Horse talk, dog talk. Nick Wratchall-Haynes would be right at home. Right class, too. Stella did at least have the advantage of having been brought up in the country, she wasn't a total townie, and she could at least understand the conversation even if her capacity for contributing to it was limited.

A young woman with dark curls, clad in a modish blue hat, approached her briskly.

"I just wanted you to know," she said, "that your pony is quite safe. He was rounded up and taken to the stables."

"It's really nice of you to tell me that," Stella said, touched.

"I would want to be assured of the safety of my mount," the girl said. "My name is Ann. Should you be concerned about him, speak to me."

"Thank you!"

Ann bustled off on another errand, leaving Stella, her hands still tied, to find somewhere out of the way to sit and work on the knots. She found a place, in the form of a window seat which looked out over the park. The sun was still quite high, but from the conversation around her, some kind of luncheon was being prepared. The knots proved recalcitrant and made Stella's fingers raw. In the event, her efforts turned out to be unnecessary. One of Elizabeth's huntsmen came up to her, brandishing a knife. Stella looked at him in alarm.

"Have no fear, maid. I am to free you, not prick you. Queen's orders."

"Thanks!" Stella said, again, although she wasn't sure whether his remark had contained some dodgy innuendo or not. "Am I joining your meal?"

"You are. We stand on little ceremony here, all together, as we hunt together."

"I bet the Queen stands on a bit of ceremony," Stella said.

"Well. Yes. She does."

At this point the subject of their conversation appeared, clad in what Stella considered to be a most unsuitable garb for the country: a gown white as ice and specked with seed pearls. Her hair stood out against it like fire. It made Stella wonder even more about Elizabeth. The Queen was, she remembered dimly from history lessons at school, the daughter of Henry the Eighth and one of his many wives. After some thought, she plumped for Anne Boleyn, but she was not sure that this was correct. A troubled childhood, anyway, if it had been Anne: Stella remembered that she had been beheaded and she thought it had been Anne who had been the ostensible reason for the split from Rome. Must talk to Davy. Must do some reading. But Stella would not have liked to have had Henry for a father and it couldn't have been great knowing that your dad'd had your mum's head chopped off.

Social services would have had a fit.

Yet seeing her up close and personal, Stella wondered if that original child of Henry's had even been Elizabeth. There was something about the Queen, not just the colour of her hair or her white, spiteful face, that reminded Stella strongly of the Hounds and of the Lily White Boys in particular. Was the person standing at the end of the room, conversing with her huntsmen, the daughter of tragic Anne or a changeling from the otherworld? Elizabeth had never married nor had children. Was there a reason for that beyond monarchical ruthlessness? Like species incompatibility? But Hob might be a Hound's child, so… Impossible to know without further evidence, but had Elizabeth, squalling and bald, been snatched through the flames of a fireplace in some great mansion rather than coming into the world as a result of Henry's sex addiction?

After all, she was pretty sure that Hob himself wasn't entirely human.

The Queen was approaching. This time, Stella managed an improvised dip at the knees, of the kind she had seen celebrities perform when presented to Elizabeth's modern namesake. Elizabeth smiled, graciously enough.

"So, little otter. You find yourself at court. We really ought to find you some better clothes. I do not even understand what you are wearing."

What was this supernatural obsession with her fashion sense?

"Clothes have changed, your Majesty. Quite a bit."

"So I see." Elizabeth pulled a sour face.

"Thank you for your hospitality, your Majesty." A bit of sucking up never hurt.

"Oh, I wouldn't call it that," Elizabeth said.

Well, that was sinister.

"My lady in waiting will seat you. You may have the honour of sitting near me."

"How extremely kind." The Queen raised a thinly plucked eyebrow at this. "Your Majesty," Stella amended hastily and to her relief Elizabeth gave an even thinner smile.

"You might be amusing. At the very least, you will be a novelty."

"Yes, your Majesty."

"I don't think we're ever sat down at board with an otter before."

"I'll mind my manners, Majesty."

"You certainly will."

Lunch was massive. Stella watched in mingled fascination and horror as dish upon dish was brought out from some kitchen somewhere by silent, capable staff. A sort of pottage to start with, followed by greens, salsify, capons and an entire roast deer, presumably the result of one of the hunting parties. Stella, unused to eating with a prong, nonetheless made short work of the pottage with a horn spoon, plus cheese, greens and bread, which was the sort of loaf you'd need a second mortgage to buy in organic bakeries in London. She didn't know what to do with the deer, slices of which were transferred to her plate without giving her a chance to refuse. She had just told herself sternly that when in Rome etc, she had eaten the mutton provided by Drum's gaoler, hadn't she? Not to mention her fish consumption, whether when otter or not – when she looked down and saw a little, terrier-like dog sitting hopefully at her feet. Stella seized a moment when the ladies were laughing at something one of them had said to slip her meat onto the floor, where it vanished. Excellent.

Wine was copious. Stella had a pewter mug of it, finding it to be like the Christmas Pudding wine that Bee had bought back in the winter for a joke, but which had actually been rather good. Heavy, though, and spiced. She sipped slowly and did not drink all of it. Some sacrifices had to be made for the sake of a clear head. Elizabeth had already swigged back three tankards, but showed no signs whatsoever of being even slightly tipsy.

And Stella was encouraged to talk. The ladies wanted to know about television, about the things of the future. She did her best to explain.

"A magic box," Elizabeth said, when she had completed a rather halting account of the marvels of modern technology. "Most diverting, Yet we have that in our day."

Stella, remembering that dark chamber glimpsed through the arras, thought she knew what the Queen was talking about.

"And now, tell me, Stella: what brings you to my hunting chase? To my time? For we have met before. Who are you? What family do you hail from?"

"My full name is Stella Jennifer F –" Stella hesitated, and pretended to cough on a crumb. The Queen's icy pearls gave her an idea. "Stella Jennifer Frost."

"A charming name."

"Thank you. Your Majesty."

"I do not know the Frosts. Are they northern, perhaps?" At this sally the Queen's ladies in waiting dutifully laughed and Stella joined them.

"Your Majesty is very insightful. Yes. From near York."

Because the Fallows had been around in Elizabeth's day, and the box which housed the gems of the Behenian stars was Elizabethan, and the last thing Stella wanted to do was to draw attention to her family.

"A lovely part of the realm." Elizabeth seemed to treat her comments, and those of the ladies in waiting, with an odd combination of malice and indulgence. This, however, was familiar to Stella: she had seen the nastier and more popular girls at school take a similar tactic. Then, her response had been snark and, in one memorable instance, a punch in the face. This was hardly on the table right now, however, and Stella opted for simple sycophancy. It seemed to be working well enough, although periodically she looked up from her plate to see the Queen's gaze upon her, a thoughtful, reflective stare which Stella did not like at all.

"And what brought you to our lands?"

"I got lost, your Majesty."

"Twice?"

"It happens quite a lot. I don't know why."

"How curious," the Queen began, but whatever she had been about to say was interrupted by a commotion from outside.

"Your Majesty," the head huntsman cried, bursting into the dining hall. "We have captured an intruder!"

He gestured to someone behind him. Two men with swords at their waists erupted into the hall, a prisoner drooping between them. They dragged her the length of the room and threw Alys at Elizabeth's feet.

LUNA

"You've got to stop adopting waifs and strays," Bee said, briskly. "First the Hound, now a ghost."

"You can talk!" Luna told her with indignation. "What about Dark?"

"I think Dark adopted *me*."

"When did that start, anyway? We've never really talked about your relationship."

"Some years years ago. I was in my twenties – it wasn't like I knew him as a child, which would have been pretty creepy. I think I might have seen him once at Mooncote and he remembers seeing us a couple of times when we were all kids, but it's actually only relatively recently that his house and ours started moving closer together in reality, for some reason. Dark doesn't know why. I've no idea. Anyway, I never thought I'd end up going out with a ghost and yet here we are."

"Here we are," Luna echoed. They were sitting on the deck, looking out over the bay. The *Stargazy* drifted at anchor and the sun was sinking down to the horizon. Rosie was asleep in a basket at Luna's feet. "I hope Sam's all right, talking of boyfriends." Bee squeezed her arm.

"I hope he is, too. I'm trying not to think about Sam, or Stella and Serena. I just keep telling myself everything's going to be okay."

"And are you convinced?"

"No, not really."

"I just feel so sorry for her," Luna said, reverting to the immediate problem of Elowen.

"I know. I do to. I think she's someone who's never been able to catch a break."

"There must have been an awful lot of people like that throughout history."

"And still are."

"It makes me really cross," Luna said. "So I want to help her but I don't know how."

"Captain Thorn's had word from the Mount, apparently. They don't know of anyone called Bersaba so it doesn't seem that she's alive now, or if she is, which is pretty unlikely but I suppose you never know, they don't know where she is. I spoke to him a few minutes ago – I came to tell you."

"So are we going to the Mount?"

Bee nodded. "Yes. He's setting sail soon."

But the Captain had a surprise for them. He came along the deck, a telescope in his hand.

"Miss Bee? You might see something of interest." He handed her the telescope and Bee put it to her eye.

"Where am I supposed to be looking?"

"See the high cliff?"

"Oh!" Bee exclaimed. "I can see Penhallow again!"

"Now bring the glass down a tad, to the beach."

"I can see the beach, a couple of gulls – ah, there's a little boat, just casting off."

"And in the boat?"

Bee dutifully scanned the coastline. "Oh my God!"

"What?" Luna asked. "What can you see, Bee?"

"It's Sam! And the dog!"

"Give me that," demanded Luna. Bee handed over the telescope and Luna held it up impatiently.

"Oh, thank God! It *is* Sam! And Serena! And – is that *Ace*?"

"Give me that back," Bee said. After a moment, she said. "Yes. Yes, it is. And someone else. Thank God. And thank you, Captain Thorn."

"I'd had word from Louisa. All's well. So far."

STELLA

If Stella had expected a 'So, Mr Bond!' monologue from the Queen, thus buying her time to think, she was disappointed. The Queen stood with a stiff rustle of silk, looked down at Alys sprawled across the dining hall boards, and said, "Drum's trollop. Take her outside and kill her."

The Hunt Master, Gregory, stepped forwards. Stella shouted, "No! Sorry! Wait, *wait*. Please, your Majesty! That's my mother. Alys Frost!"

For once, Elizabeth looked genuinely surprised. "Your mother?"

"Yes."

"And what is *she* doing here?"

"She probably came to rescue *me*," Stella said. "Your Majesty."

Elizabeth sighed. But she was hesitating, all the same.

"She's no longer with Drum," Stella told her urgently. "He threw her off his horse. She had to go to – she had to see a physician."

Elizabeth gave Stella another of those long, considering looks. Eventually, she said, "Come and walk with me, Otter Frost."

"Absolutely, your Majesty. Mum, see you in a bit."

Stella turned as they left the hall to see Gregory helping Alys into a chair. The Queen, quite alone, led Stella out into the sunshine. There was a small garden behind the lodge, with low hedges made of box. The garden hummed with bees and a curl of blue butterflies lifted up into the warm air. The Queen walked over to a seat, her immense skirts swaying around her. Stella, following, had a brief glimpse of two little ribboned white shoes.

"Sit down," Elizabeth said.

"Thank you, your Majesty." Stella did as she was told.

"So, your mother. Who are you? Your name is not Frost, for I know all the great houses in England and many beyond, and none have that name near York. I would think you of peasant stock, especially given the *most peculiar* way you are dressed, like a veritable boy, but your voice is not the voice of a peasant girl. If not quite that of a lady," she added, fixing Stella with a dark, penetrating eye.

Stella gave up. "My other name is Fallow." She dropped the *your Majesty*, but this time Elizabeth did not correct her.

"Why did you not say so?" Elizabeth exclaimed.

"I feared to get my family into trouble, in your day."

"Yet we are not quite in my day, are we?"

"Seriously, I haven't worked that bit out."

"But, *in* my day, I knew a woman named Alice Fallow. Perhaps your many times great-grandmother. Now that I think on it, she resembled your mother, and a little, yourself. She worked hard for me, Stella, and I reward those who do so. If I see fit."

"And did you see fit, your Majesty?"

"I did." Elizabeth gave a complacent nod. "She managed many things for me and when she became old and wished to return to her own lands, to her mother's house, I gave her what she had earned. A box, full of gems."

"I know that box," said Stella. She did not know whether, having decided to tell the truth, it was just simply pouring out of her, or whether the Queen's icy eyes left her no choice. "The gems are the stones of the stars."

"Yes, the Behenian stars. They used to come to the court, you know, in London. Perhaps in my younger days I did not entirely care for them, Stella. Their beauty outshone mine, you see."

"Surely not, your Majesty."

The Queen gave her a look. "Nice try. Later I came to see that they helped those whom they would and once, they helped me. They saved my kingdom. It's a long story. Perhaps I shall tell you some day. But I did not want them to remain at the court because there were those beside me who would use them for their own ends, and so with the aid of my magician, I sent them away, to be safe in the keeping of Alice Fallow, who was one of the few women I have ever truly trusted."

"They still come to Mooncote," Stella told her.

"They are eternal, immortal, as I could never be." Sitting so close to her, Stella could tell how thickly her white make up was applied, but Elizabeth seemed remarkably free of lines. Her jawline was tight, with no trace of jowls or sagging; she was faintly insectoid. It was as though her face were a mask, except for her eyes. Stella had read that the Queen applied white lead paint to cover the signs of age, but now she was not sure that this was actually the case.

"Can I ask you something?" she said, greatly daring, "Are you human?" Then she held her breath but the Queen said, without affront,

"I don't know. I believe myself to be, but perhaps there is some odd old blood running through our Royal veins. I can do things that humans cannot do, but I do not have full faery powers, nor yet the power of the stars we spoke about just now. Had we been immortal as those stars, we would still be ruling England, and many lands beyond."

"Okaaaay." Stella was suddenly reminded uncomfortably of Donald Trump. "So you come here in – what, an afterlife? In your own time?"

"I came here in my own day. But what this is now, I do not know."

Stella nearly said that it could be worse, spending your post-life period hunting and attending enormous lunches, but decided not to.

"I have a confession, your Majesty," she said instead.

"Another one?"

"I saw you take a child from the fire at a house in Clapham once."

At this, to Stella's relief, the Queen looked impressed rather than furious. She said, "*Did* you? How enterprising of you. How did you manage that?"

Stella explained.

When she had come to the end of her story, fearing reprisal and condemnation, she was interested to see that the Queen looked simply sad. It was the most human expression that had appeared on her face so far. She stared at the bees busying themselves in the lavender. At last, she said, "He was my child. As dear to me as if born from my body, as no child could be."

Stella did not dare ask why Elizabeth thought this was so.

"Two years, two years of his golden company, and then he was gone forever."

"He died?" Stella whispered.

"No. Disappeared. Stolen. Gone."

"Jesus! That must have been pretty awful for you." *Even if you stole him from his mum in the first place. Tact, Stella, remember that thing called tact?* "Who took him?"

"I do not know. Oh, my agents made all manner of searches, enquiries. You must understand, Stella, that my fingers are long. They extended into every part of England. There was, if I chose, nothing that I did not know. But we could not find the boy."

"What was his name?"

"Edward. I named him Edward. But we all called him Hob."

Stella sat very still. She, too, looked at the bees in the lavender.

"If I told you," she said, "that I could find that child, that he lives still, what would you do for me?"

The Queen seized her wrist with a hand like a claw. "I would do whatever you asked of me, if it was in my power. Can you?"

"I think so, yes."

"And what will you ask in exchange, Stella Fallow, great great great grandchild of my Alice? A mansion? Jewels? A spell?"

"Couple of things," said Stella. "Your Majesty."

"Name them."

"Please, spare my mother's life. And give us safe passage, to find Hob. Either take me to London, where he's living, or Cornwall, where we were heading. I can ask A – my friend to bring him to you there."

"Truly? We are much closer to Cornwall here," the Queen said. "But will your friend brave the otherlands to bring my boy from the capital?"

'I don't think he'll need to," Stella said, thinking of the hop to A La Ronde.

They spent the night at the hunting lodge, and rode out just after dawn. Stella was invited to the evening banquet, but declined on the basis that she had only just had lunch. How did Elizabeth remain so wasp waisted? Corsets, probably. She had feared that declining the invitation might give offence, but the Queen appeared to have taken a fancy to Stella, for now, and asked Gregory to show Stella to a bed in a room shared by various ladies in waiting. She did not see Alys again, but was assured that her mother was unharmed.

Stella did not trust this statement. If the worst had happened, she would rather know now. And Elizabeth was exactly the type of person to make a pet of you and then grow bored. So after a decent interval, she rolled up her pillow and stuffed it under the blankets, thinking vaguely that this had worked in various girls' boarding school stories. She could always claim the need for a mug of water. Everyone was downstairs, carousing. She could hear laughter and what sounded like the making of toasts, then the haunting strains of a lute. It sounded like they were having a good time, anyway. Stella crept along the corridor above the hall, hoping the boards didn't creak too much.

There was a small back staircase, possibly for the servants. Hoping she wouldn't meet someone, Stella hastened down it and found herself in a small, dark hallway. That looked like an outside door – she unlatched it and stepped into moonlight. She found herself close to the knot garden where she and the Queen had so recently conversed. The scent of lavender was still strong. Somewhere up in the trees, she heard the shriek of a hunting tawny, answered by a fox below. Stella went quickly through the garden to the buildings on the other side. The lodge itself was not big, and she had a hunch that any prisoners would be kept away from the main house.

The buildings were unlit, save for the moonlight, but it was bright enough to see. She slipped around the side of a wooden structure and found the stables. A horse shifted in its stall, hoof thudding against wood. Stella froze. Behind her, a voice said,

"Stella?"

Stella jumped, clutching at the wall. "God!"

"Oh, sorry." It was Laura, in human form. Stella threw her arms around her.

"I'm so glad to see you! Are you all right?"

"Yes, and so is the rocking horse, and so is your mother."

"Do you know where she is?"

"Yes, she's in that building over there, but locked up. She's got a hay bale to sleep on, though, and they gave her some food and some milk. She's actually fine."

"What about Kit?"

"They didn't get Kit. He's still at large," Laura said, sounding like someone in a police procedural.

"Great!"

"Are you going to make a break for it?" Laura asked. "Because I was quite glad to be captured, ironically. We made it to the oak and then we saw the hunting party coming and I thought – sorry, Stella – that there was no point in all of us being taken, so I bolted, with Alys, thinking we could double back and find you later."

"Very sensible."

"But when we got to the edge of the woodland, we saw these – things – in the trees. I think they're shucks. I've met one before. Like very deep shadows that swallow light. And they really scared me – when I'm a horse, I'm more of a horse than a woman, in some ways. I have a horse's instincts. So I just fled and that took me right into the path of the Queen's hunt, and they rounded us up."

313

"Well, this is the thing, Laura," Stella said. "I've sort of got on all right with the Queen. She hasn't had me beheaded, anyway, but I wouldn't bet on her staying White Queen and not suddenly turning into Red Queen, if you know what I mean. But for the moment, she's been quite reasonable and I have got a bit of leverage – she wants Hob, you see. I told you about him, remember? And I know where to find him, more or less. So I asked her to give us safe passage to Cornwall, and once we're there, we can get in touch with Ace."

"Why not to London?"

"London's a possibility, but we're apparently closer to Cornwall, which was where things started kicking off and I want to make sure my sisters are all right. Once we're in Cornwall and safe, Ace can bring Hob via the follies and so on. Assuming Hob will come, mind you."

"At least if we were riding with the Queen, we might be safer from whatever's lurking in these woods," Laura said.

"And they'll know the way. So on balance I think it's safer to stick with Elizabeth than not."

"She could have just threatened your mum, though, if you hadn't told her where Hob was."

"She could have but she didn't. I'm not sure why."

"Maybe she actually does have a sense of honour," Laura remarked, dubiously.

"Maybe. She does have a sense of *humour* but it's pretty dark. Did you see her?"

"Only in the distance. They dragged Alys off my back and took me to the stables. They treat their horses very well, I must say."

"I'm wondering if she'll know you're a human, once you're back into horse? She saw me in the Thames, in the spring. She knew I wasn't really an otter."

"But Stella," Laura said, "You really are."

"You know what I mean. She seems to have the ability to see through magic, to see through glamour. Maybe she can cast it herself. But whatever... Either I can just come clean and tell her upfront or we'll risk it."

"I don't know what's best," said Laura. "If she knows I'm a horse she might, I don't know, put me on show or something."

"But if we don't tell her and she finds out..." Stella looked back across the garden. In an upper light, a candle was now burning and she could hear voices. "I think I'd better get back. Sounds like the party's breaking up."

Laura nodded and retreated into one of the stalls. Stella sneaked back to the lodge and went in the same way she had come out. There was definitely movement from downstairs and she glimpsed one of the men going into a bedroom, but when she found her own chamber, her pillow still artfully arranged, it was empty. Stella climbed into bed and feigned sleep as the ladies in waiting, chattering and giggling, came in a few minutes later. And despite all the noise, Stella did not have to pretend to be asleep for long.

Elizabeth's court headed out at dawn, riding through a long shallow valley between wooded slopes. Towards midmorning, the ground began to rise, and then they were heading up onto moorland: bare, bald country where the skylarks sang and Stella heard cuckoos in the dark groves of oak in the folds of the moor. This was, she thought, surely the otherlands version of Dartmoor and she was reminded that this was where Alys had, some time ago, been trapped. But she was separated from her mother and not able to hang back and ask: she knew, without being told, that the Queen would take a dim view of this. But she was happier up here on the heights: too much lurked in the woods of the otherlands, in Stella's opinion. It felt more normal, up here among the heather and the gorse, winding between the old stone bones of the moor with the shining sea once more a glimpse in the distance.

They paused for a brief noon picnic, and pressed on. Towards sunset, a river came into view, winding between low patchworked hills. It was familiar to Stella.

"Is that the Tamar?" she said to Ann, who rode beside her and with whom Stella had struck up something of a friendship.

"It is. My mother's people are from Cornwall."

"It's changed a bit. But perhaps not so much the otherlands version." She could see no sign of modern roads or bridges, only a small sailing boat making its way downriver. They had seen no more shucks. But twilight was falling now, a purple mist over the distant moorland heights, and Gregory decreed that they would strike camp. Tents were raised in what seemed to Stella to be remarkably short order. Elizabeth's resembled a small pavilion. Stella herself was put in a large tent with the women, including Alys, but an older maidservant was set on guard. Since the court seemed to Stella to be her best chance of getting back to Cornwall, she had no intention, for once, of making waves.

That night, however, Stella woke. Something had disturbed her, a dream, perhaps, of a bird plucking at her sleeve – but then a voice whispered, "Don't move. It's only me, old Kit."

Very cautiously, Stella looked across the tent. Everyone was asleep, including Alys. A candle burned low and the guardian maidservant was no longer there.

"Milady's nipped out for a piss," Kit's voice said. "So I chose my moment. You seem to have palled up with the Queen. Are you all right?"

"Yes." In as few words as possible, Stella explained.

"Then I'll leave you be, but follow on, like."

"Brilliant! I'm glad you're okay, Kit. It'll be good to know you're out there."

The tent flap opened and the guard, rearranging her skirts, came back in to stare around. Stella feigned sleep. Kit spoke no more. And then she blinked and it was dawn.

Stella had wondered how they were going to cross the Tamar, but it appeared that the Queen had no such intention.

"South," she told Gregory. "To Plymouth and Sir Francis!"

Was Plymouth in the otherlands, Stella wondered? But perhaps the Queen meant the past. It seemed that this might be so, for the land no longer shifted and changed, but remained constant. They passed through scattered villages, whitewashed hovels from which inhabitants spilled to stare and marvel at the Queen as though she were an alien. Perhaps, to them, she was not far off. A small daring child ran up with a bouquet of wilted daisies, which Elizabeth received as graciously as if they had been a golden crown. Stella was beginning to see why she had inspired such loyalty among her subjects. She was alarming, true, and capricious, but she had a generosity which looked spontaneous even if it was not, and a chilly, intermittent charm which got under your skin, made you eager to please. Stella, however, remained on her guard and Alys did not attempt to speak with the Queen at all.

After following the twists of the Tamar for some distance along a track, which could hardly be described as a road, the smell of the air and the light told Stella that they were nearing the coast. Soon,

Plymouth itself came into view: tall half timbered houses and a throng of masts. A number of rather nervous dignitaries, one wearing a mayoral gold chain, appeared in a cluster, clucking like geese. Stella deduced that the runner who had been sent ahead to let the port know of its monarch's arrival had only just made it ahead of them, and Elizabeth's appearance had come as something of a shock, quite possibly an unwelcome one. When Gregory informed them that her Majesty would, after a brief respite, be taking ship for the Cornish coast, there was a distinct rustle of relief. The party was ushered to a large and imposing building which was, apparently, the Mayor's own house and issued with a hastily prepared meal of local delicacies (excellent cheese, Stella noted) and, after a request, water to wash in. She was accompanied by Ann and the guardian maid, who kept a watchful eye, but Stella, never overly concerned about modesty, stripped off her top and then her jeans and made as much use of the hot water as she could. There was even soap, of sorts.

Feeling a lot more socially acceptable, even if some of the company weren't that fragrant themselves, Stella went back downstairs to join the party and found that they were ready to embark, along with the horses. In the general melee, she finally had the chance to speak to her mother.

"You all right, Mum?"

"Yes. I came to rescue you, Stella, and now you've had to rescue *me*."

"Don't worry about it. We should be able to sort things out. All we have to do is find Hob. I'll explain later."

"And is this Hob findable?"

"He should be." But the hard faced maid, Margaret, was coming back, so Stella broke off. Meekly, they boarded.

She had been on the *Hind* before, but its captain showed no signs of recognising her. Perhaps that still lay in the future, or perhaps she just wasn't very memorable. Or Drake's type. Stella could live with that. Whatever the case, Drake's fierce eye passed over her with indifference; he was, naturally enough, focused on the Queen.

The *Hind* cast off, gliding out into the harbour. Stella looked back: Devon's green hills and red earth had not greatly changed, and she could see the Hoe receding into the distance. Plymouth soon became lost in a mild and smoky haze, the result of a town full of wood fires. By now, Stella was growing sea legs and she marched up and down the

317

deck, noting things of interest. Alys, however, huddled on a coil of rope, was pale.

"Are you all right?" Stella asked again, risking Margaret's ire.

"Bit queasy."

"Oh dear. I don't remember you being seasick before."

"Yes, you do. Remember that ferry to Dieppe?"

Now that she had been reminded, Stella did.

"Oh yeah."

"Weirdly, I'm fine on smaller boats."

"It's probably something to do with your inner ear."

"Are you ill, Mistress Fallow?" Margaret asked.

"She's feeling sick," Stella supplied.

"I can take her below, if she wishes," Margaret said, not unkindly.

"Actually, that might not be a bad idea."

Freed of the responsibility of looking after her parent, Stella wandered about and found Elizabeth installed in state on the poop deck, beneath a sunshade. They were now rounding Rame Head, and proceeding, if Stella remembered correctly, towards Polperro. She collared a passing sailor and asked.

"Why yes, lady. Looe and then Polperro, and then Mevagissey."

"Did her Majesty instruct Dra – the Captain to head on to the bay where St Michael's Mount lies?"

"She did."

"How long will it take?"

The sailor squinted up into the rigging. "We have a good wind in our sails. Perhaps tonight?"

"Sounds good," said Stella. She found a sunny spot on the deck and dozed for a while, waking to find that it was quite late in the day and they were still skirting the coast: the great granite cliffs reared up out of the foam, and she could see pale crescent moons of sand between the rocks, but she did not know the Cornish coast well enough to be able to tell exactly where they were. At this point Ann appeared with something wrapped in a cloth and a mug of water.

"Want some?" She handed over what Stella initially thought was a pebble, but which turned out to be ship's biscuit.

"Does it have weevils?"

"I don't think so," Ann said. Stella checked it carefully all the same but it appeared to be weevil-free. She sopped it in the water and forced it down. If it sustained the Royal Navy, it was presumably filling enough.

"Your mother is feeling a little better," Ann informed her.

"Oh, good. Thanks for letting me know." Stella got to her feet. "Do you know where we are?"

"Yes. See that headland? That is the Lizard."

"Phenomenal. Not so far away, then?"

"Not so far."

By the time they came round the Lizard, at a distance, the sun was sinking into a smoky bank of cloud and Stella shivered: it was colder now, with a stiff breeze blowing from the east. However, that wind was driving the *Hind* onwards. Alys appeared on deck, accompanied by the grim Margaret.

"How are you feeling now, Mum?"

"Better than I was. Where are we?"

Stella pointed out the Lizard, now falling behind. "We've made good time."

"That looks like Porthleven – that long stretch of beach."

Alys joined her at the rail. Margaret frowned, but in earshot as she was, she could hardly object to this anodyne conversation. "Fancy that, a trip on Drake's ship. Although you've been on the *Hind* before, haven't you?"

"Yes. I'm sort of avoiding the captain, though. I don't think he remembers me but that might be because he hasn't met me yet. If you see what I mean."

"And Dark's not here?"

"No, I checked. I don't know if this is the otherworld or just the past. Or are they even different?"

"I wonder that myself. But we're in the otherworld now, Stella. Look."

She pointed. Another ship was sailing to meet them: much bigger than the *Hind*, with unfurled white sails.

"That's a much later ship," Alys said.

"Someone's waving," Stella said, shielding her eyes. "Oh my God. Is that *Bee?*"

And it was.

BEE

It was very close to sunset now. Bee looked west, to where the sun was touching the horizon and turning the cloudy sky to fire. High in the east, the Evening Star was trembling out. She stood with Dark at the prow of the *Stargazy*, heading east to the Island. After an emotional reunion, Serena and the others had gone below, to be debriefed by Captain Thorn.

"I can see a sail," Bee said. Dark, who had been adjusting something on the deck, straightened up and followed her gaze.

"It's the *Hind*," he said.

"What, Drake's ship?"

"I'd know her anywhere." He ran below deck, to fetch Captain Thorn.

"I envy you those travels, Ned," the Captain said as they rejoined Bee.

"They weren't always so fine. Drake could be – not kind. And I did die. But the *Hind* is the ship of my heart, all the same."

"Then we'll sail out and welcome her in," Captain Thorn told him.

The *Stargazy* changed course, tacking around the bulk of the Mount. As Bee looked up at the island, Ace appeared.

"Are we not landing, then?"

Bee explained.

"And he's sure it's Drake's ship? Stupid question, probably. He ought to know his own boat."

"Quite sure. I've been on it before, too," Bee said.

"So why Drake? And why now?"

The reason was soon obvious.

Bee burst into tears when Stella stepped on board.

"Take it easy, Bee" her sister said, pleased if embarrassed. "Like Granny Weatherwax, I ate'nt dead."

"Oh, Stella. I *am* sorry." Bee sat down hard on a nearby bench. "We thought you might be, you see."

"Nah, I'm harder to kill than that. Hey, Luna, Serena." She hugged them all, including Davy, and briefly explained.

"Mate, I'm so pleased to see you."

"So where's Mum?"

"Right. Mum has to stay on the *Hind*, until you and I, Ace, can come up with Hob. She's a hostage, essentially."

"Ah," Ace said, 'I thought that might be the case as soon as I spotted her Majesty there. Good thing Hob's here."

"What? You're kidding me!"

"No, he isn't, Stella. They rescued me," Hob said, emerging onto deck.

"Well, that's gonna save a lot of inconvenience."

Hob looked puzzled. "Why?"

"Er, long story."

Dark was staring over at the *Hind* and the white clad figure at its prow. He looked stunned. "I thought I would never see her again," he said. "She is as bright as the moon."

"If we can get Hob onto that ship," Stella said, "She might even give you a knighthood."

STELLA

They were heading towards the *Hind*. Stella had finally told her story, to a white, bewildered Hob.

"So I'm – what? The son of this woman and a… a being of some kind? And Queen Elizabeth snatched me from my cradle? And then someone *else* took me from her?"

"I know it's a crazy story, Hob, but seriously, your best mate could turn into a seagull. And look at the rest of us."

Hob concurred that she had a point.

"So where's my real mum, then?"

"In Captain Thorn's cabin."

Hob gaped at her.

"Yeah," Ace said. "*That's* going to be awkward."

BEE

The turrets of the castle were wreathed with seagreen flame, through which the sun shone, casting the sward of grass in a watery light. They had arrived half an hour or so before, the *Stargazy* following the *Hind* in, and they had found many people there before them. Now, the platform of grass was crowded. At one end, by the gate stood the Hunt, dismounted. Drum was scanning the faces of the crowd, impatiently tapping one hand against his cloak. At the other end of the grass stood the Morlader. His sparks were extinguished: he was a column of shadow, his face hidden by the wide brim of his hat.

In between, Azenor had been carried in on a chair and now sat with foam at her feet. A second small band occupied another stretch of the grass, centred on a red-headed woman who wore a gown as white as winter. As Bee watched, a small number of people came from the castle courtyard to join them.

Luna nudged Bee. She had left Rosie on the *Stargazy* with Sam and Ver, to accompany her sisters up to the castle.

"Bee! Is that *Mum?* And is that actually *Queen Elizabeth* talking to Mum? I still can't believe Stella hitched a ride from Good Queen Bess."

"I think it must be her. She's got red hair, anyway. And look, there's Laura."

Azenor raised a hand. Above their heads, the flames faded and died. Two banners now hung from the turrets: one white, with a scarlet dog running across it, and one black, bearing a castellated ship in dull gold. The Hunt, and their opponents.

"Could both of them lose?" Luna asked hopefully.

"Fingers crossed."

"The Island court has assembled," Azenor said. At this distance, she should have used a megaphone, but Bee could hear her clearly. "The challenge has been made. We come as witness to the land challenge made by the Morlader, to Aiken Drum, Master of the Wild Hunt. The wrecking tribes ask for soul hunting rights on the moors of Kernow."

"Rights we have held since time immemorial," Aiken Drum said. He strode forwards. "Rights we have held since the end of the ice."

"And who gave you those rights?" Was the Morlader indeed one of the Gentlemen, Bee wondered. She'd had a conversation with Luna about this, the previous night. The Morlader was like a ghost, a spirit. Drum was nearly preferable. Nearly.

"The land itself!"

"So say you," the Morlader mocked. "The land whispers differently to me, to mine."

"You have the sea." Drum swept his hand to the curve of the bay and the glassy sea beyond. "You have more than we."

"The Hunt's champion found my mother," Azenor said. "Should there be any doubt, the vote will be mine: I will find for the Hunt. But first you must set your challenges."

"What does that mean?" Luna asked.

"I don't know."

"It was so nice earlier on," Serena said. "There's a mist coming in."

She was right. Streamers of black fog were twining around the towers of the castle; the shore could no longer be seen. Bee reached out and took Dark's hand and Luna's. Serena took Luna's free hand and Louisa Thorn took hers in turn, until they were linked in a chain. No one, Bee knew, wanted to be separated and the mist was coming down quickly now. The sun shone penny-bright for a second, a white disc, and then was swallowed. Bee saw Serena's upturned, worried face and then that too was blotted out. If she had not been able to feel the clasp of hands, Bee would have thought she was quite alone. Then someone ran past her through the mist. She glimpsed through the ragged streamers a man, barefoot and silver eyed. He leaped high, twisting in the air, dispelling the mist for a moment so that Bee could also see the remaining Hound, the Lily White Boy. His hands were outstretched, his lips moved, and tatters of fire flared out and blew the mist away.

The running man dropped in a blaze of flame but a shadow came up behind the Hound and seized him and dragged him backwards. He vanished into the fog. Dark squeezed Bee's hand, she felt him pull her. She took a step. The mist lifted again: Bee stood in a circle of people: Elizabeth and Alys were among them. The grass in the middle of the circle was empty, but the mist shifted again and Aiken Drum and the Morlader stood there. The Morlader was now much less human than Drum, Bee thought. His black coat had a chitinous gleam, like overstretched plastic, as though his clothes were not separate from his body. He doffed his hat and tossed it to one side: beneath, his scalp was bald and mottled. His lips pursed and he whistled: a thin, dreadful sound. Bee tried to wrench her hands free but Dark and Luna held on tight – she did not think she could bear it but she gritted her teeth and gripped their hands. Drum staggered back. The whistling spoke of the deep sea, the dark sea: the night storm that swallows ships and men. Bee's lungs felt as though they would burst. Drum drew a pistol and, moving with effort, fired. The Morlader's bald skull split apart, reformed, but the whistling stopped. Drum spoke a word and Bee was suddenly high in the air, looking down through thunderheads. Lightning boomed around her. She knew what it was like to ride with the Hunt, that savage thrill, the glimmers of souls fleeing before their rade, and then she plummeted to earth – no, water. The sea heaved and churned below. Beside her, Luna gasped. The Morlader stood before them, shadow tall and growing taller. He reached out a hand and Bee struggled back, for she could feel the ice in his fist, the killing deep sea cold. The Morlader's mouth opened, the air crackled, frost spread beneath Bee's feet and then the wind got up.

It blew from the direction of the setting sun, a strong westerly, stirring Bee's hair and then whipping it around her face. It caught the Morlader and tore him into rags of shadow. He cried out, reached out, his arm was ripped bloodless from his shoulder and whirled away over the cliff. The mist was gone. The Morlader was blown backwards. Bee saw his mouth open wide but the wind filled it and blew him apart. Dark and Luna released her hands; the circle was broken. Drum gave a great shout of laughter.

"Well done, Stella! My champion indeed!"

Bee, startled, looked across the grass. Beyond the circle, not far from where Azenor sat, stood her sister, and by her side, Elowen. The ghost girl was holding a small piece of string. The wind that Stella had bought in Tretorvic had been released.

"Well, that worked," she heard Stella say.

"The Hunt wins the challenge," Azenor said. She started to rise. Ace and Davy stood behind Stella, along with Hob, Bee realised. He looked stunned. But a figure ran past Bee, knocking her to one side. She fell heavily to the grass and Dark, cursing, pulled her up. Bee saw a Hound, a Lily White Boy, caught sight of the scar on his face. His fellow, snarling, was running along the grass but the Hound whom Luna had tried to help leaped, became dog in mid-air. The powerful hindquarters bunched as he sprang and he struck Drum in the chest, bowling him over. Bee had a final glimpse of Drum's face: he was still grinning. Then the Hound tore out his throat. Someone gave a hoarse cry – Alys? The second Lily White Boy, dog in turn, was upon the Hound. They rolled over and over, teeth locked in each other's flesh.

"Stop it!" Luna screamed.

"Gregory!" A chilly voice, knife quick and accustomed to command. Bee, horrified, turned to look at Elizabeth. A man stepped to the Queen's side, an arrow nocked to his long bow. He took quick aim and let it fly, silver through the air. It pierced one of the Hounds, the one without the scar, and he vanished, along with the body of Aiken Drum. Gregory took another arrow from his bow, but the remaining Hound, in his human form, was already running towards the Queen. Hob shouted out. He sprang in front of her and Bee saw then the resemblance to the Lily White Boys. But before the Hound could reach them, Elowen was there. She threw her shadowy arms around the neck of the Hound, turned, gave Hob a long, longing look and then a slit in the air opened and she jumped through it, taking the Hound with her.

"No!" Hob cried.

"Elowen!" shouted Luna.

But they had gone. Only the blood remained, staining the grass for a moment, before it, too, drifted away like red smoke.

The remainder of the Hunt stood clustered in dismay. A figure stepped out of the air, and Bee felt the weight of her presence immediately. Her hair was aflame, her eyes as green as marshfire. Antlers crowned her brow. Laura stepped forward to her mistress.

"At the death of the Helwyr, I claim –" Noualen started to say, in a voice as sweet and ringing as a bell. Then she paused. Bee tried to look to see what was happening but she could not seem to move her head. She heard music: faint at first, then twisting and winding through the air, binding their hands and lips like wild rose briar, catching them all out of time: Bee and her sisters and their friends, the white and silver Queen, Gregory with his bow, and seaclad Azenor upon the turf of her own castle.

Alys Fallow walked forwards with the old bone flute at her lips. Bee did not know the tune, only that it was familiar, recognised somewhere deep and ancient within. Its music held her as her mother walked across the sward to where Drum's great chestnut horse stood uneasily waiting. Alys put a hand to its neck, calming the stallion. Then she put her foot in the stirrup and vaulted onto its back.

Once astride, she blew a final note on the flute and tucked it inside her coat. To the Hunt, she shouted, "To me! We ride!" Spurring the chestnut around, she galloped past the Hunt, who, mounting swiftly, fell in behind her, and went straight over the edge of the cliff. Bee, abruptly released, shouted "Mum!" and ran with her sisters to the granite lip. But they need not have worried. The Hunt rode the air, streaming in a flurry of riders and runners down the cliff and out across the sea. The sun caught the silver of their bridles, flashing in the morning light. And then they, too, disappeared.

STELLA

"Would you like another flagon of wine?" Snipe said.

"Maybe share it between all of us. I'm not sure I should drink one on my own. Even if I feel like it." Stella was sitting with her sisters and their friends in a high, sunny chamber, overlooking the bay.

"I really ought to get out of London more often," Davy Dearly said.

"Haven't you got time off? I'm sure there's room at Penhallow."

"That's nice of you, Serena – I might do that. I might take next week off as well. We've just finished a biggish project and I'm owed some leave. I'll have to run it past my manager, obvs."

'Ward's due to come down with Bella tomorrow. I think it's tomorrow – perhaps it's today. I've lost track of time."

Stella snorted. "Who hasn't?"

"I wonder how Hob's getting on?" Bee said.

"In need of extensive psychotherapy and family trauma counselling after this, I should think."

"He's a big lad," Ace remarked. "He'll handle it."

But Stella was not so sure. Hob had now been closeted with the Queen and Azenor for over an hour. She would have loved to have been a fly on the wall, but had not been asked.

"Azenor thinks she can get you your shape back," Ace said to Jane Thorn, who had joined them by boat after all the fuss. "Special boon. Stella asked Azenor."

"I haven't done anything to earn it! Although it would be nice."

"You've helped us," Stella said.

"I couldn't rescue you from Drum, though."

"In the end, I rescued myself. And that's just fine."

"And Mum's gone off again," Bee said.

"Leader of the Wild Hunt, eh? So much for 'no woman can rule us'. I bet Noualen's pissed off."

"I spoke to her, actually," Ace said. "When you were introducing Hob. I thought, since I'm more used to goddesses than a lot of people, that I'd have a quiet word with Laura and she made the introductions. Noualen seems to have taken it well. Says the Hunt will do better under your ma than they did under Drum, and she'll open peace talks in due course. She's gathered a band of her own – it was that which chased the Hunt out of the wood at Midsummer, by the way."

"I think she's pretty reasonable as minor deities go," Stella said. "I hope."

"Talking of which," Davy poured more wine, "Azenor. Is an actual mermaid, or what?"

"I'm not sure. I've never been able to see her feet."

"In legend she is a mermaid," Louisa said. "She married a man from Zennor, so the old story goes."

"Wonder what happened to him?"

"I don't think we should ask." Maybe she'd eaten him, Stella thought ungraciously.

"Oh, Hob!" Bee said.

The young man, incongruous in t-shirt and jeans, had come back into the room.

"Is there any of that wine left, Stella? I bloody need a drink." He collapsed into a seat.

"Have as much as you want! What did they say?"

"I think it's sorted," Hob said. He looked very drained, but less stressed. "I'm going to spend a bit of time with the Queen. Then I'm going back to Blake's house and see what I can do for him. The court's all been very nice to me. I just feel terrible about my actual mum."

"Hopefully she's gone to a better place." A different place to the Hound, anyway. Stella was by now convinced that one of the Hounds had been the 'devil' who had fathered Hob but she didn't like to say so. He'd had enough emotional overload that morning and perhaps he'd worked it out, anyway. He had spoken to Elowen, Stella knew, but that had been another conversation to which no one else had been privy. It would keep. And perhaps Elowen had had a kind of revenge, at the last.

"I mean, she waited all this time for me, and then she – well, she died once and then she did it again, to save my life."

"Do we have any idea who took you from Elizabeth?"

"No. But Gregory says that he spoke to Dee – the magician, Doctor Dee – and Sir Francis Walsingham, that's the Queen's spy master, when I disappeared, and there had been a lot of trouble, magical stuff, with the Hunt and Gregory says he'd always had the impression that maybe they had a hand in it, took me through time to get me out of the way and didn't tell the Queen. She's been really nice to me," Hob said proudly, and Stella knew that Hob had, at least for now, found the family and the Miranda substitute that he had so craved. Even if it was a rather peculiar one. Still, there was always Blake.

Meanwhile, Hob would join the royal party on the Hind. The Queen was anxious to leave soon; she had business to attend to, she said, and she would be returning to Buckland Abbey, Francis Drake's home on Dartmoor.

"You do know, right, that local folklore says that Drake leads a pack – the Whisht Hounds – up on Dartmoor? And that he's another one who is said to be able to turn himself into a seagull?"

"The Captain could do a lot of things," said Dark.

Stella and the others gathered on the castle ramparts to watch the *Hind* sail into the eastern distance. She nudged Dark.

"Do you miss it? Sailing with Drake?"

He smiled. "I have plenty of other adventures."

Azenor spoke to Stella before they, too, left: matters had worked out to her satisfaction.

"My mother is safe. The Morlader has gone. Drum has gone."

"I'm hoping the Wild Hunt will be less of a problem under Mum's guidance. But I could be massively wrong."

"We'll just have to wait and see. I will see you again, Stella, some day, I am sure."

Captain Thorn returned them to the shore, in their own day. They stood on the harbour arm, watching the *Stargazy* depart: it was a fine sunny day on this Friday in July, but there was suddenly a bank of mist, out across the bay. The *Stargazy* sailed into it and out of sight.

"Weather can change on a sixpence, down here," an elderly salt said to Stella, as they walked back down the harbour arm to the shore road.

"You're not wrong."

But by the time they reached the Smugglers' Arms, the bay was bright and blue once more.

"We'll say goodbye for the moment," Jane Thorn said. "Would you be up for Sunday dinner in the Smuggler's? One o'clock-ish? My treat."

"You're on!"

"Jolly good. See you then." And a herring gull was sitting on the low harbour wall, regarding them with a cold yellow eye. It gave a scream of triumph and soared upwards, until it was no more than a white speck in the summer air.

BEE

Bee was making a list. It included:

Adrian and Lily: dinner Tues.
Pick Ward/B up from station: 4.40.
Thorns: Sun din, Smugglers at 1.
Reservation Rick Stein's for Fri

And that, Bee thought as she closed the notepad, would be quite enough for one week. At least they had some holiday time left. It was mid-afternoon, and still Friday. Stella, Davy and Serena had gone down to the beach for a swim. Luna and Sam had taken Rosie for a walk with Moth. She did not know where Dark and Ace might be, but she suspected that the Smugglers' Arms might be a part of it, in whatever day or age. Bee could see Ver in the garden; she had gone to sit in a deckchair with a book, she had said, but Bee noticed that the book lay splayed, on the grass and Ver was fast asleep.

But not alone. Two people were walking along the lavender bed. Bee thought, "Oh God, what now?" She went to the window to look. A young woman, modishly dressed in the fashion of a hundred years ago or more, accompanied by another girl. The girl wore a flowery dress and carried a pretty parasol. It was only when the parasol turned in her hand to show her face and hair – flame red, no longer straggling – that Bee recognised Elowen. She was laughing at something the other girl – that must be Lucy Hallow – had said.

Bee ran out through the kitchen door.

"Hello! Please don't disappear!"

Elowen exclaimed when she saw Bee, and hugged her. She felt as solid as Dark.

"Oh Bee! Thank you, thank you."

"Are you all right? What happened to the Hound?"

"I left him – there," Elowen said. A shadow flitted across her face. "Then I came back. Lucy says I can live here – I never saw such a wonderful house, it's like a palace. You will tell Baby, won't you? When you see him? So he knows where to find me?"

"Absolutely. We'll get a message to him somehow. He's quite safe." She did not like to tell Elowen that her child had gone happily off with the woman who had stolen him in the first place. The girl seemed at peace at last; perhaps things had been explained to her in the otherworld? The afterlife? By whom? Bee felt a shiver of cold in the sunny garden, but she ought to be used to it now, after Dark.

"Well," she said. "I'm very glad you're all right. I hope we see you again."

"I'll look after her," Lucy said. "Don't worry." They began to fade, until they were as pale as lavender, and Bee went back into the house. Someone must have turned the radio on, for the Shipping Forecast was singing out:

"*Fastnet westerly, two to four... Lundy, Lyonesse, sea state, slight or moderate, becoming slight later, visibility good...*"

Visibility good sounded fine to Bee. She went outside again, to enjoy the afternoon.

Lammas tide

Last month, Bee thought, they had still been in Cornwall, the last week passing eventfully, but in a human, holiday way. Serena and Ward had visited St Ives; Stella's gig had been well received at Coastival. They had left having made firm friends, and with plans to return to the yellow house on the cliff someday. The London dwellers had gone back to the city; Bee and the others to quiet Mooncote. The clock of the year had turned through August: wheat ripening in the fields and the verges purple with willowherb, the apples ripening in the orchard, the days a little shorter now. Today was the last day of summer: August 31st and the old festival of Lammas, when John Barleycorn is cut down and the harvest properly begins.

It was dusk. Bee and Dark and Sam and Nick Wratchall-Haynes and Ver sat in the spare room of Mooncote, waiting and watching.

"I wonder if they'll come," Bee said. "After all, this is still Mum's home."

She had not seen Alys since that morning on the Mount. During the month or so that they had been back, she had seen only one thing out of the ordinary, if it could be called that: a star, sitting in the spare room by the rocking horse, now back where he belonged. Bee thought she might be Procyon; there were buttercups in her hair. She had been convinced that the star had been talking to the rocking horse, but when she went into the room, Procyon had vanished.

"Had your ma always planned this, do you think?" Ver said. "To take control of the Hunt?" It was not the first time they'd had this conversation.

"I don't know." Bee was still uneasy about Noualen. Laura had not seen her for a month or so, either.

"The moon's coming out." Nick was right; a faint thin crescent hung just above the hills. And there at last was the Hunt. Bee caught her breath as they poured out of empty air: the riders, the runners, the great bull-headed man and the dogs which sped alongside like a Medieval miniature. But no Lily White Boys ran behind them and the woman who rode at their head had a companion: an antlered girl in green on a moon-grey mare.

"Ah," said Nick.

The Helwyr raised a hand to the house, an obvious salute. Then the Hunt ran swiftly along the edge of the field and the air of the night opened and took them up, up and away among the last of the summer stars.

About the Author

Liz Williams is a science fiction and fantasy writer living in Glastonbury, England, where she is co-director of a witchcraft supply business. She has been published by Bantam Spectra (US) and Tor Macmillan (UK), also Night Shade Press, and appears regularly in *Asimov's* and other magazines. She has been involved with the Milford SF Writers' Workshop for over 25 years, and also teaches creative writing at a local college for Further Education.

Her novels are: *The Ghost Sister* (Bantam Spectra), *Empire Of Bones, The Poison Master, Nine Layers Of Sky, Banner Of Souls* (Bantam Spectra – US, Tor Macmillan – UK), *Darkland, Bloodmind* (Tor Macmillan UK), *Snake Agent, The Demon And The City, Precious Dragon, The Shadow Pavilion* (Night Shade Press) *Winterstrike* (Tor Macmillan), *The Iron Khan* (Morrigan Press) and *Worldsoul* (Prime). The Chen series is currently being published by Open Road. Her next novel, *Comet Weather*, was published by NewCon Press in 2020 and was followed by *Blackthorn Winter, Embertide*, and now *Salt on the Midnight Fire*.

A non-fiction book on the history of British paganism, *Miracles Of Our Own Making*, was published by Reaktion Books in 2020, *Modern Handfasting* was published by Llewellyn Worldwide in the USA, and a third non-fiction book on folklore will be published by Reaktion in 2024.

Her first short story collection *The Banquet Of The Lords Of Night* was also published by Night Shade Press, and her second and third, *A Glass Of Shadow* and *The Light Warden*, are published by New Con Press, as is her novella, *Phosphorus*. A fourth short story collection, *Back Through The Flaming Door*, will be published by NewCon Press in 2024.

The *Diaries of a Witchcraft Shop* (volumes 1 and 2) are also published by NewCon Press.

Her novel *Banner Of Souls* has been nominated for the Philip K Dick Memorial Award, along with three previous novels, and the Arthur C Clarke Award.

ALSO FROM NEWCON PRESS

The Book of Gaheris – Kari Sperring
Gaheris of Orkney, one aof the less celebrated knights of Arthur's court, finds himself up to his neck in intrigue, deception, violence, murder, and old secrets. Clouds gather over Camelot, threatening to destroy all that Arthur and Guenever have built, and Gaheris may be all that stands between Arthur's noble kingdom and disaster.

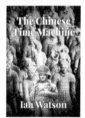

The Chinese Time Machine – Ian Watson
A new collection from one of science fictions most inventive writers; a volume released to celebrate the author's 80th birthday. Features ten stories published over the past five years in *Asimov's*, *Analog*, and elsewhere, plus a new 34,000 word novella that is original to this collection. Ian Watson at his entertaining best.

The Double-Edged Sword – Ian Whates
A disgraced swordsman leaves town one step ahead of justice. His past, however, soon catches up with him in the form of Julia, a notorious thief and sometimes assassin. Thrust into an impossible situation, he embarks on what will surely prove to be a suicide mission. "A cheerfully brutal story of betrayal and skulduggery, vicious fun." *– Adrian Tchaikovsky*

Sparks Flying – Kim Lakin
A first ever collection from critically acclaimed author Kim Lakin, spanning fourteen years of writing. Her very best short stories, as selected by the author herself. Fourteen expertly crafted tales that span myth, science fiction, industrial grime and darkest imagining. "Kim Lakin's imagination sets sparks flying indeed." *– Alison Littlewood*

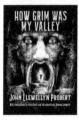

How Grim Was My Valley – John Llewellyn Probert
After waking up on the Welsh side of the Severn Bridge with no memory of who he is, a man embarks on an odyssey through Wales, bearing witness to the stories both the people and the land itself feel moved to tell him, all the while getting closer to the truth about himself.

Milton Keynes UK
Ingram Content Group UK Ltd.
UKHW040650110823
426718UK00004B/216